Lexington
CONNECTION

M.E.Logan

Bella
BOOKS
2013

Bella Books, Inc.
P.O. Box 10543
Tallahassee, FL 32302

Printed in the United States of America on acid-free paper.

Editor: Katherine V. Forrest
Cover designer: Linda Callaghan

ISBN: 978-1-59493-323-3

About the Author

M.E. Logan has wanted to write all her life, but it wasn't until retirement that life got out of the way. With all of her life's varied experiences to draw upon—from charter airlines to universities to high tech—she's happy telling stories from warm, sunny Florida with two dogs and numerous cats for company.

Acknowledgments

I would like to thank Gail who was the first one to call me a writer.

I would like to thank my writing group, Joan, Sherri, Lisa and Terri for encouraging me to submit this for publication.

Vicki, Dennie, Lynn, Nicki, Pat, Laurie for their comments, their support and encouragement.

Sherry, Donna, Cheyne and Pat, for their technical advice.

Katherine V. Forrest, my editor, for her kind comments.

And Charli, just for being there.

CHAPTER ONE

Nice little place, Diana DeVilbiss thought as she pulled open the heavy wooden door with the glazed glass window and the name "Bungalow" written in Old English stylized script above the door. She stood inside the darkened vestibule, letting her eyes adjust from the bright sunlight. All she wanted was a quick drink, let her day settle and then she'd go back to the hotel.

She'd heard the lawyers at the courthouse mention this place so she thought she'd try it out. She didn't know what else she was going to do on a Friday night in an unfamiliar town. At least it wasn't some small burg in the middle of nowhere. Lexington was the second largest city in Kentucky, home of the University of Kentucky, had two horse racing tracks, and drew international attention with annual horse sales and world-class equestrian trials. A lot of money, Diana considered as she took a seat where she could see the door but wouldn't necessarily be seen herself. It was international money here but money just the same. There were pubs and eateries all through the downtown area and the city was old enough to have more than a few historical spots. Surely she could find something to do over the weekend.

Papa, I don't know why you've got me sitting in on a drug trial for some low-life drug runner, but you ask a favor of your darling daughter and, of course, I will do it. But damn, it's boring. Would be different if I had an interest in the horses.

The waitress came, took her order, brought her drink, and she began to relax. Things began to look better. *Classy little place here, small, looks like old money, polished wood and brass, almost like the old gentlemen's club.* When the waitress came back, she commented on it off-handedly, "Quiet little place you have here."

"Only until seven."

"Why? What happens then?"

The waitress really looked at her then, saw her. "Tourist?"

"Passing through."

"All the lawyers hang out here during the day because we're across from the courthouse." Diana nodded; she'd understood that. "After six or seven, the gay crowd comes in. Dance floor is downstairs, opens at nine."

"How nice. Thanks for the info, saves me asking." She settled back in the seat. Maybe it wouldn't be just a quick drink after all. Maybe things were looking up.

Another drink, a sandwich from the bar—the last of the late lunch dishes set out for the patrons—and Diana watched the crowd change. The suits filtered out and the casual wear started coming in, some blue jeans, college crowd, young professionals. Her favorite pastime of people watching was hitting big time.

Then Diana saw her. Came in with sunglasses on, but she shed them quickly in the darkened interior. Worn blue jeans, not the ones bought that way for show but the kind that fade from hand rubbing, stretching, daily use, fit like she lived in them every day. White shirt, rolled up sleeves. Tall and lean, dark hair, just to the collar, maybe military. Nice, very nice movement, good balance on her feet. Diana watched her go to the bar, greet the bartender like a regular, get her beer and go sit at the end of the L-shaped bar, her back to the wall. Good spot, she could see everyone come in before they saw her, she could see the whole room. And she did observe the room, watching to see who came in, her eyes following the single women. A Romeo on the make, Diana decided. She had time to kill, she'd sit back and watch and see how this played out. Might be interesting.

Romeo knew lots of the women, indicated by a nod, a lifting the beer to those who knew where she would be sitting and looked for her. Soon Diana realized that she was watching the same women Romeo was; maybe they had the same taste. Of course, such a thing would be noticed, and when she tore her eyes away from one marvelously attractive redhead who had a warm hello for everyone as she came in, Diana felt eyes on her, watching her, taking her in. Diana brazenly returned the compliment, and was gratified to see the response as Romeo picked up her beer, and walked over.

"I don't believe I've seen you around here before."

Not an original opening line but honest enough. "I'm just passing through."

"Here for the Blue Grass Stakes?" When Diana simply looked at her with a blank expression, she added, "Horse races?"

Diana shook her head. "Business. I didn't know anything about the races until I hit town. Made a reasonable hotel hard to find. Had to upgrade."

"Oh, I bet. Mind if I join you?" She slid in beside Diana. "I'm Jessie."

"Jessie?"

"Jessica Ann. Always so hard to fit in the little bitty name spaces so I shortened it." She said it with a warm smile.

"Well, Jessie, I'm Diana."

"Ahh, another Princess."

Diana shook her head.

"Tired of that one, aren't you?"

Diana nodded.

"So you're stuck here for the weekend?"

"Pretty much so. Couldn't wrap it up today so I guess Monday before I can get on the road."

About that time, the band started downstairs and Diana jumped at the sudden blast. "Damn!" She bit her lip, she didn't like surprises or to be startled.

Jessie chuckled. "Band kicks in loud to start with. Want to go down and see? I could give you the grand tour."

"Oh, I bet you could," Diana laughed in return. She has a nice voice, she thought, warm, nice eyes. Damn, nice isn't the word for it. Wonder if…Patience, darling, patience.

Patience had its own reward. After a few dances, Diana was more than ready to drag Jessie back to the hotel. She liked the way Jessie moved against her, liked the intensity of her dark eyes. She liked the question, the mystery, the speculation. She began to wonder if all those dance moves could carry over to the bedroom.

She had no question about Jessie's availability, even if she couldn't feel the attraction radiate from her. She had seen the glances they got, some a little irritated, some a little puzzled at their contrast. Here

Jessie was in jeans and white shirt, and she was still in her heels, hose, business suit. They must make a sight. And Diana, normally wanting to melt into the wall and be invisible, didn't give a hoot. No one in this town knew her and it was unlikely she would return. Jessie had strong arms around her, she was a comfortable height to fit against, her hand on Diana's back was firm without being overly possessive, and when she finally bent to Diana's upturned face, her lips were soft and warm, inviting. It was an invitation Diana decided not to resist.

Diana broke away breathless, meeting the question in Jessie's dark eyes. "Bedroom eyes," she murmured, all the time thinking *Where is my head?*

"What?"

"A look my mama told me about that indicated someone was good in bed."

"We could test it out."

No, no, no, Diana's logic was saying, but every other part of her was pressed against Jessie's lean, warm body. "That could be interesting. I always like proving theories." She felt Jessie's hand slide down to her ass, a little possessive now. Her own hands were stroking that white shirt that covered Jessie's breasts. She could feel hard little bumps come up. "And if we weren't sure about the first test, we could repeat?"

Jessie had a nice warm laugh but Diana was more interested in her hands; damn she felt good. "I guess so." She could imagine those nice strong hands other places.

Jessie slid her arm around Diana and guided her through the crowded dance floor. When they reached the stairwell, which was unexpectedly empty, Jessie pressed her against the wall, her hands on Diana's ass, kissing her deeply, her tongue exploring Diana's lips. And Diana welcomed her without hesitation.

This is not good, Diana thought, thinking of their exposure, *but God, this is wonderful.* She broke away and leaned against Jessie, trying to regain her senses. "I've got a hotel room down the block. Great location for testing."

The night air should have cooled them as they walked around the block and down the street. Diana shivered but it wasn't from the night air as Jessie took her hand and kept her close. She was conscious of the long strides beside her, those long legs, that marvelously firm body she had felt. This breathing spell and time for second thoughts only made her even more eager to reach her hotel room while she could still concentrate. She quickened her step only to be doubly frustrated when Jessie caught her arm in the hotel stairwell.

"Look," Jessie said in a ragged voice, "before we get totally carried away, there's something you need to know."

"What?" Diana hissed as she pushed Jessie back against the wall. *There's nothing I need to know.* She ran her hands all over her and slid her leg between those jeans-clad delightful legs. "Are you married?" she demanded. Her blood was already pounding and she ached with wanting.

"No," Jessie stammered as Diana's eager hands fumbled at her shirt buttons.

"Steady girl?" Buttons came undone as Diana burrowed against Jessie's neck.

"No." Jessie caught Diana's shoulders. "You?" Then Diana's hands slid inside her jeans against warm flesh and firm muscles, against wet tightly curled hair. Jessie moaned and gripped Diana tighter.

"No. So what else?"

"Why are we in the stairwell?"

They stumbled through the door, down the hall to the room. Diana fumbled with the key card, shaking with predatory desire until Jessie jerked it from her hand and slammed it in to unlock the door. They were barely in the door before Jessie had Diana against the wall, her hand wound through Diana's thick hair. She pulled Diana's head back and her lips were claiming, possessive.

Diana slid her arms around Jessie, pulling tight against her. She wanted to feel Jessie against her, wanted to feel her weight, wanted. She slid her hands under Jessie's shirt against warm flesh, one hand going down into the jeans to squeeze her ass, the other hand caressing, stroking the bare breast. This woman had better not be all promise and no delivery.

Jessie broke away from Diana's lips, held her still by the hair. She shivered, shuddered as Diana watched her through half-closed eyes. Deliberately, as if waiting for Diana to stop her, Jessie returned, her lips just as warm and as promising as Diana had anticipated. Then she broke away and Diana turned her face away. Jessie left a trail of kisses along Diana's jawline, along her sensitive neck as Diana pushed Jessie's shirt off her shoulders so she could caress the sides of Jessie's slight breasts.

"You keep doing that," Jessie warned, "and something's going to happen."

"Promise?" Diana leaned back, exposing her throat as she reveled in the sensations that Jessie's lips elicited. She dropped her hands down to unsnap, unzip Jessie's jeans. Wetness greeted her fingers as

Jessie groaned in her ear, leaned against the wall. She didn't let go of Diana and in seconds she turned Diana's face back to her to kiss her passionately.

Diana pushed away from the wall and Jessie moved back. If they didn't head for the bed soon, she was going to sink to the floor. She felt Jessie's fingers fumble and then a hand on her breast. "Oh, God," she murmured, moving in against that hand, those fingers massaging and pinching and promising.

"You got a bedroom?" Jessie muttered into Diana's neck. Diana shuddered, struggling to think coherently and not just be swept away with Jessie's touch. They did an awkward, stumbling, dancing two-step into the bedroom, refusing to let go of each other, unable to get in step.

As they stood at the foot of the bed, Jessie pulled off Diana's blouse, her bra, taking Diana's face in her hands to kiss her. Diana just as quickly, as awkwardly, pulled Jessie's shirt and jeans off.

"Tell me what you like," Jessie said as she crawled over Diana on the bed, her thigh moving high between Diana's legs.

Diana's fingers tangled in Jessie's hair. "You," she said. "Anyway, anyhow. Take me, love me, fuck me." She shuddered as Jessie stroked her, light caresses over her arms, her legs. She whimpered as Jessie's tongue caressed her nipples. She closed her eyes, which intensified the sensations that were lightning flashes down to her clit. Jessie slowly moved down her and Diana felt she could come apart. Jessie held her, firm hands, a strong yet gentle touch. Just when Diana thought she couldn't stand it anymore, Jessie parted her lips and sank in against her.

She came sudden and hard but Jessie didn't stop. Diana rose up on her elbows, parting her legs to watch Jessie, who looked up at her without leaving her. Diana's head tipped back and she closed her eyes again, lost in the exquisite pleasure. Then she felt the penetration, the thrust, the withdrawal, and it was enough to take her over the edge again. She collapsed onto her back, gripping the coverlet with one hand and reaching for Jessie's head with the other.

She was shuddering, trying to catch her breath, Jessie's legs wrapped around her, Jessie's arms wrapped around her. "Oh, God," she muttered, shaking her head as she came down from that marvelous high, feeling Jessie still against her. She arched, lifted and turned, so that Jessie was on her back. She smiled at Jessie's surprise when she looked up at Diana. "I want to please you," Diana said breathlessly.

Jessie opened, offering as Diana straddled her, took her wrists and pinned them down against the bed. Diana bent down to suck the darker upright nipple, then worked her way down Jessie, tongue touching, tasting until she lay between Jessie's legs. She listened to Jessie, used the sounds to guide her toward Jessie's need. When she let go of Jessie's wrists, sought out her center, felt her wetness, Jessie's hands entangled in her hair, pushing her where Jessie wanted her to go. Taste, penetration, feeling the woman open for her, arch against her, the frantic movements that Diana managed to move with, the crest, the outcry that Jessie quickly muffled by pulling the pillow over her face, and then the spasm as she came, sudden, hard, gripping Diana's hand to hold her in place.

When the aftershocks finished and Diana could withdraw, she crawled up to lay beside Jessie, their heads on the pillows as they watched each other. "You said," Diana was able to speak with some sanity now, "there was something I needed to know. What was that?"

"I don't remember," Jessie confessed.

Diana laughed, reaching up to touch Jessie's cheek. She felt unbelievably light, free. "You are marvelous."

"You're pretty good yourself." Jessie reached for her, slid her arm around Diana, pulled her close so they were nestled against each other. "This theory we're testing, is it proven on just one trial or does it take multiple tests?"

"Confirmation tests are always good."

"Maybe in slower, exacting detail?" She cupped her hand around Diana's breast.

"We do want to check out all the contingencies." She pulled Jessie down to her breast. She closed her eyes, intensifying the feeling of Jessie's hand sliding down her side, her hips, down her thigh. This was just what she wanted, if it got any better, she'd shove Jessie in a suitcase and take her home with her. And then Jessie moved against her and she didn't think anymore.

***

Diana woke up, stretching, reaching and coming awake when she felt the empty bed. "No," she said sharply and sat up to see Jessie standing at the corner of the bed, already dressed. "Oh, tell me you're not leaving."

Jessie shrugged. "Got to. Big doings in town this weekend and I have a part-time job at one of the horse farms. I was just trying to decide whether to leave you a note or wake you."

"Oh!" The disappointment was sharp, unexpected. Diana got out of bed, not caring about her nudity. "I'm so glad I woke up then.

I'd have been so disappointed to wake up and find you gone." She approached Jessie and slid her arms around her neck. "Do you really have to go?"

Jessie pulled her arms down. "Yes, I really have to go." Just the same, she didn't look disappointed at Diana's coaxing.

"I mean," Diana said in a coy voice that she didn't believe was coming from her, "I knew this wouldn't be more than just a one-night stand, you don't have to make excuses." She ran her hand up Jessie's arm. "But I'm only in town for the weekend. We could make it a weekend fling. If you want to. No strings. Just warm memories in our golden years."

Jessie chuckled. "And I thought you were a reserved little tourist who just stumbled into the wrong bar." She shook her head.

"I can be, if that's that you want," Diana said with a sideways look at Jessie. Then she stepped away and slid open the closet door for her silken kimono. "Or I can be more forward." She slipped into the knee-length kimono and turned back to face Jessie, who had a bemused expression on her face as she watched Diana. "I thought last night was great. Besides being a beautiful woman, you proved Mama's theory correct. I'd love to spend more time with you. No strings. Just a good time. But if you've got things to do and places to go, then that's fine too. Last night was truly a pleasure."

Jessie shook her head in an amused way. "Can't get more direct than that." She wrapped her arms around Diana when Diana came back to her this time. "It was great for me too, but I do have to work. How about dinner tonight? Maybe tomorrow I could give you a tour of the area. How does that sound?"

"Wonderful." Diana didn't hesitate. This woman was something to enjoy. She wasn't going to bypass this opportunity.

"I've got to run. Pick you up here tonight. Okay?"

Tonight. Diana shivered with gleeful anticipation as she stepped into her shower a few minutes later. *Damn, I never expected anything like this!* She had thought it was going to be a dull time when Papa had asked this favor. Of course, she would do anything Papa asked for… but Lexington? She let the hot water run over her as she closed her eyes and thought about Jessie's hands on her. Long and lean. God, she loved women like that. Firm touch, like she knew what she was doing, confidence in herself. A certain amount of boldness. None of this hesitation, tentative stuff. Give and take. No, Jessie was the best she had found in a long time, a long long time.

Diana shivered as she turned off the water and stepped out. She wrapped the towel around herself and stared at herself in the full-length mirror. Sometimes she wished she were tall and lean like the women she was attracted to, but she liked being an inch or so shorter; then she fit better against them. And she liked having some meat on her bones, a cushion, although she guessed that as she aged, she might have a problem with the weight. That was a future she really didn't worry about now.

She dried herself, still examining herself in the mirror. She had nice legs. Was Jessie a leg woman? She hadn't said anything about Diana's appearance. Maybe she liked asses. Diana turned around to examine her tush. She wasn't bad in that department, considering she hated exercising. She turned back around, cupped her breasts. Jessie had caressed her breasts, oh, Lord, that had been nice. She was glad that she wasn't so big in that area either; she knew that some of the sensitivity was sometimes lost. She shook off this self-assessment. What difference did it make anyway? In all likelihood, she would not be back to Lexington. If goofis hadn't been driving around with a broken taillight, he wouldn't have gotten pulled over. And if he hadn't gotten pulled over, he wouldn't have gotten nailed. So the odds of her coming back to Lexington were somewhere between slim and none. She looked in the mirror again. Vanity, Margaret said it was. Beauty didn't last and she supposed Margaret was right. She'd seen a lot of good-looking women who had nothing when they lost their looks. Papa's holdings were littered with them.

She leaned forward to examine her face, just the same. Dark curly hair, the high cheekbones, the tawny skin, the slanted green eyes. Past lovers had said she had an exotic look, and Diana had been flattered. She didn't want to be like everyone else; she liked being different. But that had its drawbacks too. She liked being attractive; she didn't want to be memorable. That could be dangerous.

Diana realized as she dressed that Jessie hadn't been impressed with the suite. Diana wasn't even sure that she had seen it, but then wait, Jessie had been up before Diana had woken up.

Stupid! She should have thought of that. Diana hurriedly went through her luggage, checking. Not that there was anything there this time, but she still should have been more careful. No, it didn't look like anything had been touched. All her little traps were still intact. She paused, nodding. That was good. Trusting could be dangerous in more ways than one.

Her mind went back to Jessie. Another good sign was that Jessie had gotten up and showered. She said she was going to the job. Responsible. Didn't let a night's drinking and carousing detour her from her responsibilities. Diana nodded. Promising. Then she had suggested dinner, so she wasn't hiding from anyone. Had offered to give Diana a tour. That meant there was something else on her mind besides bed sports. On the whole, Jessie did appear promising. She might even be a keeper. If only Diana were around.

Realistically, it was only a Friday night pickup, a one-night stand. She had been on both sides of the coin for one-night stands, and she was well aware that sometimes it was never more than one night. Yet she found herself remembering a movement, a touch, a look. Jessie had definitely made an impression on her, on her libido. She had never had anyone affect her like this. One full night of lovemaking and she still had a hunger for the good-looking dyke. She really wanted Jessie to show up again.

She spent the day being a tourist. The Hunt-Morgan House, the walking tour of downtown, the Henry Clay House. Weather was pleasant, temperature was good. Diana made sure she was back at the hotel by three, anticipating with a tingling pleasure.

When early evening came and no Jessie, she was first disappointed but tried to be philosophical. As much as she enjoyed Jessie she could chalk her up to experience. After all, what could she expect from a one-night stand? She was getting ready to order a movie when there was a knock at her door.

"Hi," she greeted her, trying not to sound too eager. She drank in the sight of Jessie like a tall drink of cool water, a cliché she knew, but oh, my. "And how did your day go?"

"Busy. Big day for the farm. Did you see anything of the races?"

"Well, I had to see what the big doings were in town," Diana answered, although she hadn't.

"And how was your day otherwise?"

"Oh, this and that," Diana said with a smile. "Got all my little details done. I like to have everything taken care of so I'm not rushed. All free and clear now."

"I thought I'd show you our women's bar. It's out on the edge of town. That is, if you're still interested. I thought we'd go out for dinner and then to the bar, maybe some dancing."

"I'm in your hands," Diana answered with a smile.

Diana did another assessment as they approached Jessie's vehicle. Without really considering it, she had expected a passenger car, not the Jeep Cherokee. Then again, she watched Jessie unlock the passenger door for her, Jessie might have looked strange in a car. The Jeep Cherokee fit, a little rugged, sporty, town and country, yeah, it was a good fit.

"You travel a lot?" Jessie asked after she got behind the wheel.

"Pretty much."

"Thought I'd take you to something local. I always hate going somewhere and eating at the same kind of place that I could have gone to here." She looked over at Diana with a smile.

The restaurant was a local steak house, very tied into the local horse scene as Diana surmised from the pictures and décor. Earth tones, horse pictures, riders, racing saddles on the railings. Diana had to smile.

"Did I miss something?" Jessie asked as they sat in the wooden booth set up like a horse stall.

"When I was in France, I was on a tour with some exchange students," Diana started as she opened the menu. "Marie was the tour leader, she was an American but spoke excellent French. She—we were having a meal at one of the pensions and Madam Derosiers said something that none of us could catch but Marie just got this strange look. She gave some answer and we went on. She told us later that Madam was just asking if we like the mean, which was very good. I knew there was something Marie wasn't saying and I got her alone later. She finally told me that the Madam had asked if we liked the meal, she understood that horsemeat was not knowingly served in America."

Jessie's eyes widened as she glanced around at the horse pictures and then back down at the steak menu. "Ahhh, should I ask how it was?"

"Not as good as it was when I didn't know what it was." Diana laughed. "So coming in here and seeing all the horse pictures and steak for dinner, it just triggered the memory."

"Oh." Jessie shook her head. "I don't think I could have eaten anything there again." She gave a small grimace and changed the subject. "So you were in France?"

"Yes. I played tourist, did some studies. My papa thought it was a good idea." *To be out of the way, way out of the way. There was something going on he didn't want me to know about.* She shifted away from that thought; it wasn't something to remember now. "It was an experience but I was glad to get home, see familiar things."

"Speak French?"

"Not well. That was one drawback. I couldn't get into the French mentality, always felt like I was missing something. Of course, I've had that feeling traveling here in the States too. We're one country but there are such different regions."

"Sounds like you've traveled a lot."

"Yeah, I get around." The waitress came and they turned in their orders. "How about you?"

Jessie shook her head. "No, with the horse races and the sales, we get the worldwide travelers coming here. Don't need to go there and see them. Everyone comes here."

"It's a nice place to visit. There seems to be a lot of history here. I did some of the tours this morning."

"Lots of history. We may not have the nightlife of a big city but we're not a small town either."

"As long as you like horses and basketball," Diana teased. "I've seen that much."

"It's a good place to live."

Conversation continued over dinner. Diana talked about places she had been and Jessie talked about Lexington. Jessie was clearly a hometown girl, she liked where she was, didn't put it down like so many women Diana had met who had been eager to escape their home and go somewhere else. Comfortable in her own skin, Diana decided. No pretense. She liked that. They went to the bar afterward.

The women's bar was a comfortable place also, bar down one side, dance floor at one end, platform for a band which performed occasionally, Jessie explained. Cement floor and plastic tables and chairs, nothing especially sophisticated but neighborly. There was a good turnout, and Diana noticed that she got more than a few curious glances. Jessie was obviously known as a Romeo here too. She was greeted often and in a friendly enough manner but everyone left them alone. Fast and loose was Diana's guess. No need to meet whoever Jessie was with because it would change quick enough. Diana didn't mind being the latest conquest; she also had a little black book.

Dancing was good, crowd was friendly in an impersonal way. The place heated up in more ways than one and it was after midnight when they left. Diana moved closer to Jessie as they walked to the car, Jessie's arm easily resting across her shoulders. The night air was chillier than Diana had expected and Jessie was warm. She moved even closer.

"Cold?" Jessie asked as she unlocked the car door.

"A little."

Jessie reached into the backseat for a denim jacket. She draped it around Diana's shoulders. "Feel better?"

"Feels great," Diana could answer in all honesty.

"Are you coming in?" she asked when they got back to the hotel.

Jessie looked uncertain. "I'd like to," she said cautiously.

"Well, come on in," Diana invited.

"I need to make a couple of calls," Jessie said as Diana unlocked the door. She sounded reluctant.

"Of course." Diana waved to the phone on the desk. "There's the phone. I've got to make a pit stop."

"No, I'll use my phone."

From the bathroom, she thought about Jessie's change of attitude. Damn, she had thought it was going so good. She listened to hear the soft murmur of Jessie's voice and then she evidently made another call.

Jessie stood awkwardly in the center of the room, frowning at the phone as Diana came back out. "I'm sorry," she said as she looked up. "I can't stay, something's come up and I've got to go."

At two in the morning? But Diana hid her disappointment. Maybe this was something Jessie had set up to get her out of saying a point-blank no. But the evening had gone so well, dinner, conversation, the bar, dancing. "That happens," she said. "I'm sorry."

"So am I."

If Jessie had set this up, Diana thought, she was putting on a good acting job. She looked sufficiently unhappy as she took her jacket back when Diana coolly handed it to her. Diana didn't want to even use a ploy to see her again if Jessie wanted an out. She wasn't that desperate to hold on to someone.

They said goodbye at the door, Diana becoming cooler by the minute even as Jessie was reluctant to go, dragging it out as much as she could, a lingering kiss, inviting, considering she was leaving. Diana ended it.

"Goodbye." She almost shoved Jessie out the door and closed it.

Oh, well, she thought leaning against the door. *It was nice while it lasted.*

There was a sharp knock at the door. Diana turned, checked the peephole. Jessie?

She opened the door.

"Look," Jessie said quickly, "I really had a great time tonight, but I've really got to go. Wanted to ask you: a lot of the horse farms are open tomorrow for tours. Did you want to go on one?"

"Well, sure," Diana said with some bewilderment at the change.

"I'll pick you up at one, no, make it twelve thirty. That all right?"

"Fine."

"Great." Jessie leaned forward to give Diana a quick kiss. Then she turned and almost ran down the hall to the elevator.

Diana closed the door, leaning against it in bewilderment, shaking her head. So much for bailing out. *But what the hell goes on at two in the morning that she has to leave?*

***

Jessie did try to explain the next afternoon when she came to pick up Diana at the hotel. Jessie sat down on the small loveseat as Diana went back to the table by the window. "About last night," Jessie started. "I need to explain."

"No you don't," Diana cut her off. "You don't owe me any explanation, ever." Jessie looked at her in a puzzled way. "Besides, don't you know? Your friends don't need it and your enemies don't believe it."

Jessie looked even more puzzled as she leaned forward, her legs spread, her elbows on her knees. "And what class does that put you in?"

Diana shut the lid of the laptop. "The here and now. Last night's past. You're here now. That's all that matters."

"You don't want to know?"

Diana shook her head. "Why should I? Your life. You don't owe me anything." She walked over to stand between Jessie's legs. Jessie leaned back to look up at her, scooted back as Diana rested her knee on the seat. Jessie shook her head, giving Diana a sideways puzzled look. "All right," she said. "If that's your philosophy."

"That's my philosophy."

"You don't want to know anything else?"

Diana shook her head. "No." She searched Jessie's face. "Is that a problem?"

Jessie shook her head but she seemed uncertain. "I just thought you'd want to know more."

"Why? Are we going to see each other again, run into each other at the grocery store? Or the neighborhood bar?" She began to have second thoughts about this horse farm tour. There were better ways to spend a Sunday afternoon. She took Jessie's hand and brought the fingertips to her lips. "Tomorrow I'm gone." She examined Jessie's hand, long, slender fingers, delicate but strong, neatly trimmed nails. "I didn't think you were interested in exchanging life histories." She could feel Jessie's pulse increase. "Was it boring, darling?" She tongued the center of Jessie's palm.

"No." Jessie shivered as Diana slid her tongue down to Jessie's wrist. Jessie closed her eyes as her fingers curled.

"Did you have a good time?"

"Oh yes."

"Isn't that all that matters?"

With a sudden twist of her hand, Jessie caught Diana's wrist and pulled her down across her lap. She ran her hand up Diana's arm, went around her neck. She held her there a moment as Diana smiled at her.

"Isn't it?" Diana repeated softly.

Jessie slowly pulled Diana to her. Diana welcomed the caresses, ran her fingers through Jessie's short hair, ran her finger around Jessie's ear, trailed her fingers down Jessie's neck. This woman was so good; she knew just what to do.

"Did you really want to see the horse farms?" Jessie asked breathlessly when she broke away.

"Seen one horse, seen them all," Diana responded. She pulled Jessie's face back to her. As she pressed against Jessie's lips, she came up on her knees, straddled Jessie. When she broke away, she looked down into Jessie's face. "But you, darling, you're one of a kind."

***

Interesting, Diana thought as she drove away on Monday afternoon. Not exactly what I expected. Amazing what gems one can find in the hinterlands.

She glanced at her watch, already dismissing Lexington. If she pushed it, she could make it home by midnight. It would be good to sleep in her own bed even if it was late. And she could make her report to Papa in the morning. She must remember not to glow. Doing a favor for Papa promised payment. She wouldn't want him to think she got something great out of it and he could escape any obligation.

She settled back into the seat, a little sore but with a great sense of well being. The road was good, traffic was light. She should be able to make good time. Life was good, sometimes very very good.

CHAPTER TWO

Diana moved in and out of traffic once she got on Interstate 65. *It's like a racetrack out here today. Why all the traffic?* She had gotten a late start, not as early as she wanted to be on the road. Her thoughts drifted back to last night's pickup. Short, compact, blond, a little firecracker. Diana smiled at the memory. An entertaining evening to be sure, but what was her name? She played softball, had come into the women's bar after the game. Shorty? Sasha? Sue? Diana shook her head. It didn't matter. Diana wouldn't be seeing her again even if she did return to Mobile. Hadn't even been tempting enough to stay over another day. Not like that woman in Lexington, tall, dark, and handsome. Jessie, that was her name. Worked at the horse farm, something or other. Boy, she had been something. Diana had been dreaming of lean women in blue jeans ever since, gave her an itch she couldn't quite scratch. Which was strange because Jessie had been different from any of her other encounters.

"Gotta get out of this traffic," she muttered as she pulled onto the exit. "Just take a breather."

A cool drink sitting at the picnic table under a shade tree. Just what she needed. She had picked up a newspaper to browse through. Race qualifications in Indianapolis. Well, that explained the traffic. Maybe she needed to get off I-65. She pulled out her interstate map, traced out the lines. Ahhh, take I-40 over to I-75. That would go all the way up to Detroit. She traced the route with her finger. Added bonus, it would go right through Lexington. Well, now, wouldn't it be a nice place to layover and see if tall, dark and handsome was still available?

She gathered up the newspaper and tourist travel book. If traffic wasn't perfectly awful, she should have a nice evening in Lexington. Now that was something to look forward to.

However, much later, hopes dimmed. The Bungalow was as dark as she remembered and the crowd as professional until the changeover hour. Diana sat in the corner, nursing the high-priced drink, watching women come in, casually searching faces, and then turning away in dismissal. Interesting, but no Jessie. Waiting gave her time to think.

When was the last time she tried to hook up again with a one-night stand? Had she ever? Well, not anyone on the road at least. At home she remained aloof. Papa's warnings were paramount: trust nobody. The ones closest are the ones most likely to betray you. So don't let anyone get close.

She examined her drink, thinking about her papa. There was a whole lot of Papa's world she didn't want, but it was hard to reject it without rejecting him and she wasn't ready to do that. Not yet. Maybe someday. Maybe that was why she liked being on the road so much. An escape. On the road, everything seemed more normal. She could even leave Margaret at home; pretend she was just on vacation, going to visit family, friends. She could drop the suspicious attitude that was becoming second nature; stop the paranoid feelings that were becoming a second skin. She could forgo the cynical outlook she knew she was developing and just accept things at face value. Like Jessie.

That weekend had been a jewel. And it wasn't just the sex, although that, admittedly, had been mind-blowing. She had never before let anyone dominate her, take control the way Jessie had. Yet there was something else. It was just... She paused. She wasn't sure what it was. Jessie asking her out to dinner, going out dancing. It was so normal, getting-to-know-you stuff. Tourist stuff, a tour of the horse farms. When they finally got there, Diana had to chuckle. Small-town girl showing off the sights of her hometown. The cynical part of Diana was amused when she thought of all the sights she had seen, but another part of her was touched. Jessie treated her like a person, not just a sexual conquest. Maybe that was how Diana viewed it, a casual sexual encounter; maybe that was how it should remain, but when was the last time someone had treated her like someone they might want to know?

As the hour grew later and later, Diana began to lose hope. Maybe it had been just a one-time deal; but it would have been nice to repeat. Maybe Jessie had found someone; it had been several weeks. Things do change, sometimes quickly. Maybe her coming to this bar was a sometime thing, but Diana couldn't remember the way to the women's bar Jessie had taken her to, and she didn't want to ask.

She listened to the women's band, watched the dancers. Even if she didn't see Jessie, this was better than sitting in her hotel room. She would wait until midnight and then she would go. An early morning start, and then she would be home within a time frame that wouldn't require any explanation.

Midnight came and still no Jessie. Sighing, finally admitting just how disappointed she was, she picked up her jacket, checked her wallet and turned to leave.

"Leaving so soon, princess?" An arm slid around her so unexpectedly, so firmly that she just caught her reaction before she did something she would regret.

"Well, there, imagine running into you," she could say with a smile as she turned within that firm arm and met Jessie.

"Didn't expect to see you here. Thought you didn't come back this way."

"Oh, I was in the area and thought I'd make a detour." She looked Jessie over; surely she couldn't look as good as Diana remembered. Memories had a way of improving, but no, Jessie looked just as good. She was dressed again in those jeans and white shirt, must be a uniform with her, it probably was if she worked on the horse farms.

"I'm flattered—unless of course there's another reason for your coming and you're just stroking my ego by implying I might be the reason."

"Oh, you figured in," Diana said as she stroked the white shirt. "Had to check this out and see if you were really as good as my memories said you were."

"Mmmmm, memories improve with age; I might find it hard to live up to them."

She tossed Diana's jacket back on the chair and pulled her to the dance floor. It was a slow dance, they could have their arms around each other. The crowd had thinned out considerably, although it was still early.

"I don't think so," Diana said with a smile. "But then you never can tell. We might have to test the theories out again." Jessie chuckled, pulling Diana tighter against her. Diana pulled back to look her in the face. "You haven't gotten married, have you? Sneaking out on the poor wifey after she's gone to bed?"

"Hardly. Working late tonight." She pulled Diana against her and her hands caressed Diana's back. "But I like testing those theories again. Never can tell, things can change." She nuzzled Diana's ear. "I've dreamed of you," she whispered.

Diana smiled, immensely gratified to know she wasn't the only one touched. "Wet ones, I hope."

"Were yours?"

"Oh, God, yes."

Jessie chuckled as she whirled Diana around.

Yet when it came time to speak, Diana was strangely shy. That was a new emotion for her. She tried to be arch, running her hand up Jessie's arm. "I don't suppose you're available?"

Jessie caught her hand, brought it to her lips. "Not for the weekend." She kissed Diana's palm. "But tonight, yes." She lightly touched the center of Diana's palm with the tip of her tongue. "Is that all right?"

"Yes," Diana breathed. She was curious to know but she had her own rules. No questions, so she didn't ask. "I'm not at the Hilton this time. Rooms were easier to find."

"Not so crowded now," Jessie said as they walked out onto the street. "Where at?"

"The Inn over on Broadway. You know it?" Jessie nodded and Diana pointed to the late model blue-gray Chevy Cobalt parked across the street. "That's mine."

"Rental," Jessie observed.

"No sense putting business mileage on my car. Besides, it's a business expense. Shall I meet you over there? I assume you'll want to drive."

"Right." Jessie stopped at the Jeep, which Diana recognized.

Diana frowned as she walked across the street to her car. Not surprising someone would notice it was a rental, but she was surprised Jessie would mention it. She glanced back as she got in the car and saw Jessie still standing at the driver's door, watching her. Curious? Or protective? She had mixed emotions. She had a good feeling someone was watching out for her; a little uneasy someone was that observant about her. Then she remembered Jessie's kiss on the palm of her hand and she forgot about the cars.

"Mind if I bring this in?" Jessie asked after they parked side by side under one of the hotel parking lot lights. She indicated a small backpack she had slung over her shoulder.

Diana shook her head as she carefully locked the car. *Confident, weren't you? Of someone being available for you at least.* She felt a faint twinge of jealousy of some unknown woman and then she pushed it away. She was in no position to be jealous of anything or anyone.

"I thought about you after our weekend." Jessie leaned against the wall as Diana unlocked the door to her room.

"That's nice to know." *Just don't get too curious, sweetheart.*

"You never really said much about yourself." Jessie followed Diana into the room.

"I'm a modest sort of person."

Jessie looked around the room, another two-room suite. She reached over the back of the loveseat and set her backpack down. "Most modest people don't pick up one-night stands. Experience tells me they're self-confident, full of themselves." She turned back to Diana, leaned back against the loveseat.

"Like you?"

Jessie shrugged. Her dark eyes were curious, speculating. "I'm on my home ground. It's easy to be confident."

Diana advanced on Jessie. She ran her hands over Jessie's shirt. "A lot of people do things out of town they would never do on their home stomping ground. You know that."

"Is that what you're doing?" Jessie wrapped her arm around Diana. "Is there something back there I should worry about?"

"Like what?" Diana kept her voice light and even managed to chuckle.

Jessie brought Diana's hand up to her lips, looked over her fingers. "Jealous husband? Jealous girlfriend? Jealous boyfriend?"

Diana laughed almost in relief. "No, no and no. I'm free, unencumbered and I intend to stay that way." She ran her hands up over Jessie's shoulders. "Why the questions? I would think you'd be the last one to ask." She ran her fingers through Jessie's short hair, anticipating more. "Aren't you doing the same thing?"

"You're different," Jessie said flatly. "You're not like me."

Diana stepped back, stepped out of Jessie's arms. Maybe this was a mistake. Jessie wasn't asking questions, at least not the usual kind, but she was pushing. "Is that a problem? Because if it is, maybe we just don't need to go any further."

Jessie frowned. "I thought about you after that weekend. Every time I thought I knew where you were coming from, you changed. I thought you were a tourist just wandering in but it wasn't that. I thought maybe you were exploring something different but no." She shook her head ruefully, flushing a little. "No, you knew what you were doing all right." She was visibly puzzled. "I thought it'd be all sex but you enjoyed dinner, going out. You weren't in a real hurry to get back to the hotel." She stopped and frowned again. "When I bailed out, you didn't ask any questions."

"Wasn't my concern," Diana said shortly.

"'Never explain'," Jessie quoted. "You said that was your philosophy. So I gathered you weren't going to explain anything you did either."

Diana said nothing, waiting. Jessie clearly wanted to ask questions but she didn't.

"You made the entire weekend pleasant, both in and out of bed, like, like…" Jessie fumbled for a comparison. "Like someone I simply met and would want to get to know and just happened to have sex with." Then she stopped.

Again Diana waited; she'd had her share of waiting out people who made leading statements. Jessie watched her curiously but didn't say anything. "So?" Diana said finally.

"You came back," Jessie said in a puzzled tone. "I didn't expect that."

That makes two of us. Diana didn't have a response, not one she was ready to give. Jessie was thinking just like Diana had been thinking earlier. She had never looked up someone again. Why did she do so now? "Neither did I."

"So." Jessie looked like she was struggling with something. She looked away, around the room and then came back to Diana. "I mean." She stopped again. She took a deep breath. "It was a real nice weekend, Diana. Don't get me wrong. And I clearly got the idea that you were the 'love 'em and leave 'em' type, the mysterious stranger. That was the way you wanted it." She hesitated and then went on. "So why are you here?"

It was Diana's turn not to have an answer. She looked Jessie up and down, remembering all the pleasures that body had given her. There were so many things she could say but wouldn't be wise. "I just happened to be coming through again and wanted to see if you were available."

The look Jessie gave her said she didn't believe her. "Is that all?"

No. Diana walked away, half turning away from Jessie. "It was a very nice weekend for me too," she could finally admit. "I enjoyed all of it." She turned back. "I thought it was worth repeating."

"Worth enough to make a special trip?"

"I didn't make a special trip. I really am on my way from one place to another."

"And just happened to stop in?"

"No. Deliberately stopped. I wanted to see you again." *This really was a mistake. I need to keep my wants tucked away better and stick to my needs.* "But like I said a minute ago: if that's a problem, then maybe it needs to stop here."

"I don't know what you want from me."

"Nothing." *She didn't say there was a problem,* some part of Diana's mind latched onto. Diana moved to stand in front of Jessie again. She could see Jessie's tension, her indecision, but she didn't get the feeling Jessie was ready to leave. "If you're here, we can have a good time, whatever we want to do. If not, then maybe another time." She really wanted to touch her now, touch her and make her respond and drive her crazy and leave her wanting more. For the next time. *Now where the hell did that come from?*

"Your terms."

"You can always say no." *But you won't. Will you, darling?*

Jessie appeared to think about it. "What would you have done if I hadn't shown up?"

"Gone on my way." *But you did.* Diana began to unbutton Jessie's shirt, already feeling possessive.

Jessie's head came up but she made no move to stop her.

Diana ran her fingers over Jessie's collarbones, she spread the shirt open and slipped it off Jessie's shoulders. She watched Jessie's eyes turn darker, heavy lidded as Diana caressed the sides of Jessie's breasts. Jessie's breath quickened and she made a little convulsive movement to hunch her shoulders and then deliberately relaxed. She swallowed.

"Are you sure someone didn't put you up to this?" Jessie's voice was slightly huskier.

"Like who?" Diana pushed up the sports bra to uncover Jessie's breasts. The dark nipples popped up as Diana deliberately dragged the cloth taut.

Jessie reached back to grip her hands on the back of the loveseat. "Oh, I don't know. Someone who'd like to see me strung out."

"Jessie. Are you telling me that you've been elusive with women?" Diana moved in closer. She thumbed Jessie's nipples, her fingertips caressed the soft flesh of her breasts.

Jessie closed her eyes, leaned forward slightly into Diana's hands. "Maybe one or two." She licked her lips. "Sometimes you can say it's just fun and games but someone always thinks it's just a ploy and they want more."

"I know." Diana tugged at both nipples. "They start calling you romantic names and expect you to be there for them." Jessie shuddered and Diana moved closer. "But you wouldn't do that, would you, Jessie?" She bent down to take the nipple in her mouth as Jessie's hand snaked through her hair. With her other hand, Diana unsnapped, unzipped Jessie's jeans.

"Here. And. Now." She pulled Diana's face onto her breast.

Diana pushed down Jessie's jeans, lightly ran her fingers over Jessie's stomach. She felt Jessie's breath quicken, her hand in Diana's hair pull her closer. Diana lightly bit the taut nipple. Jessie groaned.

"Diana."

Diana ran her fingers through Jessie's wet hair, slid in between her lips. She was swollen and wet. She stiffened at Diana's touch, Diana felt Jessie's knees lock. Diana stroked lightly the full length of her clit, circled lightly, deliberately keeping her touch light, teasing. She pulled away from Jessie's breast and Jessie clutched for her. "You like it light to start with, don't you?"

"Yes." Jessie threw her head back as Diana knelt before her. Jessie reached behind her for support against the loveseat.

"You like to be teased and tormented, don't you?" Jessie grew even wetter. "Yes, I thought so." Diana parted the thick, dark hair. "So if I show up again, whenever, maybe, if." She lightly blew on the swollen clit. "Then it's just another layer of teasing, isn't it?"

"Y-yes, I g-guess so."

"Never knowing. Never for sure. Just waiting." Diana leaned forward to flick her tongue out. Jessie cried out at her touch. "You like that idea, darling?"

"Torture. Uncertain." Jessie was breathing hard and she was having trouble standing up.

Diana could feel Jessie shake and realized Jessie's pleasure was her pleasure. She never felt like that before, and in some corner of her mind she wondered where that feeling had come from. Then Jessie jerked her hips and Diana was waiting for her, wrapped her arms around Jessie's hips and held her still. "Just the way you like it, isn't it?"

"Oh, God, please." Jessie sank to her knees and Diana caught her. Together, they sank to the thick carpet. Jessie was reaching for her. "Diana."

"Yes, Jessie." Diana parted Jessie's legs, settled back against her, held her.

Jessie twisted and reached for Diana. "Oh, God," she repeated, her voice fading into inarticulate sounds until she finally arched and stiffened.

Diana rested her head against Jessie's hip until Jessie's breathing slowed. Then she moved up her and wrapped her arms around Jessie, pulled Jessie's head to her shoulder. "Definitely worth repeating," she murmured into the dark hair.

Jessie lay there, her eyes closed, until her breathing steadied. She opened her eyes and pushed away to meet Diana's gaze. "You like taking me apart, don't you?"

"I surely do," Diana agreed with a smile as she raised up on her elbow.

"You're going to ruin my reputation."

Diana gave a self-satisfied laugh. "Oh, no, darling. Your reputation is part of you. I'll protect that." She reached out to touch, brush back Jessie's hair. "I'll always protect you." With one finger, she traced down the side of Jessie's face.

Jessie rolled over on her back and Diana let her hand fall away. Jessie kicked off the jeans that were down around her ankles. "Why does everything you say sound like it has a double meaning?"

"My mystique."

Jessie got up, picking up her shirt and bra. "When did these come off?"

"I don't know. I wasn't paying attention." She took hold of Jessie's hand and let Jessie pull her to her feet.

"I don't know about you," Jessie said even as she slid her arm around Diana and pulled her tight against her. "I let you do things that I've let no one else do."

Oh, you too? "Oh, really? What's that?"

Jessie bent down slightly and bit lightly against Diana's neck. Diana gasped in surprise. "Who are you? How do you manage to do this to me?"

Diana laughed softly. "Because you let me; because you want me to." She wrapped her arms around Jessie. "Can't you feel it, this attraction between us?"

"Yes." She turned Diana's face to her, her gaze intent and Diana stopped her laughter. "I do. I just don't know if it's good or not." She held Diana still and kissed her hard, claiming, as if she were trying to take back what Diana had taken from her. Diana understood the feeling exactly.

Later, as Diana drifted off to sleep, all she could think was, *Definitely a keeper.*

***

The next day, Jessie took Diana across town for lunch, another pleasant excursion. "Not so crowded now," Jessie explained. "The claiming races for the horses are over. And the Derby's over so the horse crowd has left."

"Yeah," Diana said with distaste. "All the traffic is switched to car racing. You wouldn't believe the traffic up to Indianapolis." She shook her head. "It's so nice and quiet, peaceful here." She sat back in the seat and watched Jessie drive. "What's wrong?"

Jessie looked at her and raised her eyebrows. "What makes you ask?"

"You look sad."

"Mother's Day weekend. My mother died three years ago. That's why I can't stay the weekend. I promised I'd be with the family."

"I'm sorry about your mother. Had she been sick?"

Jessie shrugged as she pulled into the parking lot. "Cancer. It happens." She changed the subject. "Now this might look like a little hole in the wall but they have the best food."

Diana shook her head. "You're going to spoil me."

"Keep showing you a good time, you'll keep coming back." She gave Diana a mischievous look as she opened the door for her. She licked her lips and wiggled her eyebrows, which made Diana laugh. Jessie was so open, so enjoyable. And she had family loyalty.

Yeah, Diana thought, I'll probably be coming back.

CHAPTER THREE

After getting her sister to bed, Jessie wandered out to sit on the back deck. The neighborhood was quiet; Nicki was ready for the next day. She could take a breather. She sat down on the top step, leaned against the support post and stretched out her long legs.

"Strange to have you home on a Friday night."

She jumped; she hadn't seen her dad in the lounge chair in the corner. "Oh, Dad. Didn't see you there."

"That's bad, could be dangerous." He paused. "Got something on your mind?"

"Yeah, guess so." She pulled some chive out of the flower pot, Nicki's school project. She didn't say anything more.

"Want to talk?"

Jessie didn't turn around to face him. She and her dad were close but some things, well, he was her dad. "You want to deal with it?"

"Work problems? Someone hassling you?"

Jessie shook her head. "No, no more than usual."

She had two advantages in the department, three maybe. She was family, police family. Her father and her grandfather were Lexington cops. Okay, she was a dyke, but for the old-timers who had watched her grow up, she was still Matt's daughter. They gave her a rougher time over her age than being a dyke. For another segment of the department, okay, she was a dyke, but she was "our dyke" and while they might razz her, it wasn't bad. The new ones coming in, well, there were a few bigots but for the most part her being a dyke was like her having dark hair. Immaterial. And she was a good cop. She worked hard. She went the extra mile. She did the extra duty as much as she could with her time available. She earned everything she got.

"Mother's Day bother you?"

Jessie shook her head. "No, well, not like last year. They tell me it gets better. I just think I'll always miss her. And certainly Nicki misses her mama." They both fell silent then for a few minutes.

"I guess that leaves your love life."

Jessie gave a chuckle. Love life. Such as it was. More like her sex life.

"No denial there, must be it. Guess that means you don't want to talk to your old man about it." His voice was quiet, a reassuring presence in the darkness.

"I met someone." Images of Diana came up, not just Diana in bed, Diana on the dance floor, Diana sitting across the table from her, Diana listening to her, her head slightly bent like she did when she was intent. Diana touching her. "How'd you know Mom was the one?"

There was a big sigh—regret? Sadness. Loss.

"I just knew. She just touched me. In ways that no one else ever had. And I knew. And I never looked back."

Jessie sighed. She thought that. But she had thought that before.

"She's different."

"How so?"

That was the problem, Jessie mused. She didn't know.

"How's she feel about you being a cop?"

"She doesn't know." Jessie threw the chewed leaf away. "I haven't told her."

"Why not?"

Jessie leaned her head back against the post, looked up at the night sky. Stars were coming out. "Oh, Dad, you know sometimes that uniform is a chick magnet. I wanted to be sure it was me, not the uniform."

Matt chuckled. "And I thought dykes were different."

Jessie shook her head and then realized her dad couldn't see her. "Not so much. Some are attracted to authority, those power dynamics, want to be protected just as much as straight women. Or to challenge you." Jessie thought she had seen all the types.

"I would think," Matt said slowly, "that you being a cop would be difficult to keep secret."

Jessie blew out a breath. "She's not local. And we haven't exactly been out in public."

"Ohhh."

There was a long silence and Jessie wondered how he would take that information. Her not coming home had always been ignored, well, not ignored. She had her cell phone, she'd text a message. Sometimes he even pretended she had been out early when she came in. Sometimes he assumed she had gotten called out and she didn't correct him.

"What do you know about her?"

That was the crux of the matter, Jessie thought. "Damn near nothing." Her dad said nothing and Jessie didn't have to hear him say anything to know the arguments. She had made herself vulnerable. She had gone with someone she didn't know, she didn't know Diana's history, her connections, where she lived, what she did for a living. Nothing. His next question truly surprised her.

"Is she good to you?"

Good? What a question from your daddy. She thought about it. Well, aside from the sex, Diana was good. Diana talked to her like she had a brain. Even though Diana had traveled, she didn't treat Jessie like some country hick. She could carry on an intelligent conversation and assumed Jessie had opinions and could defend them. She definitely had her own opinions and could also defend them, but that hadn't stopped her from listening to Jessie's opinion. "Yes," she finally answered. *Except for not telling me anything about herself.*

"How does she feel about cops?"

"I don't know. Hasn't exactly come up."

"How's she feel about authority?"

"Doesn't seem to have any more gripes than the general population."

"Check her out?"

"As much as I could; couldn't even find a traffic ticket."

"Drugs?"

"Haven't seen any evidence."

"Track marks can be hidden."

"Trust me, Pops. I've seen everything."

"Oh." There was another silence. "What's your gut say?"

"No warning signals, nothing except nice." She smiled in the darkness ruefully. Nice, indeed.

She heard her dad start to say something, stop. Finally he came out with it. "What's the problem?"

How to explain? Jessie hesitated, not sure if she wanted to be this open with her dad. She had come this far, might as well. "We met at the bar, everything really clicked. I spent the weekend with her. This was three months ago."

"Uh-huh." He was uncomfortable, Jessie could tell. She decided to leave the details out.

"We had a good time. That seemed to be it. She left town, on her way."

"Was that wise? Going with someone you didn't know."

Daddy-role just kicked in, Jessie thought. "Probably not," she admitted. *Wasn't the first time, Pops. Probably won't be the last.* "I thought that was the end of it. She came back through town Mother's Day weekend. She came back to see me."

"Why?"

Jessie turned her head, surprised. Her initial reaction was *why not?* And then she realized her dad's suspicion was a cop's suspicion, something she had lost when she was with Diana. "She said she felt a connection."

"And you?"

"There's something." She turned back to look down the row of houses. "That's what bothers me." She stood up, automatically brushing off the seat of her pants. This conversation wasn't giving her any answers, just showing her how little was really there. "She says she does a lot of business travel, may or may not come this way. Promised nothing. Asked for nothing. If she comes through and I want to see her, great. If not, well, that's life. I may never see her again and all this is just a bunch of worry about nothing." She went to the sliding glass door and slid it open.

"So what's the problem, Jessica Ann?"

Jessie paused, her foot already in the door. She looked around to where she could barely see him in the corner. "I want to, Dad. I feel such a strong connection that I want more. And I know so little about her that I'm afraid of what might be there." She waited, hoping for pearls of wisdom, something that would tell her what to do, something that would shed some light on her puzzlement and show her which way to go.

"I don't know what to tell you, Jessie. You know all the pitfalls. Being gay doesn't make you immune from being used. Just be careful."

"Yeah." And she went inside and started a load of laundry just to have something to do.

***

"Is there something going on in Lexington I don't know about? New client maybe?" Margaret carefully asked her employer. "Seems like Lexington is turning up on a lot of hotel receipts."

Diana uttered a noncommittal sound. They were working out in the exercise room, Diana walking on the treadmill, Margaret on the weights.

"Your papa's starting to ask questions. What am I supposed to tell him?"

"What have you told him?"

"Gave him some song and dance. You know that's hard to do. And dangerous."

Diana shut off the treadmill and stepped off. "We agreed. This was my business, my concern. He isn't to be involved."

Margaret put aside the weights and reached for the towel. "This may not be family business, but he's still your papa." She wiped her face off. Being caught between the strong-willed father-daughter duo was not an enviable position even if she had been doing it for years. The position was just getting more complicated lately. "The next thing he wanted to know was why I wasn't along. That was a little harder to explain."

"Oh, that's the easy part. I didn't want you along."

"That's not always your choice," Margaret said carefully. "Or mine," she muttered under her breath.

But Diana heard her. "Yes, it is. My clients, my deliveries, my conditions. I'm a college kid on vacation. College kids don't have bodyguards." She gave Margaret a conspiratorial smile to take the sting away. "Or chaperones. Or secretaries. Or assistants. Or any of the other roles you might suggest." She threw the towel over the handlebars. "Ready for the swim?"

"Inside or outside?"

"Guys around?"

"Off grounds."

"Outside then."

Diana led the way to the outside pool. She casually stripped off her shorts, top, and turned to watch Margaret. The older woman glanced around, checking the perimeter. She stripped off her clothing, revealing narrow hips, small breasts, flat abs. She was muscular, strong, and capable. That's what bodyguards were supposed to be.

"So tell me what's going on in Lexington."

Diana made another noncommittal sound.

"You've been going back quite a bit, even when you don't have a run in the area. This one's lasting longer than usual."

"Lexington has lots of history, lots of attractions." She gave a slow smile. "Need to explore it all." She gave Margaret a wink. "Don't want to miss anything."

Margaret cocked an eyebrow. "Must be very interesting."

Diana dived into the pool and Margaret followed her. Laps later, they were in the showers and then retired to the bedroom to dress for dinner.

"He's going to start insisting I go along."

"Margaret, I love you. You've been at my back one way or the other all my life, but I'm not taking you along. A bodyguard will cramp my style."

"I can be invisible."

Diana laughed. "Not where I go, darling. Where I go is just two of us. Three would really be a crowd."

"This is not good, sweet pea."

"Good is not the word for it, Margaret. It's—it's…" She closed her eyes and searched for the word.

Margaret sighed and sat down on the bed. "Sounds like love." She shook her head. "Just don't lose your head, child. I'm real fond of mine and your sweet papa will have mine on a silver platter if anything happens to you."

Diana laid her hand on Margaret's knee. "No one knows about me, Margaret. I'm papa's secret child; I don't exist."

Margaret caught Diana's hand. "You feel real to me."

***

Diana had made detours to Lexington for months, even met Jessie's father and sister. That had been unplanned or she would have begged off. Meeting the family was just too close, and as fond as she was growing of Jessie, she just couldn't foresee dealing with Jessie's family. *I mean, what's to say? I come to town just to sleep with your daughter?* She shivered at the thought, but the event had come up so unexpectedly she was taken off guard, something she really didn't like.

They had gone out for an afternoon, sightseeing. Jessie was so good at knowing places of historical interest to show Diana when she came to town. They were on their way back and had driven past a park.

"Ahh, there's Dad," Jessie had exclaimed and whipped into the park entrance. By the time Diana gasped and even halfway formulated an excuse, Jessie parked the Jeep and got out. She paused, one foot on the parking bumper, looking over her shoulder, and Diana could see there was nothing to do but go through with it.

The man sitting on the park bench watching over the kids in the creative playground glanced around and smiled when he saw Jessie. When he saw Diana and, more importantly, saw Jessie take hold of her hand, he got to his feet.

"Ahh, Jessie." He glanced at Diana. "So this is the person who keeps you busy."

Diana was amused to see Jessie's flush, but at least, she realized, she didn't have to hide the fact there was some sort of attachment between the two of them.

"Ahh, Diana, this is my dad, Matt Galbreath. Dad, this is Diana DeVilbiss."

Diana held her hand out to the somewhat stocky dark, haired man who had a broad, cheerful, ruddy face. Clearly Jessie might have gotten her coloring from her father but not her body build. His grip was firm, strong, direct, much like his daughter's and Diana had an initial good impression. "Good to meet you," she greeted him even as she began to casually look around the park. The hair stood up on the back of her neck, and her stomach clenched with a vaguely familiar unease. She felt like she was being watched, something she really didn't like; like when she went over to her papa's and he was under surveillance. Her warning radar was going off like mad and she didn't understand why.

"Where's Nicki?" she heard Jessie ask her dad. Diana took the opportunity to look around when Matt turned to point at the kids at the wooden castle inside the fence. She scanned the entire area, didn't see anything that should have made her uneasy. There were no parked cars with drivers just sitting in them, no one on park benches just casually reading the newspaper. Still she turned, trying to act as if she were looking at the kids. She gripped her unease and clamped down on it when she saw Jessie give her a curious glance and she stood still, focusing on the playground.

"Which one is she?" she asked.

"She's the one up on the rampart," Jessie replied slowly, turning from Diana back to the castle.

"She looks like you, from what I can see from this distance." She looked over the playground again. "You have a castle to climb when you were a kid?"

"No. There was a community group came in and built it, all the bridges, ramps, a couple of years ago. I think I was jealous. I only had trees to climb."

Her dad laughed. "And monkey bars and swing sets, and ladders. Caught her up on the roof one time when I forget to take the ladder down. She was six."

"Dad!" Jessie playfully punched her father's arm, and Diana was surprised to see a comfortable, open relationship. She could not imagine, even as much as she loved her papa, ever playfully punching him in the arm.

Matt suddenly turned at some ruckus on the playground where two little boys were a little too spirited with their sword play. "Hey! You stop that!" He started toward them with a firm step and Diana had the impression of authority and firmness. Matt glanced over his shoulder. "You going to be late coming in tonight? Or won't I see you until tomorrow?"

Jessie flushed again. "Tomorrow," she answered. She had an embarrassed laugh and he was laughing too until he got closer to the boys.

"That is not knightly behavior," he chided them.

"Good meeting you," Diana called, relieved more than she could say at the fact they were leaving, and he answered with a wave.

"You were uncomfortable," Jessie said as she unlocked the Jeep and opened it for Diana.

Diana thought of several things she could say and discarded them all. "Yes."

Jessie went around the Jeep and Diana leaned over to unlock the door. "How come?" Jessie asked as she got in.

Diana shrugged. "Didn't expect to meet your family. I always find meeting families, especially fathers, a little nerve-racking when I'm sleeping with their daughters."

Jessie grinned. "Yeah, I guess that can be a little unsettling. Sorry about that. I didn't mean to take you off guard."

"I never like surprises, Jessie." Diana paused. "Your mother must have been the tall and thin one."

"She was, but I've got Dad's coloring. I've got a lot of Dad in me."

They went back to the hotel, to their favorite spot, favorite activity, but at some level they were both distracted.

"Need to ask you something," Jessie said finally.

Diana looked up at her. Jessie was straddling her, across her stomach, most of her weight on her knees but just the same, Diana was pinned down. Jessie drew a finger down between Diana's full breasts, and Diana wondered if her sudden pounding heartbeat was visible. "What's that?" she managed to ask in a light tone. She stretched out more, arms wide, legs open, a physical exposure even as she mentally barricaded herself for questions.

Jessie came up on her hands and knees, teasing Diana's mouth with her breast. Even as casual as her voice was, even offering herself, Diana knew that Jessie's coming question would be serious.

"I know your philosophy is never to explain, and you're always in the here and now. We don't talk about anything else, you've made that clear, but I need to know something."

"What's that?" Diana asked as she attempted to mouth Jessie's nipple that she kept just out of reach.

"You're not doing anything illegal, are you?"

"Like what?" Diana said with a half laugh as she just missed mouthing Jessie's breast. "I must admit, I'm not up on Kentucky sodomy laws but I'm willing to bet that since we're in the Bible Belt, some of this isn't exactly kosher."

Jessie did laugh, which relieved Diana even as Jessie pushed her back down into the bedding and came down on top of her. She lay over Diana, arm to arm, leg to leg. She bent down to run her tongue over Diana's lips. "No," she said in a quiet serious voice, "I mean serious things, like drugs, or guns, or I don't know, stolen items, or you're some secret assassin going or coming from an assignment." She nibbled on Diana's lip. "Maybe money laundering or some such thing. I don't know." She ran her fingers through Diana's thick hair, sliding under Diana's head and holding her still so she could kiss her.

Oh, God, if I ever do anything and the police interrogate like this, I am so sunk! Diana opened her mouth to take Jessie in, feeling the kiss down to her toes, and she curled them until they cramped.

"No," she said breathlessly when Jessie released her.

"Not into drugs or bootleg liquor or anything like that?" Jessie still asked seductively.

Diana drew back. "Are you crazy? Drugs'll kill you, later if not sooner. I've never even tried pot!" She looked up at Jessie, who pulled back from her in obvious disbelief. "Have you?"

Jessie came up on her elbows, evidently surprised at the question. "Yeah," she said reluctantly. "Once or twice in college. It didn't do anything for me." She blinked. "Well, actually it did. It put me to sleep."

Diana laughed, relieved. She shook her head. "No, I've never done anything. I have this control thing; I know it's foolish. The idea of putting something in me that would make me out of control." She shuddered. "Can't imagine why anyone would even want to do that deliberately." She shook her head but turned back to look up directly into Jessie's face. "As for any of the other things you mentioned, no." She made her look as direct and as open as she could. "And I'm not even going to ask where those questions came from." She wasn't laughing now, she wasn't angry; she knew she had done nothing to arouse suspicions except not explain anything.

Jessie searched Diana's face, then bowed her head to kiss between Diana's breasts. "I'm sorry. Sometimes I have a suspicious mind. I thought it better to ask rather than let it nag on me. I didn't want something like that unspoken to lie between us."

Diana deliberately relaxed. How could she be offended? She reached up to caress Jessie's face. "I don't want that either," she said. "I've done nothing illegal; I'm not doing anything illegal. I just don't want to talk about the life I have away from you. It's very different, and coming here to see you is a marvelous release, an escape, a restorative, and I don't want to bring any baggage with me. I promise you, it's not anything that will touch you. I just think being with you is one of the best things that has happened to me and I need to keep you this way."

She realized even as she spoke the words that seemingly came from nowhere that they were the truth. She didn't realize her eyes had filled with tears until Jessie wiped them, bent down and kissed her neck. "I'm so sorry," Jessie whispered. "Suspicious minds. Forget I said anything."

Diana lifted Jessie's face to her. "Make me forget," she commanded. She slid her arms around Jessie and pulled her down. "Pull me into your world, hold me there. I want to be with you." She shuddered when Jessie shifted her weight downward and Diana opened up to welcome her.

This was what she wanted. Jessie's tongue drove away all thoughts of past and future, just the present and as Jessie's hands slid under her ass and lifted her, she lost all coherent thought. She was conscious of Jessie's hair tickling her, her hands strong enough to hold her and the heat flowing between them. She raised up, propping herself on her elbows, looking down at Jessie's dark head buried between her thighs, wanting this moment to last forever. She shuddered as she dropped her head back, giving herself over to Jessie, Jessie of the dark eyes, Jessie of the strong hands, Jessie of the quick tongue. Her entire world consisted of this moment, this woman, this loving.

The visits continued throughout the winter, Diana coming through town and meeting up with Jessie, usually at the Bungalow; Jessie with her little black bag with a change of clothes and whatever else she needed waiting for her in the Jeep, and then they went off to wherever Diana had rooms this trip, spending a great deal of time in bed. Diana marveled at her luck. Jessie was almost always available, maybe not the whole weekend but some of it. No one had ever held her attention this long much less this intensely. Sooner or later, with everyone else, there had been questions, demands, wanting more and Diana would disappear. Jessie did none of this. She asked no questions, volunteered few things about her life. She seemed quite content with Diana dropping into her life for a weekend here and there and then disappearing for weeks on end. Her only indication that she enjoyed Diana's attention was a folded piece of paper she handed Diana with her phone number.

"Here," she said, her dark eyes direct. "Call me when you get to town next time. I may not make it down to the bar."

"All right," Diana had said. She tucked the number in her wallet but hadn't given her number in exchange. She was smitten but she still wasn't ready to take chances.

This came at the end of a good weekend. Jessie had taken Diana on a personal tour of the horse farm, white fences, long low barns. Diana had decided springtime in Lexington was a beautiful time of the year, the grass really was blue. The white board fences looked fantastic against the fields and watching the long-legged new colts and fillies discovering grass and trying out their spider legs was a public relations dream. Jessie had been very much at home as she led Diana through pastures and fields. Then she had taken her to a secluded spot, and pulled out the picnic basket and blanket from the back of the Jeep.

"Well, aren't you a wonder," Diana marveled. "It's been ages since I've been on a picnic."

"Ages for me too," Jessie replied. She handed over the blanket for Diana to spread as she pulled out the small cooler, retrieved the bottle of wine, the chilled wineglasses.

"Oh, aren't we doing this in style?" Diana sat on the blanket, watching her lover pour the wine. Jessie just got better and better. "You are a treasure." She took the glass of wine, tasted, nodded in appreciation. "I don't understand why you're still fancy free. Why someone hasn't snapped you up. Not that I'm complaining—I love the time we spend together. But, Jessie, even at the risk of shooting myself in the foot, you deserve to be appreciated full time."

There was a ripple of discomfort, of closure across Jessie's face and she busied herself emptying the picnic basket. She only looked up when Diana laid her hand on Jessie's forearm.

"I didn't mean to pry. You are just so good, not just in bed. You're thoughtful, considerate. You're beautiful." She smiled at Jessie's flushing. "I can't imagine there is no one out there trying to win you." She turned over Jessie's hand, bent down and kissed her palm. "I've seen women fall over you at the bar. You like the solitary life?"

Jessie pulled away and went back to the picnic basket. Diana watched her, seeing the unease, the discomfort. It was the first time she had seen Jessie uncomfortable and as much as she regretted saying anything that might spoil their time together, she was curious. "Jessie?"

"I don't live alone, I'm not solitary," Jessie said abruptly. "I live with my dad, with my little sister." She looked up at Diana as if seeing how she took that information. She sat down cross-legged on the other side of the picnic basket. She took a gulp of wine, set it down on the closed portion of the picnic basket. "I know, you're wondering why a woman of my age is still living with her dad instead of having her own place."

"No," Diana answered quickly. "Not at all. I still live with my dad. We're very close. Rather than him live alone and me live alone, why shouldn't we live together?" And that was true for her, as far as she went.

There was some small relief in Jessie's eyes but there was also pain and guardedness. "If you don't want to say anything," Diana said carefully, aware that she was close to breaking her own rules for living in the here and now, "that's fine. On the other hand, I'm a good listener and you know you won't have to face me with the knowledge you've spilled secrets. I know sometimes that makes it easier to talk."

Jessie nodded. "I know." She wouldn't look up at Diana. "It just touches a lot of things and I haven't really been able to talk about it."

Diana immediately thought of any number of things a woman wouldn't be able to talk about. Her little sister was really her daughter. She had an incestuous relationship with her father. Her mother didn't die, she ran away with Jessie's boyfriend. Her father was abusive and she was guarding her sister. *Stop it*, she told her galloping imagination. *You've been reading too many lurid novels, too many tabloids, watched too many soap operas. Stop and listen to her because if she talks, you really need to listen.*

"I guess you would say I'm waiting." She drank some of the wine, stared at the glass. Diana knelt beside the picnic basket and pulled out the plates, the crackers and cheese. She laid them out, set the plate close to Jessie and sat back down. She was interested in whatever could upset this calm, self-contained woman.

"For?" Diana finally ventured to ask.

"When I was in college," Jessie finally said slowly. "I met someone." She glanced up at Diana and Diana nodded, encouraging. "I mean, I knew about myself and I had fooled around some but I was waiting."

"For the special someone," Diana supplied when Jessie paused again.

"Yes," and there was relief in her voice that Diana understood.

"And that was?"

"Julie."

"Julie." All right, Diana thought. Throw away all the soap opera ideas and think instead that Julie really did a number on you. "And Julie hurt you?"

"No." Jessie looked up in quick denial. "Julie would never do that."

"Oh, I'm sorry. Wrong guess," Diana apologized. *Well, that was a quick defense*, she thought, more curious now. "Tell me," she commanded. "I mean, we've got the afternoon, don't we? And you haven't talked about Julie to anyone, have you?"

Jessie had this puzzled expression. "It doesn't bother you that I would talk about another woman?"

Diana smiled. "Honey, you and I have this thing: when we're here, we're *here*. Otherwise, we have lives that don't include each other. For whatever reason, that's been working for us. You want to talk about Julie; what have I got to lose by listening?" She watched Jessie mull this over. She took a cracker and cheese, nibbled on it, as she let Jessie think. "I take it Julie's no longer in your life?" she asked after what she thought was a sufficient amount of time.

Jessie shook her head. Clearly this was difficult for her.

Diana was curious now; at the same time, she was inviting confidences she had no intention of reciprocating. "Honey, if you don't want to talk about this, it's okay. We can have a marvelous picnic."

"No," Jessie said reluctantly. "It's just, you're right. I haven't talked about Julie to anyone. And," she looked up at Diana, still putting things together, "we do have this strange thing, don't we? I feel more comfortable with you, and it's because I know we can have a great time and then you're gone. You're not in the rest of my life. We have these great times in bed and that's it."

Most women want more, Diana thought as she sipped her wine. I know why it's good for me. I wonder why it's good for you.

"We met at a ballgame," Jessie started slowly.

Diana lay down on her side, her head propped up on her arm. It was a familiar story, meeting at school, then running into her at the gay bar. They got to know each other and one thing led to another, they discovered over Christmas break they really missed each other and then the friendship went to a deeper level. Over spring break, they became intimate and it was glorious.

"Then finals week, I got a call from home," Jessie said slowly. "Julie and I had been planning on spending the next week together before we went home. My finals were finished before hers and I was waiting. Mom called, said that Dad had a heart attack, a bad one. I needed to come home right away. I couldn't get hold of Julie, left her a message but I was on the road within twenty minutes, max. I couldn't get home fast enough." She stopped there, took out one of the ham sandwiches.

"But your dad was all right, he made a recovery."

Jessie handed off a sandwich to Diana. "Yes, but everything else went to hell in a handbasket." There was strain on her face that warned Diana to be patient. "It was a bad one; he had to take an early retirement. He needed care and before he was up and around, Mom got sick. There was Nicki to take care of, Dad to take care of. Mom was going to doctors all the time, in and out of the hospital as they tried to find out what was wrong with her. She was getting sicker. I was taking care of everyone. It's hard being a caretaker." She looked up at Diana. "No one understands what it's like unless they've been there."

"It's hard," Diana agreed. "I've only been there part of the way, but enough to know it's difficult." There was a moment's silence. "How old was Nicki?"

"She was eight." Jessie smiled as she spoke of her sister; there was real affection there, not just duty and responsibility, Diana realized. "My folks got teased that they couldn't stand the empty nest so Mom got pregnant when I hit high school. She thought she was going through menopause but she was pregnant instead."

She sighed and continued. "I didn't make it back to school. Mom got sicker, chemo, just went downhill so damn fast. Before we even had time to adjust, she was gone."

"I'm so sorry." Diana reached out for Jessie but Jessie didn't see it.

"I never made it back to school. Dad still needed care; he couldn't handle Nicki by himself. We were all shaken by the loss of Mom. I went from college student to full-time mother of Nicki, caretaker for

Dad. When he recovered more, I was able to finish up my college credits here at UK."

"What happened to Julie?"

"I tried, I really did. There just wasn't enough time; there was so much that first year, Dad, Mom, Nicki. Julie was still in college, she had nothing but college. She couldn't understand that my time wasn't my own. I didn't have time for her."

"Shit!" Diana sat up. "You probably didn't have time for *you*. Good God, woman."

Jessie looked up at her as if confessing a grievous sin. "I abandoned her."

"*Abandoned?*" Diana's jaw dropped. "Good God, Jessie. You took on a lot at an age when most of us are just learning how to manage our own lives. You took on a kid, two sick parents. And you think you abandoned her? My God, I'm more inclined to think she abandoned you."

"I loved her so much, she was so special." Jessie's eyes were filled with remorse and Diana realized she had never been able to grieve. Or let go.

"Honey." Diana sat up, moved close to Jessie. "Surely she understood."

Jessie shook her head, looking down into her lap.

"But you talked to her, explained how things were."

"I tried, there just was never enough time. I couldn't get away to spend any time with her. And once or twice when I did see her, I had to bring Nicki."

"Did she come see you?"

Jessie shook her head.

Diana was quickly forming her own opinion of Julie and it wasn't a positive one. She knew better than to say anything negative. "Honey, I'm so sorry it turned out so badly."

"I felt like I didn't have time to devote to anyone else."

"And you're still waiting for Julie," Diana said with sudden realization.

"I guess so."

"Ohhhh." Well that explains a lot, Diana thought. "Honey, how long has it been since you've seen Julie?"

Jessie stopped to think. "Well, let's see, Nicki was eight, maybe nine. She had just started the new school so I was having more time. That was, oh, maybe four years ago, maybe five."

"Honey, that's a long time to wait."

Jessie shrugged in helplessness. "I still love her," she said sorrowfully. "Every time I think I'm over her, something happens and it hurts all over again, like it happened yesterday." She buried her face in her hands.

Diana moved close to put her arms around Jessie. "Oh, honey, I'm so sorry you're still hurting." Here she had thought her Romeo was so self-sufficient and instead she was a woman hiding a broken heart. It didn't put her off that Jessie was crying on her shoulder; it only endeared her more.

"I didn't want to abandon her," Jessie protested. "Mom, Dad, they all needed me."

"And you didn't fail them," Diana soothed. "Families are important, they need our loyalty, our love. I'm so sorry Julie didn't understand that. That's not a failing on your part; it's a good trait, an admirable trait. And you can only do so much. Jessie, you did what you had to do."

Jessie closed her eyes, took a deep breath.

Diana turned Jessie's face up to her. "You showed strength and resiliency and responsibility when the majority of us are still trying to figure out what life is about. You took on responsibilities beyond your years. You're a good person. I can never see you abandoning anyone when they need you. You've got character."

Jessie flushed and looked away. "Now you're just trying to flatter me."

And now it's time to let go. Diana released Jessie. "No, just calling it the way I see it." She sat back, watching Jessie gather herself together, put her shell back on. "I'm very flattered you let me see that part of you."

"Well," Jessie said casually as she poured another glass of wine. "As you said, you're here today, gone tomorrow."

"That does make it easier." She decided it was time to change the subject, let Jessie out carefully. "Did your dad make a good recovery?"

"Yeah, he's fine now. He took weight off and exercises more and has regular checkups but his last checkup was fine. And Nicki's doing great in school." She looked up at Diana with her usual cocky grin. "And I get around all right."

"Oh, yes you do," Diana agreed. She guessed the disclosures were finished for the day. "A terror to the community and unstable relationships."

"Well, it's gotten much better since you've been in the picture," Jessie said. "You know, a nice distraction. All the insecure women breathe easier when they see you in town; we seem to have become somewhat of an item in certain circles."

That's not good.

"Then there are those who think you're just a cover; and some who even doubt your existence. They just know something has occupied me for the weekend."

"Well, I'm so glad I can aid the insecure," Diana drawled back. She met Jessie's smiling eyes. "I can well imagine what Jessie on the prowl does for them."

"I know," Jessie breathed, moving in on Diana. "I'm terrifying."

"A big pussy cat."

"Tiger pussy cat."

"Oh, is it safe to have felines on a horse farm?"

Jessie put Diana on her back, straddled her, looked down into her face. "The horses are safe," she said in a husky voice. "Can't speak for other life forms."

Diana shivered, laughed as she looked up at her lover. "I'm terrified." She watched Jessie lower herself to bring their lips together. Oh, what was it about this woman who could just touch her and do this to her? She lifted her head, exposing her throat, shivering as Jessie kissed down her neck. She wrapped around Jessie, with new appreciation for the woman behind this long lean body. "Oh, God, Jess." She could feel this woman's strength and tenderness, wanton sexuality and responsibility. She felt lips at her breast without realizing Jessie had unbuttoned her shirt, unsnapped her bra. Warm breezes wafted against flesh not usually exposed and she knew she was helpless, deliberately so, with forethought and with abandonment, in Jessie's hands. And she knew she was safe there.

She thought of that again as she knelt between Jessie's long legs. Safe wasn't a feeling she was accustomed to having outside the family, but she felt safe with Jessie. She glanced up at Jessie's lean naked body stretched out before her, Jessie moaning as Diana touched, sought out her center.

"Ohhh, baby," Jessie moaned, reaching out to grip the blanket edges.

"You like that?" Diana found Jessie's center, slid in through the wetness, used her thumb to caress her swollen clit. She shivered as she watched the tall woman writhe at her touch. She bent over to run her tongue right above Jessie's hairline, held on to Jessie's hips to hold her steady.

"Oh, God, you know what I like, baby."

"Oh, I try." Diana added her warm breath on wet tissues. "For you, I try real hard." Jessie started to say something and then gasped as Diana spread Jessie's lips, bent lower to use her tongue. Jessie moaned, a long low sound that resonated into Diana.

It was when they were saying goodbye after this weekend that Jessie had pulled a slip of paper from her visor, folded it and handed it to Diana. And that was when Diana was sure it was a two-way attraction.

CHAPTER FOUR

Diana pulled into the parking lot just as it began to rain. She had wrapped up one delivery early, one eye on the clock, the other on the road. She wanted so much to make it early enough for a good evening. She checked into the hotel, called Margaret to let her know she was safe and sound. That had been one of the conditions for coming alone. "I'm fine, I'll call you tomorrow. Promise."

She took some deep breaths. She had never called Jessie before; it was almost unnerving. Maybe it would be better just to go to the bar and wait, but that meant it would be hours before she saw her. She was excited at the thought of seeing Jessie again. She was already anticipating their evening together as she looked around the room. She had taken the suite tonight, let the business pay this bill. After all it was business. The suite consisted of a small sitting area with the wet bar and a sleeping room. Would they go out to dinner? Order room service? Oh, what was the purpose of getting here early if she had to wait to go to the bar? She would call.

She dialed the number, amused at herself. She was shaking. The phone rang once, twice, three times, four, five, six.

"Galbreath!" came this bark into the phone.

"Jessie?" Diana didn't recognize the harsh voice.

"Yes!" There was a lot of noise in the background, people talking, calling. "Who is this?"

"This is Diana. Have I called at a bad time?"

"I can't hear you. Just a minute." Then as an aside, "Honey, go ask Aunt Irene if she'll look for your suitcase in the front closet." Then the noise faded. "I'm back, this is Jessie."

Diana's heart sank. "I'm sorry, Jessie. Obviously I've called at a bad time. This is Diana."

"Diana! Are you here in town?" Jessie didn't sound exactly eager.

"Yes. But it's okay. I just wanted to see if you were available. You sound busy. It's all right."

"No. Let me think. I'm sorry, Diana. It's—it's just been a madhouse here. Let me think." And then there was a distraction again. "Harry, I'm so glad you could come by. No, I'll be there in a minute, need to take care of this. Yes, I understand."

Jessie came back to the phone. "I'm sorry, Diana."

Diana gave up any ideas she had. "No, I'm sorry. You're clearly into something. Don't bother with me. We just didn't connect this time. I'll call again when I'm back." She was already tearing this page out of her little black book.

"No, Diana, please, wait, let me think. Are you there?"

"Yes, I'm here."

"Where are you?"

"I'm at the Hilton."

Jessie took a deep breath. "Yes, it is a very bad time, but I really need to see you. Can I come by?"

"Of course you can. You know you can."

"I don't know when it will be; it might be very late." Her breathing was heavy, she sounded distressed. "Maybe it'll be too late."

"You come when you can. I'll be here. Room Two Sixteen."

"Diana?"

"Yes?"

"I'm glad you came." Then there was some shouting and Jessie was distracted again. "I've got to go. It may be late, but I'll be by." The connection was broken.

Diana stared at the phone as she hung it up. Maybe this calling wasn't a good idea. She went to the window. This wasn't what she expected. Jessie sounded upset, hassled. She shook her head. She had been lucky every other time, Jessie had been readily available. Now? She didn't sound pleased to hear her. It sounded like there was a party going on. Yet Jessie had said she really needed to see her. In spite of everything going on, she *needed* to see Diana. But what was going on? Diana didn't like things happening she didn't know about. A good part of her, the logical part, said it was time to go, no matter what she had told Jessie, it was time to check out, hit the road, not come back. The other part, the part that responded to Jessie, couldn't do it. Jessie said she needed her. She couldn't run out on Jessie and that's what it would be if she left now. She would have to play this out. She could leave immediately after.

The hour grew late. Diana ordered room service, not daring to leave the room. She had told Jessie she would be there. She ordered a movie and then couldn't watch it. She paced, her imagination going all sorts of directions as she reined it in again and again and again.

Midnight came but no Jessie. Diana tried not to get angry; Jessie had said it might be very late. She twiddled her thumbs, lay down on the couch, dozed off and jerked awake. She had only been asleep for ten minutes. She couldn't have missed her in that time.

She's getting too close, she ended up telling herself. This isn't just fun and games now. I'm waiting on her, and I'm worried about her and that's not supposed to happen. I'm supposed to come to town and if she's here, she's here; and if she's not, then maybe next time. So why am I pacing, waiting, worried?

Just when she was convincing herself she needed to pack and get the hell out of Dodge, there was a light rap on the door. She raced to the door but she hadn't lost sense entirely. She checked through the peephole to see Jessie, jeans, white shirt, long raincoat, complete with sunglasses. Then as Jessie waited for Diana to unlock the door, she removed the sunglasses. Her face was swollen, her eyes red, dark circles under her eyes. Diana couldn't get the door open quickly enough.

"Jessie! What's wrong?"

"You're still here. I was afraid it was too late." Jessie stood back. She looked at Diana as if at a stranger. She shook her head. "I shouldn't have come. I'm sorry." She turned to go and Diana caught her arm.

"No, you're not leaving, Jessie. What's wrong? What's happened?" Jessie stood there, frozen, not turning back. Diana tugged on her arm. "Jessie, come sit down," she implored in a more gentle voice. "Come talk to me. You look like you need to sit down in a quiet place. Come in with me."

Jessie rubbed her face. "Maybe for a little bit." She allowed herself to be drawn into Diana's rooms.

Diana locked the door without releasing Jessie's arm. "Let me take your coat. It must still be raining out." She hung up the coat, put her arm around Jessie and led her to the sofa. She picked up the television remote, switched the channel from the action movie to soft soothing jazz. Jessie sat down without any awareness. "Do you need something to drink? Have you eaten?"

"That would be nice. I think so, I don't remember. There was so much food."

Diana went to the wet bar, poured two drinks, the cold 7-Up Jessie preferred and then a straight shot. She looked like she needed it. She brought them both over, held them both out. Jessie reached for the straight shot, brought it to her lips slowly, uncertain, unseeing. Then she took it straight down, closing her eyes, shuddering as it went down. She handed the glass back to Diana.

Diana set the soda down on the table beside the sofa. She sat down beside Jessie, sitting on one leg, half facing Jessie. She took hold of her hand. "Honey, what happened?" She brushed Jessie's hair back. It had been recently cut, neatly trimmed. She stroked Jessie's face. "Talk to me."

"You just get to town?"

"Yes."

"Did you go to the bar?" Jessie rested her head back on the sofa.

"No, I came right here." She watched as Jessie tried to speak, started several times but nothing came out. Whatever it was, it had hit Jessie hard. Diana decided she would have to be more direct. She came up on her knees beside Jessie, straddled her so she could look into her face. She slid her hands around Jessie's jawline, lifting her head. "Tell me," she commanded quietly. "Did something happen to Nicki?"

"No, Nicki's fine." Jessie closed her eyes, her head limp in Diana's hands, not resisting, letting Diana's fingers massage the back of her neck.

"Where is Nicki tonight?"

"She's over at Aunt Irene's."

"That's who I heard you talking about on the phone," Diana remembered. Jessie nodded. "Honey," she said cautiously, guessing. There could only be one reason why Jessie could be so shattered and Nicki at her aunt's. "Did your dad have another heart attack?"

Jessie's face crumpled but she nodded.

"Did he not make it this time?"

Biting her lip, Jessie shook her head, and she began to cry.

"Oh, honey, I'm so sorry." She pulled Jessie to her, wrapped her arms around her as she felt Jessie's arms encircle her. Jessie cried, breaking down completely. She clung to Diana and Diana held her, rocking her, holding her, brushing back her hair, making soothing sounds. "Shhhh," she soothed after a while. Slowly Jessie stopped crying but Diana felt it was more exhaustion than anything else. "Do you want to tell me what happened?"

"Happened Monday," Jessie choked out. "Called me. He was at the horse farm. Couldn't get there in time." She looked up at Diana, stricken. "I didn't even get a chance to say goodbye, to tell him I loved him."

"He knew you loved him," Diana reassured her. "You've told him every day. You took care of him. He knew."

Jessie shook her head. "I met the ambulance at the hospital. He was already gone."

"Oh, honey, that must have been so hard."

Jessie closed her eyes, losing some of her composure again. "Not as hard as telling Nicki. I don't even know what I told her." Diana slowly rocked Jessie, feeling Jessie rest against her. "The funeral was just yesterday."

"I'm sorry I didn't come into town earlier."

"I couldn't have seen you yesterday; so much was going on." Jessie rested her head on Diana's shoulder. "There was so much to do, so many people. It's been a nightmare." She relaxed a little. "I'm so tired but I needed to see you."

"I would have waited for you, dear." Diana could feel Jessie's exhaustion. "You said Nicki was at her aunt's?" Jessie nodded. "So there's no reason for you to go home, is there?"

"No."

"Then why don't I put you to bed?" Diana said quietly. "You're exhausted. You need to sleep. You go home, you'll be alone. You don't need that tonight."

"That's what I told everyone, that I needed to be alone. Otherwise they wouldn't go away." Jessie was relaxing without even realizing.

"Yes, you needed to get away."

"Nicki may call."

"She has your cell phone number. You brought it, didn't you?"

"Of course."

"Then let me put you to bed. I'll hold you. You can sleep. I'll wake you in the morning so you can be at home when Nicki comes home."

Diana stepped backward off the loveseat and pulled Jessie to her feet. Jessie was pliant; Diana led her into the bedroom. Jessie stood unmoving beside the bed, her eyes closed. With tender care, Diana undressed her.

"Bathroom," Jessie said in a tired voice. Diana pointed her toward the bathroom and Jessie obediently padded her way. Diana pulled out a nightshirt, knowing it would be a little short for her. Any other time she would think it was alluring; tonight, she just wanted to tuck her in.

Jessie returned, drooping with exhaustion. Diana helped her into the nightshirt, pulled back the covers for Jessie to crawl in. Jessie stretched out, sighing as she relaxed against the fresh sheets, her arms stretching out and under the pillows. Diana sat on the bed beside her.

"When did you sleep last?" She brushed Jessie's hair back.

"Ahhh, I slept some Wednesday night, but not much. Nicki slept with me; she cried herself to sleep." She reached out for Diana.

"Who was there for you?" Diana asked rhetorically.

Jessie squeezed her hand. "I was hoping you would come."

Diana smiled as she examined Jessie's fingers. "I guess you called me."

"And you came." She sighed again and her breathing evened out, signifying she had fallen asleep, still holding onto Diana's hand.

Diana watched over Jessie, the light from the bathroom shining on her enough that Diana could see how exhausted she was, how she relaxed as she slept, her hand reaching out for Diana's. Every time Diana tried to withdraw her hand, Jessie gripped it tighter until finally Diana gave up. The light was still on in the other room, the television gave the soft murmur of modern jazz. She couldn't leave Jessie but she wasn't sure she could sleep either. She bent down and kissed Jessie's shoulder.

Watching over her that night, worried about her, she slowly came to the realization that she loved this woman. At some point, sometime when Diana hadn't even noticed, she had crossed the point where Jessie was just a fine contact for bed sports. Diana was truly concerned about what happened to her, wanted to take care of her, wanted to be with her.

Whoa, she caught herself. *This is not good.* At the same time, as she watched Jessie sleep, holding on to her, she could think, *This is wonderful.*

***

"I'll be fine," Jessie assured Diana the next day. She covered Diana's hands holding her face. "I had a good night's sleep, thanks to you." She kissed Diana lightly on the lips. "Don't worry about me."

Easier said than done. Diana searched Jessie's face. Jessie did look better; the circles under her eyes weren't as dark. She still looked like she had cried a lot, but the exhaustion was gone. Diana released Jessie, glancing at the clock, going around the room, gathering her belongings.

"I'm so sorry I can't stay," Diana apologized for what must have been the umpteenth time. "I've got a deadline this trip. I've carved out as much time as I dare." She shook her head. "I hate leaving you."

"Oh, and has it been easy every other time?" There was a twinkle back in Jessie's eyes. She grabbed Diana's hand and pulled her close. Standing together, face to face, holding hands, Jessie turned serious. "You don't know what last night meant," she whispered. "I know we've had great sex every other time, and we didn't do anything last night. That wasn't the point. I could sleep because I knew you were there. I had someone who was there for me. I didn't have to ask or explain. That was important. I've never had that before."

Diana glanced at the clock again. "I've got to go." She pulled away only to come back, distraught as she ever remembered being.

Jessie grabbed her by the shoulders, shook her slightly, held her firmly. "Diana, I'll be fine. You got me through the bad part." She caressed Diana's face. "You've got to be careful." Diana gave her a startled look, caught her breath. "You worry like this and I might think your heart is involved."

Diana let out a sigh of relief. "Yeah." She pulled herself together. "I can see how you might get that idea." She ran her fingers over Jessie's lips. "I hate leaving you."

"Go," Jessie said. "Things to do, places to go."

Diana left, but leaving Jessie standing alone in that hotel parking lot was the hardest thing she had ever done, and it was miles and miles before she could get the image out of her mind.

***

"Something happen in Lexington?" Margaret asked. "You seem—I don't know, unsettled."

"Didn't go the way I planned, some things came up." Diana passed it off. "Everything quiet here?"

"Pretty much. It's beginning to be noticed how much you're gone."

"I like to travel. Business is picking up."

"Being predictable is dangerous."

Diana paused. "I'm careful."

"Be very careful," Margaret warned.

CHAPTER FIVE

Making connections was even harder after that. It didn't matter. Diana understood family responsibilities and obligations. Those virtues had been hammered into her since childhood. What puzzled her most was her own behavior. Her contacts with Jessie had become even briefer than she would have thought possible and still she came back. All she wanted was to see Jessie, be with her for a while. A late afternoon lunch, coffee at midnight. A walk in the park, watching over Nicki. Each time she saw the tall, dark-haired woman who must live and sleep in blue jeans and a white shirt, she felt her heart leap. It had nothing to do with any sexual contact although they still flirted, still wanted, but just couldn't. There wasn't enough time.

With her father's death, Jessie had become, in fact, a single mother. And she was responsible. Nicki was very dear to her. She went from being the Romeo who terrorized the gay community to being a single parent trying to hold everything together. Diana had nothing but respect and admiration for what she was doing. And what she didn't want to admit was a growing love and tenderness.

Diana checked in at the hotel; it was never certain how long she would stay but she could be hopeful. She crossed her fingers as she called from the hotel house phone.

"Galbreath."

"Hello, beautiful."

There was a faint gasp. "How do you do that?"

"What? Call you beautiful? Why it's easy, it's just—"

"No, I mean, call like this. I was just thinking of you this morning."

"That's why I called," Diana almost purred. "How's your time, darling? Lunch, coffee, a walk in the park?"

There was a strange sound, clicking, like a pencil tapping on the desk. "How long are you here for? Just overnight?"

A possibility? Diana's heart leaped. "I'm available for the weekend." There was hope, she knew, in her voice.

"Really? Can you call me back in twenty minutes?" Jessie's voice was rushed.

"Sure."

"Let me make some calls, let me think. Yeah, call me back. Gotta go. Bye."

***

Diana moved around the room. She had taken the business suite this time, there was a little more room without the expense of two rooms. Candles, soft music from the TV. She had brought gifts, they were there on the desk, something for Jessie, a smaller package for Nicki. She wrung her hands, nervous, expectant. A weekend. It had been months and months since they had been alone together. She had a feeling in her that this was a turning point. She had these feelings occasionally, gut instinct her papa called it. He told her always to listen, that the subconscious knew what the mind did not and this should not be ignored. Now her gut instinct was talking to her libido and they were having a great conversation.

There was a soft rap and she threw open the door. They stood there looking at each other.

"Well, are you going to invite me in?" Jessie asked with an uncertain grin after a minute.

Diana dragged her eyes over the taller woman. "You're not in jeans." She took a long look at the black tailored pants, still a white shirt only now it was white silk, the leather jacket. "I didn't know you owned anything else." She stepped back from the door, inviting her in.

"Got a promotion at work, splurged on an expanded wardrobe." She seemed a little hesitant.

"You look fantastic." Diana couldn't get over the change. "Turn around." Jessie turned around, posing. "Damn, I thought you were hot in blue jeans."

Jessie laughed. "No one has called me 'hot' in ages. I'm not sure I know what that means any more."

"God, Jessie, you've got to get out more." Diana took hold of Jessie's hands, stunned by the change. "On, second thought, maybe not. You'd have to beat them off with a billy club." She brought Jessie's hands to her lips. "Where's Nicki?"

"She's spending the weekend with a friend. I called Paula and said I had a chance to go out, could she keep her for the weekend. We're both single mothers, have this system worked out." Uncertainly and with almost shy eagerness, she pulled her hands free of Diana's, took Diana's face in her hands. She searched Diana's face before she kissed her, her lips warm and trembling. "I've missed you."

Diana moaned. She had forgotten what this woman could do to her without even trying. She closed her eyes, drank her in. She didn't move, even when Jessie released her. "Oh, God, Jessie. I had planned we'd go out to dinner, but with a kiss like that, I could skip the preliminaries and go right to bed."

"I'm not hungry," Jessie said in a husky voice, "at least not for food."

Diana stepped back, opening her eyes, shook her head to clear it. Jessie was right in front of her, watching her, questioning. She was trembling. "I'm not kidding, Diana."

"Neither am I." Diana moved away from Jessie, locking the door. She moved to the closet, pulled out a wooden hanger. "Let me have that jacket. It's much too nice to throw around." She took a deep breath, calming herself. Had it been that long since they had been together? "Damn, I didn't realize leather jackets were so heavy. What have you got in there, lead weights?" She hung up the jacket and turned around.

"No." Jessie pulled the shirt over her head, pulled her bra off. "Just my—" She seemed to lose all train of thought and words when Diana slid her hands around to cup her breasts, to pinch the upright nipples. Her hands immediately covered Diana's, and she whimpered. She threw her head back against Diana's shoulder and shuddered as she turned her face into Diana's neck. "Oh, God, Diana. It's been so long."

"I can tell," Diana whispered in her ear. "Too long." She ran her tongue around Jessie's ear, felt her whimper.

"I need you," Jessie almost sobbed.

"Have you been without all this time?" Diana asked, more to tease than anything else, and she was shocked when Jessie answered.

"Yes."

"Oh, baby, that's not good." She wrapped her arms around Jessie and pulled her tight against her, hands stroking her, caressing her. She could feel Jessie shaking, unable to move. "Why?"

Jessie shook her head. "Just—just not enough time." She arched her back and pushed against Diana's hands.

"Let me take care of you," Diana promised. "Don't worry—don't worry about doing anything, sweetheart. We've got all weekend." Jessie's only response was a moan. Diana stroked down Jessie's abdomen. The woman must still be working out. She felt in great shape. She unfastened the pants at Jessie's waistband. "Show me you want me, hon. Open your pants."

Uncoordinated, moving against Diana, Jessie managed to unzip her pants, push them open, whimpering as Diana's hand dropped. No more cotton panties, the logical part of Diana's brain noticed. Hip riders. Silky. She nibbled on Jessie's neck as she pushed the tailored, lined trousers down. She felt Jessie moving against her, caught a motion out of the corner of her eye. She glanced at their mirrored reflection, herself still completely dressed holding the almost naked woman against her. She shivered at the sight, at Jessie's soft sounds in the back of her throat, at the feeling of the woman in her arms.

"How do you want it, darling?"

"I don't care," Jessie moaned. "Just—just take me, love me."

Diana slid her hand inside the silky hip riders, finding the wetness she had expected. She didn't expect Jessie's cry at her touch, her sinking to her knees.

"Oh, God. Please, Diana. Don't tease me. I can't—can't stand it."

Diana bent Jessie over the foot of the bed, releasing her to caress her ass, to lean against her, to find her center, to hear Jessie cry.

"Oh, God, yes, please, don't stop." And then it was just sounds as Diana found her center, found her wetness, stroked her, parting her legs more, finding her swollen, highly sensitized clit. Jessie ground herself against the bed, clenched the bed covers in her fists, panting, lost to her surroundings as Diana held her, focused on her, penetrated, stroked. "Ahhhhhhhhhh!"

Diana lay over Jessie, her head against Jessie's back, feeling her heart race, feeling her panting. She lifted up as Jessie turned her head, reached back for her. "All right?" she asked. Jessie nodded, unable to speak. Diana still hadn't let her go. "Appetizer?" Jessie gave a weak laugh.

Diana got to her feet, withdrawing. She was surprised, even shocked at Jessie's raw need. She flexed her hand, loosening tight cramps. Jessie pushed herself to a sitting position, rolling over. Her bright red panties were pooled around her ankles and she examined them in embarrassment.

Diana sat beside Jessie and took her hand. "Why so long?" Jessie didn't look up, gave a little shrug. "Honey, that's not good for you."

"Busy schedule, things to do." She still didn't raise her head.

Diana was puzzled over several things, but now she was concerned because Jessie seemed embarrassed. She brought Jessie's hand to her lips. "What's wrong?"

"Just—just." Jessie closed her eyes. "I feel like I used you?"

"Used me?"

Jessie drew a deep breath. "I just needed." She had tears rolling down her cheeks.

"Jessie!" Diana's voice was sharp. "Look in the mirror. Just look at that."

Reluctantly Jessie looked up. "Now tell me, sweetheart," Diana said gently, "if someone walked in on us, who would they say was the user and which of us got used?"

Jessie's answer was muffled in Diana's shoulder. "I guess it would look like I'm the one who got used."

Diana turned Jessie's face to her. "Do you feel used?" Jessie shook her head. "Me neither." She let go of Jessie, got to her feet. "Now we have to face the big question," she said lightly. She walked around the bed to pull the bedcovers down, came back to stand beside Jessie.

"What's that?"

"Are we going out for dinner or are we going to be each other's main course?"

Jessie blinked. "You're not upset with me?" she asked in puzzlement.

"What for? For your need for immediate gratification? Jessie, we did that for months. We could hardly wait to hit the bed when I got into town. We might have met at the bar but we both knew where we were going to end up. And probably pretty damn quickly."

"But we changed," Jessie said. "We haven't done that in a long time."

"Well, no, not with any white heat, but we've gotten older. Circumstances have changed. We've made adjustments."

Jessie got to her feet. "Are you sorry?"

"About what? Circumstances changing?"

"No, about always ending up in bed." She rested her hands on Diana's hips, stood close to her.

Diana gave a big sigh and stepped back. "I recognize that look." She pulled her shirt over her head, unfastened her bra. "No dinner out tonight; maybe later." Jessie caught her, pulled the lacy bra off, caressed, squeezed Diana's breasts.

"You didn't answer my question." She pulled Diana against her, nibbled on her cheek, rubbed her face through Diana's hair. "Still wear the same perfume, have I ever told you how much I love it, spent all afternoon in Surry's once, trying to identify it."

"Savannah Gardens." Diana stepped into Jessie's embrace. "They take it off the market periodically. I have bottles of it."

"You didn't answer my question: are you sorry?" She slid her hands down the inside of Diana's pants, squeezing her ass, pulling her tight.

Diana looked at Jessie directly, her arms around Jessie's neck. "I haven't been celibate when we're not together." She felt Jessie's hands stop. "I didn't promise faithfulness and I didn't ask for it. I've traveled this whole country. I've seen lots of women and yes, I've had my share. I've always been clean when I came back to you. I haven't found anyone anywhere who can turn my head and fill my senses the way you can Jessica Ann Galbreath. So I've always come back. No, I'm not sorry. If something happened and I never saw you again, you would still go down in my book as the best woman I've ever known."

Jessie looked away, trying not to look immensely pleased and extremely flattered at Diana's words. She began to knead Diana's ass again, and they moved against each other as only long-term lovers can do. "So why haven't we done anything about that?"

Diana thought her heart would stop. Of all times, of all things, yes, she needed to listen to her gut more often. But the logical part of her was still working. She pushed herself back so she could see Jessie's face. "Jessie," she said softly. "I'm not saying this to hurt, and I can't tell you in how many dreams I have wished for everything you seem to be implying, but it's not going to happen."

Jessie pulled away sharply. "Why not?"

Diana looked at her in some disbelief. She didn't want to say what she knew to be true, could not believe Jessie could be so blind. "Because you're still waiting for Julie."

CHAPTER SIX

They went out to dinner. Diana watched Jessie carefully. Had she read her wrong? She didn't think so. This weekend wasn't turning out the way she envisioned. "I didn't say that to upset you, Jessie." She watched Jessie's smooth motions as she drove through town in the late-model car. Absently, Diana wondered if she'd gotten rid of the Jeep. Then it didn't matter, any more than where they were going. Diana really didn't care.

"Then why did you say it?" There was a hard edge in Jessie's voice, not anger exactly, more like protection against future blows.

"Because it's true. I know your life has changed since your dad died, but even before that you weren't going out. You weren't dating. You may have gone out on the prowl and may have made your way into many beds, but you weren't trying to meet someone. You weren't trying to make a relationship."

"And that bothers you?"

"It just told me that you weren't interested in a relationship; you were still waiting."

"And you were looking for a relationship?"

"No. I never said I was. I told you what we had was in the here and now, no strings, no holds. If I came back and you were available, we had a great time. If not…" She shrugged and turned away to look out the window in the gathering dusk.

"I was always available for you," Jessie said defensively.

"And I keep coming back," Diana said in a weary voice.

Jessie pulled into the parking lot of a small restaurant at the edge of what looked like a small community. Diana looked around with some dismay. She had been so upset that she had broken not one but several of her cardinal rules. She wasn't driving. It wasn't her car. She didn't know for sure where she was. She was too upset to care.

Jessie shut off the ignition and sat there a moment, not moving. "What do you want from me, Diana?"

"I'm not asking anything from you, Jessie. I come to town, I call. Whatever you've had to offer me, I've accepted. It used to be we had a great time in bed. You want to talk, I listen. You have five minutes, I don't ask for ten."

Jessie frowned as she sat back, spread her arms, one across the back of the seat, the other on the steering wheel. "I used to think it was the sexual excitement. One more conquest, even the beautiful stranger who comes to town. But then slowly it wasn't just sex. You've given me more support these past few months than my so-called long-time friends. They dropped me like a hot potato when Nicki became my sole responsibility."

Diana pushed herself back into the seat. "You changed; you had to. You weren't Romeo any more; you had responsibilities. When there's a kid, you can't go out drinking and dancing all night, partying. You can't go out at the drop of a hat."

"It didn't bother you."

"Families come first. They're not just there when you need them. You need to be there when they need you. It's a hard lesson for some people to learn. You learned it younger than most."

Jessie bowed her head. "So what have you gotten out of it?" she asked finally. "There's got to be some reason you keep coming back."

Diana shoved her hands into her jacket pockets. *Good question.* "Fantastic lover, a woman with character, who's charming and sweet and intelligent, who knows who she is. Who is loyal and has a sense of responsibility. Why wouldn't I want to keep company with someone like that?"

"And why don't you want a relationship?"

Diana turned back to the window. In the gathering darkness and the parking lot lights she could see her own reflection and behind her,

Jessie's. "Because the one I love isn't free to make a commitment, she's bound to another."

Jessie seemed to digest this for a few moments. "Does she know you love her?"

Diana didn't turn around to look at her. "I don't know."

"Why not?"

"As long as she's committed, I can't honorably speak about how I feel. Until she tells me she's free, I won't say anything."

"That's not giving her a choice."

"No, probably not, but that's the way it is."

The car was silent for several minutes as each woman mulled over their words, the feelings they expressed. "Then I guess I owe her a lot," Jessie said finally.

"How so?"

"As long she's unavailable, you'll keep coming back to me."

Diana closed her eyes, bit her lip. She hoped the darkness would hide her tears. "Yes," she managed to say without her voice breaking.

"I'm right, aren't I?" Jessie pressed. "If she were free and accepted you, you would be faithful to her, wouldn't you? Tear up your little black book."

"Of course."

Jessie sighed. "She would be a lucky woman." She ran her fingers through her hair. "Look, do you really want to eat? This place is really good, but to be perfectly honest, I don't have any appetite. If you want to eat, we'll go in, but otherwise…"

Diana pulled herself together. "No, let's go back. I don't feel like eating either."

Jessie started up the car. "I'll just drop you off at the hotel," she started.

"Drop me off? Why? Aren't you coming in? I thought we had the weekend?"

"I didn't think that you'd want me to stay after all this."

"Jessie, I'm always going to want you."

Jessie paused at the edge of the parking lot. Even though the road was clear, she turned to look at Diana. "Why couldn't we have found each other when we were free?"

Diana couldn't answer, she turned away to look out the window again.

Once they were at the hotel, Diana wasn't sure how much more she could take. She excused herself and closed herself in the bathroom.

She turned the water on full blast and buried her face in the thick towels, wondering how she had even gotten into this mess and how she was ever going to get out. At length, she knew she was going to have to continue. She didn't want Jessie to leave; it wasn't white-hot sex she wanted now. She wanted to curl up with the woman she loved, feel her warm body next to hers, be able to reach out and touch her, be able to hear her breathing, be able to pretend at least for the night they belonged to each other.

She dried her tears, washed her face, splashed it with cold water, examined herself in the mirror. Jessie wouldn't be fooled any, but maybe she would be able to coast by. She came out of the bathroom to find Jessie sitting on the bed. The woman had changed; now she was wearing a University of Kentucky T-shirt over those red hip huggers. "You okay?" Jessie asked.

Diana nodded.

"I took you at your word that you wanted me to stay. If you've changed your mind, tell me now."

Diana shook her head. "No, I haven't changed my mind."

"Good. Now I need the bathroom."

Diana changed into nightclothes feeling totally depressed. If she thought it would have done any good, she would have left, but a weekend with Jessie was scarce enough that she didn't dare pass it up. There was no telling when it would come again. She put on music trying to cheer herself up but could only find country, which at least for the stations she was hitting seemed to focus on love gone wrong or lost love. She settled for the soft jazz that was soothing, just not cheering. She was looking out the window when Jessie came out of the bathroom.

Jessie came over and slid her arms around Diana. "I'm sorry," she apologized. "Here I wanted this weekend to be totally physical and all I've done is pour cold water over everything. That wasn't my intent, Diana. You know how much I enjoy you."

Diana gave a small rueful smile. *Enjoy*, she thought. "I know." She settled back into Jessie's arms. "Maybe instead of coming back here, we should have gone out. Loud music, all that sexual energy on the dance floor. That might have helped."

"It's been ages since I've been to the bar, even before Dad died. Just didn't seem any point." She fell silent, and neither one of them moved.

Diana took a deep breath. She was going to have to do something, this could not go on like this. "I brought you something," she said abruptly. She broke free of Jessie's arms and went over to the desk.

"You did? It's not my birthday, not Christmas."

Diana opened the drawer and took out the wrapped present. "I don't even know when your birthday is. It's appalling what we don't know about each other." She handed it to Jessie. "I've got another one in there for Nicki, not quite the same but enough to match."

Jessie looked at her strangely as she sat down on the bed. "You've never brought me anything before."

"Oh, I saw this, could just see you wearing it with your blue jeans. Bought it before I could change my mind."

She leaned against the dresser as Jessie unwrapped the gift, glancing at her and then back to the wrapped box that was obviously jewelry. "I don't think that I've ever seen you wear jewelry so I tried to keep it simple, but I thought it'd be just right with your coloring."

"You're right, I don't wear much." She opened the velvet box to expose the spider web turquoise stone set in silver. "I love turquoise!" She picked up the silver chain, examining the silver bezel setting. "This is beautiful. Where did you get this?"

"I was out in Albuquerque a few months ago."

Jessie jumped to her feet, dropped the necklace over her head. The fine silver chain was long enough that the stone dropped just to the hollow of her breasts. She examined herself in the mirror.

"I got Nicki just a single nugget on a leather thong. You were saying she was in the back-to-nature movement." They both watched their reflections in the mirror.

"She will just love it. You are the sweetest person," Jessie said. "I can't remember the last time anyone bought me anything that wasn't for Christmas or birthday or some gift-giving time." She turned to Diana, turned Diana's face to hers, smoothed back her hair. "That woman you love doesn't know what she's missing."

"No, she doesn't," Diana said evenly.

"But I'm here," Jessie whispered. She brushed Diana's lips with her own. "Will I make a good substitute?"

"You'll never be a substitute for anyone, Jessie."

Jessie held Diana still as she kissed her, and Diana accepted her. Wanting, needing to feel her, Diana ran her hands up under the T-shirt. Warm flesh, she wanted her more than anything, not in the sense of hot sex, not in the sense of physical desire, but to have her and hold her, to love her for the sake of her own completeness. She pulled Jessie to her. "I want you," and even to her own ears, her voice sounded strange. Jessie drew back and looked at her.

"I'm right here, babe."

Diana shook her head, not sure of this feeling washing over her. She pulled Jessie's hands down from her face, held her hands with interlaced fingers. She had never let her emotions go with Jessie, she had never been angry, never pushed. This weekend hadn't been the relaxing, fun-filled time she had envisioned. Instead talks of deeper emotions thinned her self-control. Wanting her, not having her, that hadn't helped. Instead of release, she had frustration. Instead of relaxed communication, there was nothing but missed cues and misunderstandings. Every bit of her logic told her to leave, this was foolish, this could be dangerous, wanting someone so much as to be predictable. And she couldn't. She didn't even try anymore. She wouldn't until Jessie sent her away. But this in between thing was tearing her apart.

"I want you," she repeated, and if there were dark overtones, Jessie seemed not to hear them.

"I'm yours for the taking," Jessie whispered.

Diana shook her head. "You don't understand," she said in a low voice. "You don't understand how much I want you." Unconsciously she turned her hands, Jessie's arms so the woman couldn't pull away, couldn't escape her. "I don't want to please you, I want to claim you, I want to possess you. You have no idea how much."

"No, but you'll show me, won't you?" If Jessie was afraid, she was hiding it and at the fringes of Diana's awareness, she knew Jessie was unafraid, which was good, because she was. "I want to be wanted. I want you to show me how much you want me." Jessie moved closer to her. "Show me, Diana. Show me what I mean to you."

Diana shook her head. She wanted control over her, she wanted to dominate her. She wanted to demand so much of her that Jessie would be unable to think of anyone else, to remember anyone else. She wanted to be the only one in Jessie's world. She could feel herself take on the persona where she could do that, take what she wanted, without concern for her lover. She had never done anything like that with Jessie before but her control was slipping quickly. "No. I want you so much I'm afraid I'll hurt you."

"I won't let you hurt me," Jessie promised. Her voice dropped into that husky register that did things to Diana's libido. "If you need my permission, I give you my permission. If you want my consent, I freely give it."

Diana shivered and closed her eyes. Why did Jessie have to say that, as if she knew what gave Diana permission? She could feel Jessie's body heat, could imagine her whimpering. All sorts of images came to mind, desires unleashed that she had never before brought with her when she saw Jessie.

"Let me be whatever you want me to be, Diana," Jessie offered, her breath hot against Diana's neck. "Take me, use me whatever way you want me. I want that. You've given me so much, I want to give you what you want. Just tell me."

Diana groaned as she gave in to her desire. "Take off your shirt," she ordered hoarsely as she let go of Jessie's hands.

Jessie pulled the shirt up and over her head, her breasts brushed against Diana's. She tossed the shirt onto the dresser behind Diana, her eyes on Diana, expectant.

"On your knees," Diana ordered in a shaky voice.

Never breaking her gaze from Diana's face, Jessie went to her knees in front of her, her arms at her sides, waiting. Diana looked down at the long leanness that was Jessie, her breasts with the dark upright nipples. What was the hold this woman had over her? What was her allure? Diana pulled off her shirt, she could feel her own arousal, she could see it reflected in Jessie's dark eyes. Bedroom eyes. She shivered.

"Take down my pants." Diana settled herself against the dresser, gripped the edges to hold on. She threw back her head, closed her eyes as she felt Jessie's hands at her hips. Jessie's fingers hooked the elastic, slid them down. The silky material glided over tortured flesh. Jessie's hand was at her calf. She lifted Diana's leg, held her foot by the instep, first one leg, then the other as she removed the panties, tossed them to one side. Jessie ran her hands up the outside of Diana's legs before she dropped her hands and waited, her breath warm on Diana's belly. Diana spread her legs, braced her ass against the cool wood. "Go down on me."

Time hung still an eternity before Jessie moved. Diana waited, every nerve she had tingling in anticipation. She sucked in her breath when Jessie feather-touched inside her thighs, at the tantalizing brush of Jessie's hair, the tentative feel of Jessie's fingers as she parted her lips, and then Jessie's warm mouth. She almost came undone and she thrust her hips forward. She threw back her head, a low sound escaped her throat as she felt her lover's ministrations. She stood there, shaking, waves of pleasure spreading out along nerve pathways, totally lost in the sensations.

She drew a shaky breath, opened her eyes. She bent her head down to watch Jessie between her legs, watching her, feeling her as Jessie became more certain of what Diana wanted, less tentative in her desire to please. Diana closed her eyes and gripped the dresser tighter, concentrating on Jessie's lips, Jessie's tongue, Jessie's fingers, Jessie's arm wrapped around her hip, holding on to her, moving with her. Spasms shook her and she relished them, pleasure like a strong drink at one central spot and then spreading out all over her, all in her.

"Stop," she ordered abruptly just before she came. She didn't want to come. When she came, it would be all over, and she didn't want it to be over. She wanted it to go on and on. She wanted to feel like this all night, maybe forever, this elusive spot of pleasure, of a high no drug could give, this bliss.

Jessie stopped immediately.

"Get on the bed, on your back, spread out." She watched through half-closed eyes as Jessie got to her feet, moved over to the bed, crawled to the center and rolled over on her back. She repositioned herself to lie diagonally on the bed, pulled the pillow out and tossed it away, stretched out her arms and watched Diana's face as she spread her legs, exposing herself, her dark pubic hairs peeking out around the red panties.

Diana watched her, still supporting herself on the dresser. She needed to get her breath, control her shakiness before she could continue. "You looked so good that first night," she said finally. "Animal magnetism. Like watching a horse move, strong, graceful, controlled. Like a cat on the prowl, watching, searching for prey, stalking. You moved like you owned the place, like everyone was there for your enjoyment, your pleasure. Confidence oozed out of you, promises of pleasure, enjoyment, fulfillment surrounded you. And there was danger too, that element so tantalizing. Can't catch me, corner me and I bite. Corner me and I slip away but not before I have you." She shivered. "Watching you was like watching a nature film, so—so raw, natural, compelling."

Diana moved from the dresser, came over to the bed, leaned one knee between Jessie's legs, watched Jessie watch her. "And then I was the prey. Fun and games, challenge. I'd done that before, the local Romeo. They're fun, let them have their conquest, let me have mine. They're great in bed, experience makes them polished lovers, always pleasing, earning their reputation." She ran her hands over Jessie's legs. "No strings. They want the conquest, I wanted the pleasure. Then we move on." She spoke in a hypnotic way, as if she were drugged, which in a way she was. "So why did I come back?"

She moved over Jessie, straddling one thigh that Jessie brought up to press against Diana's wetness. "What's one Romeo in some town I had an assignment in and probably never would come back to?" She leaned forward on one arm, her other hand gliding over Jessie, up her leg, up her torso, caressing first one breast, then the other. She licked her lips as she paused. "What was it that would wake me up in the middle of the night from a dream of blue jeans, white shirts, dark sunglasses?" She drew back from Jessie, rode her thigh. "What made me come back to see if you were as good the second time as you were the first?" She pulled down the red panties just enough to slide her hand in, ignored the wetness, slid into her, quickly penetrating before Jessie could even draw a breath, raise her hips. They both shivered as Diana crouched over Jessie.

Jessie's breath quickened as Diana's breath was on her belly, as Diana's hair caressed her flesh, as her fingers parted her lover's lips, her breath on the throbbing clit. "And damn, you were." She claimed Jessie yet another way, her mouth, her hand. Jessie arched, moaning, coming up on her elbows, her head thrown back, whimpering as Diana's tongue stroked.

Diana felt Jessie's surrender, felt her passion, felt the gathering muscles, felt her fingers captured and held, tasted her, tantalized her and broke off, denying herself and well as her lover. "No! You cannot come!" She felt, heard Jessie's sob, held her as Jessie twisted and fell back against the bed. Then Diana took possession again. "You cannot come until I tell you that you can." Jessie shook her head from one side to the other, a sob torn from her. Diana moved up over her, looking down into Jessie's face, the glazed eyes, the slack mouth.

Diana slapped her, not hard, just enough to bring her back to the present. Jessie looked up at her, her eyes focusing, widening. "Not until I tell you that you can," Diana warned. "You hear?" Unsteadily, Jessie nodded. "You understand?" Again, still breathing hard from frustration, Jessie nodded. "As long as we both understand," Diana said reasonably as she examined Jessie's face, slowly came down to kiss her, to claim her mouth. Jessie started to wrap her arms around Diana and Diana broke away again. "No." Jessie froze. "No," Diana repeated in a warmer voice. "Not yet, darling. Not yet."

Diana went back to Jessie's mouth, exploring, tongue wrestling, tasting. She stretched out across Jessie, feeling her flesh, her knee drawn up between Jessie's legs, pushing the panties down. Her hands roamed over Jessie, her arms, feeling her hands, until finally that wasn't enough. She broke away from Jessie's mouth, began to taste her all over, the palms of her hands, the inside of her wrist, the inside of her elbow. She nibbled on Jessie's shoulder, her tongue sliding across Jessie's collarbone. Jessie laid there, gripping the sheet, her legs drawn up. She whimpered as Diana moved around her, nibbling, kissing. She was surrounded by Diana.

Diana moved down, still exploring, still kissing, still tasting. Her dialogue stopped but her thoughts didn't as she finished exploring, tasting the exposed half of Jessie's body. She felt Jessie whimper, felt her want to move, but she remained anchored to the bed. When Diana finished up, licking the inside of Jessie's thigh, tasting the passion that had flowed, Jessie was aquiver.

Diana moved around again, her eyes still on her naked lover. She laid a hand over Jessie's dark triangle, watching Jessie's face, her need for release. Diana smiled, still in control over her own desire, still split between the emotional and the mental, still able to control and be aware of her actions. She bent over Jessie, pulled the panties down and off her, threw them in the corner. She knelt between Jessie's spread legs, sat back on her own, watched Jessie move restlessly, watched Jessie watch her to see what she would do.

"This time," Diana told her, "you may come. Think you can do it?"

"Oh, yes," Jessie replied in a shaky voice.

"We'll see." She bent over her lover. Slick, wet, swollen lips, glistening engorged clit peeking out through dark hairs.

"Every time," Diana began the dialogue again. "Every time, I'd be sated when I left and I'd tell myself, all right, that's it. Nothing there that no one else can't do." She heard Jessie whimper as she explored, caressed her. "And every time, it would wear off." She found Jessie's center, slid in, wet and warm and eager. "Do you want more?" She watched Jessie suck in her stomach, the ripple of muscles.

"Yes." Jessie shivered, licked her lips, closed her eyes. Her nipples were in hard little points, she was flushed. Diana watched all these changes.

"So I'd find someone else, someone with a nice ass, pretty little boobs." She pulled out, added another finger, carefully slid back in, finding a rhythm with Jessie's hips. "Maybe they had dark eyes, run their fingers through their hair like you do. Maybe they'd swing their hips on the dance floor the way you do. Maybe have good balance. Need more, darling?" She watched Jessie's hands clench, unclench.

Jessie licked her lips, closing her eyes, lifting her hips. "That would be nice."

"Got tossed out of more than one bed because at the wrong time, I'd call for Jessie, getting it almost there, almost right, and just not quite." She added the pressure. "Can you take it all?"

"Think so," Jessie groaned. "If you're careful."

"Ohhhh, yes." Diana withdrew her fingers, used Jessie's passion as lubricant, went back with gentle insistent pressure. "Almost but never quite right, tantalizing, tormenting, and I knew Lexington would be in my planner soon, maybe very soon, maybe later if it had to be, but soon." She felt Jessie resist her, trying to open, careful, and then she was in, her hand squeezed to a fist, feeling Jessie hold her, moving her. "And then." She bent down to kiss Jessie's abdomen, feeling her hand against her lips through the abdominal wall.

"Oh, God," Jessie sobbed. "What have you done to me? Oh, God!" Her frenzied movements bounced them both on the bed.

"No," Diana crooned, her breath on Jessie's lips. "What have you done to me?"

She felt the gathering climax, felt the tightening of Jessie's muscles, felt the tightness and she slid her arm around Jessie's hips to hold her when it finally came. Jessie sobbed with the release, coming up, trying to sit up and Diana pinning her down.

"I'm not done yet," Diana told her. "And neither are you." With gentle administration, with tongue and hand she put Jessie in a cycle of pleasure. Jessie came up crying out, her words becoming less and less intelligible with each cycle until at last she fell back, exhausted, her eyes closed. She lay still, breathing hard, wrung out, limp. Diana carefully withdrew.

She slowly got off the bed, padded into the bathroom. She washed her face, hands, held her head in her hands for a moment to regain some sense. Then she pulled down the hand towel to soak in warm water. She wrung it out and returned to the bedroom where Jessie still laid. She hadn't moved. Diana sighed as she crawled up on the bed beside her lover. She brushed her face.

"You okay?"

"Uh-huh." She still didn't move.

Diana tenderly wiped Jessie's face, then leisurely, gently, took the warm towel over Jessie's entire body. Jessie was limp, half dozing as Diana handled her. When Diana finished she tossed the towel in the bathroom sink. Making sure Jessie was still, she went to the small refrigerator and pulled out a 7-Up. Then she moved to the small bar and mixed a hefty shot of Seagram's. She came back to the bed and sat on the corner. When Jessie began to stir, Diana put aside the drink and leaned over her prone lover.

"Roll over, darling. Come up on your knees."

"I can't," Jessie protested weakly, even as she rolled over. "I'm done."

"But I'm not," Diana came back with reasonably. She cupped Jessie's breast, the nipple coming up against her palm. She caressed Jessie's ass as Jessie came up on her knees.

"God, Diana." She rubbed her face against the sheet. "How much do you want?"

"Everything. All you've got. And then some."

"I've given you everything." She pushed herself up on her arms.

"No, darling. You've got so much more." Diana reached around to cup Jessie's breasts and pulled Jessie against her. She nibbled on the back of Jessie's neck. "Unless you're telling me no."

Jessie shook her head. "No, I'm not telling you no." She leaned back against Diana, pressing against her breasts.

"That's good, sweetheart. Because you know I would stop. I would never want to hurt you. I just want you so much."

Jessie stretched her arms, reaching behind her to touch Diana, who still nibbled on her neck. "What more can I give you?"

"Oh, I don't know. You like dildos?"

Jessie shivered. "Yes, but usually I'm the one using them."

"You like having your ass fucked?"

This time it was a spasm. Diana tightened her arms. "I've never done that," Jessie confessed.

"Ahhhh." Diana breathed in Jessie's ear. "Virgin territory."

"Diana, I don't want to be damaged."

Diana ran her hand over Jessie's body. "I would never hurt you," she promised. "I would never let you be hurt if I could do anything to prevent it. I just need you, more than air. I want to be a vampire and take in your life's blood. I want to take you like you've never been taken before. I want you to shiver at the memory and remember that Diana did that to me, with me, for me."

"Di, let me love you," Jessie implored.

"No, not now. Later. After I've shown you everything you can give me."

"There won't be anything left of me."

"Ahhh, really?" All the time she spoke, Diana's hands roamed, caressing, squeezing soft flesh. "That's a thought." She brought her hands back to squeeze Jessie's ass. "You want to lie on the bed or bend over the bed."

"For what?"

"When I fuck your ass."

Jessie bent over, her forehead touching the mattress. "You will be gentle, won't you?"

"Gentle and thorough." Diana waited. She knew Jessie would consent, but it was important that Jessie consent. She felt her resistance, felt her struggle with this.

"Over the bed," Jessie finally said.

"Very good." She kissed the back of Jessie's neck, squeezed her breasts, pinched her nipples. She left the bed then, going into the bathroom. Behind her, she heard Jessie getting off the bed, kneeling down beside it, leaning over it. She pulled down her makeup case, unzipped it, and then it hit her. What was she doing? This was Jessie. She shivered, shuddered. This was Jessie, not some casual woman she would never see again, not someone she might hurt and then take care of but never see again. This wasn't some scene staged for someone to be shaken to their soul. This was Jessie. Where was her head? She moaned. What had she been thinking of?

There was a crash in the bathroom, and Diana found herself on her knees. Then Jessie was there, and she was on the floor, her arms around Diana.

"Honey, what happened?"

Diana's head rested on the cold tub, it felt great to her heated face. She felt Jessie's arms around her, felt Jessie take her in her arms. Diana buried her face in Jessie's shoulder. She gripped her hard, seeking an anchor, a way back. She was shaking. She had been right earlier: this middle space was tearing her apart.

"Are you all right?" Jessie asked when Diana tried to sit up.

"Are you all right?" Diana asked in response. She faced Jessie directly. She searched Jessie's face. "I didn't hurt you, did I?"

Jessie shook her head. "You didn't hurt me." She in turn examined Diana's face, looking intently at her. "It was intense," she admitted. "It was different than you've ever been before." She stroked Diana's face, reassuring. "You didn't hurt me. I told you I wouldn't let you hurt me." She held Diana a few more minutes. "Now, are you all right?" Diana nodded. "Can you tell me what happened?"

"Probably not." Diana sighed. She pushed back her hair. "I just wanted you, terribly."

"You said that."

Diana shrugged. "I can get possessive."

Jessie's eyebrows went up. "I see." She sat back, still holding Diana. "Well you said you weren't concerned tonight about pleasing me, you wanted to take possession."

"I'm sorry." Now it was Diana's turn to avoid Jessie's look. "I shouldn't have treated you like that."

"I told you I wanted you to show me how much you wanted me."

"I doubt you had this much in mind," Diana said despairingly.

Jessie caught her face, made her look up. She was shaking her head, her expression bemused. "Is there no end to those still waters?" she asked. "The first time I see you, I think you're some tourist going exploring. You blow me away with coming on like a sailor who has someone in every port of call. And then I think it's just a one-night stand, okay, a good lay when you're in the area. Fuck buddies when we're in the same vicinity. Fair weather friend. And you show up when I need someone, and you understand about family and loyalty and family responsibility. And then when I think no sex, therefore no Diana, you show up for lunch, for coffee, for a thirty-minute chitchat. Every time I think I've got you pegged, you do something to surprise me."

Diana gave a small chuckle. That hadn't exactly been her aim but it was flattering. It was good to be able to do that.

"So tonight, first you zap me about Julie. You were right of course. I didn't think of it that way but no, what I was doing certainly didn't encourage any kind of relationship, except for being the Friday night brass ring." She caressed Diana's face. "So you rip me for that and I figure, well that's over: I've lost a friend and a—a—" She stumbled for a word. "Just what the hell are we anyway?"

"I don't know." Diana shook her head. "Lovers? Friends with Benefits?"

"That'll do. I think I lose a friend and a lover and you still want me to stay, you still want me, even though you've already said I'm in suspension because of Julie. You bring me a gift. And then you tell me you want me, you want to claim me, possess me." She shook her head in puzzlement. "What are you when you're not here? Some kind of dominatrix?"

Diana had to laugh although it was an uneasy laugh. "No, just a spoiled kid who's accustomed to getting her way."

"Well, I can see you've been getting it."

"Pretty much," Diana admitted.

"Diana." Jessie made Diana look at her. "You did not hurt me. I wouldn't let you hurt me. Do you really think I'm so weak I would let you abuse me? I gave my consent, my permission. At any time I could have stopped you. You didn't tie me down to the bed, you told me to stay there." She kissed Diana's forehead. "No harm done. Actually it felt pretty good."

"*Pretty good?*"

Jessie looked a little arch. "I've been telling people what to do for months. It was sorta nice not to have that responsibility. And I came over with the intention of getting laid. I certainly did." She looked at Diana. "You still don't believe me."

"It's not your behavior I'm concerned about," Diana said. "It's mine."

"And what bothers you about yours? Can we get off this floor? It's cold, and it's hard. I don't have enough cushioning on my butt, not like some people I know." She patted Diana's ass.

"Watch it," Diana warned.

"I try, all the time I can." Jessie looked positively relieved at Diana's faint smile. They both got up and Jessie retrieved the kit from the tub. She picked up the dildo, glanced at it and the other items in the bag, looked over her shoulder at Diana. "I would have, you know. I haven't before, but I trust you." Diana winced and Jessie shook her head. She put everything back in the zippered pouch. "Maybe next time. Now tell me why your behavior bothered you. Let me be the one who listens this time."

They returned to the bedroom. "This is uncomfortable," Diana said in an effort to delay.

"I know. You've had me in this position several times. Paybacks are hell." Together they picked up the blankets, the bedding and remade the bed.

"Sometimes," Diana said, "when I have a difficult task or really focus on something, I get into this mental zone and that's all I focus on. Call it tunnel vision or whatever you want. While I can do whatever I'm doing, sometimes I miss things. I wanted you." She closed her eyes for a moment then shook her head. "Maybe too much. Anyway, it would have been real easy to miss something, like you were being hurt. And being that I was ready to do something that was a first for you, I could have easily hurt you. And I wouldn't want to do that." She looked up across the bed. "I really wouldn't want to do that."

"I believe you," Jessie said. She went around and turned off the lights, checked the room. "Get into bed, Diana." She slid into bed beside Diana after she turned off the bathroom light. She put her arm around Diana, pulled her close. "But you see, my dear, I hear what you say, and I remember all the things you've done for me and how you've treated me for what, these past two years—three years, whatever it's been. I trust you, I don't think you would hurt me." She rolled over, put Diana on her back. "And now, I'm going to hold you to your promise."

"What's that?"

"That I could love you. You said later, after you showed me everything I could give."

"You said you wouldn't have anything left."

Jessie bent down to kiss Diana. "I was wrong."

CHAPTER SEVEN

Diana moved around the room while Jessie was in the shower. She tossed the pillows and the covers back on the bed, picked up the glasses, the fast-food wrappers from their three a.m. foray out for something to replace their missed dinner. Jessie had been relaxed, congenial, not like she had been in the early evening, hesitant and needy. Maybe she was right, a session of sexual domination was just what she needed. Didn't have to be responsible for anything for a change, didn't have to worry about pleasing Diana, just be fucked, even told when not to and when to come. She said it was very freeing. Diana wasn't so sure. Yes, she believed what Jessie said. She just wasn't sure about her own behavior.

She had never brought that part of her personality to Jessie. That was the part she was leaving behind. Jessie was so far away from Diana's life that she was a breath of fresh air, a getaway from all the issues and motivations that were beginning to surround her at home. She would have to start making choices soon, choices she wouldn't be able to take back, life-changing choices. It would be so much easier if she knew Jessie wanted to be in her life, but Jessie was waiting for Julie. Damn that woman. Julie, not Jessie. Diana admired loyalty. She would never interfere with it. Sometimes loyalty was all there was. Even misplaced loyalty. If it weren't for Julie.

Diana picked up Jessie's clothes. Jessie never hung them up, just threw them on whatever was handy. That was why Diana had hung up the tailored leather jacket the night before. It was much too expensive and whatever she was carrying would have pulled it out of shape. She spread the silk shirt out over the chair, running her fingers over it. Such a change from cotton shirts, but so sexy. My, my, Jessie could dress up impressively when she went about it. She shook the trousers out, lining up the pants legs, when something fell out of the pocket, a credit card or something.

The shower was just stopping when she bent down to pick it up. It became one of those moments remembered with such clarity that every little thing registers, the sound of the shower, the lighting in the room, the texture of the light wool pants still in her hand, the dark stitched leather, the silver color of the metal, the shape, the engraving, Lexington-Fayette Urban County Police Department.

Diana literally lost her breath and her initial fight or flight response set her heart pounding before her quick thinking stifled all reactions, or at least most of the drastic ones. She stood up, still staring at the badge when Jessie came out of the bathroom, wrapped in the big bath towel.

"What's wrong?" Jessie asked.

"What's this?" Diana was able to say with some calmness.

"My badge."

"Your badge," Diana repeated like she didn't understand the word. "You're a *cop?*" She hoped it sounded surprised rather than horrified, but from the change in Jessie's expression she didn't quite pull it off.

"Yesssss," Jessie said with some guardedness. Diana just stared at her, like she was seeing some stranger. "Is there a problem with that?"

"When did you become a cop?" Diana asked, trying hard to give an even inflection to every word.

"I've always been with the police department."

Diana closed her eyes, trying to shift all the mental gears, to take this in and not panic at the same time.

"Where did you think I worked, Diana?" Jessie moved cautiously, taking several steps toward her.

Diana opened her eyes, let out a long breath. She needed to treat this casually, act casually, not like she just got caught red-handed doing a criminal act. She shook her head and looked at Jessie in puzzlement, innocent puzzlement. "Every time we were together and you had to go to work, you were going to the horse farm. I thought you worked at the horse farm, the one you took me to when we had the picnic." She put the badge back in the trouser pocket with great deliberateness. "You really need to learn to hang up your clothes when you take them off. I'll have to use the steam iron on these."

"Don't worry about it," Jessie replied, her senses still on alert over Diana's changed behavior. "You always came in on the weekends. The horse farms usually hire off-duty police when there are big doings going on. Extra pay. And Dad was head of security for Broadrick. He worked there after his heart attack forced his retirement from the police."

"So he was on the force too?" Diana said, turning back. "Family tradition." She shook her head again, trying to clear it.

"What's wrong?" Jessie took Diana by the arm. "Is this a problem?"

Diana looked her in the face. Probably it wasn't best to freak out a cop even when she was standing there in nothing but a towel and you were standing between her and her gun. "I don't think so," Diana could say honestly. She deliberately relaxed. "It—it's just a shock."

An understatement if there ever was one. "I mean, all this time, when I've been away and thought of you, my image has been of you in blue jeans and a white shirt, working around horses, riding, walking them, grooming. I've pictured you on a horse farm even if I didn't have a clear idea of what you were doing."

She could look at Jessie in honest bewilderment. "And now I find out you're a cop and I see you in a navy blue uniform and carrying a gun?" she asked in a questioning mode. Jessie nodded, with some caution, still watchful, still holding onto Diana, but with a more relaxed grip. Diana let out another breath, in understanding. "That's what was in your jacket last night when I thought it was so heavy. Ahhh." She stepped away, out of Jessie's grip. She sat down on the bed. She shivered. All those months and she had been bedding one of Lexington's finest. She gave a shaky laugh.

"What now?"

"Oh, shit Jessie," Diana said with forced deprecation. "Learning you're a cop, and thinking of everything I did to you last night?" She brought her hand to her mouth, half laughing, half crying.

Jessie squatted down in front of Diana, with a reassured look. "I'm still Jessie," she pointed out. "I'm still the same person. Just because you know something about me that you didn't know yesterday doesn't change anything."

Just everything, Diana thought. "Changes all my memories," she said aloud. "I realize it's hindsight, but still."

"Does it change how you feel about me?"

"No," Diana answered instantly and realized only after she said it, that it was true. But the ramifications, they were mind-boggling. "No, it doesn't change my feelings at all."

"I'm glad," Jessie said with relief. She stood up. "Sometimes when I've dated someone, there's been issues. And I've lost some friends who discovered what my job was. Problems with drugs sometimes, maybe problems with authority."

"Well," Diana said with forced casualness, "now I might have a problem with that." Jessie gave her a quick questioning look. Diana shrugged. "Like last night, sometimes I like to be in charge."

Jessie chuckled. "And sometimes I like not to be," she said carefully.

Diana stood up. "Like I said last night, it's appalling what we don't know about each other. I mean, I'd recognize your voice, your walk anytime, the way you move." She chuckled, revising images as quickly as they came to mind. "I wonder if I would recognize you in uniform." She looked up at Jessie in puzzlement. "I thought you had to carry your gun and ID all the time."

"My little black bag," Jessie answered. "My change of clothes."

Diana slowly nodded in realization. Of course, Jessie always had her little black bag. Diana had thought it was because she was so confident of scoring when she was on the prowl. *God, talk about only seeing what I wanted to see.* She kissed Jessie quickly rather than follow that train of thought. "So where are we going today?" *Some place busy, active, so we don't have to talk.*

Jessie drew Diana back for a longer kiss. "Are you all right with this? Really? I'd be upset if I lost you."

Diana closed her eyes, lost a little apprehension in that kiss. She waited until Jessie let her go. "Well, we don't want to make you upset, do we?"

"You know, we don't have to go anywhere." Jessie again wrapped her arms around Diana.

"Tempting," Diana ran her fingers across Jessie's face. "But we need to do something, go somewhere. I need to see you out and about, process all this," she said honestly. "Seeing you naked in bed and getting lost in you won't do it." Just the same, she still ran her hand under the towel. "I should have it processed nicely by the time we get back, get adjusted, you know." She looked up at Jessie as if with a sudden thought. "Does that mean you have handcuffs?" she asked playfully.

Jessie laughed, back to her old laughter, Diana was relieved to hear. "For me or for you?"

"Oh, honey, I don't think I could stand the cuffs on me. I was thinking more for you."

"Maybe we'll just skip the cuffs. And maybe it's better we go out today." She kissed Diana again. "I was thinking of taking you to Berea."

"What's Berea?"

"It's a little town about thirty miles from here. It's full of craft and folk art shops. There's a college there originally founded for the mountain folks and there's lots of craftspeople. I thought you'd like it."

"Sounds like something Nicki would like," Diana suggested oh so casually.

"No. She'd find it boring and then we wouldn't have tonight, which I'm really looking forward to." She leered at Diana. "God knows how long I'm going to have to store this up for."

Diana chuckled and shook her head. She'd manage some way.

***

Diana pulled into the driveway with a sigh of relief. It had been a weekend, about as far away from her expectations as it could have been and yet still be with Jessie. God, Jessie a cop. Never in her wildest dreams. She really had put Jessie in some small secret part of her mind where the world didn't exist. Margaret was right. That really was dangerous. Maybe she should be glad Jessie had been a cop and not any of Papa's rivals. A cop was bad enough but it could have been worse. The world did exist, and Papa's part of it wasn't always a pleasant place.

She walked into the house, dropped her suitcase, surprised to see bigger suitcases packed and lined up by the door.

"What's up?" she asked as soon as Margaret entered.

"We're going to Wyles."

"In Miami?"

"You're good," Margaret pointed out with respectful sarcasm. "Have a good weekend?"

"Eventful." Diana passed off, not ready to confess to Margaret her lack of caution. "What's up with Wyles?"

"Your papa thinks someone's cooking the books, wants you to examine them."

"Who's going with us?"

"Franklin."

"Okay."

"And then we're going directly to the West Coast."

"Why?"

"We'll find out when we get there."

"Okay."

CHAPTER EIGHT

Four months later Diana examined the changing colors as she drove back into Lexington. Autumn already. Right from spring flowers to fall colors. It had been a while. Big changes coming. She frowned. Big choices too. In or out. She had to decide while she still could, before it became an offer she couldn't refuse. Papa had been clear on that: she could still choose. But what kind of choice did she have? All she knew was the Family. Except for Jessie.

On the other hand, this was a nice town, she wouldn't mind living here. Lots of history, nice year round weather. The horse farms were beautiful, white board fences, grass really was blue. She still remembered her surprise at that. She eased into the traffic on New Circle Road. Wouldn't be bad at all. She could like it.

She drove through downtown. She wondered if she would need the hotel this trip. Maybe, maybe not. She glanced at the sidewalks. Nice day for the outdoor café. Ahhh, and look who was there. And a parking place. Well, this was her lucky day.

She watched her at the café table as she walked up the block. Dressed in civvies, she was reading something, one leg stretched out to the other chair, the other leg drawn up, and whatever she was reading resting against her leg. She was frowning in concentration, only slowly turning the pages. Black slacks, off-white Irish fisherman's sweater. Coat thrown back over the chair. Coffee cup on the table. Diana walked right up to her without being noticed.

"Hello, beautiful."

Jessie looked up, annoyed at the interruption, then did the classic double take. "Diana." She leaped to her feet, greeted her with a hug.

"I'm not interrupting anything am I?"

"No, no." There was a flicker of dismay across Jessie's face and then it was gone. "I've got to meet someone for lunch but that's later. Have a seat."

There was a distance there, and Diana had the first inkling of something wrong. Jessie's openness was gone. She was more guarded.

"So you came back?"

"Well, yes," Diana said, sitting across from Jessie. She began to have a bad feeling in the pit of her stomach. "Did you think I wouldn't?"

"I didn't know," Jessie said frankly. "You haven't been gone this long for a long, long time."

"I had a deal on the West Coast. I just got back a couple of days ago." Jessie nodded, but there was disinterest there. "How's everything going with you?" Diana fished.

Jessie nodded. "Can't complain."

"How's Nicki?"

"Doing good. Likes school this year." Jessie met her gaze. "She wears the necklace you got her almost every day."

Diana couldn't see with the high neck of the sweater whether Jessie was wearing hers. That would have helped, because this conversation was much too casual to make her feel comfortable. "Did you think I wouldn't come back, Jessie?" she asked again.

Jessie made that expression she had when she wanted to be casual. "I didn't know. I thought you might have called since you were gone so long."

"Would that have made a difference?"

"Maybe. I don't know." Jessie moved around the coffee cup, the notebook, not looking at Diana. "So what now?"

Maybe she was imagining things, maybe Jessie was just pissed because she had been gone for so long. "I have," Diana searched for a word, "an opportunity. I wanted to talk to you about it. But I think you've got news to tell me, don't you?"

Jessie shifted her gaze, still avoiding Diana's. "You ought to be in my line of work. You read people very well."

"What's up?" Diana asked, inwardly bracing herself even though she wanted to get up and run away rather than hear whatever Jessie was going to tell her. She did not think the news was going to be good.

Jessie licked her lips, watched the traffic in the street for a minute. Then she finally looked directly at Diana. "Julie came back to town. She was never able to get over me either. She understands now what I was going through. We're working things out, getting back together."

"Oh," was the only coherent thing that Diana could get out. There wasn't anything else she could think to say. "Well." She paused again as she searched for some coherency. "I guess that makes you unavailable."

"Yeah," Jessie said with a little relief, as if she had expected something more.

"Well," Diana repeated. She sat back in the chair, looking at but not really seeing Jessie. "Working out well for you?" she asked for lack of something better to say.

Jessie nodded. "It's rocky," she admitted. "There have been a lot of changes. Julie's a doctor now. We're not kids anymore."

"But your feelings have lasted this long." Somehow Jessie didn't look as happy as Diana would have expected. "Well."

"You've said that," Jessie said with some irritation.

Diana took a deep breath, pulled herself together. "I imagine that after this many years and changes, things may be rocky for a while. I'm sure you'll work all of those problems out." Jessie looked up in some surprise and Diana went on. "You've waited for Julie a long time. You've demonstrated your loyalty and how important she is to you. I have nothing but wishes of happiness for you, Jessie."

"Really?"

Diana's voice softened. "Jessie, we've shared a lot. I knew all this time you were waiting for Julie. The last time I was here, that came up and you were so upset when I said you were waiting. Why wouldn't I want you to be happy?"

"I almost wished you hadn't come back," Jessie confessed. "I dreaded telling you. I feel bad because now my waiting has been rewarded and yours hasn't."

Diana forced a laugh. "Don't worry about me. You just focus on Julie. Not everyone gets that second chance. Make the most of it. Grab the chance to be happy." She got to her feet, and Jessie followed.

"You're not leaving?"

"What reason do I have for staying, Jessie?"

"You didn't tell me about your opportunity."

Diana shook her head. "It doesn't matter."

"I don't suppose you would want to meet Julie."

Diana shook her head. "I don't think so." She leaned forward to give Jessie an air kiss. "Give my best to Nicki." She reluctantly released Jessie. "You take care."

"Diana, I don't know how to get hold of you."

"You don't need to now. You've got Julie. You be careful. It's a rough world out there." Then she turned and walked away, quickly, while she still could.

***

She was drinking coffee in the kitchen when Margaret came down. "Well, you're back early. I didn't expect you back for a week."

Diana shrugged. It had been a very long drive home.

"Did you decide what you're going to do?"

"I'm going to take the job. I've already told Papa."

Margaret poured herself some coffee. "You are? You did?" She looked at Diana curiously. "How was Lexington?"

"Lexington is over."

"What happened, sweet pea?" Diana shook her head. "She dump you?"

"Not exactly. She—an old flame showed up, they are working things out."

"I'm so sorry." Margaret watched Diana over the rim of her cup. It was not Diana's way to take it so calmly.

Diana drank some coffee, picked up the paper. "Just as well. There would have been problems. Real difficulties down the road."

"Most problems can be worked out if you're determined."

"That's what I told her about her old flame. I don't think it would have worked for us."

"Why not?"

"She's a cop."

Margaret spit coffee all over the counter, looking at Diana with complete disbelief. "A cop!" Then she lowered her voice, glancing around. "Are you out of your mind?"

Diana didn't look up from the paper. "Yes, one of Lexington's finest and no, I'm not out of my mind. It doesn't matter. It's over and done with."

"But it went on for a long time!" Margaret hissed.

Diana still didn't look up. "I didn't know for a long time. But don't worry. It was a strange relationship: she didn't ask any questions and I didn't volunteer. If she had asked, I would have split. And if I had asked, I would have known much earlier."

"What the hell happened to your radar?" Margaret demanded, fear coloring her voice. "Didn't I teach you anything?"

Diana looked up. "I'm afraid I had other radar working that was stronger, Margaret. Now calm down. Nothing was compromised."

"My God," the woman muttered. "You, the daughter of Czar Randalson, and sleeping with a cop, a female cop."

Diana banged her coffee cup down on the counter, sloshing some out. "Enough." Margaret looked at her in startled surprise. "Yes, my father is a crime lord. Yes, my lover was a woman; and yes, she is a cop, a good cop, I might add. One who knows nothing about me. And you will not say anything. You will not mention Lexington again, Margaret. It is to be forgotten. Do you understand?"

"Yes, Miss Diana."

"Don't get smart with me," Diana snapped back. "I haven't been Miss Diana to you since I was sixteen, when you became my bodyguard instead of my nanny." She closed her eyes, willing tears away.

Margaret went to her, put her arms around her. "I'm so sorry, Diana."

Safe there, Diana would let herself cry.

CHAPTER NINE

Two years later

"Then that's the plan. Any questions?" Captain Conrad looked around the table at the six officers, finally resting his eyes on Jessie. "Jessie?"

Well aware she was the keystone, that if she couldn't do it, the whole sting would fall apart, Jessie shook her head. For the past two years she had created the persona of a college kid, skinny, awkward, geeky, first to buy drugs, then do a little selling. Now was the opportunity to go to a higher level, to find out just who was bringing the drugs into the area.

"Then let's get set up, everyone in place."

The group broke up, Jessie and Pete going out the door together.

"You mention this part to Julie?" Pete asked.

Jessie shook her head. "We talked about this a long time ago, at the beginning. She said she didn't want to know."

Pete gave her a questioning look. "That can lead to problems or a hell of a surprise."

Jessie agreed. "She said that was the only way she could handle it. So." She turned away.

Two years with Julie and Julie still hadn't been able to adjust to Jessie's choice of a career. She tolerated it, in her own way, but it hadn't been easy. Julie could deal with devastating illness, struggles for survival, but she could not deal with the idea that Jessie could possibly go out the door in the morning and never return.

"Nicki?" Pete pulled Jessie back to the present.

"She doesn't like it, but she can deal with it better. Guess that comes from growing up in a cop family." Jessie glanced at the clock. She still needed to go pick up the money then get wired, pick up the car. Time was passing so quickly.

When the call came through, she was alone and she grabbed it eagerly, assuming it was a call saying the money was ready. "Galbreath."

"Detective," came an unfamiliar even metallic voice. "Don't go on that drug buy."

Jessie stopped dead, all her senses came alert. "Who is this?" she asked sharply.

"Doesn't matter. Just don't go. You've been made."

Jessie turned in a circle, ascertaining she was alone. "What do you mean I've been made?" She quickly went down the short list of people who knew of this covert operation even as she weighed the value of this call.

"Hey, I'm calling, ain't I? Got your number, know about the two o'clock. Got your life insurance paid up?"

"Who is this? And how do you know?"

Low throaty laughter. "Wouldn't you like to know?" And then the voice turned ominous. "You're warned: Don't go." There was a click.

Jessie stared at her phone. Ominous, but how credible? Unknown number? No identification. From someone who disguised their voice. Did that mean it was someone she knew? Someone she trusted? She stood there, her hand over her mouth as she considered.

Regulations required she go right to Captain Conrad and tell him about the call. And he would cancel the entire operation. Was that the purpose of the call, not to warn her but to keep her from finding out who was behind bringing the drugs into town? Was it simply a warning they were getting too close to the source?

Damn, she had put a lot of time into this. Who would be in the position to know about her? Only a handful of people. The caller even had a mocking tone as if he, she, it, knew Jessie would doubt the source. Was it just someone trying to screw the deal? But how did they get her number?

Jessie stood there, considering. She had confidence in the plan, confidence in the team they had put together. She trusted everyone.

At least she had thought they were trustworthy. Now she wasn't sure. The phone rang again.

The money was ready for pickup, time to decide. A risk yes, but a calculated risk. She had put a lot of time in this, a lot of herself. She wouldn't be scared off. She put the phone back in her pocket. She would go with it.

"The money's ready," she told Pete as she came out.

"Something wrong?"

She shook her head even as she evaded his gaze. Years of working together had made them a team. Sometimes they could almost read each other's minds. She didn't need him to read her mind now.

"You using your weak ankle brace story?"

"It's worked so far, ever since I really twisted my ankle that one time."

"Still confident?"

She nodded as she wrapped her ankle where she had strapped her Ruger LCP. Small enough to be concealed under her jeans, compact to fit snugly against her ankle, curved edges enough not be noticed during a quick pat down. She was already turning inward, projecting how this would go, the meeting, the buy, ticking off her list as she wrapped the other ankle so they were equal. Money for this operation came from previous drug raids. Seemed only fair. Counted, recorded, and stuffed in the backpack, an old army green one picked up at the surplus store. Body wire, new type, not on her this time, but in her belt. Test it out. Pick up the car, make sure it was scattered with evidence of her use, candy wrappers, drink cups, school notes.

"Ready?"

She nodded, and they started out. She paused before she went out the door, shook herself to dispel the tension. A little was good but she needed to be looser for her "character." She took a deep breath, deliberately relaxed and went out the door.

She drove around town, arrived from the other direction. The meeting spot was isolated, a construction site that had been halted when the builder ran out of financing. Fence was down on the back side and she pulled up and got out of the car.

Johnny pulled up a few minutes later, his car directly in front of hers, nose to nose like he always did.

"You got the money?" he greeted her.

She picked up the backpack off the hood and unzipped it enough so he could see cash, just not how much. "You got the stuff?"

"Not here. I'm to take you to them."

Her stomach lurched. This wasn't in the plan.

He came around the car. "Didn't want to meet you here. Too public. I'll take you to the spot." He gave her a cursory pat down, even more casual than usual. "Let's go."

She knew the wire couldn't be detected but she always had a faint feeling of contempt that he believed her ankle story. She got into the car, the backpack containing the money resting between her feet. As they pulled out and went out Richmond Road, she hoped her surveillance could keep up.

The uneasy feeling grew when they pulled behind an abandoned gas station. They hadn't anticipated the switch to yet another vehicle. She hadn't anticipated being blindfolded. The thought occurred to her she should have listened. They continued for miles and turned off the road, driving over rough ground and then came to a stop.

"We're here." He leaned over and took off her blindfold.

Jessie blinked, her eyes adjusting to the light as she looked around to see the wooded area. They were on an old logging road. From the growth, it hadn't been used in a while.

"I don't see anyone," she said nervously as she wondered if she should have listened to the phoned in warning, should have passed on this one.

He pointed down the track through the trees. "He'll meet you on the other side. Once the deal's made, you come back here and I'll take you back."

She tried to read him, uneasy. She wondered if her surveillance had been able to keep up. Damn, she should have believed the call.

She looked around as she got out, listening but there was nothing to hear except the wind in the trees. Johnny sat still, seemed poised to wait. She pulled out the backpack, and started down the lane. As she started down it, the car pulled away.

She jerked around but the car was already gone. She circled, not liking anything about this. She was in an open space, a long drive between the trees. Something was wrong, no one was there.

"Hello?" she called, not liking the silence. Even the birds were quiet. She was out in the open, exposed.

A car pulled up at the far end of the road where it looked like it opened to a meadow. A man got out, too far away to be able to identify. "Down here," he hollered with a wave of his arm.

With more than a little misgiving, Jessie started down the road, nervous now, wondering how this was going to go down. All she could hear was the crunch of the gravel, a light breeze through the trees. No birds. Nothing. The man was slowly walking toward her.

"Jessie!"

The scream came from behind her. Nerves taut, she jerked around into a crouching position, already reaching for her weapon. The gunshot took her from behind, where she moments before had been facing. She felt the punch in the shoulder blade, slamming her forward, sprawling across the gravel. White pain took her to the edge of consciousness. Training and duty got the gun in her hand but she was unfocused, disoriented. She could hear running, the vibrations through the ground as she struggled for some grip on consciousness.

I'm going to die, she thought and focused in an effort not to go without a fight.

There were hands on her other shoulder, her weapon grabbed from her and then from behind her, above her, another voice, a male voice.

"What the fuck! What are you doing here?"

Then there was an explosion of sound, the gun going off right above her and she didn't hear anything more.

She came back, into a kaleidoscope of sounds and images, foggy and unclear. Someone was leaning over her. "Damn. So much blood," a woman was saying.

She screamed at the pressure on her shoulder.

"Jessie, Jessie!" came the demand. "Are you wired?"

What difference did it make anymore? At least the bastards would know there were witnesses. "Yes," but it took all her breath to say that.

"Thank God." Her shirt was pulled up as if to see and she moaned at the jostling.

"Officer down! Officer down! Need an ambulance. Life Flight."

You've called the cops? Then everything dissolved.

She came back to feel pressure on her shoulder. Someone, she didn't know who, was trying to help her.

"Tell—tell Julie I'm sorry," she whispered.

"Oh, fuck, tell her yourself."

Why do you sound so angry? "Tell Nicki I love her." *Never see her graduate, never see her get a life.*

"Don't you die on me, Galbreath! I didn't come all this way just to have you take the easy way out! You tell Nicki yourself! You better not abandon her, leave her with no one."

"Not easy."

From off in the distance, or maybe it was her imagination, she heard a siren.

"About damn time," came the muttering from above her and then there was the roar of engine, siren, dirt being kicked up, a police radio crackling.

"Police! Put your hands up!"

"Oh, God, a county mountie."

"Now!"

"Deputy, I take my hands off her and she's going to bleed to death. Are you the only one here? Is the ambulance coming? Oh, shit man, I'm not going anywhere. Are you alone?"

Jessie moaned and was gone again, fading in and out. Time was telescoping and she didn't know what was happening except breathing hurt. "Can't breathe—breathe," she whispered.

"Where the hell's that ambulance? Is that the helicopter?"

There were more sirens and the next thing she knew, there were white uniforms leaning over her. She screamed as they lifted her and roughly jogged her to the copter that she didn't remember landing. She thought she was going to vomit as it lifted and turned and that was the last thing she remembered until bright, bright lights blinded her and she was rushed somewhere.

She screamed when they lifted her and moved her to a table and there was so much activity around she couldn't keep track. She could hear paging echoing and a lot of confusion around her but nothing that made sense. Light flashes, confused glimpses of people, machinery, an operating room and then merciful blackness.

Delusions and hallucinations followed, glimpses of reality or maybe she only thought it was reality. Nicki curled up in a chair beside the bed, Julie standing beside the bed talking to the doctors. She even thought she saw Diana leaning over her, wiping her face. Mostly she slept. Sometimes she hurt so much she could only count the minutes, the hours until the next dose of pain relief.

She didn't even remember the first surgery, just the second where they took a tendon from her leg to repair some of the shoulder damage. Laid up with shoulder damage, leg surgery, she faced months of therapy, maybe a full year of recovery. Nothing like what you saw in the movies or on television.

"You're damn lucky," Captain Conrad told her, standing beside her hospital bed. "If that shot had taken you on the left side, we'd be going to your funeral."

Lucky, she considered. Yes, she supposed so, although there was still a mess to clean up.

"What made you turn?"

She looked away and didn't answer.

"Had to be something. Report said you were sprawled out flat on your stomach, Kaplan's body behind you on his back. You took the bullet in the back."

Jessie could still hear that shout of warning. "There was someone else there," she said slowly.

"Yes, someone Kaplan recognized, a woman." He cocked his head and looked at Jessie. "Any idea who?"

Jessie shook her head. "I turned, got hit almost immediately. Everything's fuzzy."

"Surprised you can remember that much." He gave Jessie a speculative look. "She called you by name." He paused. "She knew about you. She said you couldn't die and leave Nicki alone."

Jessie blinked and looked up in surprise.

"Is there something you're not telling me, Detective Galbreath?"

Jessie gave a rueful shake of her head. "Probably a lot. I can't remember, just bits and pieces, fragments." She looked at Conrad directly. "I don't know who the woman was. But I'm grateful."

He let it go at that, but she knew there would be more questions later.

Finally weeks later, she was home, although she still faced more therapy. But not back to work. Not yet. Fragments of memories surfaced, and then the nightmares began.

***

"Jessie! Honey! Please wake up. It's Nicki. I'm right here. You're home. You're safe." Jessie came awake, her hand on the back of the couch, pulling herself up, her legs already swinging to the floor. She was breathing hard, her heart pounding as she wildly looked around.

Nicki stood there, distraught, hands clenched, as she watched her sister. "Jessie, it's okay. It's only a nightmare. It's all over."

Jessie looked around, grounding herself. Her living room. Her house. Her couch. Her coffee table with the newspaper, the TV remote. Her sister, Nicki, standing back, watching her, concern written all over her face. Jessie ran her hand through her hair, closed her eyes, reached out for Nicki to let her know she was awake. Nicki took her hand, pushed her back to a reclining position, sat at her hip. She stroked Jessie's face, wiping away the panic sweat.

"Jesus, Jessie. Did the doctor say how long these nightmares were going to last?"

Jessie closed her eyes, going though her cycle of thoughts to calm her panic, slow down her heart rate. It was all over. She was out of the hospital. No more surgeries, just therapy. She was still on leave but that would soon be over. She could go back to work, desk work, yes, but she could get over this waiting, this suspended time. Get back into the rhythm of living, not of healing. "Don't swear." She drew a deep breath. "He says it'll lessen once I get back to work. Where's Julie?" He also said they would stop when she remembered whatever was eluding her.

"She went in to the clinic."

Jessie drew a deep breath. That was good. Her nightmares always upset Julie, and then she had to deal with Julie as well as the nightmare.

"Was it the same thing?" Jessie nodded. "You know," Nicki said carefully, cautiously, "you probably had this one because of the fight you and Julie had last night."

Jessie opened her eyes, looked up at Nicki. "You heard."

"Well, it was a little hard not to the way you two were yelling at each other."

"We were out in the family room."

Nicki nodded. "Yeah, you were pretty loud. Want to talk about your nightmare or the fight?"

Jessie sat up, drawing up her legs, resting her head on her knees. She was embarrassed Nicki had heard anything, not that Nicki didn't know, but still it was not comfortable your little sister hearing your lover's quarrels. "She wants me to quit the force." Nicki nodded. "She thinks I can do private security, even get a PI license, anything but being a cop."

"Your being shot really freaked her out. Didn't help that you didn't tell her about the undercover you were on."

"Cops get shot occasionally." Jessie raised her head, rested her chin on her knees. "We never like to think it's going to happen but we all know it does, and it might. That comes with the territory." She stared straight ahead.

"Was the nightmare the same?" Nicki put her arm around Jessie and gently transferred Jessie's head from her knees to her shoulder.

Jessie nodded. "The drive down between the trees, the open space. Someone screaming at me. Being hit." She shivered.

"Nothing more?"

Jessie shook her head. She had tried so hard to remember more, but everything was a blur, she had snatches of memory, bits and pieces, not enough. "There were three people there," she said. "One survivor, one dead and one unknown." She took a deep breath. "I know I didn't kill him. I couldn't—couldn't turn over. I know I got the gun out, at least I think I did. But it was my gun that killed him."

She knew she shouldn't be talking about this. And if she was talking to anyone, why not to the shrink? Or her life partner? Not to her seventeen-year-old sister. She had already failed one psych evaluation. They said it was too early for her to return. Maybe it was. She had been having night terrors then. Now it was just nightmares. What would she do if she didn't pass her evaluation? And her partner? If it was up to Julie, she wouldn't pass. Julie, she knew, would be sympathetic and say all the right things, but she would be delighted if Jessie couldn't go back. That left Nicki. And her longings for a lover who understood and accepted all parts of her life.

"Are you sure it was a woman?" Nicki asked. Jessie nodded. "Not him?"

"No, Kaplan was an executioner. We had him on file. Same MO. Lure the suspect to an isolated area." She had been so stupid but they too thought they had everything covered. "One shot to take them down, then another shot at close range at the back of the head to make sure. Always the same." She felt Nicki's grip tighten around her.

"Then whoever the mystery woman was, she had to have killed him." She paused. "She saved your life."

Jessie nodded. No matter what line of reasoning she took, it always came back to that. Who and why? She had gone over and over everyone she had come in contact with, examined them one by one and discarded the idea. Except, of course, for the anonymous tip. She hadn't told Nicki about that, certainly hadn't told Julie or anyone else for that matter. She sat up, needed to move, suddenly felt caged. Nicki released her immediately.

"Want some iced tea?" she offered. "Why don't you go sit on the deck? It's a beautiful afternoon."

Jessie nodded. Outside in the sunlight had to be better than sitting in the living room replaying memories. She went to the bathroom, stopped off in the library to pull out a book, something light and frothy to help refocus her mind somewhere else. Nicki handed her the tall glass as she went through the dining room to the deck.

The deck caught all the afternoon sun. She pushed the redwood lounge so it came out of the corner, adjusted the umbrella so it shaded the chair, and flopped down, setting the iced tea on the decking beside the lounge.

She lay back, the afternoon heat felt good. There weren't a lot of days she could do this. If she went back to work, there would be even less. The investigation was back to square one on the drugs. Now she had even greater reason to bring them down. On the other hand—an outcome she didn't even want to think about—what would she do if they wouldn't let her back? All she had ever wanted to do was be a cop, like her dad, like her grandfather. She couldn't imagine doing anything else. That was what made the arguments with Julie so painful.

This enforced leave had given her time to think. And the fact that she could have died made her reflect on her life. She had waited so long for Julie, had held on to the memory of their loving like a lifesaver when she was overwhelmed with caring for first her mom, then her dad, and always Nicki. Someone had loved her and she had loved someone. When all this caretaking was over, there would be someone there to love again. The truth of it was that Julie had not supported her then; and she wasn't supporting her now, not like Jessie needed her to.

Letting go of that memory was like saying she had wasted all those years. She had gone through so many women, women she watched find someone, settle down, have a home life, someone who loved and supported them. When Julie had come back and said she had never gotten over Jessie and wanted to try, it had seemed like justification for all that waiting, all those lonely nights. What they hadn't figured on was Julie's distaste for being a police wife.

Jessie closed her eyes and it wasn't Julie's image that came to mind. Instead, Diana came to mind. With a surprising clarity, she remembered Diana's shock when she had discovered Jessie was a cop. Jessie remembered her impression that Diana wanted to bolt out the door and disappear forever. But she hadn't, she stayed, she said it didn't change things. She just needed to readjust. She never explained why she was so shocked and then she had disappeared for months. When she came back, Julie was in the picture. Then Diana had disappeared.

Diana's shock and Julie's distaste. But Jessie was a cop, it was part of her heritage. It was in her blood. She expected problems because she was a cop. Station houses were littered with failed relationships. Her parents had made it. So she knew it could be done. She also knew how hard it was. Why did she have this vague feeling that Diana would have been able to handle it better than Julie?

She sat up and buried her face in her hands, slowly rocking. Where did it leave her now? A busted investigation, a failed relationship, a career that might or might not be there. She felt lost, adrift, with an emptiness in her she didn't know how to fill.

She jumped when her phone rang, and her first startled, eager thought was, *Maybe it's Diana.* The phone rang twice while she shook off that thought, shocked at its intensity. She checked the number as it rang again. She didn't recognize the source but flipped it up. "Galbreath."

"Well, well, well, back to the land of the living," came the unforgettable metallic voice. "Didn't believe me, did you? Had to learn the hard way."

Her heart leaped and all Jessie's senses came alert as she sat up. "Who is this?"

"Your guardian angel," the voice mocked. "Answer the question."

"It was you!" Like a burst of light, the memory returned. "You warned me." Jessie turned around to sit on the side of the lounge chair. She felt strangely exhilarated, she could remember something. Another black hole eliminated.

"For all the good it did."

"What do you want?"

"Just to know you're alive and well."

"What difference does that make to you?"

"Wouldn't want to think I totally wasted my efforts."

Jessie caught her breath. "Why?" At least, Jessie thought, maybe she could get one question answered and she could figure out the other. She ran her fingers through her hair.

"Beats the hell out of me," the woman mocked. "Stop running your hand through your hair."

Jessie froze. She turned her head carefully as she looked around the adjoining backyards. She examined overlooking windows, anyone who was working in the yard, the mowing service two yards down. She couldn't see anyone who might be watching her.

"Now that I've got your full attention," the woman went on in a more serious tone, "you've got a problem."

"No shit," Jessie retorted, "tell me about it." *Who the hell are you?* she wondered even as she answered.

The woman laughed again. "When do you go back to work?"

"Why should I tell you?"

"Ummm, let's call it a trade. I'll tell you what I know, you answer the question. I know you failed your psych eval, passed your physical. I know the second eval is coming up. I imagine you're worried whether they'll let you back in, if you've lost your nerve."

Jessie felt her blood run cold. Whoever this was, they knew her well. Or could make very good guesses. "Next week," she answered carefully.

"You'll do fine. You're a good cop, Detective. It's in the blood."

Why should the praise of someone so unknown reassure her so much? Jessie struggled to focus. "Tell me about my problem."

"You've got a leak in the department."

That was a sucker punch and yet it would explain so much. "Who?"

"Don't know. Eliminating them as I search."

"Peterson?" Jessie questioned. *Oh, please, don't make it Pete. Couldn't stand for my partner to betray me.*

"No, cleared him."

Jessie felt the relief. She saw Nicki come to the patio door with a question on her face. Jessie shook her head, waved her away, bent over, her elbows on her knees. "Conrad?" She named her captain next, because she needed to report this to someone and she needed to know who was safe. A leak, damn, that would explain so much going wrong.

"Cleared."

"So why are you telling me?"

"Can't be watching your back all the time. I got other things to do."

"How do I know you're just not making guesses, potshots in the dark?"

"Ummm, difficult. What can I say?"

"Tell me something that can't be guessed at, that I can check out."

"What? That I'm there? Really got my eye on you?"

"Yes."

There was a long pause and Jessie thought it would end there. "You'll be upset," came the warning.

"Upset me!" Jessie snapped, tired of being jerked around.

"All right. Nicki was at the Bungalow Thursday night. Remind her she is seventeen even if she looks older. Kentucky hasn't lowered the drinking age." Jessie leaped to her feet. "I told you you'd be upset."

"Hold on!"

Jessie threw the phone on the lounge chair, charged in the house and found her sister at the kitchen sink. "Nicki!" she barked. Nicki turned, her jaw dropping at Jessie's tone. "Now answer me, truthfully. I need to know: were you at the Bungalow Thursday night?" She saw the truth in Nicki's face. "Don't lie to me, Nicki, this is important." Nicki nodded, swallowing. "Shit. You're grounded. We'll discuss this later."

Jessie charged back to the patio, picked up the phone. "You still there?"

"I'm still here."

"You know I've got to take this somewhere."

"Like I said, you're a good cop. Just watch your back. I'll let you know when I find out something. Oh, and tell Nicki I'm sorry."

The connection was broken. Jessie sat there staring at the phone for several minutes, her mind a jumble of confusion. Someone who knew her. Someone who knew Nicki. Knew the Bungalow. Oh, God, who was this person?

She sorted things out, punched in a phone number. "Captain, I need to talk to you...No, away from the office, preferably with no one knowing...Yes, it's important...Fine. There's that little coffee shop on Harrisburg Road, Logan's. I'll meet you there."

***

"I got a call," Jessie started without much preamble. She knew this was not going to go over well. "Warning me not to go, that I had been made." She wasn't wrong.

Captain Conrad slowly put his coffee cup down. "I should fire you."

"Hear me out. Whether you fire me or not, you need to know this information." Jessie recounted the information the woman had given her over the phone.

Captain Conrad listened. When Jessie finished, he gave her an even, hard look. "You believe this person?"

Jessie spread her hands. "She was right that I had been made. If it was her, she was there to save me. She told me information about my sister here in town, which means she is or at least was here in town and she could recognize my sister."

"Did your sister recognize her?"

"I don't know. I haven't had that discussion with her," Jessie said forbiddingly. "Not yet at least."

Captain Conrad considered everything while Jessie waited. She was still trying to figure things out. There was some nagging familiarity about the voice in spite of the metallic sound, a pattern of speaking. It eluded her, but it tantalized.

"Any names?" Conrad asked.

"Said you were clear. Peterson was clear."

"Nice to know we met someone's approval," the captain said with some grim humor. "Did you get the idea this was inside their organization?"

Jessie went over everything that had been said. "There was nothing said and we've found no record on any women working in the groups we found. On the other hand, if the information is accurate, it has to come from the inside."

"Know anyone inside?"

Jessie shook her head. The thought that someone she knew and trusted might have a secret life was too disconcerting to contemplate. And yet there was only one unknown in her life.

"We'll continue with our investigation, of course. It sounds like she will be contacting you again. We need evidence." Jessie nodded. "It'd be nice to know who this person is."

"If she's inside, she's got to be putting herself in danger."

Captain Conrad nodded. "It'd still be nice." He gave Jessie a cryptic look. "There's still the matter of you withholding information."

Jessie nodded. "I shouldn't have." *And I almost paid a fatal price, except for someone I don't know.* "I just wanted it too badly. I'll deal with whatever the repercussions are."

CHAPTER TEN

Jessie slipped into the squad room early. She didn't want any fanfare. She felt enough of a relief just to be able return to work. Instead of drawing a suspension without pay, she could have been fired. She could have been demoted down to patrol instead of given desk duty. And she wondered how much her contact with whoever had saved her life played into that. But now all that was behind her. The extra therapy time had been good. She was cleared to return.

She'd had time for discussions with Nicki, Nicki's curiosity about herself, some long talks about sexuality, about vulnerability and any spillover from Jessie's life. They were still on the same wavelength.

Julie was another story. Julie wasn't happy with her return to the force. She would have been just as happy if Jessie had been fired, although Jessie hadn't explained the evidence withheld had been a warning phone call. There were lots of tears, some hysteria. They had seen a counselor, joint sessions that were stormy. In the end, it had come to a truce. Jessie had to finish this case. Then they would reconsider. Julie had to come to terms with the potential for loss. It was very unlikely anything else would happen to Jessie. Cops go their entire careers without getting shot. This was a fluke, a one-time occurrence. There had to be a way.

"Good morning." Pete greeted her with a grin and a hug. "Welcome back."

"Glad to be back. How goes it?"

Pete shrugged. "Same old, same old." He shoved files over to Jessie's desk.

Jessie had an interview with the captain. They did not discuss anything about the leak.

She went back to work and they waited. Every day, with a raised eyebrow, the captain asked; and every day Jessie shook her head. Every day she thought of everyone she knew, quietly investigated even people she never would have otherwise considered. She went over and over every nugget of information, tried harder to remember everything that had happened in the clearing. She grew suspicious of everyone, and she waited.

***

"You ate the last doughnut," Jessie complained. "What? I'm not special any more?"

"You were late. Teach you to be on time."

"Funny." She glanced at Pete, looked him over, his settling belly. She was conscious of those things after watching her dad. "Looks like you need to give some of those up, Pete. I'm the one who needs to put the weight on."

"Learn to cook."

"I know how to cook. That's not the problem." The phone on the desk rang and Jessie got it first. "Galbreath."

"How's it feel to be back in the saddle, Jessie?" an old woman's quavering voice asked.

Jessie signaled Pete, settled into her chair. The voice wasn't metallic this time, it was very different, but there was something in it she recognized. *Something elusive, tantalizing, just beyond her conscious memory*. "About time you called. I'd just about given up on you." She silently buzzed the captain. "You sound very different."

"Yeah, feeling old these days. Task took a little longer than I thought it would. Did you apologize to Nicki for me like I asked?"

"Yeah." Jessie really didn't like that this woman knew her sister, but it was a confirmation of identification. "How do you know her?"

"Met her at the park. Well, at my age, I don't have time for chit-chat. Maybe another time. You doing okay?" The inflection made it sound like she was really concerned, Jessie thought.

"Fine, how about you?" If she could delay the conversation long enough, maybe they could get a trace.

There was an amused chuckle. "Not bad for my age, if I say so myself. But I'll save you your time tracing. I'm at a pay phone at the strip mall at Richmond Road and Lakeshore Drive. You get someone here and I won't be here, but I'll leave you something." The tone was inviting, almost seductive.

"Don't you want to tell me who you are?"

"Only in your dreams. You get somebody here to pick this up. I don't want it to blow away. Just hope what I found is enough to give you your answers."

Then she was gone.

***

Jessie went in to join the captain. Pete went to the cited phone to join the squad car that had been immediately dispatched. They waited, making small talk, still puzzling about the caller's identity. An idea nagged at Jessie, but it was too ludicrous to contemplate. They kept watching the clock. The captain spoke to Internal Affairs but they stayed away. Everyone was trying to be very careful, and Jessie's stomach was very nervous. When Pete returned, he came into the captain's office. He had a folded piece of paper with Jessie's initials, JAG, in his gloved hand. Carefully, only the briefest touch at the corners, she opened it. It contained a phone number. They all looked at each other. No one recognized it. The captain picked up the phone, blocked his phone number and dialed. They all turned when the cell phone rang in the outer office.

"Henderson."

No one said anything.

"Henderson here."

The captain broke the connection.

"Damn fool kids." Henderson hung up the phone and went back to his paperwork.

***

There were no clear fingerprints on the note. She must have used gloves. Paper and pen could be bought in any store in town. The computer experts tried taking away the old woman's voice to find the real one, but it wasn't clear enough for any identification. The caller remained a mystery, but the information was enough to get them going on an investigation.

Even as officially the department sought the identity of the informant, Jessie privately, quietly, did the reverse. There was only one person in her life that she hadn't known much of anything about. She tried to find Diana.

She put together everything she knew about Diana, and as Diana herself had once said, they knew precious little about each other. Diana had wanted it that way and Jessie had never questioned. Now she was handicapped. But Diana did know Nicki and certainly Nicki looked enough like Jessie that anyone seeing them would have guessed they were related. Diana knew the Bungalow. Had anyone seen her there recently? Wouldn't Nicki have recognized her? Jessie didn't even have a picture of her. Diana had never liked pictures.

Jessie didn't know a hometown—hell, she didn't even know a state. Diana had talked about a lot of places in ways that said she had more than just a passing familiarity with them. Rental cars, that meant a credit card. Avis was one, Jessie remembered. She talked about going to France, that meant a passport. She started with the broadest general search and found twenty people across the country. She found a courier service, bonding information. That would have explained the traveling. Then that company disappeared. That was in Pennsylvania. There was a gun permit in Texas. That was recent. She found residences, none current, in Atlanta, Detroit and then none. No phone. No cell.

She said she lived with her father, her mother was gone. Another dead end.

Jessie ran out of ideas to search. She even went to the police sketch artist who used a computer and tried to make a composite. She was dismayed to realize that she was forgetting what Diana looked like. She could remember her touch, could conjure up an image of her but details? Her eyes, slanted or did she just remember them heavy-lidded with desire? Her mouth, were her lips so full or swollen? Her breasts, oh, shit. Jessie turned away from her memories.

There was nothing she found to confirm. Or deny. And bringing back all those memories, all those times with Diana, made a stark contrast with Julie. She finally had to put it aside, but she couldn't completely forget. The door had been opened and it was damn hard to shut.

Two months later, the bust was complete. Tracking Henderson had revealed sources, deliveries, a trail. It was a big bust and Jessie got credit. She wasn't happy about it though, seeing someone she had worked with, had over for backyard cookouts, pulled details with, being arrested. Henderson paused at her desk before he was taken away. "Jessie," he said, "the shooting. I wasn't in on that. And it wasn't personal."

"It was to me."

***

The phone call came on Wednesday night after Jessie had gotten home but before Julie did. She was tired and depressed and when the phone rang, she dreaded answering. This case had taken more out of her; in ways, even more than almost losing her life. She had survived, but everything in her life had been shaken to the core.

"All wrapped up?" The voice wasn't an old woman's this time. It was a young girl.

"Yeah." Jessie fell onto the couch, too drained to be inquisitor.

"You sound tired. I'm sorry. It's always hard to deal with betrayal."

Jessie closed her eyes. Strange comment from someone who had to be on the inside. "Isn't that what you're doing?" She didn't care if it pissed her off.

"Sometimes you have to sit back and decide where your loyalties really lie. Sometimes it's not easy."

What the hell does that mean? If you're inside…If you are Diana…? Jessie thought but couldn't say. "Are you in danger?" she asked instead.

"Why Jessie, you sound concerned." Jessie made no response and the woman went on, answering seriously. "Not yet, but it'll be too dangerous to call again."

She had to ask. If it was Diana, she had to know. "Why?" If it wasn't, she still wanted to know why someone broke ranks for her.

"Choices. Don't like seeing women cops killed."

"Thank you, you saved my life," Jessie said.

"You take care. It's a rough world out there." And then the connection was broken.

Jessie frowned, looking at the phone. Words and speaking patterns tugged at her memory, but she couldn't say for certain. Familiar phrases but that only said it was a possibility, a possibility that chilled her.

When she did do a trace, the call was like previous ones, from a disposable cell phone, locally bought, cash payment. There was no way to trace it.

CHAPTER ELEVEN

Eighteen months later

Margaret supervised the last of the packing, her eyes going over the empty rooms. The furniture had gone on ahead, these last things were those she didn't trust to the movers. There were the books, the jewelry, and the mementos from Diana's travels. Diana had said they were not important, but they were to Margaret. She packed them with care, supervised the helpers carefully, and woe be to anyone who jostled any of the boxes or was careless enough to drop one.

Suitcases and trunks of clothing were packed and carried to the truck. Margaret checked behind to make sure everything was taken care of and nothing was left. All this in addition to her usual duties and she was tired and irritable, a trait well noticed by anyone working for her.

"Oh, leave it, Margaret. It doesn't matter," Diana had said again and again about any number of things when Margaret did ask her opinion. Soon Margaret stopped asking, but she watched her ward, her employer, her mistress with worried eyes. This was not a good move.

No one knew why the old man suddenly wanted to move. It was just an announcement one morning that the family would be moving to Lexington. She immediately looked to Diana, but the expression on

Diana's face revealed nothing. It was only the set of her mouth that revealed her distress. That and her remoteness, even more than usual, told Margaret of her distaste for this move.

Other than her increased smoking, her sullen silences, she was still Diana. Yes, Papa; no, Papa; of course Papa, like some meek, mild, deferential little girl. Margaret knew differently, so did several other parties who had mistakenly believed this woman who had no name, no rank in the Family, could be ignored when she made polite requests. They did not make that mistake twice.

Margaret shook her head as she watched Diana on the gallery smoking one cigarette after another as the trucks were loaded and pulled away. That she smoked so much was a sign of strain and inner turmoil. Margaret had hoped so much that her little girl would not grow into this business. She had been such a sweet child, so beautiful, so quick to love, such a sunny cheerful disposition. She had stayed out of it for so long. There was that time she thought Diana was leaving. She had her college degree; she had stayed clean. No one knew she was her father's daughter. She could leave the Family, make her own independent life. She could be happy.

Then she had come back from Lexington and nothing was ever the same. She had accepted the position her papa offered, had carved out her own specialty. She started smoking, even started drinking more, not a problem, but she hadn't before. She had stopped talking to Margaret. There was no joy in her heart. There was a hardness in her heart. Now her papa trusted her, depended on her. She was still Margaret's princess but she was not the same. It was all because of Lexington, and now she was being directed back there. Margaret didn't like it at all.

"Is everything ready?" Diana asked as she came in the door.

"The last box is being loaded," Margaret reported.

"Did you get the hotel reservations?" Diana asked as they pulled out of the driveway. She did not look back at the home she had lived in for several years.

"Suites at the Hilton."

"I don't want them at the Hilton. Change them." There was a coldness, a finality in Diana's voice.

"Where would you prefer?" Margaret asked carefully. She watched the trucks fall into line.

"Anywhere, just not there."

"Very good. I'll have Stella change them." Diana rubbed her forehead, her temples. Margaret glanced at her passenger. "Why don't you put your headphones on and lay back. We won't be stopping for several hours." Diana shook her head. She put her head back and closed her eyes. "I picked up that new book you wanted. It's out on audio." After several minutes of nonresponse, Diana put her hand out and Margaret reached into the bin and pulled the book out. She wasn't sure if Diana really wanted to listen to the book or if she was just humoring her. It was enough that her princess was occupied. She eased onto the interstate and picked up speed. They were on their way.

***

Diana wound her way through downtown traffic. How convenient for Papa to spend Wednesday afternoons with his girlfriend. Convenient even if Diana found the idea unsettling. She found it hard to believe her no-nonsense papa would pick up and move to Lexington just to be near a woman. Not like him at all. Yet it gave her an advantage. She had Wednesday afternoon free. She didn't have to worry about him calling for her or looking for her. She could be out on her own. And Papa always returned looking both tired and yet rejuvenated. So they were both happy.

She pulled into the parking lot finding a place in the shade where she could see the outdoor seating of the restaurant. She did not know why she did this to herself. If she hadn't gone to the game at Rupp Arena and—well, she did. And if she hadn't heard Jessie's laughter, she knew it immediately, she would have run right into the woman. Just seeing her—fortunately Jessie had her head turned to listen to her companion and didn't see Diana—had been a dash of ice water. She had thought, oh what difference did it matter what she thought. The fact was that now she was obsessed with Jessie. She followed her, she knew where she lived, where she ate, where she hung out. And where she had lunch every Wednesday afternoon.

She watched Jessie park her car on the street, get out and casually look over the traffic, before she headed for the café. And from the other direction, the hospital, Diana picked out the auburn-haired woman coming to meet her.

She took a deep breath as they went inside and within a few minutes, came out on the deck alongside the café. She frowned when Jessie sat in the corner, her back to the wall. Good strategic spot for her but Diana couldn't see her.

This is foolish, Diana told herself, maddening even. Why? Why? Why? And then she waited because she knew why. Just for a glimpse.

Just to see her walk down the street. Just to see that she was alive, to see her smile, to see her laugh.

Every time she left the compound, she said she wasn't going to go looking. And sometimes she didn't. Sometimes their paths just crossed. Once as she drove down the street where Jessie was working, Jessie even looked up, looked straight at her, and Diana knew she had to have seen her. Then her partner, must have been Pete, called her and she had turned away.

"This is madness," Diana muttered to herself as she settled in to wait until they finished lunch. "Margaret would kill me if she knew." Yet she waited, hungry just to see her again. "No more," she told herself. "Last time. I'll leave now, before she comes out." But she made no move. "The last time, I swear it," she promised herself as Jessie came out the door, looking around as she always did and then turning back to her companion. A quick air kiss and then she went to the car, unconscious of the hungry eyes that followed her.

Diana forced herself to remain in place as Jessie pulled away, and then she turned back to watch Jessie's companion, lover, Julie. *Were you really worth waiting for?* She started the car and pulled out into the traffic. She stopped at the light, still watching Julie, unable not to, as she thought of all the questions she wanted to ask. Were they happy? Doctor and Cop, both high-pressure professions. Were they able to deal with that? Did Julie love Nicki or resent the little sister who was Jessie's family? All the questions she just wanted to know answers to.

She saw Julie pause at the entrance and look up the street. Diana followed her gaze and frowned. A man was walking over from the parking garage. He raised his hand to wave and Julie waved back. Diana started, all thoughts of Jessie forgotten in her shock to see her papa come up to Julie, greet her with the charm that he was capable of and so seldom displayed. He held out his arm for her to take. As she slipped her arm around his and they walked into the clinic together, Diana stared at the sign identifying the Hematology Clinic.

"Oh, good God," she said as the car behind her laid on the horn. "What am I going to do?"

CHAPTER TWELVE

Margaret drove around New Circle Road. Ten months it had been and she still hated this place. Her princess stayed in the compound, hardly coming out at all. And there was so much to see, so many things Margaret would have liked if her princess had been happy. No, she might as well been in Atlanta or Chicago or Cincinnati for all she had been out in Lexington.

Margaret had taken on housekeeper duties, not wanting anyone else around Diana. Diana ran her businesses by computer, by phone, leaving on her monthly trips to do personal checks. And other things. Sometimes she took Margaret along and sometimes she didn't. The times she didn't were the times Margaret worried. And then there were the times Diana just disappeared. Margaret would come home and Diana would be gone. Margaret had no idea where she was. She wouldn't answer the phone. Discreet inquiries revealed nothing. Diana would come back, brooding, silent, uncommunicative, depressed, angry. This was the dark part in Diana, it was growing since she had come to Lexington.

And Diana wasn't the only strangely acting one. Her papa. A girlfriend at his age. Margaret had carefully tried to sound Diana out, but Diana would say nothing. Her only change toward her papa was she was more cooperative, doing favors for him that she usually would have argued with, challenged. Like this one for Waldo. Waldo was a piece of garbage from way back that Diana would have nothing to do with until now. And this was even after Margaret had heard that rumor about his vendetta against some local cop. She didn't understand. She just knew all this was going to end badly.

***

"I'll drive," Pete said as they came out the door.

"Fine with me." Jessie got in the passenger side.

They had been assigned to investigate a body found in an abandoned house on Georgetown Street.

"You okay? Things going any better?"

"About as well as I can expect."

"Julie?"

Jessie shook her head. She still wasn't ready to talk about Julie. Even after three months, she still couldn't quite take in Julie's announcement that they were over. All the counseling, her feeling they were working things out. How could she have been so wrong?

They pulled up in front of the house, looking around. Once a prosperous area, now the narrow street was showing its neglect. There were three houses boarded up, obviously abandoned houses across the street, another one two doors down from the one they were looking at, but the remaining houses on the block looked maintained well enough, cared for.

"Looks harmless, doesn't it?" Pete said as they got out.

The single patrol officer came down off the front porch. "Glad to see you," he greeted them, looking first Pete and then Jessie over as they showed their badges.

"Anyone come around?"

The officer waved a hand at one of the houses across the street. "Neighbor came over earlier, he was home for lunch. Mr. Stoaks. He said there's been some squatters staying here lately. He sees them leaving in the morning when he goes to work. He works at the university, will be home about four thirty."

"Anything else?" Pete asked.

"Haven't seen you around before," Jessie commented, looking at his name plate. Vanderpool.

"Just started, ma'am, about a month ago."

She nodded as she and Pete went up the steps and opened the door. They ducked under the yellow tape.

The house was empty, their footsteps echoed across the wooden floor. Scattered litter and trash were around the edges of the living room and there was a stack of firewood by the fireplace.

Pete was looking through his notes. "The body was found in the back, through the kitchen. There's a bedroom in the back."

They went through the house carefully. Just as Pete was turning to say something to Jessie, there was an explosion. She was knocked down by the force. She saw Pete down, heard yelling, more than one voice, then she was grabbed, felt a blow to her head.

She struggled to get her feet under her as she was dragged away. Sunlight briefly as she was dragged out the back door and thrown through the open door of the van in the alleyway. She still struggled and another blow to the head brought total darkness.

***

"What's on the agenda?" Diana asked that morning. More and more she was letting Margaret do all the day-to-day duties. She was focused on another project and Margaret didn't like being shut out. But she never said a word, never complained.

"Waldo Tompson."

"Damn, I'll be glad when he's gone."

Margaret made no comment. She had only a vague idea why Diana had taken this one on other than a favor to her papa. Tompson was a piece of garbage.

Traffic was terrible—not that she thought it was ever really truly terrible. Lexington was a small city in comparison to some places they had been. What was disconcerting were all the police cars moving around. That always made Margaret nervous and was something she had not noticed before. She saw the news headline in a kiosk when she stopped for gas, and she picked up the newspaper. She read it quickly as she walked back to the car. Now she understood all the police activity and it gave her an uneasy feeling.

When she walked in to where Tompson was holed up, waiting, the sight was not unexpected. Never one to express emotion, Margaret made small talk with several of the men before she walked over to the woman tied in the chair. She noticed the table in front of the woman with the badge, the ID, the gun resting on it, like a taunt. Waldo had a streak of cruelty in him.

Without emotion, Margaret lifted the woman's chin. Her eyes were blackened, her cheeks cut and swollen. She was cuffed and tied to the chair. Her clothing was torn, she was bruised. She looked like she had been sick. Her hair was matted. Without much interest, Margaret picked up the ID, read it and put it down. She wasn't sympathetic but she was concerned. She took out her cell phone.

"Princess," she said when Diana answered. "You need to get down here."

"Is there a problem? I really don't want to deal with him."

"There is a problem."

"He's changed his mind, doesn't want to go?"

"We should be so lucky. No. You need to come."

"Margaret," Diana started.

"You need to come," Margaret said quietly, firmly. "And pick up a paper to read before you get here."

There was a moment's silence. "If he's screwed this up," Diana said in a low voice.

"We've got big problems," Margaret reiterated. She broke the connection, looking down at the bowed head. She sincerely hoped she was wrong, but she was afraid she wasn't. This was going to be ugly.

CHAPTER THIRTEEN

Diana came in the door in what Margaret called her kick-ass, take-names-later mood. She glared at Waldo, who was sitting at the table, his chair tipped back on two legs leaning against the wall. Several of his faction were around the table playing cards, killing time. Two of them had jumped to their feet when the door hit the back wall. She looked around the room until her gaze fell on the woman tied to the chair. Margaret was standing to one side and she nodded slightly.

Diana stalked over, flipped open the paper she had carried in under her arm, and with her other hand pulled the woman's face up by the hair of her head. The woman gasped and Diana held the newspaper beside the woman's face as if comparing her to the picture. "Detective Galbreath, I presume?"

Jessie swallowed and Diana's grip tightened. "Yes," Jessie gasped. Diana tapped the paper under Jessie's chin in a warning not to say more. Jessie's eyes widened, as much as they could as swollen as they were, and she clenched her mouth shut. Diana glanced behind her at the badge, gun and ID on the table and turned back to the woman.

"Well, well, well." Diana bent down so they were face to face. "Imagine seeing you here." Jessie's eyes were wide with surprise, with fear and if possible, she went even paler than she had been. Diana impersonally searched her face, although her adrenaline had shot up sharply when she realized it really was Jessie.

Diana released Jessie with a movement that looked much harsher than it really was. She whirled on Waldo with every bit of her papa's temper she could muster. She'd always thought he looked like a rat, so skinny as to be anorexic, with thin, slicked back hair, pointed features.

"You son of a bitch," she said in a voice so harsh he brought the chair down solidly on all four legs. "Where the hell was your brain? Or should I even bother asking? You get this close to getting out of here and you pull some goddamn stupid stunt like this?" She threw the newspaper at him, a picture of Jessie on the front page. "Bad enough to nab a cop, you have to nab a female cop? Her picture's been all over the paper for the past week! And you expect me to ghost you out of the country?"

"No one knows it's me that's got her!"

"I do. Now. And you know it's been in my rules all along. No cops. None here. No friends. No sightings. Never mind dragging them along for the ride."

"Then I'll get rid of her!"

"Fuck that idea! You think of taking her out and wasting her, I'll cut you lose so fast you'll break the sound barrier. The only thing worse than nabbing one is killing one, and I will not be a party to that!"

"You don't have to be involved!"

"I already am!" Diana shouted as she pounded the table in front of him. "I'm here! She's here! Eye to eye!" She made violent gestures pointing to Jessie, pointing to herself, tapping her temple. "What part of that can't you understand, you imbecile?"

"You weren't supposed to show up."

"Well, son of a bitch, I did!" Diana glanced around the room.

Waldo's errand boys were lined up against the wall trying to look invisible. She still wasn't sure what she was going to do. The most pressing problem was to get Jessie out of there alive. Damn, she should have moved faster on getting Waldo out of the country. She shook her head as she walked back over to pick up Jessie's badge, her identification as well as her revolver in her shoulder holster. "Son of a bitch," Diana repeated, glancing at Waldo as if she wanted to vaporize him.

Diana finally turned back to Waldo's table, even as she stuffed Jessie's badge and ID into her hip pocket. She slung the holster over her shoulder. "I'd love to be able to cancel this whole operation, let you hang by your heels, but unfortunately we're too far along the pipeline. It would be noticed if things got changed. But that's the only reason, you bastard. And you'll still pay for all this, this, this *mess* I've got to clean up because of your actions. I swear to God, you can screw up a wet dream!"

Waldo only reacted to her words about canceling. He came out of his chair and around the table. "You cancel this and you'll live to regret it!"

She laughed at him. "From who? From you? Hell, I cancel this and you'll be doing eighty years in an eight-by-eight isolation cell, a walk in the yard for an hour a day, maybe what? Ten-by-twenty? High walls, solid, can't see through them. Only thing to see is sky, overhead. Little boxes of bricky brick," she taunted, her hands up, her fingers wiggling at him.

Waldo broke out in a cold sweat before her eyes. Diana had heard rumors he'd developed a bad case of claustrophobia when he had been in prison before. Now he was due for sentencing, was likely to get a long stretch, and he was sweating like a stevedore. She guessed the rumors were true.

She contemptuously turned her back on him, glancing at Margaret. She was reasonably sure his need to escape the country would keep him from doing anything to her but it was still nice to have someone at your back. She returned to Jessie, standing over her a moment as if deciding what to do with her. She hated that she had to play this part, but now it wasn't just Jessie's life at risk. It was her own and Margaret's.

"Untie her," she ordered finally.

No one moved. Diana slowly turned her head to Waldo. "I *said*," she started, and he gave a quick look at one of his men. Two of them jumped to untie Jessie from the chair.

"Keys to her handcuffs," she demanded next. The keys to Jessie's handcuffs were immediately handed over.

As soon as Jessie was untied, Margaret came forward. Between the two of them, they half-dragged, half-walked the still cuffed Jessie to the bedroom in the back. As Diana took Jessie to the foot of the bed, Margaret shut the door.

Jessie barely made it to the bed. Diana turned her around and got her set down before she fell. Dropping her angry attitude, Diana half-knelt before her, lifting Jessie's face to look at her. Jessie's gaze slid over her.

"Let me see," Diana muttered as she gently felt along Jessie's jaw. She noted the dilated eyes and wondered if there was a head injury, or if she had been drugged, or it was just plain fear. "Did they rape you?" she asked as soothingly as she could with no idea what she would do to Waldo if the answer was yes.

Jessie shook her head. "No," she answered in a croak of her former voice. She moved away from Diana's touch. "Please, don't touch me." She looked down into her lap.

"Why? Because you don't want to be touched? Or because you don't want me to touch you?" She gently turned Jessie's face so she could see the cuts across the high cheekbones, the dark bruises, some already turning an ugly shade of yellow. Jessie lifted her chin off Diana's fingers and turned away without answering. "You didn't mind the last time I touched you, Jessie," Diana said softly.

"That was different. We were lovers then."

"Ohhh." *So she really doesn't remember*, Diana thought. "And now I'm on the other side and that's hard to deal with?" Jessie made no response. "Sorry, sweetheart. I am going to touch you. For various reasons, but I won't presume on our past relationship." She turned Jessie's face to her, wondering if there were any broken bones. No, he wouldn't have done that yet but she really looked bad. "Do you need something to drink?"

Jessie made no response, but Diana brushed a finger over Jessie's dry lips. She got up and went over to the small fridge in the corner, opened it to find an assortment of drinks, pulled out spring water. She retrieved a straw from the drawer and opened the bottle.

"Drink," she ordered.

Jessie turned away again. Diana pivoted around to find Margaret. "I've got my suitcase in the car. Go get it. We need to get her out of these filthy clothes."

Margaret went out the back door and Diana turned back to Jessie. "Drink."

This time Jessie tried but she couldn't get the suction up the straw. Diana took the drink back and started the drink up the straw.

"What are you doing here?" Jessie asked in a disbelieving whisper.

Diana shook her head and tilted the bottle back to Jessie. "Doesn't matter. I'm just here, and I'm going to get you out of here." When Jessie took what she could swallow, Diana put the bottle aside and began to examine her. She carefully felt down Jessie's arms, her ribs, noting the flinches that Jessie couldn't control. She hated to ask but she had to know. "They worked you over pretty good. When did they grab you? The paper was rather vague."

"Three days ago."

"They threaten you?" The legs felt all right too. The weakness she displayed had to be simply from being tied for so long, the limited circulation.

Jessie shuddered. "Elaborately." She turned her face away.

"Let me guess, some future point but soon?"

Jessie nodded. She closed her eyes as she shuddered again and looked like she might be sick.

"Yeah, I heard rumors," Diana went on. She rested her hands on Jessie's thighs. "What the hell did you ever do to him?"

"Busted him. My first big one, totally by accident." Jessie clenched her jaw. "He got a short sentence. Out early on good behavior." She bent over.

"He's not on good behavior now. Gonna give us a few problems."

As if on cue, Margaret came in the door with the announcement, "We've got problems." She closed the door and set the suitcase down by the bathroom door.

Diana pivoted and stood. "Margaret, if you don't stop telling me that every time I turn around..." She trailed off at the sign of Margaret's cocked eyebrow. "All right, what now? As if there isn't enough?"

"There's another woman here. I could hear her crying when I went around the house."

"Another woman?" She turned back to Jessie, a question unspoken. Jessie shook her head, but there was scared apprehension on her face. "Go check it out."

Margaret left the room and Diana put a steadying hand on Jessie's shoulder. "We don't know. The paper didn't say anything. Don't panic yet. Margaret will let us know."

As they waited, Diana checked out the room. It looked like it had been added on to the house at some time, had its own bath, small kitchenette, a door to the outside, the hallway to the house proper. Maybe a maid's room, a mother-in-law suite. Not a bad little efficiency. She strained with listening and was finally rewarded with steps down the hallway.

CHAPTER FOURTEEN

Margaret pushed the other woman in, hands tied behind her, gagged, face swollen and tear-stained, who blanched when she saw Jessie.

"Over there," Diana directed, pointing to a settee in the corner across the room. As Margaret settled the woman, Diana turned back to Jessie. The answer was on Jessie's face but she had to ask anyway. "Julie?"

Jessie unsteadily nodded.

"It's okay," Diana assured her even as some part of her railed that even here she couldn't have Jessie to herself. She bent down to eye level with Jessie. "Look at me," she demanded. Jessie dragged her gaze from Julie back to Diana.

"I didn't know she was here," Diana said evenly. "And now we know. She doesn't look like she's been terribly hurt. Now don't be going and doing anything foolish." She touched Jessie's cheek. "I'll take care of her."

"Please." There was bargaining in Jessie's voice. "I don't care what happens to me. Don't let anything happen to her."

"Jessie. It's a package deal."

She met Margaret in the middle of the room, between the two women. "Wasn't difficult. She's been hysterical, noisy, hence the gag."

She shook her head. "Waldo wasn't happy. Guess she was his back up plan."

Diana frowned at the thought.

"What are you going to do?"

"A little hell-raising, maybe throw another temper tantrum. I'm getting real good at them."

"You're going out on a limb."

"I'm already so far out there that this isn't going to do anything more."

"He won't like it."

"Tough shit."

"I wasn't talking about Waldo out there."

Comprehension dawned on Diana. "Oh." She sighed. "Well, I'll just have to cross that bridge when I get to it." She looked from Jessie to Julie back to Margaret. "I guess it's about time."

"Perhaps so, sweet pea. You ready for it?"

Diana nodded. "I think so." She glanced over at Julie. "Let's see if I can get her calmed down. Got enough problems without hysteria. Think I'll have enough time?"

"It'll take a while for him to get his nerve up. You should be able to do it."

Diana nodded. "Likely make the detective nervous. Better stand ready."

As Margaret went over by Jessie, whose gaze shifted from one woman to the other, Diana went over and sat down beside Julie. Julie immediately pushed back from her, her eyes dilating, as Diana made herself comfortable. She sat on one leg, laid her arm across the back of the settee, reaching for but not touching Julie. She just watched her, her face neutral. Auburn hair, fair complexion, probably had freckles as a kid, nice build from what Diana could see. Nice eyes, even as scared as she was. She'd trip over into panic easily and then she'd be a handful. Yet, Diana didn't get the feeling she was flighty, just strongly emotional.

"Scary, isn't it?" she said finally in a quiet voice.

Julie swallowed hard, glancing at Jessie.

"Look at me," Diana ordered quietly. "Jessie can't help you right now."

Julie's gaze shifted back and her eyes filled with tears.

"Don't cry, it makes breathing hard when you're gagged." She kept her voice soft, gentle, reassuring. "And I'd like to remove the gag, but I need to know you've got your self-control back." She slowly bent her arm, leaned on her elbow, a studied casual pose. "You're Julie, aren't you?"

Julie responded with a short jerky nod.

"And you're a doctor, aren't you?" There was another nod. The tears were controlled, that was a good sign. "Did they hurt you?"

Julie started shaking again, her glance going back to Jessie, but she shook her head. She looked back at Diana.

"Yes, they hurt Jessie. In the scheme of things, it could have been worse."

Julie's eyes widened in horror.

"I know. It doesn't seem like it could be worse, does it?" Diana spoke quietly, even as she was saying frightening things, conjuring up terrifying images for Julie. "That's why I'm so glad I got here in time." She saw the question, the sudden hope. She shook her head. "No, I'm sorry to say, I'm not the calvary coming to rescue. Let's just say right now, I'm the lesser of two evils." She saw the letdown. "Now, did they hurt you?"

Julie uncertainly shook her head.

"Scared you?"

That produced an emphatic nod. Diana nodded. "Okay," she said. "That's good. Being scared is a lot better than being hurt. Jessie's got enough to deal with without being afraid for you." There was the question, the wariness in Julie's gaze. "Yes, I know you're Jessie's lover. They know it too. That's why they grabbed you."

Julie almost lost it then. Diana leaned forward, laying her hand on Julie's thigh.

"I'm not using you as a weapon against Jessie," she said quickly. She added pressure until Julie looked at her, saw her again. "Relax, I'm not going to hurt you. Got a grip now?"

Uncertainly, Julie nodded. Diana took her hand away.

Diana took a deep breath, unsure how she was going to reach this woman. If she didn't reach her, her panic would be as much a problem as Waldo. Then she got an idea. "Did you ever work the Emergency Room?" She had the faint idea it was a necessary part of physician training so it seemed likely.

Julie nodded, frowning.

Good. Make her focus. Make it her setting. "So you know what it's like when you've got lots going on, it seems truly like a madhouse, everyone going every which way, organized chaos."

Apprehensively, Julie nodded.

"But at the same time, everyone knows what their job is, what they have to do to accomplish it and they just have to ignore the chaos and at the same time work with everyone else. Right?" Julie nodded, still puzzled looking but with greater confidence. "Of course, the patient—now he's just lying there, maybe conscious or unconscious, probably scared out of his mind, trying to answer questions, not understanding a damn thing that's going on around him, hoping they're going to help him with the pain or the sickness or whatever has happened to him, and trust they're going to do their job and he's going to survive and get better. Right?"

Julie nodded again.

"He's in a scary, uncertain position, isn't he?'

Julie nodded, calmer now.

"Well, this is going to be somewhat like the ER, only in this case, you're the patient. I get to be the doctor, and Margaret there, she's my able assistant. And you have to trust us, that our goal is to get you safely out of here. Can you do that?"

Julie's glance went to Jessie and back to Diana, clearly a question.

Diana gave a small smile. "Jessie's quite used to being the doctor, but in this case she's the patient. And you know how doctors are as patients."

Julie gave a small identifying chuckle and Diana breathed a sigh of relief.

"Now, you think that you can control your panic enough that I can remove the gag?" Slowly, uncertainly, Julie nodded. "Good girl."

Diana got to her feet and when she reached out to touch Julie, the woman didn't draw away. She moved and flexed her jaw after Diana removed the gag, took some deep breaths. "One question," she said in a strained voice.

"What's that?"

"Are you going to let us go?"

Diana tipped Julie's face up, brushed back her hair. She was an attractive woman, on that she couldn't fault Jessie's taste. "That's the goal of every doctor, isn't it? To restore the patient to how they were before? Sometimes things happen that the doctor can't control, but I don't think you'll have any grounds to sue me for malpractice."

Julie accepted this with some evidence of doubt but then she nodded.

"Will you feel better if you're over by Jessie?" When Julie nodded, Diana brought her to her feet. She saw Jessie's relief as she escorted Julie to a spot on the bed beside Jessie. "Margaret, get her something to drink. She's had that gag on too long."

***

They heard the strides down the hallway before the door even opened.

"I'm taking them back!" Waldo announced.

"I don't think so," Diana said mildly. She eyed the men behind Waldo, decided that while they might go against her, they would never go against Papa.

"No little prima donna is going to deprive me." He made a signal and his men did take a step forward only to stop when Margaret stepped in front of Jessie. Even cuffed, Jessie moved to place her body in front of Julie.

Diana gave a grimace of disgust. "Don't even bother, Waldo." She even half turned away from him.

That only invited him to reach for her and as soon as he grabbed her arm, she exploded. It was easy enough to grab his arm and twist. His forward movement only propelled him into the angle that would easily snap a bone or at least dislocate it. She brought him down low enough that she could look into his face. "Don't touch me," she said in a cold voice. "Prima donnas don't like to be touched by scum."

Margaret kept the others at bay and Waldo's past history made it unlikely he would be difficult by himself. "Now, I said I'm taking the cop. And since the other is a witness, I'm taking her too. Maybe the next time, if our paths ever cross, you'll remember my rules." She twisted again and he yelled.

"Diana," Margaret said in a quiet rebuking voice.

"But he's such a slimebag," Diana protested.

"This is a favor to your papa."

Diana breathed a heavy sigh of acceptance. "I suppose so." She released him and stepped clear. "Get out, before I forget why I'm here," she snarled at him.

Waldo held his arm, swearing, but retreating. Margaret and Diana exchanged small smiles.

"You know he'll call your papa."

"Oh, I'm banking on it," Diana replied. She turned to Jessie and Julie. "You two okay?"

Both uncertainly nodded, Julie looked even more scared, and Jessie looked at her with some disbelief. Diana looked at them both and realized they were looking at her a little differently now. That was all right too.

"Now," she said, "we'll be leaving in a little while. And Jessie, I don't mean to be offensive, but you need to shower." Jessie's chin came up. "I know, it's not your fault. Let's get it done. I've got a change of clothes that'll fit you." She took Jessie by the arm and pulled her to her feet, catching her when she swayed.

"I'll help her," Julie immediately said.

"I don't think so. I'm not ready to leave the two of you alone together. Maybe later, but not now." She glanced around the room, found the overnight bag by the bathroom door. "I'll take care of the shower bit. Margaret, you stick with Julie. If Papa calls, tell him I'm in the shower."

She turned back to Julie. "You behave. Margaret's not as patient as I am, and I will be unhappy if I come back out and find she had to hogtie you."

As if she thought it would happen, Julie pulled back, giving Margaret a fearful glance. Simply to reinforce it, Diana looked at Margaret. "Be nice," she warned and Margaret appropriately glowered.

CHAPTER FIFTEEN

Diana let out a sigh of relief when she got Jessie in the bathroom and the door closed. "Now you, are you going to be nice or be difficult? If you get by me, you've got Margaret. And if you get by her, you've got Waldo and his men. I don't think he likes you. Is that enough for a truce?"

Jessie was unsteady enough that she leaned against the wall. It took a minute for her to reassess the situation but she reluctantly nodded.

"Very good, Jessie. I appreciate that." Diana turned Jessie around enough to unlock the cuffs and remove them. Jessie's arms fell forward and she swayed, almost going down before Diana caught her. "Sit down." Diana positioned her firmly on the toilet. The bathroom was so small there was nowhere for her to fall without hitting something. Toilet, sink, shower.

"Now let's get all this crud off you and see what's underneath." The thought did occur to Diana that Jessie might be shamming but she didn't think so. She turned on the shower, adjusted it to as fine a spray as she could get, adjusted the temperature. Jessie unbuttoned her torn shirt but winced as she tried to slide it off her shoulders. "Ribs?" Jessie nodded. "Let me." What she discovered when she slid the shirt off Jessie's shoulders was not a pretty sight, bruises and cuts all over.

As she stripped off the rest of Jessie's clothing and tossed it in the corner, Diana realized Jessie would never manage the shower by herself. "Well, babe, it's been a long time since we showered together. Any problem with me in there with you?"

"Julie?"

"Not a chance. I'll send in Margaret."

Jessie shook her head. "You'll do."

Diana quickly undressed, tossing her clothing where it wouldn't get wet. She pulled Jessie to her feet, and then, maneuvering Jessie within her arms, they stepped together into the shower. "Lean over me. I'll take care of everything else."

Jessie braced her arms on the shower walls, the water running over her as Diana maneuvered in front of her. The shower was so small they couldn't move without brushing against each other.

"Too warm?"

"A little," Jessie said with a nod, and Diana reached around her to adjust the temperature. When Jessie nodded, Diana pulled down the washcloth, the soap and began to lather her.

"Is she your lover?" Jessie finally asked. She stood with her arms on the wall over Diana's shoulders. She closed her eyes and bit her lip as Diana touched her. Diana tried hard to be gentle on the bruised flesh.

"Who? Margaret? No, hard to be lovers with someone who's changed your diapers. Not impossible I understand but wasn't anything I was able to do. Margaret went from my nursemaid to my nanny to my tutor to my bodyguard. Never a lover."

Jessie held her breath as Diana moved down her torso. Diana lathered and soaped and very gently washed away dirt and dried blood from so many small cuts and scrapes. "Why didn't you tell me?" Jessie asked finally when she started breathing again.

"About my family? Well, at first it was immaterial. One-night stands don't need that kind of information. Then, it just didn't matter."

"It mattered," Jessie said. "But now I understand why you freaked out when you discovered I was a cop."

"Freak? Did I freak?" Diana gave an exaggerated response. She wanted to distract Jessie from what must certainly be painful. "And here I thought I passed it off rather well, calm, cool, collected. Just honest surprise."

"No." Jessie was able to smile a little. "You freaked."

"Damn." Diana frowned at the memory of her shock. "Another failure."

"Enough that I went back to work and ran a check," Jessie confessed.

Diana shook her head in amusement. "Knew it. Always figured whatever you did, you'd be good at it. A cop? You'd check out those suspicions. Didn't find anything, did you?"

"No, of course I didn't know if you were using your real name. When I added up all I really knew about you, I realized it wasn't much."

"Yep, we definitely did the here and now bit," Diana quipped. "The name is real, at least it's the one on my birth certificate." She pulled down another cloth and lathered it well. "Here. I don't suppose you want me to do your privates, and I said I wouldn't presume on our past relationship. You manage or want some help?"

"I'll manage."

"Thought so." Diana knelt down, taking care of Jessie's legs, ignoring what was happening at her shoulder level. Finished there, she moved around to stand behind Jessie, adjusting the spray to go over Jessie's back. "Ready to turn around?"

Jessie carefully turned with Diana's hands supporting her. Diana angled the shower to flow over Jessie, rinsed her well.

"I appreciate," Jessie stumbled over the words a bit. "I appreciate you taking care of Julie, her panic."

"No problem. Don't need Waldo in front of me and a hysterical woman behind me."

"You read her real good, but then you always were good at reading people."

"Helps. Here, bend down, stick your head under, let's get your hair washed." She helped Jessie move around. "Gotta say though, she surprised me. Thought a cop's wife would be of tougher stuff."

Jessie shook her head. "Always a problem with violence. Was an issue for years." Then she stopped as if she'd said too much.

"Jessie," Diana said carefully as she gently lathered Jessie's short, dark, thick hair. "You're a good cop."

"Some good cop. Let myself get ambushed, lost my gun, badge."

"They're secure and it's not like you just walked into something. Someone laid a trap for you."

"Got my partner shot up."

"Still Peterson?" Jessie nodded. "I can check on him for you. I do have some contacts." Diana carefully rinsed Jessie's hair. "You know, Jessie. You are a good cop, so I'm going to have to treat you like one."

"Lock down," Jessie supplied.

"'Fraid so."

"If I gave my word?"

"Positions reversed would you believe me?" After a longer hesitation than Diana expected, Jessie shook her head.

"What are you going to do with us?"

"Well, I'm not going to kill you," Diana said with a laugh. Then she sobered as Jessie turned away. "You didn't think I might, did you?"

"I don't know. Have you killed before?"

"Only to protect someone I cared about," Diana protested. "Don't hold that against me."

Jessie shook her head. "I don't understand you." She leaned over, her head against Diana's shoulder. "I loved you, but I don't understand you."

Diana blinked, caught off guard. In all the times they had slept together, Jessie had never said that. If she had. If she had, how differently things might have turned out. Diana snapped back to the present. She gently rinsed Jessie off. "Need to get you out and dried before you're chilled."

When they came out of the bathroom, both Margaret and Julie looked at them strangely, Jessie dressed in loose pants and buttoned shirt, Diana still wet from the shower. Jessie was cuffed again, this time with her hands in front of her.

"Your papa called," Margaret reported. "I told him you were in the shower, and would call back."

Diana nodded. She settled Jessie back on the bed. "You stay put," she ordered gently. "Lie down if you want but don't get off the bed."

She checked on Julie, glanced at Margaret. Then she paced around the room, psyching herself up to call her papa. She loved him, had a special place for him, but he had a deserved reputation for volatility.

She finally went over to sit at the table, at an angle so she could see Julie and Jessie. She could feel the curiosity, the wariness, the apprehension from the three women.

"Hello, Papa." Diana moved to the settee in the corner, glancing at Jessie and Julie on the bed, Margaret pacing the room. "Yes, Margaret said you called." This was going to be a hard conversation she knew, and it was a gamble. "Oh, Waldo. Yes, he was not happy."

"Now, Papa, you know when I got into this, I told you I wasn't happy about everything you did. You let me pick and choose. I told you then I didn't want to have anything to do with cops, didn't want them on my turf, didn't want to deal with them, certainly didn't want to be involved doing anything to them. And you agreed. Waldo broke those rules." She paused, listening, laughed.

"Oh, Papa. He said *what*?…Now I've never said anything about your lovers. What makes you say anything about mine?…Oh he did? And you're going to believe that lowlife? Papa, I've never understood why you let that slime bag in, but I certainly wouldn't let him lay a hand on anyone I loved." She listened, wondered if she would be able to pull this off. Margaret's pacing indicated how nervous she was. Jessie was listening intently.

"Papa, bottom line. I said no cops, didn't want any part of it. Waldo brought one in. Now I'm still willing to transport him, but I'm not transporting any cop. I don't care what he says. I'll walk first and he can do his time in his little cage…No, I haven't decided what I'm going to do but if I go to jail, it's going to be for something I do, not something I'm accessory to. Now if you won't back me on that, then I can close up shop and put my feet up…I thought you might see it that way, Papa." *Okay, first hurdle taken care of.*

"Yes, Papa, there's another woman here. Yes, I took her too…No, Papa, she's not a cop…No, nothing to do with police work as far as I know…no, Papa, I've never spoken to her before…No, Papa, I have no claim on her."

From the corner of her eye, she watched Margaret groan and turn away. She heard Jessie groan and Julie looked from one to the other, start to wail as she understood what Diana meant. Margaret was immediately there to silence her.

Diana forced herself to chuckle. "Yes, Papa, I know it's a pain. I hate that he called you. He's such a helpless prick. I never did like him. I'm only transporting him as a favor to you. After all, you're my papa… yes, Papa, I know. You value loyalty and you pay all your favors back. I understand, Papa. Good values. You've drilled that into me since I was six. Today they call it networking." She laughed. "I know, what goes around, comes around. Each generation discovers old values all over again. I know, Papa."

She glanced around the room. Julie had her head buried on Jessie's shoulder, Margaret was standing in front of Jessie and Jessie was glaring at her with murderous rage. "No, no, your calling is fine. If you hadn't called, I was going to have to call you anyway…yeah, this thing with the cop. Really came out of left field, wasn't prepared for this, screws up my plans. I'm going to have to take care of her…No, I don't know what I'm going to do. I'll figure it out. Don't worry it. I'll do you proud…yeah, Papa, something is bothering me. I'm not going to make it back to say goodbye…No, Papa, I really won't, and I'm sorry."

This was going to be the hard part, she realized, maybe harder than she thought.

"Papa. I know...I know about Wednesday afternoons. And I know about Julie." She didn't dare turn to look at anyone. She listened to his protests. "No, Papa, I didn't follow you, and I haven't mentioned it to anyone. I was out on one of my excursions, and I went by the hospital. I saw you there without Jimmy so I waited. You looked so bad when you came out that I was curious." She hesitated on some of the words. "No, I didn't say anything, not even to Margaret. I know when it started, and I know when you stopped."

There was a long pause and she listened to an open line. "And Papa," she said with a sigh, "I know the truth about Julie." She paused for a minute, trying to find the proper words. "She was sweet, Papa, wasn't she? Kind to the distinguished elderly gentleman who came in every week without any family there to support him. She made something so difficult a little easier, didn't she?"

She hated putting him through this. But she was hurt that he had not told her, not trusted her. For that, she didn't mind using him, but at the same time, she would have been there for him.

"Yes, Papa, I know she was very nice to you. So, don't you think you owe her something, payback the favor, payback the kindness...of course, Papa, I can do that for you. You know I would do anything for you. Yes, Papa, I know this is important, but I know something that you don't know.

"You see, Papa, the police detective I have here, who I said I'd take care of, has a female lover. And that is the woman Waldo picked up and planned to torture to punish the cop. Yes, I know you've heard the rumors...yes, I know you didn't like it but you would still permit it... what you don't know is that her lover is Dr. Julie Carlton, Julie who was so kind to you at the clinic."

She closed her eyes, barely hearing what her papa said, just listening to the sound of his voice that she would not hear many times more. She was a realist, knew he was not a good man, and in many eyes, deserved the painful death he was dealing with. She wouldn't bother to argue with them. He was still her papa, and she loved him.

"Yes, Papa. I'll take care of that. Yes, Papa, of course, Papa. You can trust me." She closed her eyes, trying to keep her memories of the loving papa she knew. "Goodbye, Papa. I love you, too."

She broke the connection and snapped the flip phone shut. No one said anything and she sat there for a minute, trying to regroup, to pull herself back together. Finally she let out a long breath and got up from the chair, turning. Margaret looked prepared to say something and Diana gave her a warning look.

"Not one word about this call," she ordered. "Not to me, not to anyone else. You never heard it. Understand?" Margaret nodded and at her glance, Jessie nodded also.

Diana stretched, looked up at the ceiling. "Oh, but there will be weeping and wailing and gnashing of teeth," she quoted. She brought her head down and looked at Margaret. "Ten minutes? Twenty minutes?" She was back in control. This thing about papa, she would deal with later.

"Fifteen."

Diana nodded. "Did you get a vehicle?"

"Ordered a limo instead of a van. Thought we might as well be comfortable."

"Good idea." Diana pulled the chair from the table and dragged it over to place in front of Jessie.

"I think I owe you some information," she said as she sat on the chair, leaning on the back of it, facing Jessie. Jessie still looked angry, bewildered, relieved. She glanced at Julie. The woman looked so badly frightened and Diana just couldn't say anything, not even to reassure her. She reached over and patted her knee. She just couldn't say anything.

She flipped her phone open and punched numbers, turned her attention back to Jessie. She watched Jessie as she spoke into the phone. "Hi sweets, how's it going?…Good to hear…Need some information. You had a cop come in, about three days ago, maybe…yeah, that's the one…What can you tell me?…Oh, I know information's shut down. That's why I'm calling you. Ahhh, good news, bad news…can't tell you how often I've heard that in the past couple of days…Okay, give it to me. …Good news: he's doing well." She looked directly at Jessie and Jessie breathed a sigh of relief and nodded. "Okay, let's have the flip side. …Ah, just a flesh wound, no sweat. But he had a heart attack, right there in the ER. If he hadn't gotten shot, he wouldn't have been in the ER, wouldn't have been saved. Guess it was a lucky shot for him. That's good, no, sweets. All is well…What's that? Oh, Dr. Carlton? Yeah, I just found out about that. I'm sure she's safe. No, you stay there. May take a while, you just stay there, low profile. Let me take care of everything. Thanks, sweets."

She closed the phone and looked at Jessie. "Okay? Feel better?"

Jessie nodded. "Yes." She hesitated. "Thank you," she said finally in a low voice.

"Here he comes," Margaret warned.

Diana immediately got up, put the chair back. She wanted to look casual but be prepared. He wouldn't be stupid enough to do the same thing twice.

He was. This time she put him on the floor, her foot on him to keep him down.

"You stupid son of a bitch." This time he wasn't quiet but exploded into curses, orders to his men who didn't dare move against Diana. And finally, because she had nothing else to be angry at, nothing she could safely explode at, she cursed back, twisting his arm. She called him everything she had possibly heard in the English language, and in the circles she ran in she had heard a lot. When she ran out of English curses, she used the Spanish ones she knew. When she ran out of those, she used words she didn't even know what language they were, just that they sounded ugly and he paled when he heard them and they sounded so satisfyingly bad. It took Margaret's hand on her shoulder to bring her back to the present.

"Let him go, princess," Margaret said in a calming, even voice. "You've hurt him enough, let him go, or there won't be anything to transport."

Diana fell silent, debating. The idea was actually tempting. That would solve all her problems.

"You don't want to break your word," Margaret coaxed.

Diana slowly released him. "Get him out of here," she ordered in a cold hoarse voice. "Have him at the airfield in two days. I'll let you know the time after I talk to the pilot." She walked over and picked up her phone, punched in a number as they dragged him out of the room.

"Helen? You still want that flight?…Are you current?…Can you be ready in two days? Call me back as soon as you get the time. It's all yours."

She hung up, met Margaret's gaze, took the drink she handed her. "Are you sure you can trust her?" Margaret asked.

"She'll do the right thing," Diana replied in a tight voice. Margaret shrugged and turned away. The time for arguing was past.

CHAPTER SIXTEEN

Diana and Margaret moved around the room, checking everything that might link them to the room. Diana checked the bed.

"You know," Jessie said slowly, "if you turned Waldo in, you'd get lots of brownie points. You saved us. Counts for a lot. If you've done nothing before, it'll be easy on you."

"I gave my word," Diana said in a cold voice. Wouldn't she like to turn Waldo in if she could? Or take care of him in other ways. The man was a menace.

"Diana, he's a slime bag, he's not worth your word. Give him up." Jessie came to her feet, her face directly in Diana's, searching for something. "I'd put in a good word for you," she promised. "You saved me, you rescued Julie. That'll count for a lot."

"I understand what you're saying, but I gave my word." Diana stepped back from Jessie.

"Damn it!" Jessie went after her. "Don't throw your life away. Not for some lowlife like Waldo. Whatever else you've got, you've saved me, you saved Julie."

Diana met Jessie's eyes. She knew Jessie didn't understand all the ramifications, and she certainly wasn't about to explain. She only wondered if this was Jessie the cop talking or Jessie her ex-lover, concerned for her. Probably a mixture. Wasn't she herself a mixture in dealing with Jessie? "It's not time," she said in a calmer voice. "Sit down, Jessie. This act isn't done." She stepped back but Jessie followed her, reaching out for her. Diana caught the handcuffs, her other hand on Jessie's chest.

"Sit down, Jess. Don't make a bad situation worse. There are still things I've got to do, places I've got to go. When that's done, then it might be another story. Don't make me get ugly with you. I'd really regret it."

"But you'd do it!" Jessie spit out, surprising Diana with her vehemence.

"The same as you would do what you had to do," Diana retorted in a hard voice. "Now sit down."

***

"The limo's here," Margaret announced.

Diana nodded. "That's good. You good for driving?" Margaret nodded. "Have them take our cars back, turn them in." She turned back to Jessie and Julie. "Let's go, ladies."

She settled them in the back, eyeing them both, and then resting her gaze on Jessie. "I'm sorry, Jessie. I'm tired, you've got to be tired. I can't let you go, and if Margaret's driving, I can't watch you all the time. I'm going to give you a choice: I can give you a hypo to knock you out or give you some pills."

"No, don't do that." Jessie's protest was vehement and sudden.

"Jessie. You're a risk to me. I don't want to hurt you. The only other choice is to tie you down tight, and frankly, I don't want to do that. You've been bound long enough on all your pressure points. But if that's what you want." She shrugged.

"If this is because of what I said before—"

"No," Diana cut in. "I appreciate what you said. I just can't. You're my biggest risk. I don't want any trouble."

"What about Julie?"

Diana smiled, glancing at the woman who sat on the edge of the seat, wide-eyed, watching both of them. "Not to be insulting, but Julie's no risk. If you're down and out, she's not going to leave you." She turned back to Jessie. "What's it going to be?"

"Cuffs off?" Jessie temporized.

"Once you're asleep."

"I'd probably go to sleep anyway."

"Probably. I'm just not ready to deal with probabilities. For at least one thing today, I'd like a sure thing."

Jessie hung her head in consideration. "All right. Pills." She raised her head. "If Julie says that's all they really are."

Diana gave a tired smile. "What? You really think I'd give you something else?" She passed two pills to Julie, brought out the bottle of water.

"Actually," Julie said upon examining the pills, "they're pain pills, probably not enough to knock you out except you are tired. They'll put you to sleep for probably about four hours." She looked to Jessie. "The sleep will probably do you good, you'll be able to rest. I'd recommend them."

Jessie sighed. "With both of you, what choice do I have?" She put out her hand, popped them in her mouth.

Diana patted Jessie's thigh. "You'll feel better with some sleep. Sweet dreams," she said with a smile. She looked to Julie. "Thank you."

***

By the time they reached her hideaway cabin in the mountains, Diana had a splitting headache. Two confrontations with Waldo, an emotional conversation with her papa, rearranging plans on the fly, and last of all, seeing Jessie again, had succeeded in draining her. She had checked on their guests several times to find Julie sitting up asleep with Jessie's head in her lap, also asleep. Diana shook her head. Those two had gone through hell with Waldo. No, whatever they had gone through was nothing to what Waldo had planned for them. That, she had been able to prevent.

"Are you all right?" Margaret asked as she pulled the limo in front of the cabin.

"Yes. I called and had someone come up and open up, stock it. We shouldn't have to do much besides go in there and go to bed."

"Secured?" Diana nodded. "So all we have to do is get them in?"

"Our sleeping beauties? Yeah."

Julie came awake with a start and a small cry as soon as Diana touched her. Jessie didn't stir. Even after both Diana and Julie shook her, she was only half awake. Margaret and Diana half-carried the groggy woman into the cabin and then into the bedroom. They dumped her on the bed and Julie quickly stepped to her side, taking over. Diana was more than ready to let her. By the time Margaret did her security check on the house, Diana had made her check-ins, and she and Margaret were settled in their rooms, it was almost dawn.

"Are you going to manage this?" Margaret asked.

"Of course," Diana answered, thinking longingly of fresh sheets and soft pillows.

"Is she the one?" Margaret finally asked.

Diana debated about not answering, about ignoring the question, but finally she nodded.

"I feared so," Margaret said. "Get some rest, sweet pea."

Diana went to her room and closed the door, leaning against it and letting out a sigh of relief. Dealing with Waldo had been bad enough, having first Jessie and then Julie there was more troublesome. Talk about tearing up all her well-prepared plans!

Unbidden, the memory of touching Jessie flooded her, even just touching her bruised flesh, washing her hair, her head resting on Diana's shoulder. Diana had managed to stay focused then, be impersonal, but now…She pressed her heated face against the cool dark wood. Any thoughts she had that all her desire for her ex-lover had died were just as shattered as her plans.

She pushed herself away from the door and moved into the room, belatedly realizing she did not have the master bedroom this time. She would have to go to the bathroom down the hall. She threw herself on the bed and stared at the ceiling.

Now, Jessie was under her roof; Julie too. There hadn't been anywhere else to put them, not where she thought they would be safe. She couldn't bear the idea of Waldo having his way with them. Although truth be told, she might have done the same for anyone Waldo had, she just wouldn't have brought them here.

She sat up and began to undress. Here, where she thought she would be safe, where she would be able to figure things out, she was going to have to face Jessie every day, have to look at a road not taken, have to see her and Julie. The Fates were cruel, she thought as she fell asleep.

CHAPTER SEVENTEEN

"Oh, God." Jessie awoke with a moan. "What a hangover!"

Julie choked and Jessie woke up completely, rolled over quickly, and then stopped at the resistance of all her joints and muscles.

"Be careful," Julie said, her hand on Jessie's shoulder.

Jess half raised up. "Julie?" She collapsed back into the bedding. "Oh, God, it wasn't a nightmare."

"No, I'm afraid not."

Jessie lay there a minute, her eyes closed, trying to get her bearings. All the memories came flooding back, each one more unreal than the previous: the ambush, the beatings, then Diana there, then Julie, then Diana having some position of influence, authority, enough to get them out of there.

"Where are we?" she asked.

"Somewhere in the mountains," Julie answered, sitting up beside her, leaning over her. "How are you feeling?"

"Like I've been run over."

"Well, that's about how you look. Look at me."

Julie leaned over her, felt her face, examined her eyes, moved the finger that Jessie followed.

"Seems to be okay. Sorry, dear, it's not a hangover. Don't I wish. Do you remember coming into the house last night?"

Jessie struggled for the memory. "Vaguely, very vaguely. A cabin?"

"Yes, a very nice cabin." Julie came up on her knees, leaned over Jessie, slid her hands around Jessie's face and under her head. "I fell asleep on the drive up. They didn't wake me until we got here. Took both of them to bring you in."

Julie felt down Jessie's neck, her shoulders, down her arms, her ribs where Jessie winced. "Don't think anything's broken, but you're going to be sore for a while."

"What about you?" Jessie asked. "Did they hurt you?"

Julie shook her head but Jessie could see how frightened she was. She reached up for her, trying to be reassuring.

"I'm so sorry, Jul. I never thought anything like this would happen."

Julie shrugged and turned away. Jessie bit her lip, she knew this had been Julie's fear for years and she had dismissed it unilaterally. She pushed herself up, looking around the room, not sure what to expect. They were in a bedroom, a good-sized room, king-sized four-poster bed, table and chairs in the corner, a dresser. Sliding doors against half of one wall, probably a closet, a door beside it opening to what looked like the bathroom. She managed to sit up, looked down at her tank top and panties. She didn't like the idea that someone had undressed her when she was unaware, especially under these circumstances.

"How'd you get caught?" Julie asked.

"Pete and I went out to investigate a body in an abandoned house. Ambushed. Pete got shot." Jessie struggled to her feet. "Next thing I know I'm thrown in the back of this van." She didn't bother explaining the next part, she was evidence enough. "How about you?"

"I got a late night emergency call from one of my patients, went to the clinic."

Jessie shook her head. She had warned Julie to be careful on these late night calls. But then, right now she was hardly in the position to scold anyone for their lack of vigilance. She managed to take a step but reached out for the corner post. She saw her clothes or rather the loaned outfit from Diana across the chair. "You sure you're all right, Jul?" She half turned to see Julie slide out of bed, wearing a T-shirt.

"Outside of being almost scared to death, yeah, I'm doing just fine." She came around the bed to take hold of Jessie's hand. "Stiff?"

"You could say so."

"Once you start moving around, it'll be better but I wouldn't do any heroics right away."

"Oh, I don't think I'll be up for that." Jessie coughed and quickly wrapped her arm around her ribs. She really felt like they were going to come apart. She had not felt so bad since she had gotten shot and had months of surgery and recuperation.

"Who are these people anyway, Jessie? What's going on?"

Jessie eyed the bathroom as a destination. "Waldo, he's—"

"I don't mean him. I figured he's the bad guy. I mean these two women. They walk in like they own the place, at least Diana, is that her name? She acts like that and the other one will either clear the path or cover her backside."

Jessie rubbed her face as she contemplated the distance to the bathroom. "I don't know, God, I don't know."

"But you know her, or at least she knows you." Jessie said nothing. "She's very familiar with you," Julie said slowly. "Possessive."

Jessie nodded. "Yeah," she admitted. "We had a thing before you came back to town."

"Ahhh," Julie said as if that explained everything. She continued slowly, tentatively. "I find it hard to believe you've been involved with someone of that ilk. Or didn't you know?"

"It was—" Jessie managed to get her feet moving. "It wasn't exactly the kind of thing where we knew each other's business. She didn't know I was a cop until one day my badge fell out of my pocket. Freaked her out." She looked around the room, another door on the other wall. "Are we locked in?"

"I don't know. I haven't tried the door."

Once she made it to the bathroom, Jessie found little guest packages with toothbrush, toothpaste, soap, deodorant, everything she might need. She went through all the morning motions, slowly stretching, and soon the muscles felt functional. The brain part, that part was moving slower than normal. Must be the drug. Everything was still a little fuzzy, or maybe it was all the blows to the head from Waldo. She examined herself in the mirror, raccoon eyes. She cautiously touched her nose. It felt broken.

She leaned over the sink, trying to pull together what she knew, what she could do. God, seeing Diana had been a jolt. Of all the times she had ever fantasized about running into her, this was not the setting. Explained a lot though. She was just as willful and sure of herself as she ever had been. What kind of role did she play that she could get away with that? When she screamed at Waldo, when she took him down like it was nothing to her, when she just took them away. Jessie shook her head. A mistake. *How am I going to deal with her?*

There was a quick knock on the door. "We're being called for breakfast," Julie announced.

Jessie pulled herself together as they walked into the kitchen full of breakfast smells, bacon, sausage, fresh coffee, which was the best smell of them all. She hurt like anything but she wasn't ready to be that vulnerable. Not that it mattered much, Diana knew her enough to take one look at her and know.

Diana entered the kitchen the same time from the far side, through the glass door leading out to the deck. She glanced at Jessie and Julie and pointed to the table. "Have a seat," she ordered as she took the coffee carafe Margaret handed her.

She brought the coffee, the mugs over to the table, set them down. "Still take cream?" Jessie nodded. Diana brought it from the refrigerator but she didn't join them at the table. "As I recall," she said dryly, "you're not worth anything until you have your coffee, so I'll leave you in peace. But then we need to have a talk." She picked up her coffee, went over by the stove to steal a piece of bacon, and left the room, smiling at Margaret.

Julie and Jessie exchanged glances, not sure what that meant. Jessie thought they might get some answers, but she had the feeling it wasn't going to be anything she liked. She drank her coffee, watching Margaret efficiently move around the kitchen area. Bodyguard, cook, Jessie wondered how many other things she could do.

"Jul," she said in a calm, quiet voice, without looking at her. "I didn't mean for you to get dragged into this. And it seems unfair now most of all when we're not together any more."

Julie shrugged. "Looks like that word didn't get out." She gave Jessie a speculative look. "Or they think I still matter." She had the cool, detached tone which told Jessie she was trying to hold all that panic at bay.

"You're always going to matter to me. You're still family." She reached out for Julie's hand. "I'm still sorry."

Julie gripped her hand hard. "Well, at least we're not in it alone. That's a comfort."

I hope that's what it is, Jessie thought, and not a threat.

Diana came back into the room, went to Margaret, slid her arm casually around Margaret's waist, said something in a low voice, laughed at Margaret's answer. Then she came over to the table, her gaze resting a moment on Julie's and Jessie's clasped hands.

"It's a beautiful day outside," she said abruptly. "Let's go out on the deck and talk."

Oh, God, Jessie thought. *Means I've got to move again.* She awkwardly got to her feet as Julie picked up both coffee cups. Getting up was the hard part and once she was up, Jessie decided moving wasn't bad. Maybe Julie was right, moving would limber her up. She could walk almost normally as Diana opened the door for them to go out on the deck.

Jessie automatically scanned her surroundings, with mixed emotions. Blue skies, forest as far as she could see, quiet, peaceful, away from civilization. No roads, no power lines, no towers. They were truly isolated. They weren't on a mountaintop, there were higher elevations around them but they were pretty high. There was a coolness in the air. If it weren't for the circumstances, she might have enjoyed it.

"Please," Diana said politely but firmly, just as much of an order as an invitation. "Be seated." She closed the door and waited as Jessie moved over to the redwood chairs and gingerly sat down. Julie sat, handed Jessie the coffee cup.

She's changed, Jessie decided. Yesterday there was familiarity. She knew we wouldn't give her any trouble because of Waldo. Today, she's different. Now we see what it's going to be.

Diana set her coffee mug on the railing. "Yesterday I assumed there would be a certain amount of cooperation between us. It was purely an assumption on my part that you would find me more palatable than Waldo but it seemed reasonable. I'm not going to make that assumption today."

She paused, looking to Jessie perhaps for confirmation, but Jessie kept her expression bland. She was relieved enough she had been able to anticipate Diana's reasoning.

"I don't think it's safe for either of you to be out running around. It's entirely possible you could be picked up again by some of Waldo's people and spirited away. I had enough leverage to get you out of his hands once. I'm not sure I could do that if he got you again."

"And you think that's a possibility?"

"I do. Waldo's a sadistic bastard and he'll carry a grudge to the grave. He's nailed you once. I don't think he'll give up just because you got away this time." She paused. "You made a powerful enemy, Jessie."

"And you think he won't find us here?"

"I know he won't," Diana came back confidently.

Jessie made no response and finally Diana continued. "That brings us to the second problem." Diana took cigarettes out of her pants pocket, shook one out and played with it as she spoke. "I had a few plans of my own, and as good as it is to see you again, you are major interference."

"I'm sorry about that," Jessie said dryly. "I'll try to do better the next time."

Diana chuckled and shook her head. She took the time to light the cigarette before she spoke again. "I hadn't planned on coming here so soon, but it seemed like the safest place to stash the two of you until Waldo's taken care of. The problem is that once I'm here, I'm here for a while, which means the two of you are too."

"How long a while?"

"I don't know." She leaned against the railing, relaxed, casual, confident. "So here's the deal," she said after a minute of examining them. "You can be my guests, have the run of the house, the deck. I've got a library, a theater, an exercise room downstairs. There's a hot tub you might find helpful. You can be as comfortable as you can be." She glanced skyward, looked around, came back to them. "Weather should be nice, scenery's nice. You could be in a lot worse places."

"If not guests, then what?" Jessie asked. "I'm sure you have an alternative."

Diana turned colder, her expression harder as she fastened her gaze on Jessie. "I'll have Margaret clean out a room to the bare walls and put you in lockdown for the duration."

Julie reached out to lay her hand on Jessie's thigh. Jessie laid her hand over Julie's in assurance. The motion was not lost on Diana.

"And afterward?" Jessie asked. "What happens to your 'guests' then?"

Diana relaxed slightly. "Then I guess they'll go home."

"Go home?" Julie burst out, unable to contain herself.

"Just like that?" Jessie asked with some wariness. Even considering her link to Diana, that wasn't exactly what she expected.

Diana shrugged. "I'm not sure how yet. There are details to be worked out, but yeah, you go home. Safe and sound. Unhurt." She appeared amused at Jessie's wariness. "So which will it be, ladies: guests or—" she paused delicately. "Otherwise?"

Jessie felt Julie's grip tighten, reminding her that whatever she did, she had to consider Julie. She turned away from Diana, looking out over the vista of solid trees. She couldn't even see a break in the trees that might mean something as simple as a lumber road. Besides, she wasn't exactly in any shape for hiking out, even if she did know where she was and how she could do it. "I guess we'll be guests."

Diana tilted her head in exaggerated politeness. "Why thank you, Jessie. I appreciate that so much." She turned to Julie. "And you?"

Julie nodded. "Yes, a guest," she said quickly, fumbling with the words as she looked at the tension between the two women.

"Very good. That will make life so much better." She examined them both as if threatening them if they failed. "Now, shall we go have the breakfast Margaret's holding for us? Unless either of you have anything else to contribute?"

Julie broke the silence. "You know," she said tentatively, "it's not healthy to smoke. You shorten your life by years."

Diana turned to Julie is some disbelief and then amusement. "That's what Margaret tells me," she began. "But then I don't always listen. Is my smoking going to bother you, Julie?" She seemed rather amused at Julie's anti-smoking stance. "And do you mind if I call you Julie? After all, we haven't been formally introduced. I wouldn't want to be rude."

"No, I don't mind. And your smoking won't bother me."

"That's good. I'd hate for a guest to be uncomfortable in my house." Diana folded her arms across her chest, not relaxed completely but not so tense. "My smoking, which I generally do outside, is primarily from stress. I think we can admit we're all in a stressful situation. Can't we?" Both women nodded.

"Shall we go in for breakfast?" Diana invited in a much friendlier voice.

They filed into the kitchen, and Jessie didn't miss the speculative glance Margaret gave her and Julie and then how quickly she checked with Diana.

"Margaret," Diana said as she went to the table, pointing to which chairs she wanted them to sit at. "You'll be delighted to know Julie thinks smoking is bad for my health."

"Me, you don't believe, but you'll listen to one of our guests. Humph!" Margaret brought plates of eggs, sausage and bacon, pancakes to the table as Jessie took a seat. Julie started to sit down when she realized Margaret was doing all the serving.

"What can I do?"

Margaret gave her a measuring look and then shrugged. "Orange juice, fruit in the refrigerator." She herself picked up the coffeepot to refill the insulated carafe.

"The exercise room is downstairs," Diana said as Margaret and Julie sat at the table. "The hot tub down there may help you feel better." She gave Julie a speculative look. "And later Margaret can take you to the storage room. There's a variety of clothing available. You can pick something out to be comfortable in. I'm sure you'll get tired of that outfit."

Julie looked down at the same clothes she had worn for days. "That would be nice," she admitted.

"The library holds a wide range of movies and taped television shows. Not a lot of books but some."

"Anything live?" Jessie asked blandly and Diana gave her an amused answer.

"No. Nothing live, no phone, no television, no computers."

Jessie turned her attention back to her plate. It was worth a try.

"There're board games and video games," Diana continued. "I don't generally play them so I can't tell you exactly what's there. Jigsaw puzzles. Things like that."

"You seem well prepared," Julie commented cautiously.

Diana toyed with her food. "I got caught by an early snowstorm one time. After that, I stocked up."

"You use it often then?" Jessie tried to make the question casual.

"It's been handy," Diana said. "Now I'll have to go out and find another one."

Julie looked up in surprise. Jessie surmised it was a safe house. "Seems like we've been an inconvenience in several ways."

"You could say that." Diana shoved her plate back. "Let me know when you're done, Jessie. There's something more we need to discuss." She got up, her hand on Margaret's arm. "Breakfast was great, I'm just not hungry." She took in the others. "Excuse me." And she left.

Jessie finished eating, carefully because her jaw still hurt. This Diana was going to take some getting used to. She tried to give Julie a reassuring look, found Margaret looking at her strangely. She went back to eating, realizing she was hungry. She couldn't remember the last time she ate. "You're a good cook, Margaret," she commented.

"Huumph," was Margaret's only reply.

"Julie likes to cook," Jessie said deliberately, ignoring Julie's surprised look.

"Is that so?" Margaret looked up, looked at Julie.

"Yes," Julie blurted out as Jessie nudged her with her foot. "Nothing like coming home from a long day at the clinic and cooking up a storm."

Margaret looked away, clearly disbelieving.

"Actually," Julie said in a warmer voice. "I never have time to cook. I'm always too busy, but I do like to. And when I have time, I think I do more than a halfway decent job. It's just so hard to do when you're on the run all the time." She trailed off when she realized her wording.

Margaret chuckled and she nodded. "Hard to eat healthy too," she commented.

"Yes," Julie grabbed the words like a lifeline. "Fast foods are just so—so unhealthy."

"Takes planning, can be just as quickly done, but planning. Planning is the key."

"Yes," Julie agreed, glancing at Jessie.

Jessie nodded slightly. If they were going to be with Margaret for a while, she needed to know more about her. Julie would be the perfect foil for that. Jessie could deal with Diana, if she could figure out how to.

She had put Diana out of her mind for so long it was a little hard to drag her back. Diana had been so abrupt in her departure that Jessie had been surprised, and, she could admit now, after all these years, more than a little hurt. Diana's habit of sudden appearances had always been surprising, an unexpected pleasure. Her visits were never so long that they got into real mundane life, there were never the daily problems of living with Diana, just the highlights. Then she was gone again, but there was always the promise of the return, until those last two times.

At first, Jessie hadn't been concerned. Diana's schedule, for the lack of a better word, was maybe a month, six weeks. Then she was there again. That time four months went by, and no Diana. Jessie had reconsidered Diana's reaction to her discovery of Jessie's profession. Diana had said it was just a surprise and Jessie had wanted to believe that. Someone dropping Jessie because they learned she was a cop wasn't unusual although Lexington was small enough that most women knew before they started dating. Jessie had encountered almost all the attitudes, but Diana's reaction had her puzzled and curious. They had certainly been seeing each other long enough that Diana knew Jessie, certainly she had been passionate enough, insistent enough just the night before that it didn't matter, so Jessie really didn't understand. It wasn't like it was a secret. It just never got said, like Diana never said anything about her work, except she was in the area.

When Jessie had gotten curious enough to check Diana out, but found nothing, the only thing was that she was bonded. But that wasn't unusual, depending on the job she had, and it indicated deliveries.

For months Jessie held onto the hope she'd show up again. Someone just doesn't throw all those years away, not unless Diana just saw her as a toy, something to be played with while they were both available and then discarded and on to the next one. At least that was the only thing Jessie could come up with to explain why Diana just disappeared, never wanted any contact. Jessie was just a toy. And that hurt.

"Jessie." Julie laid her hand on Jessie's shoulder and Jessie looked around to realize both Julie and Margaret were done eating, had cleared the table. "Are you all right?"

Jessie shook off her memories. "I'm okay, just trying to put everything together."

"Your bringing up the cooking was a masterpiece." Julie dropped her voice. "Margaret's really into health. Healthy food, no smoking, exercise. I can't do the exercise, you'll have to do that part, but I've made a good impression on her. You should do so good with Diana."

"Yeah." *Fat chance.* "Speaking of which, I guess I need to go see what our hostess wants." She pushed back her chair. "Margaret, do you know where Diana might be?"

"I'm right here," Diana answered from the doorway. She took in Julie helping Margaret with the dishes, Jessie awkwardly getting up. "Want to come with me?"

"I have a choice?" Jessie got up and followed Diana back out onto the deck and around the front of the house.

"You're moving better," Diana commented as they went around the far side.

"Moving helps." And the railing, she thought as she leaned on it.

The deck came to a dead-end where the house extended. Diana reached around the corner of the house and pulled out a satellite phone. "Don't bother looking for it here again: it won't be here. I owe you a phone call."

"What for?"

"I can't see leaving Nicki hanging this entire time. Not knowing and just waiting to hear something isn't pleasant." She punched in some numbers, pointed to Jessie as the phone rang. "Lean against the wall before you fall over."

Jessie moved back against the wall, puzzled and confused. Was there supposed to be a hidden message here? She folded her arms and tried to be disinterested as someone answered the ring.

"Yo! Everything quiet?" Jessie looked down at the ground, concentrating on the muffled voice coming through. She couldn't understand a word. "Sounds good," Diana was saying. "Keep a low profile. Let me know if anything rattles." She paused, listened. "Yeah, that sounds good. Chat with you later." She broke the connection.

"Nicki's been moved to a safe house. After Julie got picked up, the powers that be thought she might be at risk and moved her."

Jessie looked up at her in real confusion now. *Where is she getting this information?* "You know this?"

Diana nodded. "Nicki wasn't happy about it, gave them a bunch of gaff but she was finally persuaded. They thought she was high risk so she has a guard on her."

"You're watching her," Jessie realized in surprise.

Diana shrugged as if it were no consequence. "Figured Waldo wouldn't get through both your police and my people. What's her cell number?"

"Why are you doing this? Is this some form of torture?" Jessie demanded in a shaking voice. "Are you trying to make me believe that you're concerned?"

Diana looked insulted as she eyed Jessie. "I told you: I think waiting to hear about whether someone is dead or alive is hell. I can't see leaving Nicki hanging just wondering about you. But if you don't want to, that's fine with me." Diana started to turn off the phone.

"No, don't." Jessie reached out for the phone. "I—I was hasty. Yes, I want to talk to her." She couldn't apologize, that would be too much. She met Diana's chilly gaze and wondered if Diana would demand an apology. She waited and finally Diana turned the phone back on. Jessie supplied the number and Diana punched it in.

"You talk about you and Julie, nothing else. No matter what she asks," Diana instructed. She pulled a miniature hourglass out of her pocket. "You've got this long." She set it on the railing as the phone rang. She handed the phone to Jessie.

"This is Nicki."

Jessie felt like weeping at the sound of her sister's voice. There were so many times in the past three days she had thought she would never hear it again. "Oh, God."

"Hello?" Nicki repeated.

"Nicki, it's me."

"OMG! You're alive!"

Jessie sagged against the house, not seeing Diana step back, giving her room. "I'm alive. No, I'm not back. Julie's with me."

"Are you all right? What's going on?"

"We're okay now, just—we can't come back yet."

"Why not? Where are you?"

"I don't know, not exactly. We're safe, at least for the time being. Nicki, I'm sorry. I need to tell you I love you. I want you to know that. You've been the best sister anyone could have ever had."

"God, where are you? What happened? They said you were kidnapped. Pete was shot. Jessie, are you really all right? I've got to do something."

"No, no, Nicki. Don't do anything. Just—just stay put. You may be in danger. Just please, cooperate with them. They'll take care of you."

"Like they took care of you?" Nicki exploded.

"Nicki, please." She drew a ragged breath as she watched the sand flow. "I've got to go, Nicki. Please. Be careful. I love you."

She abruptly broke the connection and stood there. She closed her eyes, feeling Diana gently take the phone from her hand. She felt totally undone, uncertain. She had no idea why Diana had allowed the call, maybe there was still some sympathy in her. She didn't want to cry, no matter how much she felt like it, not standing here in front of Diana.

"You okay?" Diana laid her hand on Jessie's shoulder, concern in her voice. Jessie could almost pretend it was old times.

Jessie took a deep breath and tried to pull herself together. "Yes," she nodded.

"You didn't need to make it sound like a last call," Diana said quietly. "It's not."

"Why'd you let me call her?" she asked numbly.

Before Diana could say anything, the phone in her hand rang. She answered it immediately. "Yo!" She half turned away from Jessie. "Damn, she must have bolted out the door. Let me see what I can do. I'll call you back. No, keep on her tail. Treat her as one of ours. I'll get back."

She broke the connection, hit redial. She looked up at Jessie with a look of exasperation. "Your little sister is definitely a chip off the same block." Jessie reached for the phone as it rang but Diana caught her hand. "Not this time." She didn't let go of Jessie's hand. "Not a word," she warned and she put the phone on speaker.

"Jessie!" Nicki answered.

"Not this time, kid." Diana came on strong. "Now you turn that little green Honda around and get right back to where you belong."

"Have you got my sister?"

Diana held Jessie back. "Yes, I've got your sister, and you're not helping matters any. Just where the hell do you think you're going anyway? Think she's going to be waiting at the corner for you to pick her up?"

"Please, don't hurt her!" Nicki pleaded. "She's the only family I've got!" Nicki started crying and to Jessie's surprise, Diana looked touched.

"Nicki, calm down, stop crying. I'm not going to lie to you. Yes, Jessie was hurt but nothing that won't heal and nowhere close to the last time." Jessie jerked at that reference and Diana gripped her hand hard. "She's just got to be kept in a safe spot for a time."

"Please," Nicki begged, "don't hurt her! Let her go!"

"Nicki," Diana said sharply. "Go back. You've got to be safe. Otherwise, Jessie's only going to worry about you and that's going to make it worse on her. I'm not going to hurt her."

"Please," Nicki begged.

"Nicki." Diana drew a deep breath and turned away from Jessie. "You're not helping. Now stop crying," she said sternly. They heard Nicki get control, sniffle. "Now go back to your safe house and stay there."

"You know about that."

"Yes. I know a lot, and I know Jessie and Julie will be safe as long as they behave. And you know Jessie won't behave if she thinks you're in danger. So you have to do this to help her."

"Promise me you won't hurt her."

Diana sighed in exasperation. "I promise: as long as Jessie behaves herself, she'll be safe. Now you promise me you'll go back and you'll behave. Because I'll know if you don't."

"You're watching me."

"You've got a guardian angel, kiddo. Now go back."

"Can Jessie call me again and let me know she's all right?"

"Yes," Diana hissed. "Now go. Goodbye."

Diana broke the connection, bowed her head, looked at the phone for a few minutes. As if she just realized she was still holding Jessie's hand, she released her as she looked up. "She sounds all grown up," she said slowly. "I can still remember her running around the park."

"She's going to UK, wants to go to law school."

Diana shook her head. "Where does the time go?" When the phone rang again she was slower to answer. "Yo. Good. Maybe she'll stay put. Keep up the rotation. Be safe." She broke the connection.

"Why are you watching her?"

"She made too good a target," Diana said absently. "Didn't want to take a chance."

"How long—"

Diana shook her head. She lifted the phone. "One more call."

"Who?" Jessie couldn't imagine anyone else to notify.

Diana made a connection, asked for a relay, and Jessie sagged in shock when she realized Diana was calling Jessie's place of work. "Relay to the police department. Insist on Captain Conrad." She looked up at Jessie. "You need to confirm you're alive, Julie's alive," she instructed. "No message, keep it brief. You can't talk." Her expression changed, colder, harder. "You behave. Don't make me regret this."

"Conrad." Diana handed Jessie the phone.

"Captain, this is Galbreath."

"Galbreath! Are you all right? Where are you?"

"I've been allowed to call you to let you know I'm alive. Julie Carlton's alive. I can't tell you where we're at because I don't know." She watched Diana, wondering what she could say, would be able to say. "I've already talked to my sister." Maybe they could get something from those phone calls.

"Are you all right?"

"It was rough for a couple of days," Jessie said carefully, watching Diana. "Then things changed."

"Is there someone there with you?"

"Yes."

"Are they listening?"

"Yes."

"Have you been hurt?"

"Yes, but I think that part's over."

"Has Dr. Carlton been hurt?"

"No."

Diana made the cutting motion across her throat.

"I've got to go," Jessie said.

"Can you call again?"

"I don't know."

"Have you been threatened?"

"Not exactly. I've got to go. Goodbye." She closed the phone, hoping the connection wouldn't break as she handed it back to Diana.

Diana opened it to clear the connection, dialed a number. "Turn it off, shut it down. Log it out," she instructed. Then she turned it off.

Jessie tried to keep any disappointment from showing in her face.

"Very good," Diana commented. "You okay?" She picked up the timer and stuffed it in her pocket.

"I guess so." Jessie pulled herself together. "I guess I have to be." She looked directly at Diana. "So what are we? Bargaining chips?"

"No. I don't need that. Let's go back inside now."

They started around the deck, Diana walking slowly to keep pace with Jessie.

"You never asked if Julie had family to notify," Jessie commented.

"There's only a cousin she doesn't see much," Diana replied.

Jessie whirled around, her jaw dropping. *How the hell did she know that?* Diana caught Jessie before she lost her balance and Jessie pulled away immediately. "How do you know that?"

"I do my homework, I still don't like surprises." She turned Jessie around. "Don't give me any."

What about you giving me surprises? When they reentered the house, Julie immediately came over to Jessie, slid her arm around Jessie's waist. "You okay? What—"

"She let me call Nicki," she explained as she rubbed her forehead. She was still confused over that. She didn't miss Margaret's curious look as Diana came through the kitchen.

"Good," Julie agreed. "Now Nicki won't be on pins and needles. At least she knows you're alive."

"Margaret, why don't you take Julie upstairs to the storage room. She can pick out some clothes. We can't have her spending the entire time here wearing the same things."

"Yes, Diana."

Diana turned to Jessie. "Think you can take the stairs? The storage room is in the attic."

"I'll manage," Jessie replied. She wasn't about to pass up the opportunity to examine the rafters of this house.

Jessie followed Julie who followed Margaret up the narrow, steep stairs built against the outside wall. She wasn't sure what she would find, but she was surprised at the built-in cabinets down the length of the cabin. The center aisle under the peak of the roof was the only area they could stand up in without difficulty. Drawers were neatly labeled with item and size. Margaret eyed Jessie and started pulling out drawers. Underwear was still in new packages. Jeans, worn but clean and neatly folded, folded shirts, tank tops, sweatshirts, there was a reasonable variety in sizes and colors. Within minutes, Jessie had a few changes of clothing.

Curious, Jessie thought. Like they were accustomed to supplying clothing. All women's, various sizes, but not a wide range.

"Try this," Margaret pulled out an outfit for Julie.

Jessie walked up and down the length of the cabin, eyeing the drawers. *Probably wouldn't be a good idea to start going through them.* She glanced back at Margaret and Julie, who were pulling out clothing. "I'm going downstairs to change," she announced and was relieved when Margaret merely nodded, still talking to Julie.

Security, clothing, isolated. Must really be a safe house, Jessie decided as she went down the stairs. *Safe from what?* The stairs took her down through the kitchen, across the room and back up the stairs to the bedrooms. She kept looking around, wondering where Diana had disappeared to.

Nice cabin, not exactly rustic though. Cathedral ceiling in the living room, bedrooms overlooking the living room, library, glass, and what beautiful views. Got to be a power source somewhere. Can't believe there's no outside contact unless she shut it up.

She changed clothes, getting into blue jeans and white shirt, feeling more comfortable but still sore. Moving felt better than being still so she took the opportunity to wander around. She casually went through all the rooms, apparently just wandering if she ran into either of her hosts, her hands in her hip pockets, just looking and wondering where Diana had gone to, feeling her presence, still puzzling about her. With Julie and Margaret in the attic, she felt alone, and yet…she examined corners, looking for wiring. Would there be security cameras? She kept looking behind her as she cautiously went back upstairs, glancing all around as she paused at the bedroom door, waiting to be stopped. Did guests snoop in a place like this? Maybe curious ones.

She and Julie had the corner bedroom, the master with its own bath. Jessie cautiously opened the door to the next room, listening for any sound as she glanced down into the living room. This would be easier if she knew exactly where Diana was. A bedroom, queen bed, furniture, not as luxurious as the one she and Julie had. It appeared empty so she stepped inside. She caught the faint fragrance, this was Diana's room. She quickly searched, not even sure what she was looking for. Clothes in the drawers, in the closet, science fiction book on the bedside table. Very impersonal. She checked the hallway before she slipped out.

The next room was a bathroom. At least she had an excuse for being there. Cabinet held the standard types of things, aspirin, lotions, aloe cream, first aid cream. Nothing you wouldn't expect in a vacation house.

The last room was Margaret's and even if she wasn't there, Jessie could feel the atmosphere. Efficient, plain, impersonal. She was more wary of being caught here and she made a quick search but found nothing. She slipped out, not even sure what she had been looking for.

Something to tell her how Diana fit in all this, with Waldo, who her papa was. Margaret had mentioned she had promised her papa. What had she promised? Had she and Diana ever talked about her father? Did they ever talk about her? Jessie couldn't remember. She had certainly talked about herself, her sister, her father, Julie. She couldn't ever remember talking about Diana. Did she have a family? What kind of work did she do? But even when she had finally gotten suspicious, there had been nothing on Diana DeVilbiss.

She went downstairs, looked in the kitchen for Julie and Margaret but they must still be upstairs. Taking a lot of time to pick out clothes, she thought. I sure hope Julie's charming her. If she can work on her, maybe I can work on Diana.

She found the small bar in the living room between the massive windows across from the fireplace. She went out the front door cautiously and no alarm sounded. Maybe there were silent ones. She didn't even try the steps as she walked all around the deck, looking for wiring, for trip wires, motion detectors.

She came back into the house, entered through the living room, casually walked into the library and found Diana there. She stopped in slight surprise. *She wasn't there when I stepped out*, she thought in confusion. For a moment she stood there, able to look at Diana draped sideways in the wingback chair, one leg thrown up and over the arm as she was lost in a mystery. For a moment, a brief moment, the clock turned back and Jessie wanted—wanted what? She shook her head. She reached out and knocked on the door.

Diana looked up, eyebrows raised, but Jessie didn't think she had been unaware of her standing there. "Yes, Jessie?"

"Can we talk?"

"Sure." Diana closed her book but didn't put it down as Jessie came in. "You got more clothes. Back to blue jeans and white shirt uniform, I see."

"Yeah." Jessie looked down at her outfit belatedly remembering how Diana always found it a turn on. "Just picked out what was comfortable." She came over and sat on the edge of the library table across from Diana. "Bother you?" Diana shook her head but Jessie wasn't so sure. She didn't want to have to go that route. "No dark glasses though," she commented, trying to lighten the mood.

"Wouldn't want that much nostalgia," Diana said dryly. "What did you want to talk about?"

Keep it calm, Jessie counseled herself. *Two equals just talking about things going on. Don't be adversarial.* "You really going to get Waldo out of the country?"

"That's the plan."

"You know what a scumbag he is, don't you? All the things he's part of?"

"Probably better than you do."

Oh, that's encouraging. "Why are you helping him?"

"As a favor." Diana rested her head against the curve of the chair, looking directly at Jessie. As much as Jessie tried, she couldn't quite see Diana there. "And having him out of the country seemed to solve a problem."

"What problem was that?"

"He threatened you."

"I'm flattered, but that was hardly necessary." Jessie passed it off as she leaned against the table, hands holding onto the edge. "I've been threatened before. Occupational hazard."

Diana's expression didn't change. "Been ambushed before?"

Jessie paused before she shook her head. That had been unexpected.

"Seems like Waldo was getting closer than just threatening."

"If he was so close, then why didn't he kill me when he had the opportunity?" Even though she had seen Diana come in like gangbusters, she had a hard time visualizing Diana on the gory side of crime. Okay, maybe the white-collar kind, but blood and guts, no, she couldn't visualize that.

"He never intended to kill you, Jessie."

"Then what?" Diana shook her head. "Oh, don't stop now. You've been carrying on like the big tough broad up until now. Don't be getting all squeamish at this point."

"I was never told, it was just hearsay."

"But you believed it enough to move him."

"Yeah. I thought it was quick enough to prevent him doing anything." She laid the book on the floor beside the chair. "I never liked dealing with Waldo, so it was a fluke I even discovered he had you."

"So what was he going to do?" Jessie repeated, getting the feeling Diana was avoiding the question. "I mean, I'm glad you stepped in. Don't get me wrong, but if he wasn't going to kill me…"

"Oh, he wouldn't." Diana paused. "Just what did you do to cross him anyway?"

"You mean besides bust him for drugs? For possession? For distribution?" She stopped and thought about it, putting her head back to examine the ceiling. "Waldo and I seem to have been fated. A number of years ago when I was just a rookie, my partner and I pulled him over for a traffic violation. No taillights as I recall. Car was loaded with cocaine." She abruptly looked at Diana. "About nine months before I met you. Would that be purely a coincidence, Diana?"

"Maybe fate, but I had nothing to do with any of Waldo's drug dealings, if that's what you're asking."

Can I believe that? Jessie mused as she tried to read Diana's mind. It had the feeling of truth. Maybe she was grasping at straws. "Anyway, he did a short term, first offense, although he wasn't unknown to us. Then after he got out, I happened to be the one to arrest him for distributing. This last one I didn't have anything to do with so I don't know why he's pissed at me."

"I can answer that for you. During that stretch, he developed a real case of claustrophobia. Blames you for that. Sending him back to prison, locking him up, is all your fault."

"I lose sleep at night over people like him," Jessie said with some sarcasm. "Come on. I answered your questions. Now you answer mine." Diana was still reluctant. "What? Rape me? Torture me? Kill me? No, you said he wasn't going to do that. What's the deal? He didn't manage to do any of it."

Diana gave in. "Since you insist on knowing," she started. "This is only second maybe thirdhand because no one would say this to my face. He wasn't going to kill you because he wanted you to suffer, and you couldn't suffer if you were dead. Rape? Most likely. Torture? Yeah, he's always had a sadistic streak. But the kicker was he was going to rape, torture, and kill Julie, make you watch. That way you could remember for the rest of your life that you couldn't do a thing to stop him or save your lover."

Jessie stopped breathing and when she opened her mouth to say something, her mouth was so dry she couldn't get her tongue to work. Her stomach lurched and she gripped the table so she didn't pitch forward. Diana watched her without moving. Abruptly Jessie pushed off from the table and bolted down the hall to the half bath tucked under the stairs.

When she finished losing her breakfast she buried her face in the icy washcloth, then sat on the commode trying to pull herself together. Delayed panic set in. All those years of worrying about Julie and now that she was out of the house, out of Jessie's life, she was still at risk. Images came all too easily to mind, images about herself she could shut out. But not Julie.

She pulled herself together, washed her face. She was still shaken and angry as she stalked back to the library.

Adrenaline-fueled, she headed straight for Diana, grabbed her by her shirt front and pulled her out of the chair. "That son of a bitch. And how did he know anything about Julie?"

"Don't be an ass, Jessie," Diana retorted, not even struggling against her. "You think things like that aren't noticed? You think the police are the only ones who do surveillance?" She caught Jessie's wrists but she didn't try to pull them away.

"And you're letting that bastard get away?"

"If that was what I had to do to make sure you were out of his hands, yes."

Jessie was shaking so badly that when Diana pulled Jessie's hands free, Jessie let her. Diana turned her around, set her down in the chair. Then, even as Jessie tried to get a grip on her emotions, Diana disappeared. She returned almost immediately, this time with a glass of dark liquid.

"You haven't gone off the deep end and had to join AA or anything like that, have you?"

"No," Jessie said shortly as she reached for the glass.

"Just checking. Seems to be a frequently traveled road."

Jessie knocked off the glass, handed it back. She felt Diana's hand on her shoulder to steady her.

"It didn't happen," Diana said firmly. "It might have been, but it didn't happen. You're safe; Julie's safe. You got slightly hurt. She got terrorized. In the scheme of things, nothing happened. And it's not going to happen."

Jessie shuddered. All the things they had threatened, she had thought they were just saying all that to scare her.

"Stop it!" Diana's voice was sharp.

Jessie looked up at her. Diana was looking down at her, and she looked concerned instead of the bland mask.

"Breathe. Deep breaths."

Jessie obeyed, things began to fall into place again, she got her focus back. "Don't," she started. "Don't mention." She tried again. "Don't say anything about this to Julie." She closed her eyes. Poor Julie, who couldn't deal with violence.

"I wouldn't have said anything to you if you hadn't pushed."

"I know. But I needed to know."

Diana didn't take her hand off Jessie's shoulder. She gripped it painfully tight. "Now I'm going to tell you something else, so you listen up."

"What?"

"Don't you ever do that again, lay a hand on me like that. If you do that in front of Margaret, she'll kill you. Or die in the attempt. You understand?"

"I wouldn't—didn't—"

"Doesn't matter. Margaret's my bodyguard. I haven't moved in the safest circles. She'll react and ask questions later." Diana slowly released Jessie and stepped back. "It's something we all have in common: we react to protect those we care about." She leaned against the library table and watched Jessie for a few minutes. "You all right now?"

Jessie nodded. She sagged back into the chair. "Just seems so unfair now," she said distractedly.

"How so?"

Jessie closed her eyes, forgetting here and now. This was Diana, her Diana. She had always been able to talk to Diana about Julie. She didn't even stop to censure herself.

"Julie couldn't deal with the violence, even the idea I might go out the door in the morning and not come back."

"That is a hard idea to wrap your mind around," Diana said quietly.

"We separated about a year ago. She couldn't deal with it any more."

"What!" Diana burst out and quickly muffled it.

Jessie barely let Diana's exclamation register. She went on. "I thought we were working everything out, going to get back together. Then a couple of months ago she said she couldn't. It was over permanently. We could still be friends, family even, just she couldn't deal with it on a day-to-day basis." She opened her eyes to see Diana looking at her strangely.

"I'm sorry it turned out that way," Diana said in a voice that sounded hollow. Maybe it was just Jessie's listening because of this latest shock.

"Yeah, so am I." Jessie buried her face in her hands. Damn, this woman was everything she abhorred, and yet she was her friend. She felt like she needed to do everything in her power to arrest her, to take her in, to suspect everything she did, and at the same time, she wanted to sit down, talk to her, ask her how she had been. She wanted to cry on her shoulder, talk to her the way she used to, tell her all about her frustrations and her joys in life. Ask her about hers. Ask her if she ever got to be with the woman she loved. She raised her head to find Diana watching her, concern and understanding in her face, her eyes. "This is a hell of a situation, as my dad would say."

Diana nodded. "Yes, it is."

"What are we going to do?"

"What we have to."

"I don't know if I can deal with this."

"Yes, you can."

Jessie gave a mirthless chuckle. "You have more confidence in me than I do at this point."

"You've had some hard shocks, one right after another. You thought you were going to die. You thought your partner was dead or dying. Julie was pulled into it. Even me showing up had to be a shock. Give yourself a break and let the dust settle. Nothing's going to happen."

"I feel like I've been through an earthquake and all the landscape's different."

Diana gave a small smile. "That's how I felt when I found out you were a cop. Everything changed."

"And then you left."

"But not because you were a cop." She gave a rueful smile as Jessie ran her hands through her hair. "Give yourself some slack, Jessie. Things that matter will fall back in place."

"You say that with certainty."

"I am certain."

Jessie shook her head, not at all certain. Diana still looked so calm, sounded so confident. Then she saw Diana's hands, gripping the table hard enough that her knuckles were white. So she wasn't having an easy time either. She looked up to meet Diana's gaze.

"Go soak in the hot tub," Diana suggested. "Explore the exercise room. Go lay out on the deck, the sun's coming out. Should be nice."

Jessie stood up. "Do anything, just go away?" she asked ruefully.

"It would probably help us both right now."

Jessie nodded. "I guess so."

She wandered out of the room, listening, waiting for Diana to stop her, for some reaction. She paused at the door, shook her head, straightened her back. She would have to deal with this, one way or another, although for the life of her, right now, she didn't have the faintest idea how.

***

"Margaret doesn't like you," Julie said that night as they were preparing for bed.

How'd she find out so fast? Did Diana tell her? was Jessie's first thought. "What makes you say that?" she asked instead. "Did she say something?"

"No, it was more like what she didn't say."

Jessie came out of the bathroom. It hurt to brush her teeth. "How so?"

"She never says your name, just 'the other one' or 'your friend.' Haven't you noticed? She watches you but never when you're looking at her. Are they lovers? Is she jealous?" Julie sat cross-legged on the bed.

"No, not lovers, at least Diana denied that." She walked around the room. "Nice jammies."

"Silk." Julie slid her hand across the material. "Margaret picked them out for me. That was another thing: she kept picking out clothes for me, concerned about style, color, like she was dressing me for some show and she was the fashion consultant. You picked your own, she didn't care, couldn't be bothered."

"Maybe she knows how I hate shopping. I wondered what took you so long. Maybe she's attracted to you."

Julie shook her head. "No, didn't get those vibes. It was sorta fun, you always hated shopping. And I figured the longer I kept her up there, the longer you had to search the house or talk to Diana or do whatever cops do to investigate."

Jessie sat down in the chair. "Am I that transparent?"

"You're a cop, twenty-four-seven." Julie shrugged. "Find out anything?"

"Diana's room is next door. Margaret's down the hall. I get the feeling there's security, maybe closed circuit, but I couldn't find any wires, any cameras. But this house isn't a rustic cabin. If there is anything, it's probably so built-in that it's not apparent."

"Were you able to have any type of conversation with Diana?"

"Of a sorts," Jessie admitted. She shook her head. "It's really strange, like one minute I know her and the next minute, who is this woman?"

"I can imagine."

No you can't. Jessie sat there. "But I didn't find out anything. It would probably help a good deal if I could find out who *Papa* is."

"I think I can do that." Then she laughed at Jessie's expression. "Well, I'm not a ninny, Jessie. I was supposed to have treated her papa. I'll just ask. I imagine there's a whole lot she'd like to ask me."

Jessie nodded thoughtfully. "Probably so." She got to her feet and came over to the bed to crawl in. "And for the record, I do not now nor did I ever think you're a ninny." She ran her fingers over the silken material of the pearl-pink pajamas. "So what other kinds of clothes did you get out of Margaret?"

CHAPTER EIGHTEEN

Diana glanced at the kitchen clock. Nine a.m. Another six maybe seven hours and Waldo would be taken care of. That would be one thing out of the way, one item crossed off her list. She glanced at Jessie eating her eggs, Julie asking Margaret something about the coffee cake she had made. She watched as Jessie casually glanced at the clock then back into the living room. She was watching the clock also.

Diana pushed her plate away. She hated waiting, hated that she couldn't be there supervising. She had good people, she didn't worry about that. She just hated most that she hadn't been able to talk to Helen in person. There was something there she just couldn't put her finger on. She had been pissed at Waldo when she called Helen, knew Helen would jump at the chance to take that flight. Now she was second-guessing herself. Helen was a more than capable pilot. She had gone through that bad time after Jillian died when she was so depressed Diana didn't dare put her in the cockpit. She had come through that, the depression was gone, turned into grief at the loss of a partner. She kept saying she wanted back in the loop, wanted to get back to work, needed to get back to normal.

"Are you all right?" Margaret asked as Diana got up.

"Yes," Diana said shortly. The cabin was too confining, she needed to be outside.

She went out on the deck, paced from one end to the other. By now, Helen should be getting ready. Damn, she hated being stuck here. She took a deep breath. She had made all the plans, everyone knew what they were supposed to do. She just needed to let it go, but her gut instinct just wouldn't.

When she came around the corner of the house, Jessie stood on the corner of the deck, leaning back, her elbows resting on the railing. She watched as Diana walk toward her after an initial hesitation.

"Waiting's hard, isn't it?" she said conversationally. "You make all these plans and then pray everything got covered and goes the way it's supposed to." Diana didn't answer. "I guess it's the same no matter what you're planning." She turned around and leaned on the railing. "Would you be there except for us?"

"Yes."

"You could take me along," Jessie suggested slyly.

Diana laughed, just as much from tension as she did at Jessie's suggestion. "In your dreams." She leaned on the railing.

"Well, I thought I'd try."

"Good try, not a chance."

They stood there in silence for a while, a comfortable silence, Diana realized. Then something changed and Diana knew Jessie was a cop again. "You do things like this often?"

"Like what?"

"Getting people out of the country."

Diana didn't turn to look at her. "I'm not going to answer that."

Jessie ducked her head. "You know it's all going to come out sooner or later."

"Maybe. Maybe not."

"Since you're holding us here, you could still be an accessory to kidnapping."

"Better than murder," Diana commented. She straightened up. "If this is the way the conversation is going to go, Jessie, I'm not in the mood. If we were on your turf, you would only be asking if you thought a crime was being committed."

"I heard you make those plans," Jessie said carefully without turning to look at Diana.

"Then you wouldn't be talking to me. You'd be talking to my lawyer."

Jessie pressed on. "You know, if what you said was true about what Waldo planned, I'm sure a very favorable deal could be cut."

"Crap. I don't need this today." Diana turned and took several steps away before she turned back. "Jessie, you're a good cop. We've got quite a history. Don't press your luck." Then she left, jerking open the door to the living room, stepping aside to let Julie go by her to go out on the deck herself.

She needed to work off this nervous energy. If she couldn't go outside, then a good run on the treadmill might work. She went through the kitchen, where Margaret stopped her.

"Did you get a chance to speak with Helen? Was she all right with this?"

Diana paused. "Spoke to her. She seemed okay." She glanced back to see Jessie and Julie talking on the desk. "She says she got a good bill of health. She apologized for blowing up when she learned I agreed to transport Waldo. She said it was unprofessional of her."

Margaret chuckled. "Unprofessional. Is that what you call a screaming rampage?"

Diana was able to smile about that. "That pilot's license is important to her. She likes our little jet. She was asking me if there was a chance I could get another."

"Why? She wants to fly two?" Margaret shook her head. "I never thought she'd come back after Jillian was killed. She blamed Waldo for a long time, botching that deal. You know that, don't you?" Diana nodded. "You think he won't reach back here for your friend?"

Diana raised her eyebrow at Margaret's designation of Jessie. "Not if he knows what's good for him."

"I don't know," Margaret said as Julie came back inside and the subject was dropped.

Diana went on down to the exercise room and set up the treadmill. A good run, mindless, draining. That was what she needed.

Diana didn't come up until lunchtime, fresh from a shower, the towel still draped over her neck. Margaret wasn't saying anything more but then she wouldn't say anything in front of Jessie or Julie. Julie looked a little scared again, moving carefully around the kitchen as she helped Margaret. Jessie stood at the door, her hands in her hip pockets, watching as if she expected Kentucky State Police to swoop in and rescue them.

"Let's eat," Diana said abruptly although that was about the last thing she wanted to do. Salad, a clear soup. Diana recognized Margaret's coaxing to eat, to relax, to calm down. She took a deep breath. It would soon be over. By now, they should be half way there.

She was just reaching for the salt when the alarm went off, a loud blaring sound that sounded like a fire siren. Diana and Margaret both leaped to their feet, throwing back their chairs while Julie and Jessie both freaked out, came to their feet, searched for the source of the noise.

"Stay in the house, don't even try the doors," Diana ordered as she headed for the living room, the library. Margaret disappeared into the pantry. They met downstairs in the communications room, the computer up and running, phones ringing.

"She reported a mayday," the voice came over the speaker phone when Diana picked it up. "Over international waters."

Margaret took the other phone, while Diana sat down at the computer. She was still aware enough to initiate house security. She glanced at the monitor showing Jessie and Julie picking up chairs, talking to each other. Then she dismissed them from her thoughts.

"Any idea what happened?" she asked as she went through security to access links.

"Negative."

"They get off on schedule?"

"Package was picked up with little difficulty. Takeoff on time."

"Anything unusual?"

"Helen dismissed the crew."

"She what?"

"Dismissed the crew."

"What the hell…"

With some trial and effort they managed to make links to find out what was going on, but even the links didn't tell them anything.

"Should they be close enough to anywhere to make a landing?" Diana muttered. She pulled up maps of where the flight plan took them.

"Lots of open water," Margaret reported. She put on headphones and started searching. "Cruise ships should be in vicinity. They might see something." She listened. "Something's going on, lots of chatter."

Flight plans. Checkpoints. Diana went through the list, her gut instinct doing a fire dance. Weather was clear, no storms. No conflicting flight plans. No one scrambled. What would have prompted a mayday? Mechanical? Helen was a good pilot, she would manage. The ground crew was dependable.

"Lost them," reported the voice over the phone. "Diana, what happened?"

"Don't know, how the hell should I know?" Diana muttered. "I'm not there. I'm stuck here. Damn it, Helen, what did you go and do?"

Margaret looked at her. "Do you think she did something?"

"She wasn't any fan of his, but—"

"Getting something."

Hours passed before they were through sifting through reports, listening in on radio communications. Diana was still in some area of numbness that something could change so quickly, and she was conscious of Margaret covertly watching her.

"Diana, stop," Margaret said finally. "Going over it and over it isn't going to change the outcome."

"There's got to be a reason."

"I don't think you're going to find it in those reports."

Diana stopped, rested her head on her bent arm. "Damn, what the hell happened?"

"We need to go back upstairs," Margaret suggested.

**

Diana hardly noticed that Julie had cooked dinner. She was still so lost in the problem that she hardly ate. She ignored everyone, everything, her tunnel vision kicking in as she searched for an answer. Margaret accepted this, Jessie watched. Julie, only conscious of discomfort, tried once or twice to make conversation, first with Margaret then with Jessie.

"I'm sorry," Diana said as she got up to leave the table. "I know it's rude. It's not your fault, and it's nothing you've done. It'll be better tomorrow. Please just overlook my rudeness tonight." She moved her chair back under the table. "Excuse me, there're still things I need to take care of."

Things to take care of, she thought as she went back downstairs. *Like talk to papa.*

**

By the time she came back upstairs, the house was quiet. Margaret was sitting in the kitchen, waiting for her. When Diana entered, Margaret immediately got up and poured hot tea for her. She didn't ask anything, just put the mug down for Diana and pulled out the chair. Diana sank into the chair, buried her face in her hands, as Margaret moved in behind her to massage her shoulders, her neck.

"Was it bad, sweet pea?"

"Wasn't good." *Even worse was his mildness*, she thought but couldn't say. Years past, his rage, his sarcasm would have reached through the phone for her, making her relieved she was miles away.

Papa's rages had been notorious and now they were gone. She took it as yet another sign her papa was failing, a thought as depressing as anything else that had happened.

"Did he blame you?" Margaret asked with all the wariness of a protective mama.

Diana sighed. "Actually, no. In fact, he asked if it could have been sabotage. That was something I hadn't even considered."

"Sabotage? Why sabotage?"

I can think of lots of reasons, Diana thought but she shook her head. *If anyone suspects about papa's health, that would stir things up. Damn I hate being stuck here.* She sank down, her head on her folded arms. "Rub right in the middle, between the shoulder blades. Ahhh, right there." She sighed. "How's our company?"

"Quiet. Julie's a little spooked. She doesn't like these strong emotions. Or she's afraid of you. They're watching a movie."

"I'll try to be nice to her the next couple of days. Can't have her afraid of me. Don't know how long we'll be here." She moved for Margaret to rub different muscles.

"This waiting is bad."

"May get worse." She sat up. "Ohh, that felt good." She arched her back, stretching stiff muscles. "Why don't you go to bed, Margaret. Maybe I can find out more tomorrow."

"Is that just a cover to say you want to be alone and brood?"

Diana laughed. "Can't hide anything from you, can I?"

Margaret brushed back Diana's hair. "Never." The bodyguard sighed. "These two. What's with them?"

"Cold storage for a while. Once I figure out what I'm going to do, then I'll know what to do with them."

"No harm?"

"What do you think?"

"Over your dead body."

"Well, I sure hope it doesn't come to that." She got to her feet. "Do we have a cake? Cookies? Something sweet."

"In the pantry. I think Julie cooks for therapy. She baked a cake this afternoon."

"That was accommodating of her." She went into the pantry, pulled out the cake. She came out for the plate and knife.

"What are you going to do?" Margaret asked.

"Nothing I can do. The original timetable is royally screwed. I'm stuck here instead of running around getting things done. Can't meet anyone. No face-to-face, this video conferencing just doesn't cut it.

But we'll just have to go on the way we planned. I don't know what else to do."

She lifted the cake. "Not bad. I'll need to mention it to her in the morning."

"The cop," Margaret said slowly. "She going to be a problem, sweet pea?"

Diana hesitated, started to say no and then shrugged. "I don't know. Today's probably not the day to ask. She's a cop first."

"But you're still in—"

"Leave it," Diana cut in, not sharply, just wearily. "Like I said, today's not the day." She finished the slice of cake and put the plate in the dishwasher. "I told you a long time ago not to bring that up again."

Margaret shook her head, but she said nothing.

Diana stood at the sink a minute, staring at nothing. "Go to bed, Margaret. Let me brood. That's what I came here for."

She listened until Margaret went up the stairs and away. When she was alone, she could bury her face in her hands, wanting to weep but not ready to let go. Then aimlessly, she walked through the house, past the closed library door. The movie was still on, she could hear it faintly. She went to the bar and fixed a drink. She needed to be alone, and there was no place to be really alone. She went out the deck door, into the darkness.

CHAPTER NINETEEN

Jessie woke up early, lay there staring at the ceiling in the morning light. Julie was still asleep beside her, curled up on her side, wrapped up in the blanket, just like she always had. Jessie had forgotten how she always hogged the blankets. It had been over a year since they had slept together—well, mostly. There were the occasions when they tried at reconciliation. It wasn't that they didn't like each other, didn't even sometimes love each other. It was just that Jessie had the choice between being a cop and loving Julie, and she chose being a cop.

It was a quandary that had led to many sleepless nights, days of turmoil. Being a cop was part of her identity. She couldn't imagine doing anything else. Being a cop was a link with her past, it was her justification for living. Julie couldn't understand. She thought Jessie should be able to change. There had been no way Jessie could explain it to her. And now, after all the dust had settled, after they had finally found ground where they could meet, could talk, could deal with each other again, this had happened.

Such a contrast between Diana and Julie, and yet she had loved them both. She blinked at that realization. She and Diana had never talked about love. Diana always insisted on the here and now. Clearly Jessie was just someone to fill the time until whoever Diana really wanted was available. Until Diana was gone, Jessie never even thought about whether she loved her. Then when time went by and it was clear she wasn't coming back, Jessie began to realize she missed Diana. That passionate willful self-confident woman who would simply appear in town and sweep Jessie off her feet. She always had such great timing, never frequently enough to disrupt Jessie's life and never so long between that Jessie felt like she wasn't coming back. Until she didn't.

Jessie folded her arms up and over her head. All the times and ways she had ever wondered if she would run into Diana again, this was not the way. Whatever had she missed all those days with Diana? Surely there was something. And now, she knew what she had to do. She just wasn't sure how much she wanted to do it. And there was the small matter of how.

"What are you thinking?" Julie asked.

Jessie turned toward her. She hadn't even felt Julie wake up and turn over. "I think," she said with slow consideration, "today might be a good day for you to ask Diana about her papa."

"Oh, really?" Julie got out of bed. "After her rudeness last night? She's more likely to bite my head off." She went into the bathroom, leaving Jessie to think some more.

"No, I think she'll be conciliatory," Jessie said when Julie came out.

"You sure about that?" Julie's tone was one of disbelief.

"Yes. She really doesn't want you to be scared of her."

"She told you this?"

Jessie got out of bed. "No, I overheard it. She came upstairs when I was in the john. I decided it wasn't a good time to come out, so I waited. She and Margaret were talking in the kitchen."

"Wondered what took you so long. Began to think you fell in. Almost came looking for you."

"I'm so glad you didn't. Ever notice how women like to talk in the kitchen?"

"I've noticed."

"They talked for quite a while. Then Margaret finally went to bed. Diana went out on the deck. I didn't get the idea she had a good day. Something happened to Waldo's plane."

"What?"

Jessie shook her head. "They didn't say, but she's real upset. I guess it was something bad."

"Hmm." Julie thought about it. "Maybe Margaret will say something."

"Margaret doesn't strike me as the type to talk much."

"Margaret thinks Diana walks on water, would do anything for her. The only time her face comes alive is when she talks about Diana." She cocked her head and looked at Jessie. "Did you do something to hurt Diana?"

"Me? Not hardly," Jessie answered in bewilderment. *More like she hurt me.*

Julie shook her head in puzzlement. "Can't figure out why she doesn't like you."

"Cops sometimes get that reaction," Jessie pointed out. "After all, if I can, I'm the one who's going to arrest and take them to jail."

Julie shook her head. "I don't know. It seems to me that would come with the territory. Margaret seems like too much of a realist to hold that against you. No, I think there's something else."

***

Diana was the last one up again and she looked like she had a bad night. Jessie noted the concern on Margaret's face as she handed Diana her morning coffee, which made her wonder about their relationship. Diana had mentioned Margaret had changed her diapers, had been her nanny. That didn't seem like what was expected of a bodyguard.

"Good morning," Diana greeted them as she sat down at the table. "I had some of your cake last night, Julie. It was very good."

Julie gave an uneasy laugh, glancing at Jessie. Jessie smiled encouragingly. "Thank you."

"Julie bakes when she's upset," Jessie supplied.

"Oh." Diana nodded. "Well, I'm sorry you were upset, but I can't complain about the cake." She sipped her coffee. "You know, Waldo was being transported yesterday."

Jessie tensed but managed to stay leaned back in her chair. However Diana explained it, it would be telling. She nodded.

"Something happened. I still don't know what, may never know, but anyway, the plane went down. No survivors."

"Search parties?" Jessie asked casually. She wondered where they had been heading.

"It was over international waters," Diana said. "I don't expect anything will be found."

"Should I say we're sorry?"

Diana looked up at her with some of her old cynical amusement. "Not if you want to be believed. Waldo is no great loss to anyone, and

I imagine many people will sleep easier." She frowned and her face held more than a trace of sadness. "But the pilot was an old friend of mine."

"We're sorry to hear that part," Julie said with compassion. "It's always a shock when something like that happens unexpectedly."

"Any idea of the cause?" Jessie asked, not looking at Diana directly. She didn't miss the dirty look Julie gave her.

"No. We may never know."

The shock had worn off Diana, that was what made her rude the night before, Jessie realized. Why hadn't she recognized it? Now Diana was getting her footing again and an opportunity had passed. "So what now?" she mused without realizing she had said it aloud.

Diana looked at her, evidently taking it as a question directed at her. "We wait."

Jessie tilted her head. She hadn't expected an answer. "For?"

Diana shrugged and got up. Jessie took it that the conversation was over. Diana went and said something to Margaret and then she disappeared downstairs.

Margaret cleared the table. "You ask too many questions," she said flatly, looking at Jessie.

Jessie drank her coffee and decided Julie was right: Margaret didn't like her.

She thought about it as she wandered around the house. If Margaret had always been there, then she had to know about Jessie and Diana's relationship. She hadn't been along—at least Jessie had never seen her and she didn't think she had been that blind. So Diana had been off by herself when she came to Lexington. Business? Or just pleasure? She never knew when Diana came into town, she usually knew only when Diana left. And she was always alone. Rented cars. She never had any idea where Diana had come from or where she was going. She had said business trips brought her into the area and Jessie hadn't questioned. Damn, she was stupid. Or trusting. Maybe a mixture.

She went down to the exercise room. She needed to start moving again or she'd stiffen up too much. And she always did her best thinking when she ran. She just had too many questions. They were in a safe house, there were communications. They would be released, unhurt. What was Diana waiting on?

She wasn't physically ready for a run, she discovered almost immediately. She slowed it down to a walk, had been walking about fifteen minutes, when Diana came in.

Diana stopped at the door when she saw Jessie and then came in. Ignoring Jessie, she chose the elliptical for her exercise, and for a few minutes, they worked out side by side.

"Margaret says I ask too many questions," Jessie ventured finally.

"Probably right."

"Doesn't seem to bother you." Diana made no response. "I am sorry about your friend." Diana still made no response. "You always were a good listener, better than a talker," Jessie went on. "I didn't realize until afterward how much you knew about me and how little I knew about you. You knew about my dad, you knew about my sister, you knew about Julie. You knew I liked sweet wines, you knew I liked Chinese better than Mexican food. You knew I exercised regularly, I worried about my weight, I was afraid of dying alone."

The more she thought about it, the angrier she became. She stopped the treadmill, used the towel to wipe her face, came around and stood beside Diana. "Why didn't you talk to me? Was it because you were there on Family business? Was I some little toy you used to while away the time while you waited for something to happen?"

Diana said nothing, her expression closed and noncommittal, but her eyes met Jessie's with some defiance.

"Damn it!" Jessie turned the elliptical off, caught Diana by the arm and jerked her off, catching her when she lost her balance and stumbled against her. "Answer me!"

Diana didn't try to pull away. "Why?"

"Because you owe me that."

"I don't owe you anything," Diana retorted. "You were the one who used me while you were waiting, but you were pretty clear on that. I knew it and I still came back. So why should I bother talking with you? It would have been just a waste of breath." She jerked her arm out of Jessie's grip.

"I would have listened," Jessie protested.

"Yeah." Diana grabbed her towel off the treadmill. "I saw evidence of that. You listened, you just didn't hear."

"What's that supposed to mean?"

Diana stepped back, took a deep breath. "You were in the 'here and now,' nothing but the present mattered."

"That was what you said you wanted."

"So I did." Diana wiped her face. For an instant, she looked like she might crumple and Jessie reached out for her. "No." Diana stepped back. "I've got enough going on in my life right now, I don't need you as another complication." She looked around the room as if she wanted to escape. "I'm going upstairs. I'm going to take a shower and then I'm going to the library. Just leave me alone."

"Diana."

"No," Diana said firmly. "Just—just stay out of my way."

Jessie watched her go up the stairs, puzzled and upset. She shouldn't have gotten angry. She leaned over, her arms on the treadmill. There was too much going on that she didn't understand. She straightened up and got back on the treadmill. She'd deal with everything else later.

As soon as she entered the kitchen, Julie grabbed her arm and dragged her out onto the deck. "What happened downstairs?"

Jessie shook her head. "Nothing." Julie glanced up and down the deck and through the glass to the interior rooms. "Why?"

"Diana came running up here, went upstairs, slamming doors all the way. Then when she came down and went into the library, Margaret went in, came back out in about ten minutes, looking like a thundercloud. She was working in the kitchen but I heard her muttering something about 'stupid dumkopf.' I just figured you had said something or done something downstairs."

"Thanks a lot."

"Well, I don't know what happened, but if I were you, I'd stay out of Margaret's way for a while."

"Great, why don't I just retreat to the bedroom and hide from everybody?"

Julie gave her that examining look she had when Jessie was trying to hide something. "What happened?"

Jessie shook her head. "I brought up that when she and I were together, I talked a lot about me, and she didn't talk about herself. I wanted to know why. She said something to the effect that I listened but didn't hear."

"You do that occasionally," Julie observed dryly.

An old unresolved issue with Julie, Jessie admitted. She just didn't expect it to come up with Diana. "So what am I supposed to do?" she asked.

"Well, I think you might be right." Jessie looked up in surprise. "I think we need to find out about her papa. Did she ever say much about him?"

"Just that she was very fond of him, they lived together. She seemed respectful, but, I don't know, cautious. Mixed impression, I guess."

"I get the same from Margaret. She's very respectful of him around Diana, but she doesn't like him." Jessie looked up in surprise. "Dislike is to put it mildly. But she's really afraid of him too."

"Can you do it?" Jessie asked. "Ask her about her papa? She'll be upset and that might set Margaret off."

"I don't think Margaret sees us the same. I think she might see me as trying to help." She gave a half-smile to Jessie. "You are the black sheep in the lot. Isn't this what you do with good cop, bad cop?"

"Yeah, but usually it's an act. I'm just not sure what I did to be the bad cop."

CHAPTER TWENTY

Diana avoided everyone through lunch. She went over and over the plans she had made to get Waldo out. She had always been a meticulous planner, down to the finest detail. That was how she survived. This was not the time in her life for things to come unraveled. She reflected that in the past week, so many things had gone awry. All because of Waldo. She had only agreed to transport him after Margaret had told her what she had heard. Papa had been cooperative by asking her to do this for him, and her reluctance had convinced him she was doing him a favor. Now, Waldo was gone, and she had no regrets about that part, but he'd left her one hell of a mess to deal with.

She wasn't going to get back to see papa, to say goodbye. There were still things she had wanted to say, but they would go unsaid. If she only had some indication of a time line. The first unknown.

There was the matter of the plane. Would there be any way to tell if it had been sabotage? No black box, deep waters. If they had to go, that was probably the best way; if it weren't only for the nagging suspicion about Helen. Another unknown.

She would have liked to have met with the lawyer face-to-face. There were always nuances of body language she liked to see. So much was lost on the phone, even on the video phone. Even if everything was pretty much set up, another meeting would have made her more comfortable. She didn't like going into something blind and she felt like that was what she was doing.

And then last of all, there was Jessie. Diana had really wanted Waldo out of the way so she didn't have to deal with Jessie. Now she had not only Jessie but Julie under her roof, in her safe house. How ironic, now that Jessie and Julie weren't a couple. Wonder how that went across the years? She didn't want to know. It was difficult enough as it was.

Damn, this is not going the way I want it to go.

Her brooding was interrupted by a soft tentative knock at the door. Diana gave serious consideration whether she wanted to be interrupted. It had to be Julie and she would be easy enough to scare away. On the other hand, Julie was Papa's doctor. Such a source of information should not be ignored.

"Come on in, Julie."

The door opened and Julie slipped in with all the appearance of coming into the lion's den. "Can we talk?"

"Of course." Diana invited her in with a wave of her hand, indicated a chair for her to sit.

"How did you know it was me?"

"Process of elimination. Margaret wouldn't knock; Jessie wouldn't bother me." She sat down in the chair across from Julie. "What did you want to talk about?"

Julie was shaking, Diana could see, and she had a hard time looking at Diana.

"Julie," Diana said slowly in an effort to put Julie at ease. "I'm not going to bite. I really am a nice person most of the time. It's just that some people are not nice and those people I tend to speak to in their own language. There's no reason for me to be 'not nice' to you."

Julie uncertainly nodded but Diana could see that she wasn't reassured. "You said you wanted to talk. Why don't you tell me what you wanted to talk about?"

"Your father." Julie looked at her, glanced away, and looked back, as if trying to gauge her reaction.

Diana stiffened. Her first reaction was to say nothing; she never talked about her papa, especially to someone outside the family. Then she reconsidered. She needed information, this was Papa's doctor. Julie had come to her. It wasn't like she was asking for information. Years of secrecy warred with a need to know before she finally gave in. "What about Papa?"

Julie sighed in relief and she settled back into the chair. She stopped shaking as the roles changed from reluctant guest and hostess over to doctor and patient's family. "You said earlier he came to see me, and you know if he came to see me, he was very sick."

Diana nodded. "Yes, I knew."

"It's always a strain on the family when illness gets to this stage. There are so many variables we don't know. I'm more than a little handicapped because I don't know who your papa is. I don't have any patients with your name."

Diana considered this. "I have to ask you this, Julie. If we talk about this, are you going to tell Jessie?"

Julie took a deep breath. "I won't if you ask me not to."

"Puts you in a conflict, doesn't it?"

Julie nodded. "Some, but I'll deal with it."

Diana thought about it a moment. Papa had described Julie well. He always did have an eye for the ladies. Attractive. Charming. Told it like it was, was what he said. Didn't sugarcoat when there was bad news. It hadn't made sense then, when he was trying to imply that his Wednesday afternoons were trysts. Now it made sense.

"You know, Papa didn't tell anyone he was sick," Diana said slowly. "I found out by accident. So when he was going somewhere somewhat regularly for whatever, he made up a cover story. He said he had a new girlfriend." She watched to see Julie's reaction. "Her name was Julie."

Julie's jaw dropped a little and her eyes got big. She even flushed a little, a charming sight, Diana thought.

"He was very complimentary, just dropped little things here and there, enough to be plausible. He'd pick something out, a piece of jewelry, some little gift, and ask me if I thought Julie would like it. He always came home looking better, but tired also."

"Blood transfusions," Julie said faintly.

Diana nodded. "He probably didn't use his name. Considering what I've learned about you the past couple of days, you probably wouldn't have recognized it anyway."

"But Jessie would," Julie surmised.

Diana nodded. She finally got up and went over to the bookcase. She took down the picture of colorful hot air balloons against clear blue skies and turned it over. "We went to the balloon festival in Albuquerque a couple of years ago," she said as she slipped out the hidden picture. "He never wanted to be photographed so I have very few pictures of him. I coaxed a couple out of him that trip, but then when we got back he destroyed them all. He didn't find this one." She pulled it out and brought it over to Julie.

Julie took the picture of Diana and her father, the balloons in the background. They had their arms around each other's waists, both were laughing. She examined it carefully. "When was this taken?"

"We went about six years ago, then again maybe two years ago. I can't remember. He was just beginning to get sick."

Julie nodded as she tapped the picture. "I remember him. Very charming, soft-spoken. Distinguished looking." She looked up at Diana and handed the picture back. "You don't look much like him."

"No. He always told me I look very much like my mother."

Julie nodded. "He used the name Petree." Diana sat down again, the picture still in her hand. "It's not good news, Diana."

"He's dying," Diana said slowly, maybe so she didn't have to hear Julie say the words.

Julie nodded in confirmation.

Diana closed her eyes for a moment, took a deep breath. "I knew that. He's changed, personality wise as well as physically. He's been wrapping up details. I've watched him get frailer and frailer." She shook her head. "We always think our parents are going to last forever, and then one day we turn around and they are old and frail and we have to take care of them."

"Your papa didn't want anyone to know, not even his family. In fact, he said he didn't have any family."

"I'm not surprised. His death..." She thought about what it would mean. "He has a position that many are going to try to fill," she said finally, carefully, even realizing Julie didn't understand. "What does he have?" she asked after a few minutes.

Julie looked uncomfortable.

"You can't say." Julie shook her head. "You mentioned blood transfusions. You're a hematologist. Leukemia?" Julie made no response, her eyes filled with compassion. "I guess it really doesn't matter. The fact is he's dying, and there's nothing I can do."

Diana got to her feet, paced around the room as Julie watched her. Diana had managed a fair amount of research on the computer with the details she knew. If she could just get them narrowed down. She slowly walked over to stand over Julie. "I know you can't say much but maybe you can confirm or deny." Julie made no response. "He's getting weaker and weaker, although he hides it. He has a nurse now, almost constantly. Is this something that he's just likely to die in his sleep? If it's with the blood, is it just going to be heart failure?" Julie raised her head a little. "Do you think it will be soon?" Julie looked away and ducked her head.

Diana leaned over her, her hands on the chair arms, pinning Julie in. "Julie," she said quietly. "I'm not asking you to violate a confidence." She took a breath, reconsidered. "Yes, I am. I'm asking because I need to know. When Papa dies, there's going to be a big reaction in certain circles. It may have already started. That's one of the reasons I'm sitting here in a safe house and can't take you or Jessie back yet. Is this going to happen soon?" Julie said nothing but her scared look was back. "I'm not threatening you," Diana went on in an effort to reassure her, not frighten her. "But the information would be very helpful for me, and in turn, for you and Jessie." Julie made no response; indeed, closed her eyes.

Reluctantly, Diana straightened up. She couldn't browbeat Julie into telling her what Julie felt she couldn't ethically reveal. If Diana were more like her papa, she probably could, but she had resisted for years taking on those traits and she couldn't change at this late date. She walked away, realizing she didn't know any more now than what she had before.

"Diana, who is your father?" Julie asked behind her.

Diana shook her head. "Let Jessie tell you. She can give you a more accurate picture of him than I can. He's my papa, that's the only way I can see him."

The room was silent.

"He's lasted longer than I thought he would," Julie said in a very quiet voice. "I really thought he'd be gone by now. I think he could leave any time."

"Thank you," Diana said without turning around. She felt rather than heard Julie come up behind her, lay her hand on Diana's back.

"Are you all right?"

"Yes." *No, but I have to be.* "Go on out, Julie. Just leave me alone." She heard Julie walk away. "Thank you for the information, Julie." Then she heard the door close.

Even less time than what I thought, she mused as she watched the sunlight and shade on the trees below. *This is going to get tricky.* She needed to talk to Margaret.

When she opened the library door, the first thing she saw was Julie and Jessie standing there, talking. Jessie had the picture in her hand and she looked up guiltily as Diana came out of the library.

"Your father is Czar Randalson?" she said in disbelief as if she expected Diana to deny it.

"Yes."

"Czar Randalson doesn't have a daughter," Jessie protested. "He has wives, he has girlfriends, he has mistresses, he has whores, he has junkies, he has—" She broke off, shaking her head. "He doesn't have a daughter."

"He has a daughter," Diana corrected. "He had one wife, only one lawful wife, and she died. He never took another. He has a daughter."

Jessie still shook her head, refusing to believe. "No, you can't be."

Diana nodded. "Yes, I can. Yes, I am." From the corner of her eye, she saw Margaret come in from the kitchen.

Jessie looked back down at the picture. Diana was sure she knew the significance. She had purchased a necklace for Jessie there, the only gift she had ever given Jessie.

"No wonder you acted like you could take anyone you wanted," Jessie said in a low voice. "No wonder it was so casual, just when you were in the mood. No wonder it was always on your terms. Just like your father."

"Jessie, it wasn't like that."

"Then what was it like?" Jessie demanded, advancing on Diana, shaking off Julie's arm. "Tell me what it was like for you when I was so glad to hear from you, to know I had you for a few days. Tell me what it was like when I came to you, wanting you, trusting you." She forgot Diana's warning about Margaret, or didn't consider it when she took hold of Diana, so she was totally unprepared for Margaret's hands on her when Margaret jerked her away from Diana and slammed her against the wall.

"No!" Diana ordered as she stepped in between the two women. She felt someone at her back and realized that while she was pushing back Margaret, Julie was preventing Jessie from coming back at them. "It's all right, Margaret," Diana assured her bodyguard and hoped she was right. "Just a little knowledge."

"A little knowledge," Jessie spat out over Julie's shoulder. "A little knowledge would have been you had another girlfriend. A little knowledge would have been you were married." Jessie was shaking, but letting Julie keep her back against the wall. "Being the daughter of one of America's regional crime lords is not a little knowledge."

Diana turned around, dismayed to see the anger, revulsion on Jessie's face. "Neither was you being a cop," she said calmly, surprised at her relief it was out in the open now.

"I never hid that. It just didn't get said. You assumed I worked at the horse farms because we never talked about our jobs. However, we did talk about our families!"

Julie still stood between them, she still wouldn't let Jessie away from the wall as she looked over her shoulder at Diana and Margaret.

"Yes, we did," Diana agreed quietly.

"And you never said—" Jessie broke off, unable to even say anything else. "You never—All those times—" She closed her eyes, breathing hard, still angry. "Damn you, Diana. Damn, I wish I'd never laid eyes on you!" She turned away then, hiding against the wall as Julie put her arm around her.

Diana took a step forward only to be stopped twice, once by Margaret's hand on her arm, the second by the look Julie gave her as she protectively stood in front of Jessie. She gave a last lingering look at Jessie and turned toward Margaret. *Too much, too much happening all at once. Maybe jail would be peaceful and quiet.*

"Come away." Margaret drew Diana out of the room. "Come out into the kitchen."

***

Jessie reeled from the shock, unable to fully comprehend, and yet it explained so many things. No wonder Waldo was cautious; no wonder Margaret was a bodyguard; no wonder Diana needed a safe house. No wonder. She just couldn't believe it. She slid down the wall, crumpled into Julie's arms.

The worst of it was remembering how open she had been with Diana, how she had trusted her. She had talked about her father, talked about Nicki, talked about Julie, she had laid bare her emotional vulnerabilities, and Diana had sat there and listened. Oh, God, she had even *wanted* her, *desired* her, and now it was like—like something sordid and revolting.

"Calm down, Jessie," Julie soothed as she stroked Jessie's hair.

Jessie shook her head. "You don't know, you don't understand."

"I understand you've had a shock," Julie spoke quietly, soothingly. "I understand you're upset."

"Upset!" Jessie raised up to stare into Julie's face. "Upset? I'm upset when I can't find my car keys, I'm upset when I spill the milk, I'm upset when I'm overdrawn at the bank. This is way past upset."

"Yes, I understand," Julie repeated.

"No, you don't." Jessie leaned back against the wall. "You don't understand about Czar Randalson. He's had his fingers in every piece of criminal pie in the entire region. Drugs, gambling, prostitution, trafficking. You name it, and he's into it or behind it or bringing it here." She shuddered at her contact with it. "We've been after him for years but he's always had slippery lawyers, or scared off witnesses, or paid people off. We've been thwarted at every turn."

"But that's him," Julie pointed out carefully. "We're dealing with Diana."

"It's the same thing!" Jessie got to her feet, shaking in her emotion of mixed rage and newfound fear and even shame of her association with Diana.

"No, it's not." Julie got to her feet and still faced Jessie.

"Are you defending her?" Jessie challenged her.

Julie looked confused. "Not exactly," she said. "But yes. For as scary as Diana is, she is the one who took us out of Waldo's clutches. She didn't have to, not if she's as terrible as you say her father is."

"We take a dim view of cop killers," Jessie said menacingly.

"He wasn't going to kill you, Jessie," Julie said slowly. "And I'm not a cop."

"*What!*" Jessie gasped, unable to believe that Julie knew. Diana had said she wouldn't tell her. Did she lie about that too?

"They threatened me with a lot of things, but they assured me they weren't going to kill you." Julie swallowed, paused in an effort to regain some composure. "I think Diana can be scary as hell when she wants to be, but I don't think it's in her nature. She came in and got us both away, not knowing for sure if she could cross her family. Even now we're sitting in her safe house, hiding from everyone, your people and her people. That doesn't sound like her father to me."

Jessie refused to even think there might be something good. "We're just bargaining chips!"

"For what? With whom?"

Jessie made no response. She had no answer.

Julie went to Jessie and put her arms around her. "Jessie, I know you feel betrayed. I understand that. I would be, too. But I'm not sure Diana's betrayed you. Yes, she didn't tell you, but what would you have done if she had?"

Jessie tried to think but she couldn't, not coherently. "I don't know." She was calmer now, at least if she tried to think of Diana and not her father. Right now, she didn't want to think. If she thought, all she could see in her mind's eye was Diana, bigger than life.

"Come, sit down," Julie coaxed. "You need to absorb this." She looked. This room didn't have many chairs, which meant the library or the kitchen. Margaret decided for her when she came to the door.

"You need to come in here." It didn't sound like an invitation.

Jessie shook her head. Margaret's attitude was probably going to change now. She'd really screwed it up this time, but maybe it was just as well. It would be hard to be treated as a "guest" with the way she was feeling about Diana.

"Come sit down," Margaret ordered, pointing to the chair at the table. There were already two mugs waiting for them. "I brewed tea, lemon balm, soothing. Relaxing. You need it."

Jessie sat down, not sure about Margaret's changed attitude. Maybe she needed to check the tea for poison. No, the way she felt right now, she'd drink it.

"You too," Margaret pointed to Julie. "Have some tea."

"Where's Diana?" Julie asked.

"She had some things to take care of." Margaret looked at Jessie but she spoke to Julie. "She tells me her papa is dying." When Julie made no response, Margaret turned to look at her. Jessie even turned to see what her answer would be.

"Is that true?" Jessie demanded.

Julie opened her mouth but said nothing, shook her head. "I can't say," she said finally.

"That was not a question. Diana said it was so." Margaret leaned back in the chair. She didn't look displeased. "That means changes."

"Yeah." Jessie sat up, still upset, but the ramifications sank in. She looked at Julie, back at Margaret.

"I know you are upset with Diana," Margaret said slowly. "That's how I felt when I found out about you." Jessie bristled. "I thought you would get my Diana killed." She looked Jessie over. "Now, how many years later, I still have the same fear."

"Look," Jessie protested. "I never put Diana in danger."

Margaret stared at Jessie for several minutes. "You listen," she said finally. "You don't hear."

"Damn it!" Jessie shot to her feet, glancing at Julie. Diana had told her the same thing. Julie had even said the same thing. She was tired of hearing this. "What's that supposed to mean?" She glared at Margaret. "If you've got something against me, then spit it out in plain language. Maybe I'll hear it then."

Margaret didn't even look perturbed. "Against you? I could write a book, but I'll start with the simple things so even a smart cop like you can understand." Her sarcasm was scathing.

Jessie drew back, surprised at the depth of Margaret's animosity. Julie caught her by the arm. Margaret saw and didn't even blink. "You got a warning that your undercover role was blown, a big risk to

Diana. And did you listen? No, you knew better. So how did you like the months in the hospital? Surgeries?" She sneered. "Maybe you still have nightmares from it. Maybe you see the whole thing again. Maybe even today, you wake up in a cold sweat."

Jessie fell back into the chair, unable to comprehend what Margaret was saying. "Diana?" Julie looked from Margaret to Jessie, but Jessie couldn't drag her eyes from Margaret's face. She shook her head. "No," she said in disbelief.

Margaret watched her. "She told you point-blank, 'Don't go. You've been made.' Did you listen?" Margaret shook her head. "No. But Diana knew. She knew you. So she goes to see for herself. She loses all common sense when you're involved."

Jessie was stunned into silence.

"I couldn't believe it when she disappeared that day," Margaret went on. "She'd never done anything in the field before, a babe in the woods. And hit men like Kaplan never leave witnesses, no matter who they are." She continued to glare at Jessie. "As soon as I heard, Kaplan killed, female cop in the hospital, oh, I knew, I knew then where she was." She glared at Jessie. "Such a risk, she didn't even know how big a risk. For you."

Jessie reached out to take hold of the table. She had to hold on to something solid. All of it came flooding back, the informant, the familiarity, the little things she couldn't put together. She had had the idea it might be Diana. She found nothing to prove it. Or disprove it. "Margaret, I didn't know. Really."

Margaret folded her arms. "She warned you."

"I didn't know where it came from."

"You were *warned*?" Julie burst out as she finally realized what they were talking about.

"It was an anonymous tip," Jessie said as an aside to Julie.

"Did you really expect a name and address?" Margaret mocked.

Jessie searched Margaret's face. She had to be lying, but how could she be? Who knew? "Then she was the one who tracked down the inside leak, Henderson, the dirty cop," Jessie said suddenly. "How did she do that? What did she know?"

"My Diana, she knows a lot," Margaret started.

"Margaret!" A cold, emotionless, hard voice from the hallway door. They all jerked around to see Diana there, an angry Diana who fastened her equally cold gaze on Margaret. "You talk too much."

"Maybe you don't talk enough."

"Is that true?" Jessie stood up, just as much to deflect Diana's anger from Margaret as to elicit more information. "Were you the woman in the clearing?"

Diana never took her gaze from Margaret, who didn't move. "Yes."

"But why didn't you tell me?"

"Why should I?"

"I would have believed you."

"You don't think I was taking enough of a risk that I should reveal my identity to someone in a department where there was a leak?" She finally looked at Jessie. "God, Jessie, get real."

"I wouldn't have identified you."

"Well, I figured what you didn't know you couldn't say." She looked back at Margaret. "Not like some other people."

Margaret braced herself. Diana looked over at Julie, who looked from one of them to the next, completely confused.

There was a moment's silence when no one spoke and they all stood looking at each other, waiting. Then Jessie managed to put things together even more. "You used my gun."

"I didn't carry a weapon then. It wasn't until after that I thought it might be more prudent on occasion." Diana came on into the kitchen, walked by Margaret and opened the cabinet for a glass, opened the refrigerator for the pitcher of iced tea. "A lot of things changed after that."

"You killed him," Jessie repeated, still trying to put the final pieces together.

"Considering he was standing right over us, I didn't have many options." She took a drink, turned around to face Jessie. "You think I had any other choice?"

Jessie shook her head. "I—I couldn't remember, just him asking what you were doing there."

"Yeah, he was a little surprised." Diana drank the tea. "Then you were bleeding like mad, your backup wasn't anywhere close. Thought Life Flight would never get there. I was never so happy to hear sirens in my life, before or since."

"How'd you get away?"

"First one there must have been a rookie. Put him on you so you didn't bleed to death. Told him I'd direct the others in. Pointed them in and walked into the trees. Guess I got lost in the confusion."

Jessie shook her head. Every time she thought she knew everything, something else was revealed. "You could have gotten killed."

"It never occurred to me." Diana looked directly at Jessie. "Remember, I have tunnel vision." Margaret made some unintelligible sound.

"Why did you do it?" Jessie asked in bewilderment.

Margaret made some sound of disgust as she got up and even Julie looked at Jessie in amazement.

"And what was I supposed to do?" Diana asked. "Let them kill you?"

"You could have—" Jessie started her stock answer of calling the police but stopped before she finished it. Diana raised her eyebrows and shook her head. Jessie collapsed back into the chair. "I didn't know," she said weakly. She buried her face in her hands.

Her mind was a whirl, she could not take it all in. First, Diana's father. She still couldn't get a grip on it, like someone beloved turned into a monster right in front of her. Then right on the heels of that, the monster turned into the guardian angel. How was she supposed to cope?

She listened to Margaret and Diana talk in a low voice, felt Julie's hand on her back. She stood up. "I need to—" To what? she thought. The four of them were in this house. There was no place to get away.

"The exercise room," Julie suggested.

"Yes," Jessie agreed. "That would be good." Julie started to get up and she laid her hand on Julie's shoulder. "No, I need to be alone. For a while, work this out. I'll be all right."

**

The treadmill was not the same as an open run, and that was what she wanted. She wanted to run away. When she went into the closet, she found the gloves, and she glanced at the punching bag. That was something she usually didn't do, but today, maybe.

Hitting something felt great even if it hurt, even if she wasn't clear what or who she was hitting. Czar Randalson's daughter was a nice target. Why hadn't she mentioned that little fact? Why had she hidden it? Well, duh, that was a stupid question. *Hey, lover, even though you're a cop, how would you like to meet my dad, the kingpin of crime?* That would go over well.

Jessie shivered. She could have lost her life. She could have lost her career. Just being remotely associated with anyone from the mob would have cast shadows on her reputation. After just two more punches, she clung to the punching bag, leaning her head against it, smelling the leather, her sweat, a faint fragrance of Diana's perfume.

She wanted to cry. She'd almost died, she would have without Diana there. How was she supposed to deal with that?

She sat down and cried, not even sure why she was crying. What had she lost? Diana had been gone for a long time, it wasn't like they were still lovers. Her career was intact. Diana had saved her not once like she thought, but twice. How could she be angry with her? Why did she feel like she had lost something precious, that something she remembered as so good never was?

She went upstairs, showered and changed clothes. She was clearer in mind now, almost crystal clear. She came back downstairs to find everyone in the kitchen.

"We need to talk," she was able to say, calmly fastening her gaze on Diana.

"All right."

Margaret half turned, but Jessie forestalled her. "I'm not angry. I'm not going to do anything rash. I just want some answers. I think I deserve that."

Margaret and Diana exchanged glances and Diana nodded. Jessie looked at Julie and she appreciated her concern more than she could say. "I'm all right," she told her. "I just need to do this."

When Diana started for the kitchen door, Jessie stopped her. "Can we go out front? I know Margaret's going to watch, but I'd rather her not be hanging over my shoulder."

Diana changed course and went through the living room and out the front door. Jessie followed, pausing at the bar long enough to pull out a bottle of Seagram's and two shot glasses. She had the feeling they might be needing it.

Diana sat down on the top step and Jessie came down to sit beside her. "I'm not going off the deck," she protested in anticipation of Diana's warning.

"I know."

They sat there, side by side, looking down the drive through the trees in silence for a few minutes. Neither one spoke and the sounds of nature were their only background.

"Why didn't you tell me?" Jessie asked finally, never looking at Diana.

Diana shrugged. "About what? My Family? At first, it didn't matter. Brief encounters. By the time it mattered, it was a little late to say anything. I mean, what was I supposed to do? 'Hi, Pops, here's my lover, and oh, by the way, she's a cop.' That would have gone over big."

Jessie didn't turn to look at her. She couldn't argue. As she had figured this out downstairs, she had envisioned an almost identical introduction.

"So that was really you who called in the tip and then at the clearing?" she asked without turning around. She could deal with all this information if she didn't have to see Diana, watch her formulate an answer, see whatever emotion she was hiding. She didn't want to see if she was lying.

Diana picked up the bottle and broke the seal. She filled both shot glasses. "Yep," she answered like she was confirming a mail delivery.

"You saved my life."

"Someone had to. You didn't have anyone else at your back." She handed Jessie one of the glasses.

Jessie knocked it back. She should have had one of these earlier instead of the tea. She swallowed, examined the glass. "The follow-up calls, you stayed around to check."

"I needed to cover some tracks, and I wanted to know you survived."

"Wasn't that a little dangerous?"

"As compared to what?" Diana drank her shot a little slower. "That was a piece of cake. Tracking down Henderson was the dangerous part. There, I went poking into areas I really didn't have any business in."

So many questions, Jessie thought. "Do I want even want to know what your business was?"

Diana chuckled. "The dull part, I kept Papa's books."

Simple enough, into nothing and knowing everything. "So how'd you find out I'd been set up?"

Diana looked down at the steps. "Papa wanted me to attend this party. I didn't want to go. He did some arm twisting. I kept wandering around the fringes trying to escape. Overheard Sticks and Monahan talking about this guy they brought in from out of town, setting up this Lexington female cop. It pinged my radar. I started snooping around, figured out it had to be you."

Jessie thought about it, the clearing, the bad feeling she'd had coming through the trees. It would have been a fatal shot if she hadn't turned around; wouldn't have turned around except someone, Diana she now knew, had yelled at her. She calmed the flutter of panic in the pit of her stomach. "You could have gotten killed yourself."

"Never occurred to me. Not until about six months later, then I had a panic attack."

"Yeah," Jessie agreed, "sometimes it's like that. You're not scared until everything's over."

Jessie looked out over the trees, trying to incorporate all this new information. Diana was the daughter of Czar Randalson, she kept his books, but she had tipped Jessie about a deal destined to go sour, had been there to save Jessie's life, had exposed a leak in the department and then disappeared again. Jessie rubbed her temples. "Tell me something."

"If I can."

"When we first met, there at the Bungalow, were you there on Family business?"

Diana hesitated. "No, not exactly. Papa was using me but I didn't know that, not until later. He asked me to do him a favor, just go and sit in on this trial that was going on. Seemed harmless enough."

"That was Waldo's first trial."

"Figured that part out later. My being there, just being there was a message to him from Papa that he wasn't forgotten, that he wasn't in any trouble."

"I didn't see you."

"Were you looking? We didn't know each other until afterward. I'd never sat in on a trial before, thought it was interesting. God, was I naïve."

"And later, when you kept coming back. You always said you were on business, were in the area. Was that so?"

"Yeah. My business. I started up a courier service, very select clients, very lucrative." She smiled at the memory as she set the glass down on the step.

"Drugs?" Jessie asked tentatively.

"Drugs might have been safer," Diana said with a rueful laugh. "I transported gemstones. Sometimes when I stopped in Lexington I may have had a couple hundred thousand dollars worth of gems either on me to deliver or I'd already delivered."

"Jesus!" Jessie shot up, her anger forgotten. "Are you kidding me? Stones are untraceable. You could have gotten robbed."

"Did once. Went crying home to Papa. The stones were returned the next day. The insurance companies loved me. I looked like a college girl out on a lark, vacationing, going on a shopping spree. Except for that once, which I really think in hindsight was just a fluke. They had no idea what was in my jacket when they lifted it, just an expensive jacket."

Jessie shook her head. Diana's revelations were just one shock after another. "What made you get into that?"

"Met someone who needed some gems transported. I'm not even sure if that first one was legal. I mentioned I was going to Atlanta, he asked if I'd deliver a package. It seemed like a fun thing to do, harmless, so I said yes. When I delivered it, the jeweler asked was I taking on any other clients. He thought I was in business, so I said yes, and started up the service. Just sorta fell into it. Used the money to put myself through college. By that time I knew about Papa's money. Didn't want it. This paid lots of money for very little work, and I got to see different parts of the country."

"I never would have dreamed," Jessie said slowly.

"Well, that was part of it too. I never looked like one would expect. Still waters and all that. Remember?"

"Yeah, I remember." For the first time, she turned and looked at Diana. She still felt the rush of anger at Diana's deceptions, but she didn't see Diana as a monster any more. "What happened to your mother?"

Diana poured herself another shot. "She went into a depression after I was born. Probably postpartum. She committed suicide." She slowly drank.

"I'm sorry."

Diana set the half-drank glass down. "One of the things we had in common: motherless, with great relationships with our dads."

Jessie bristled at the thought of her father being compared with Czar Randalson about anything.

"I'm not stupid or naïve," Diana went on in a low voice before Jessie could protest. "I know what Czar Randalson is. I know he could be a cruel and vicious man. I know he did terrible things, things I turned a blind eye to. But he was my papa, and he loves me as much as your father loved you. And in turn, I love him as much as you loved your father."

If he loved you, why is he leaving you in this position? Jessie wanted to demand but she couldn't say it. All she could think of was the legacy her father had left her, his good name, and how supportive and sympathetic Diana had been when Jessie's father died. And now Diana's father was dying.

"You don't have your father's name."

"He made me take my mother's. I'm not sure Randalson is even the name he was born with. He always talked that my mother's name was a good one for generations, I could be proud of it."

Jessie didn't make any response, unable to say anything positive. She was silent for a few minutes before she spoke. "This is," Jessie started slowly, "really hard for me to take in."

"I understand."

Probably not, Jessie thought, but left it alone.

"Your papa…" Jessie discovered she could not refer to Czar by name, not without anger coming back. "Your papa," she repeated carefully, "when he dies, there will be a lot of changes."

"That's true." Diana sounded noncommittal as she took out her cigarettes.

"Your position will change."

"Yes." Diana lit her cigarette.

"Is that going to be a problem?"

"Could be."

"Do you have a plan?"

"Maybe."

"Can I ask?"

"No." Diana sounded firm. She picked up the rest of the drink. "It took me a little while to figure out how much this could reflect on you and your job," she said after she finished it. "If you don't know, you don't have any conflict. If you do know, I'm afraid there might be some idea of collusion from your peers."

Jessie nodded, surprised Diana had thought of that. She breathed a little easier that Diana had thought of her. But she still needed to think about how she felt. That would come later, when she was home safe, and Julie was home safe, and she didn't have to worry about what might happen next. "How long are we staying here?"

"Until Papa dies," Diana said simply.

"Are you ready for that?" Jessie could ask with some sympathy.

"Yes, I'm ready for it to be over, get things settled. No, I don't want to lose him." Diana drew up her legs, wrapped her arms around her legs. "Always mixed emotions." She rested her forehead on her knees.

"I have to ask one more thing, Diana," she said quietly. "There'll probably be more later, but I just need to know one thing."

"What's that?" Diana didn't raise her head.

"Was I just a toy, something to play with when you felt like it?"

"You were never a toy, Jessie."

Somewhere deep inside, Jessie breathed a sigh of relief. And with that settled, she could move over to Diana, set the bottle on a lower step, and put her arm around Diana's shoulders. "I'm sorry you're losing your papa," she could say with some sincerity.

And I hope Czar Randalson dies soon, and we get through this.

CHAPTER TWENTY-ONE

That night, Jessie dreamed of Diana, old dreams of her Diana, when they were young and together. She was holding her again, wrapped around her, burying her face in soft flesh. She moaned, holding tight, not wanting to leave even though someone was calling her, repeatedly, insistently.

"Jessie, Jessie, you've got to wake up."

She came awake abruptly, looking around, staring unbelieving at the pillow in her arms. She shook her head, shaking off the dream.

"Something's going on," Julie was saying. "You've got to be awake."

Jessie rolled over, still trying to acclimate herself to wakefulness. She sat up, put the pillow down. It was early morning, the room was just barely light. Then she heard it, vehicles, voices.

"Get dressed," she ordered Julie. She was already reaching for her clothes. Damn, she was a fool. Diana had said she had a plan, and with the old man dying, she wouldn't delay.

"What do you think is happening?" Julie asked even as she dressed. "I hated to wake you, you were dreaming."

"Yes." Jessie didn't even want to go there. "How long?"

"Dreaming?"

"No," Jessie rasped, glaring at Julie. "Cars. How many did you hear?"

"Two, then a third one. But there were more voices than three."

"Could you understand what they were saying?"

"Sounded just like greetings, friendly sounding, like old friends greeting."

Just then they heard another car pull up. Listening carefully, Jessie could hear car doors slam, one, two, three. She moved over to the door, tried it. It was locked. She pressed her ear against it.

"God, I hate these early morning things," she heard someone say, an unfamiliar woman's voice.

Jessie went to the windows. They faced away from the parking area, and all she could see was the back end of an SUV, red. She pressed against the glass, trying ineffectually to see around the corner.

"Damn it," she muttered, going back to the door. She tried the doorknob, tried shaking it. It didn't budge. Julie stood off to one side, watching her. "Damn it, damn it, damn it." To know there was something going on, and not being able to do anything. She pressed her ear back to the door. They were probably coming in through the kitchen but where would they meet? The library? And it was right underneath them.

Jessie went over the room, the bathroom, listening at the vents, anything. The house fell silent.

"What do you think is happening?"

"I don't know. Diana said last night she had a plan."

"About?"

"What she was going to do." She searched the room, checking each wall, even the floor to see if any sound traveled. She heard muffled conversation and then it moved away. There had to be a fake door in the library somewhere. Diana had disappeared there or appeared there more than once. She was stupid, she should have checked the bookcases. There had to be something from this room. It was the master bedroom, Diana wouldn't let herself be trapped. She went over the entire length and width of the flooring, stamping.

"Isn't someone going to hear you?" Julie demanded.

"They're too busy elsewhere." She moved the bed, the dresser, gritting her teeth and ignoring the pain until finally Julie helped her. She finally sat down on the corner of the moved bed, exhausted. She had to think. She was surely missing something. A sharp knock on the door brought her to her feet, her heart pounding. Julie looked fearfully first to the door and then the reorganized room. Had someone finally heard something and come to investigate?

"Yes," Jessie called, determined to get some answers.

"Ready for breakfast?" Margaret called.

"Yes," Julie responded at Jessie's direction as Jessie moved up against the wall, beside the door.

"Very good. As soon as both of you sit on the bed."

Jessie immediately looked around for the camera. Stupid, why didn't she think the bedroom would be under surveillance? She had let Diana lull her into false security. She shrugged and walked back over to the bed. When Julie sat down on the bed, they heard the lock in the door.

Someone else opened the door but it was Margaret who brought in the card table. She carefully set it up then reached back for the tray of food that someone handed her. The door closed, and they heard the lock click.

Margaret glanced around the room. "Been busy this morning, haven't you?"

Jessie said nothing, the time for congenial conversation was over. Julie looked from one to the other.

"Go ahead and eat," Margaret invited. She stepped back against the wall. "Diana sends you a message."

"And what might that be?"

"She's sorry for the inconvenience. It just seemed best this way." For the first time, Margaret looked sympathetic. She glanced around the room again. "Glad you're feeling stronger, Jessie."

"How long do we have to stay in here?" Julie asked.

"Until her meeting is over."

"And then?" Jessie asked. She hadn't overlooked that Margaret had used her name. The old girl was softening in her attitude toward Jessie.

"Then we wait for the end."

Julie slowly went over to the table to see their usual breakfast, eggs, bacon, pancakes this morning instead of french toast. "Why aren't you in the meeting?"

"Diana will tell me what I have to do."

"And you'll just blindly do it."

Jessie got up and went over to the breakfast table. Maybe she could needle something out of Margaret.

"Not blindly." Margaret watched as they took their plates. "You underestimate Diana. She is her own person, and she has a good heart."

"Perhaps you don't have the best perspective," Jessie replied caustically.

"Perhaps better than you. I've known her longer."

Jessie took her plate and went back to sit down on the bed. "That's right. You were her nursemaid, weren't you? So how did that happen? You seem about the same age."

"Don't say that to Diana, please. She'll think you think she looks old. She would be upset."

"So?" Jessie sat back, trying to look relaxed. If she could get Margaret talking, perhaps, well, if nothing else, she could learn something. Maybe. "How did you come to be Diana's nursemaid?"

"Her papa bought me." She watched them for their reaction.

Jessie stopped eating but Julie was scandalized. "Bought you?"

So they are into trafficking, Jessie thought, feeling sick. She really had been blind to Diana.

"You know Czar?" Margaret asked and Jessie realized the question was directed to her.

Jessie nodded. "Know of. Saw him once or twice."

"He's not charming," Margaret commented, glancing at Julie.

"No," Jessie agreed. "He's not charming."

"I was born in the Ukraine," Margaret said slowly. "My name was Margarta. We were very poor." She gave a cynical smile and shook her head. "Poor there is not like being poor here where you can get food stamps, go to school, and get government aid. No, we were poor because there was no work, no money, no nothing. I was always hungry, there was no education. It was terrible."

She took a deep breath and went on. "My—" She stopped to rephrase. "The man who was my father sold me. He promised I would work to pay off the debt. The money he got for me fed the rest of the family. So I went away. I was fourteen. The man who bought me had brothels. He decided I wasn't pretty enough for the sex but there were other things to do." Jessie watched the tough, contained woman shudder at the memory.

"One day, this man comes in. He's well-dressed, nice suit, very polite. He wants to buy a woman, a girl. He has very specific conditions. Young, impressionable, not stupid but not smart, not pretty. Must be a virgin, healthy. Virgins in a brothel." Margaret shook her head and laughed, but it was a bitter laughter.

"He had eyes like ice, cold, devoid of feeling. A lot of the girls hid. I did too. But they brought us all out. He went down the line. Too pretty. Too smart. Too flirty. I was so scared as more and more of them went away and I was still there. This man was not good." Margaret paused, lost in thought. Then she came back to the present.

"He picked me." She looked up at Jessie and Julie. "He took me to one of the rooms, took my clothes off, looked at me, felt me. Felt my hair, looked at my teeth, my fingers, my toes. Like he was buying a horse or a cow. Then he nodded. I got dressed and we left."

She paused again, perhaps lost in memories, perhaps trying to find the words.

"I was so afraid, but I thought, at least he is just one, not like different men each night. He's rich so maybe I would have better food, more clothes. We went to a hotel, and there's all these men around him. Then one woman comes in, and he gives her instructions. I didn't understand any of this. She took me away. She gave me a bath, brought me new clothes to wear, brought me a big dinner. I did everything she wanted but I was so scared. I waited, waited, and I waited. And finally I fell asleep."

Jessie went back to eating. They had long suspected Czar had his fingers in the Eastern European trafficking. This seemed to confirm it. "What's this got to do with Diana?"

"Oh, you're interested now?" Margaret asked with some sarcasm.

"I'm listening. And I hear you."

Margaret shook her head but she moved over to the chair. "Do you mind if I sit? It can be a long story."

"Go ahead," Jessie said. "Have some coffee. It appears we have time."

Margaret poured coffee from the insulated pot. She sat down where she could see them. Then she began again.

"When I woke up, I wasn't there anymore. I felt terrible, I had a headache, I was hungry. Everything was different. It was very bright. I was in this room all by myself in some strange house. A woman came in, took me to the bathroom, checked me over. She took me back to the room, brought me a meal. She won't talk to me. Well, she talked but I don't understand. She was speaking some language I never heard. I was terrified. I had no idea what was going to happen.

"Later, the man you know as Czar comes to see me. He took me downstairs to a nursery. This little baby was in a crib, laying there, bright-eyed, kicking, dark hair, gurgling. He picked her up and there was no ice in his eyes. 'This is Diana,' he tells me. 'You're to take care of her, all the time. If anything bad happens to Diana, it will happen to you. Understand?'

"I understood. So I took care of this little baby, me who never had babies." Margaret's face softened. "She was such a good baby, a happy baby." She looked up at Jessie. "At first, it was hard for me, tied down, but then one day, she grabbed my finger in her tiny little hand and wouldn't let go, like she was telling me that we were in this together."

"Bonding," Julie said.

"Yes. So I cared for Diana, and anything I needed I could have, as long as Diana was taken care of, full time, twenty-four hour a day job." She drank some coffee. "He didn't like my Ukraine name so I became Margaret. When she started to talk, he doesn't like my accent, so I must learn proper English. And then I must do this or do that, all for Diana." She looked at Jessie. "And this man who can look at you and your blood turn to ice turned to mush when she looks at him. Oh, yes, I took great care of Diana."

Julie began to eat again, and Jessie began to relax a bit. Interesting about the old man, but she saw lots of men melt at babies, daughters and sons. Interesting side to the old man. God, what a scary thing for a fourteen-year-old. "Then what happened?"

"When Diana was three…" Jessie noticed her tone changed. "Czar sent me away. He said Diana didn't need a nursemaid anymore. He sent me to one of his sweatshops. After three years of having almost everything I wanted with Diana, that was hell. Within three days, I knew I had to get out of there, one way or another. Before I could do anything, I saw Czar's right-hand man. He came back for me. Took me out of there without a word. I'd been gone for four days. He told me Diana had been screaming for three, regular little temper tantrums. Czar was beside himself. She'd hold her breath mid-scream, pass out, come to, look for Margee and start all over again. Wouldn't eat, wouldn't go to bed, searched the house over and over again, cried for Margee. Czar was furious. He could make men wet their pants with one look, and this little three-year-old screams at him demanding where has he hidden Margee."

Jessie bit her lip. She thought of the time she had called Diana a spoiled rich kid used to getting her own way. Evidently it had started early.

"She was coming down the stairs, big wide fancy stairs, when I came in the front door. She catapulted off those stairs; she hit me so hard she knocked me down. She was hysterical. Czar followed her down and I remember laying on my back looking up at him. 'You seem to have a champion,' he said, looking at me. 'You'd better make sure you're worthy.'"

"Yes," Jessie agreed. "I've noticed Diana can be demanding upon occasion." She ignored Julie's look. "So you've been with her ever since?" Somehow she thought Margaret had a stronger point than talking about a three-year-old, even if it was Diana.

"When Diana was fifteen, he tried to send me away again. This time he told me in advance, but I was not to tell Diana. He would send her on a trip and I'd be gone when she got back. By that time, I knew a lot of what he was doing, if only to keep Diana from knowing what her father did. She adored him."

She looked up at Jessie. "I hate that bastard," she said flatly. "There's not a day goes by I haven't looked forward to his death, but he doted on Diana. He was as good a father to her as any girl would ever want. He would spoil her rotten and then I would have to clean up the mess when she had her tantrums, and she had her tantrums. That seems to be part of the deal. In any other area..." She didn't finish the sentence. It was a moment before she started up again.

"I had interfered with something, I can't even remember what. Maybe insulted one of his girlfriends or did something that bothered him. I don't even know. It was hard to tell what motivated him. He just said he was getting rid of me and I wasn't real sure just what he meant. It could have meant anything in those days. I was real upset, had nowhere to turn, didn't dare talk to anyone, afraid to stay, more afraid to run. Diana found me crying one night. She wouldn't stop in the next days until she got the story out of me, and then the whole thing came out, how I came to be her nurse and everything. She didn't believe me, not about her papa. She withdrew from me, wouldn't talk to me. Czar was delighted I'd lost my champion.

"Then one afternoon, she came in. She had been out and about. She wouldn't let me go along, said she would use one of the guys with her because she wasn't to go out alone. He said she went shopping but I don't know where she went. It wasn't shopping. She came right up to me and apologized, said she believed me now. She would take care of it. The way she said it gave me chills: it was just what her papa would say when he had a problem. He would take care of it."

"What did she do?" Julie asked cautiously.

"Her birthday was coming up. She teased and tormented Czar so much about how he was going to celebrate her sixteenth birthday." She paused as if remembering and smiled. "She could wrap that man around her little finger. He thought she wanted a car, so he promised, publicly promised, that she could have anything she wanted. We had a big dinner party in the Family. She dressed like a coming-out party, I could see she would be a beautiful woman but I knew she was going on a trip and I wouldn't be there to see her. She looked lovely and I saw more than one man look at her and think about marrying into the Family. Czar was so proud of her, so pleased with her, pleased with himself. He had a car all ready for her, keys in hand, ready for when she would ask for it. So when he turned and asked, she had only one word for him. She said 'Margaret.'

"He didn't believe her. She told him she was sixteen, she thought she could take over the responsibility of my behavior. I thought he would have a seizure and that was the first time I knew she was Czar's daughter for sure. She didn't budge an inch, even when he said they had to retire to the library for a discussion. There were a dozen of us at that table and we all ignored the shouting from the next room, and it wasn't only Czar shouting. But when they came out, Diana was just as calm and as pleased as the cat who swallowed the songbird, he had given her what she wanted."

"So," Jessie said slowly, "you're with Diana because she 'owns' you."

"That's barbaric!" Julie burst out.

Margaret gave them a look of disgust. "Barbaric is not seeing the lengths that even a sixteen-year-old Diana would go to in order to get her way. No, Diana does not own me." Margaret shook off the story, got to her feet. "Her papa gave in rather than lose face on breaking his word in front of his people but he wasn't happy. He canceled the big trip he had planned for her. Diana wasn't stupid about it. She packed her bags, had me pack mine, and we went on a road tour instead. We traveled for six weeks, just going wherever the way looked interesting. One of the places we went was Canada and when we re-entered the country, I was legal. I got a green card, Diana was my employer and she found someone to sponsor me. She went on to make sure I got my citizenship papers. She pays me to be her bodyguard, pays taxes. No one owns me. I would do anything Diana asked me to do because no one else in the world has done as much as lift a finger for me."

"And how old was she?" Jessie couldn't believe a sixteen-year-old could formulate all this.

"She was sixteen," Margaret confirmed as if she read Jessie's mind. "That was when she separated Czar Randalson from her papa. I don't know how she did it. I don't know how she does it in her mind now. But I do know that whatever she says she will do, she will do. And no one will stand in her way."

Jessie set her plate back on the table. Yes, she could see Diana doing that. Stubborn, unreasonably so, loyal, determined. "So you're saying Diana will deliver us back safe and sound because she told us she would."

"As soon as her papa dies. She's finalizing the plans now."

"So we should just sit here and wait."

Margaret shook her head. "That's up to you. It's simply my responsibility to make sure you don't cause her any more problems while she makes plans."

Stalemate. Jessie nodded.

"Very good. I appreciate that. I could go to any length, but Diana would not be happy." Margaret got up and knocked on the door. "Now that we have this new understanding, is there anything I can bring you to help pass the time?"

"Any idea how long it's going to be?" Margaret shook her head.

The day lasted forever. Margaret brought up a jigsaw puzzle, several books, the small personal DVD and several movies. She brought up lunch, watched Jessie pace. Julie requested some journals and Margaret even downloaded them for her, brought them up on the disabled laptop so she could read them. Jessie took a nap, putting together the new information she had about Czar, about Diana. She still had trouble sorting it out.

Dinner was late, after dark. They watched the cars pull out, four of them, enough distance between them that the headlights didn't shine on the one in front. Jessie bowed her head against the glass in frustration. There were so many answers right there, and she couldn't get to them.

They turned at the sound of the lock. There was a knock and then Diana opened the door. She looked drawn and gray although, Jessie considered, that might be exaggerated by her black clothing. Her shirtsleeves were rolled up, and there was a dishtowel tossed over her shoulder, but otherwise, the tailored clothing denoted power and authority. However, when she spoke, the weariness was also in her voice. Whatever she had done that day had drained her. "You can come down for dinner. I'm sorry it's been such a long day. I don't want to leave you in here longer than necessary. Cabin fever is bad for you."

"You sure it's all right?" Jessie asked caustically.

Diana didn't even seem to have the energy to take offense. There was no challenge in her gaze when she looked from one to the other of them. "Look, I've had a long tiring day. I'm really crabby. I'd really appreciate it if you don't be shitty. Now do you want to come downstairs or not?"

From the disarray in the kitchen, it was clear a group had been there. There were stacks of plates, silverware and cups. Margaret was filling the sink to start dishes as Diana pointed for Jessie and Julie to sit at the table. While Jessie and Julie sat down, Diana pulled out filled plates from the oven that obviously had been prepared and saved for them. Without saying a word, she brought everything to them, drinks, silverware, anything they might need.

Jessie thought Diana looked exhausted, resigned, but not upset or angry, and she wondered what this meeting today had entailed. She exchanged glances with Julie but even Julie remained silent. There didn't seem to be anything either one of them could say that wouldn't seem like they were fishing for information.

"Can we help clean up?" she asked as she and Julie finished eating.

"If you want," Diana said. "I wouldn't ask but I wouldn't turn it down either."

CHAPTER TWENTY-TWO

Diana was up at dawn, the first one up. It was not often she could beat Margaret to the kitchen. She started the coffee and when it brewed, she took her cup and went out on the deck. The sun was just coming up, nature was awakening, the morning was still cool, the morning fog not yet burned away. It was quiet, peaceful, and maybe she would have the opportunity to think. This was not what she had planned. What she had planned was being able to sort out all her options in a quiet, leisurely time frame. What she got instead was a house full of tensions. Julie was still scared of her. No, not scared. Wary was a better word. Even with her wariness, she had been helpful, providing information about papa.

Jessie was friendly one minute, still a cop the next. Her blowup at papa's identity hadn't been completely unexpected. It was just stronger than Diana had been prepared for. Even though Jessie had calmed down and they had been able to talk, Diana realized she was going to have to let go of any fantasies and dreams she had about having Jessie in her life. It just wasn't going to be possible. And Margaret? Whatever had possessed Margaret to tell Jessie about Diana's role in Jessie's shooting? Margaret had a dislike for Jessie. Diana chuckled a little. Margaret sometimes still thought of herself as the mother figure and woe to anyone who hurt her Diana. It was nice to have someone like that in her corner, but sometimes it was a liability. Well, there wasn't much else she could spill. There was one more thing to consider, and soon enough, that too would be taken care of.

She heard Margaret come downstairs and start breakfast. Diana knew she should go in and help, Margaret had caught so much of the work, but she just couldn't stir. As soon as she finished her coffee, she'd go in. More than anything, she just wanted a quiet day.

Much to Diana's amazement, the day was quiet. Now that everyone knew they were waiting for Czar Randalson to die, some of the apprehension was gone. Even though the timing was uncertain and the waiting brought its own tension, everyone in the house was able to deal with it. Admittedly each felt differently about the death but they all knew when it happened, they would be leaving.

It was late that night before Diana was alone, and she mixed her evening drink and went out on the deck. Julie's information about papa and how long he might or might not last had been very helpful. Although she felt guilty about it, she wished the end would come. It wasn't just that he was in pain or she wanted him out of the way; she couldn't bear to see him so helpless, so failing. In that way, her isolation was a good thing. She could remember him from younger days, when he was healthy.

She heard the door open but didn't turn around. "I'll be there in a minute, Margaret."

"It's not Margaret," Jessie said. She came out on the deck. "Can we talk?"

"Sure." *Perfect end for a perfect day*, she thought. "What's on your mind?"

Jessie came out and went to the railing in front of Diana. For the first time in a long time, Diana could see her old lover. She hadn't realized just keeping secret her involvement in Jessie's shooting had put such a block on her feelings. Now that it was out in the open, she could really see Jessie.

"Do you know what you're going to do now?"

"About?"

"When your papa dies. What kind of position does that leave you in?"

Such a good question, Diana thought.

"I mean, I know you killed Kaplan but considering the circumstances, that's hardly a crime. And you were instrumental in bringing down a drug ring. Even keeping us here is sorta gray."

"Still, not exactly the sort of thing to win any friends in the Family," Diana pointed out.

"Witness Protection?"

"Thought about it. Thought about buying an island and just retreating there for the rest of my life. Thought about retiring to Europe but the Family has long arms."

"So you want to leave the Family."

"Without papa, there's no reason to be there." She pulled out her cigarettes again. "Didn't like what they did, don't like what they do. Managed to tiptoe through the minefield and not get involved, unless knowing is involved."

"Can I ask something?"

"Can't say I'll answer, but go ahead."

"Why'd you get involved? From what you said the other day, you had your own business that was legit. You put yourself through college. What made you throw it all away?"

Diana looked away. "Stupidity. I came to a crossroads and I thought I had only two choices. The Family was one, and the other was—" She picked her words carefully. "Closed to me. I didn't realize there were other choices."

"Was it really closed?" Jessie asked unknowingly.

"No, probably not. I just took it as a closed door and didn't take the risk. Stupidity in hindsight, but then we make those kinds of stupid mistakes when we're young."

"What about that woman you were in love with?" Jessie asked.

Diana paused to light her cigarette before she answered. "What about her?"

"Did you ever get a chance to speak to her?"

"No," Diana answered shortly.

"Never an opportunity?"

"No."

Jessie shook her head. "I'm glad some couples can work everything out." She stood there, thrust her hands in her pockets. "I always wanted something like Mom and Dad had. I know Mom was worried sometimes, but she always put on a strong front. She told me once she had to. She couldn't help him any other way except to make him believe she was confident, she had faith in him, everything was going to be all right."

"Sounds like a remarkable woman," Diana was able to say.

"Oh, I can't say Julie and I have had a bad relationship while it was there. We've had a lot of fun. She took well to Nicki. Not everyone could step into a relationship with a half-grown kid. We've had some good times." She stared off into the trees. "I guess I just wanted more."

"I'm sorry it was less than what you wanted."

"And you had no one." She turned around and looked at Diana. "Am I right?"

"No one who really mattered."

Jessie shook her head. "Is there anything I can do?" she asked after a moment.

"I don't see there's anything you can do," Diana said slowly.

"I can put in a good word for you."

Diana chuckled. "Tell me, Jessie, are you familiar with the Stockholm Syndrome?"

Jessie looked at her strangely, frowning. "Of course, it's where hostages bond with the kidnappers, think well of them, even take their side." She paused. "Oh."

"Oh," Diana echoed.

"But that doesn't exactly fit us. We knew each other before this. And you've saved my life before."

"And tell me, would you like our previous relationship to be the front page news on the tabloids? I'm sure it would make good copy."

"Good God, no."

Diana laughed. "That's what I thought."

"But even that would be worth it," Jessie said after a moment.

Diana sighed. "No, Jessie, I think the best way you can help me is by doing what you do best, being a good cop."

"Can't talk you into letting me take you in?"

"We'll see."

"You have something."

"I have something. And that's all I'm going to say, and you're not going to ask anything else."

They were silent a few more minutes, a comfortable silence. "I missed you," Jessie said slowly as if she hated to admit it. "I kept hoping you would come back through town or call or something. Even if it was just to talk. You always understood." She bowed her head. "I could talk to you about anything."

"It was better this way," Diana said slowly. How could I watch you and Julie? she thought. And Julie seems too likeable to even dislike.

"Well, knowing everything, that's probably right," Jessie agreed. "I still missed you," she said softly, wistfully.

Diana got up. This conversation needed to be nipped in the bud before it went someplace Diana really didn't want to go. "It's late.

We've had a long day. It's bedtime." She ran her hand over Jessie's back as she started by.

Jessie turned, catching Diana's arm, reaching out for her so they were in a partial embrace. "Why didn't you tell me?"

Diana froze, caught her breath. "Tell you what?"

"That you were the woman in the clearing, that you came to town to see how I was."

Diana gave a small sigh of relief. "It would have put us both in danger."

Jessie drew Diana to her. "You still wear the same perfume."

Diana drew back, her logic still working even though she wanted, oh, how she wanted. "Jessie, don't."

"Why not?"

"Because I need you to be a good cop. And this isn't…"

"Is that the only reason?" Diana didn't answer. "I can't believe you'd still be holding on to that fantasy for that other woman." She nuzzled Diana's hair.

"I'm not," Diana said slowly. "But this is not the time." She took a deep breath and stepped back. "I told you earlier, I've lots of things going on. I don't need any more complications."

She examined Jessie's face in the moonlight, in the half light from the kitchen. *And I can't trust you*, she thought. *Not at this point, not with everything going on.*

"Time for bed," she said in a steadier voice.

They went in the house, and Jessie went on upstairs as Diana shut up the house for the night. She put her glass in the sink, looking at her reflection in the window. She shook her head, still feeling Jessie's hands on her, feeling Jessie's nearness. "God, Jessie, your timing sucks," she muttered.

***

"Margaret, you seem like a reasonable person," Jessie said carefully.

Getting to see Margaret alone had been tricky. Diana was off doing something somewhere; Jessie suspected she was finalizing plans in one of her rooms that was off-limits to Jessie and Julie. Julie had succumbed to Jessie's suggestion that now was the time to catch up on her journal reading. Margaret had been very generous in downloading much information for their restricted afternoon and since Julie had always complained she never had time to do all the reading she wanted, why didn't she take advantage of this time? After Jessie had assured her she wouldn't cause any problems, she would be on her best friendly behavior, Julie had given in, so she was ensconced in the library. That left Jessie in the kitchen with Margaret. She picked up the dishtowel and began to dry the dishes as Margaret washed them.

"I mean," Jessie went on. "I can understand now your loyalty to Diana. I don't even question it. Considering the circumstances, yes, she went way out of her way to do everything she could to protect you. Not many sixteen-year-olds would be able to do that, much less face down someone like her father." Even now, Jessie could not say his name.

"I told you, she has a good heart."

"And a lot of nerve," Jessie admitted. "It looks like she could do anything she set her mind to. She always talked about family loyalty and taking care of each other. I guess it's not surprising she joined the Family."

"I didn't want her to," Margaret said slowly. "I thought for a long time she would not. She made her own money to go to college."

"Yes, she told me. Transporting gems." Jessie shook her head. "That really surprised me and yet, you know, when I thought about it, it seemed just like her. Like she had that secret no one else knew and she could just breeze through."

Margaret gave Jessie a measuring look. "Diana always liked her secrets."

"Well, she did keep those," Jessie said, thinking what an understatement that was. "I knew there was something in her life, never dreamed she was in the Family."

"She wasn't."

Jessie stopped. "She wasn't?"

Margaret shook her head, continuing the dishes. "No. She knew what her papa did, and didn't want to know. To his credit, he didn't flaunt it in front of her. Maybe he wanted to keep her out of it. He encouraged her to travel so he could operate more freely. There were just things he didn't do when she was with him."

"Did he know she was a lesbian?" Jessie could imagine how someone like Randalson could react if he disapproved.

"Yes. I think he was pleased."

"Pleased? Why?"

"His ego. If she never married, he would not be replaced as the man in her life."

"So he knew about me?" Jessie said cautiously.

Margaret shook her head. "No one knew about you," she said firmly. "Diana traveled a lot, she saw lots of women. I was probably the only one who knew there was someone special and even I didn't know you, I only knew *of* you. I didn't know who you were until last week."

Jessie put the plate down, totally confused now. "Margaret, if you didn't know me, why don't you like me? I mean, I know, I'm a cop. You're not predisposed to like cops, but that's not the reason, is it?" Margaret said nothing. "Diana and I, we were lovers a long time ago. That's over and done with. Diana walked out of my life and didn't even want to be friends." Margaret still had nothing to say, just set her mouth in a grimmer and grimmer line. "You said the other day that I put Diana in danger. I appreciate her saving my life, but I didn't know she did it so it wasn't like it was something I asked her to do."

Margaret set her jaw firmly. Jessie had the feeling she really wanted to speak but was holding back.

"Margaret, what's the deal?"

Margaret turned on her. "If it wasn't for you," she spit out, "my Diana never would have joined the Family."

Jessie stepped back from Margaret's anger. "I don't know anything about that," she protested. "I didn't know about the Family. I don't know when she joined. How did I cause that?"

Margaret glared at her. "We took a trip out west, we were there for almost the entire summer. Her papa, something changed. Maybe it was just because she was getting out of college. Maybe people were noticing. It was getting dangerous for her just to be around. He told her she would have to decide, to join or to leave. It was her choice but she had to decide. She said she would have to think about it." Margaret shook her head. "She didn't have to think. I knew she didn't want to join. She went to Lexington. I assumed she went to see you."

"To see me?" Jessie thought back and she nodded. "That's right. She was gone the entire summer. I didn't think she was ever coming back. She had just found out I was a cop. I knew she was upset but I didn't understand why. She had never been gone so long. Julie came back that summer."

Margaret nodded. "Yes. I know." She went back to the dishes. "My Diana can do anything, but she cannot be alone. She needs to have someone there for her even if only in the background. She had her papa and she had you. When you turned her down, she had only her papa. That's when she joined the Family."

"Turned her down? What are you talking about?" She stopped and thought about that day. "Diana said there was something she wanted to talk about with me," she remembered. "She said something about an opportunity, she called it. But she said she thought I had news for her. So I told her about Julie." She stared at Margaret. "She never told me about her opportunity then, she said it didn't matter."

"It mattered," Margaret said in a hard voice.

"Are you saying that it was joining the Family—that was her 'opportunity'?"

"Yes."

"And so you think that was why she came back and joined?"

"No, I don't think so," Margaret said in a chilly voice. "I know so."

"No!" Jessie was emphatic, almost shouting. "No, you are not blaming me for that!" Margaret said nothing. "Margaret, she didn't tell me anything. She didn't ask me anything. She just said she hoped Julie and I could work things out and then she got up and left."

"You could have stopped her," Margaret said stolidly.

"Margaret, I didn't know. She didn't say anything. You can't blame me for her joining the Family. That was her choice."

Margaret shook her head. "No, she felt she had no place else to go."

"That's not my fault!" Jessie almost shouted back at her.

"What's not your fault?" Julie asked from the doorway.

Jessie gave her a quick look and turned back to Margaret. "Margaret doesn't like me because she blames me for Diana joining the Family."

Julie came into the kitchen. "How is that your fault?"

"She said Diana came to talk to me about it. Her father gave her an ultimatum. But Diana never said anything to me that day. She said she wanted to talk to me about something but then when I told her about you, she said it didn't matter." Jessie turned from one woman to the other, disbelief on one face, surprise on the other.

"When was this?" Julie asked as she came further into the kitchen.

"That summer you came back. We were just beginning to work things out; we hadn't even moved in together. She came to town and ran into me downtown."

"And up until then?" Julie asked. "You never said much about your relationship about Diana."

"We got together whenever she came to town," Jessie said with some discomfort. Talking to Diana about Julie was a whole lot easier than talking about her relationship with Diana to Julie. "Just friends."

"Who slept together?"

"Well, yes, there was that. But not always. Sometimes we just talked, had lunch, did things. I had told her all about you, how I felt about you. She always understood I was waiting for you."

"And how long did this go on?"

Jessie shrugged, shook her head. "Whenever she was in the area, a number of years, I don't remember how many off hand."

Julie's and Margaret's gazes met through Jessie's bewilderment.

"And how did she take the news about me?"

"She was a little surprised, okay, speechless maybe."

"I'll bet," Julie muttered.

"She said her news didn't matter. She hoped you and I would be able to work everything out. She was confident we could if we worked at it. And then she left."

"And that was all she said?" Julie asked. "You never mentioned any of this before."

"I told you there had been someone but never anyone serious."

Julie closed her eyes and shook her head as she leaned against the door frame. "Jessie, you're one good cop but in other areas, you are blind as a bat."

"What do you mean by that?"

"She means that besides not hearing real well, you don't see so well either," Margaret said with some bitterness.

"No," Jessie protested as she threw the dishtowel down. "No. I know what you're thinking. You're thinking she was in love with me. She wasn't. There was someone else, she would never tell me who, someone who was committed. Diana's always been loyal, you know that, Margaret." She turned back to her for confirmation.

Margaret dried her hands and leaned against the counter, looking at Jessie with a look of profound exasperation.

"She told me she couldn't tell this woman how she felt as long as the woman was committed. Even the other night, on the deck, she said she'd never been able to tell her because of that." She looked from Margaret to Julie. "She didn't see her anymore," she added weakly. "You know she wouldn't say anything to someone who was committed."

Julie folded her arms and leaned against the door frame, shaking her head.

Unbidden, phrases came back to Jessie now. "You'll never be a substitute for anyone, Jessie—I haven't found anyone anywhere who can turn my head and fill my senses the way you can Jessica Ann

Galbreath, so I've always come back—I just need you, more than air—I want to be a vampire and take in your life's blood—I want you like you've never been taken before. I want you to shiver at the memory and remember Diana did that to me, with me, for me.—I would never ever let you be hurt." She turned again from Julie to Margaret.

"When she came back," Margaret said, "she was different. She turned harder, colder. It wasn't just joining the Family. She had no joy in her life. Even her papa noticed."

The front door opened and Diana came in. They all turned toward her as she crossed the great room and came into the kitchen. As soon as she stepped in, she realized everyone was looking at her and she stopped. Jessie and Margaret at the sink, Julie across the room, all looking at her.

"What's wrong?"

"Revelations," Julie said cryptically.

Diana immediately looked at Margaret, who straightened up and braced herself. Finally she looked at Jessie.

Jessie didn't know what to say. She stood there for a moment, completely blank. Neither Margaret nor Julie were going to say anything, they were looking to her. "Margaret was telling me she dislikes me because she blames me for you joining the Family."

Diana frowned. "Margaret talks too much. We're going to have to come to a new understanding about that."

"Margaret says you came to talk to me about, how did you word it, an opportunity? But you never said anything to me."

Diana glanced at Margaret and back to Jessie. "That's right."

"Why not?"

"You said Julie had come back to town, the two of you were working things out."

"What did that have to do with your opportunity?"

"You just weren't available anymore."

"And so you couldn't talk about your opportunity to a friend."

Julie moved backward into the hallway.

"I didn't want to talk to just a friend." She watched as Margaret moved around them and went into the pantry.

"Margaret and Julie think you were in love with me. I told them that you were in love with a mystery woman who was committed to someone."

Diana made no response.

Jessie took a step toward her. "Are they right? Or am I?"

Diana opened her mouth but said nothing. When Jessie advanced another step she finally spoke. "I guess both."

Jessie digested that. "You were in love with me," she said in a disbelieving voice. "Not just 'here and now.' You were in love, like in a relationship." She waited for Diana's denial but nothing came. Then she looked into Diana's face, and she knew it was true. "Why didn't you say something?"

"You were waiting for Julie. You made that clear all along. You never said anything to indicate you had stopped."

"And then you found out I was a cop."

Diana shook her head. "It didn't matter anymore."

Jessie thought over that entire weekend, how much she had wanted Diana to come to town, how eager she had been. In light of Diana's mob ties, she shivered. But no, Margaret said Diana didn't belong then. Jessie remembered how she had wanted Diana that weekend, she wanted Diana to want her and Diana had shown her she had. "You said," she said slowly, remembering something else, "that my waiting for Julie was what stood between us." The expression on Diana's face confirmed it. "I was the woman you loved, and you wouldn't say anything as long as I was waiting for Julie." She closed her eyes. "God, how stupid I was."

"You could say that," Diana said sadly. She turned back to the living room.

"No, wait." Jessie grabbed hold of Diana's arm and turned her around. "But then you found out I was a cop. And you left. And you didn't come back. I didn't think you were ever coming back."

"Damn it, Jessie." Diana jerked her arm away. "You waited how many years for Julie to come back? And you couldn't wait four months for me? Even to see if I would return?"

"I didn't know if you were ever coming back!"

"And I wasn't worth waiting for!" Diana filled in.

"That's not what I said."

"Yes, it is, it was. We said everything that weekend. You asked why we hadn't done anything about a relationship, and I said that it was Julie between us. And you blew up like I threw a bomb instead of just stating facts. Even then, I did everything I could that weekend to eliminate her."

"And then you found out I was a cop."

"I told you it didn't matter. I simply had to adjust to it."

"I thought you were running away."

"Like you do?" Diana sneered. "Jeeze, Jessie. You nursed the idea of Julie for years. You're a cop. You have access to information the general public doesn't have. Julie's one of the leading hematologists in the country. Are you going to tell me that in seven years you couldn't find her?"

Jessie let her hand fall. "I didn't know where to start," she offered.

"You didn't want to," Diana stated. "At first because you were too overwhelmed, and then because you couldn't stand the possible rejection. So you became Romeo, the Friday night brass ring." Jessie winced even though that's how she had described herself. "And I tried to be there for you, not for some brass ring, not just sex. I might have started out enjoying Romeo but I ended up loving Jessie."

Jessie swallowed, unable to comprehend. Diana had loved her. And she knew that. She had always known it somewhere deep inside her. But what to do now? By her own admission, Diana was in the Family, and the Family was not some minor little problem. And Jessie was a cop, all she had ever wanted to be was a cop. She met Diana's gaze and said nothing.

Diana waited, watching with this knowing look in her eyes. She finally shook her head and turned away. "See? I loved you then and I love you now, but that's not enough."

She turned and walked out the door and down the steps where Jessie couldn't follow.

CHAPTER TWENTY-THREE

Diana sat at the base of the tree. Safe house. She had never felt as alone as she did now, never as low. She had been afraid, adrenaline-rushed, panicky even, but never so totally alone. Everything she ever thought she had was gone. Papa, Jessie even in her dreams, and she was sending Margaret away. A person of interest, she was being called by the Feds, and she knew what they wanted. The men who were already jockeying for Papa's position were calling her a marked woman. That South Sea island escape was looking better and better.

She had called the meeting of her shadows to make one last request before she cut them loose. To her relief, they had agreed, and for that she was grateful. They had protected each other's backs for how many years? She had helped them, they had helped her. She wondered if they would continue without her, if there would be anyone who could or would step into the leadership role.

The shadows had been Margaret's idea, starting out just as someone to cover their backs in ways the men didn't dream of. When she brought Diana in, Margaret had abdicated her position and Diana had worked them. She had used them very quietly. Some of them, like the now-dead Helen, had been with her from the beginning. A shadow was at the hospital, she had a shadow on Nicki. She had shadows in almost all the women's organizations in town, the battered women's shelter, a midwife. She had set up self-defense classes, seed money for business, drug abuse prevention in the bordellos, anything she could do quietly to prevent Papa's Family from getting complete control. She'd had to do it in order to live with herself. Now she wondered if they would continue without her or like so many things, just disappear until the next person came along and saw the need.

She lowered her head to her knees. She had so many secrets and she was going to have to give some of them up, but not necessarily all. Right now she just really wanted to disappear but that wasn't possible. She had Jessie and Julie to return. She leaned back against the tree. Places to go, and things to do. Wasn't that what she and Jessie always said? And the other thing, it's a rough world out there.

She got up and started back for the house. She would have to face Jessie sooner or later. Nothing new, just old news recycled. Well, maybe Jessie knew it now. That was different.

Her phone vibrated, and she pulled it out of her pocket to read the text message, stopping in a shady spot so she could read the small text. Papa was taken to the hospital. It wouldn't be long now. She leaned against the tree and wept.

***

By the time the next call came in at three in the morning, Diana was all cried out. She lay there for a moment. "Goodbye Papa. Godspeed." She felt guilty for her sigh of relief and then she got up.

Margaret was sound asleep but came up like a catapult when Diana shook her. "It's time," she said quietly. "The call just came through. I'm going to shower downstairs."

"What about them?" She indicated down the hall with her head.

"Let's get things started first. We'll be able to move around better if they're still asleep."

"Are you all right?" Margaret asked.

Diana nodded. "Fine," she said simply. "Let's get moving. We're on a time schedule now."

At six, she knocked on the master bedroom door. She hesitated just a moment before she swung it wide. "Good morning, ladies," she greeted. Jessie sat bolt upright, Julie stirred sleepily. "Time to rise and shine. I want to be on the road in an hour and a half."

"On the road?"

"Coffee's brewing. Shake a leg."

Diana seemed to be on the move constantly, skipping breakfast except for coffee which she drank standing up, her gaze constantly roaming the house. The additional difference was that she had a phone in her hand all the time. She looked Jessie and Julie up and down like a mother sending her kids off to church. She wanted a good impression. She pointed to Jessie. "No blue jeans," she said, sending her back to change. "I'm not going to have anyone say you were treated badly." Even then, she stepped in front of Jessie at the door, impersonally turning her face one way then to the other. "Well, at least it was long enough for most of the bruises to heal."

"What?" Jessie couldn't resist saying. "Don't you want us to look like you rescued us from something bad?"

"I've got pictures," Diana commented. "Now go change." She went on to examine Julie, nodding in approval.

"Diana," Julie said in a passing moment.

"What?" Diana said curtly.

"I'm sorry you lost your father."

Diana took a deep breath. "Thank you," she said. And then she went right on. "Are you ready?"

The SUV pulled up, the driver got out and disappeared somewhere around the house.

"Let's go, ladies," Diana ordered. She opened the back door for them to slide into the late-model SUV. "Seat belts," she ordered. "Now, I'm asking for cooperation on this." She pulled out two blindfolds. "Just put these on, lay back and take a nap."

Before Jessie and Julie could as much as really catch their breath, they were on the road.

"You didn't forget the box, did you?" Margaret asked.

"Right here."

"Are you sure you want to do it this way?"

"Nope," Diana said briefly. "I just don't know any other way." She looked over her shoulder to see both women had their nightshades on. They were both leaning back, for all the world looking like they were sleeping. Diana, for one, did not believe it.

When they came out of the mountains, before they hit the highway, Margaret pulled over. "You're sure, last chance?"

"Last chance. This is the best way. You can take your blindfolds off, ladies."

Diana got out of the car, went around to the driver's side. Margaret got out. Diana and Margaret hugged tightly.

"Be careful," they both said at the same time.

With great reluctance and just as strong purpose, Diana got in on the driver's side and slowly pulled away. Jessie and Julie looked at each other and then both turned around. Diana drove slowly, just long enough to see the other vehicle pull up and Margaret got in.

"What the—?" Jessie turned around to Diana who looked at her in the rearview mirror.

"Don't ask," Diana said. "That's a request, not an order." She picked up the metal box in the passenger seat and passed it back to Jessie. Rectangular, locked with a combination, Jessie felt the contents slide. "Your weapon, your identification, your badge, all intact. I'll give you the combination when we get there."

"Get where?"

Diana gave her a warning look.

When they got into the area Jessie began to recognize, Diana made two phone calls. "Don't turn me in because I'm on the phone while driving," she said with a smile as she caught Jessie's eye in the mirror. The first call went to Nicki.

"Yeah, who is this?"

"You want to see your sister?"

"Yes, where? Who?"

"Three o'clock, Two Ten High Street. Be there." She hung up even as Nicki was sputtering.

The next call went to the police department. "Peterson, please." She listened. "Patch me through." There must have been a protest. "Regarding Galbreath." It took a moment but he came on. "Peterson. You want Galbreath? Three o'clock, Two Ten High Street. Be there." Then she hung up on him as well.

"What are you doing?" Jessie asked.

"Taking you home."

"But—but—"

"Just hush, Jessie. There's nothing you can do at this point anyway. It's all arranged."

They drove through town in after-lunch traffic, without speaking. Diana pulled around to the back of a three-story house that had been converted to offices. Jessie glanced at the attorney's name as they pulled in.

"Showtime, ladies. Please smile pretty for the cameras." Diana opened the door for Jessie and Julie scooted across the seat to come out the same side.

"Diana," Jessie said as she got out. "Are we going to have a minute to talk?"

"Time for that is past," Diana said without looking at her.

She left the keys in the car and pointed to the side door where a woman was motioning them in. "Combination for the box is your birthday. I finally learned when it was."

Inside, the office was organized chaos. Nicki hit Jessie with a hug, grabbing Julie also. They were pulled across the large room and then Peterson along with Captain Conrad was there, grabbing her arm. Jessie turned frantically around to see what happened to Diana, where she was, what was happening to her, only to see her being led away by two men and a woman, all dressed in black suits, looking like Federal agents, along with one man in a gray suit who looked like an attorney.

Diana didn't look back.

CHAPTER TWENTY-FOUR

Three years later

Diana unlocked the door to her apartment. She had made it through another week. Friday night movies and pizza beckoned. She mixed her first drink of the evening and took it with her to the shower.

Something raunchy tonight for the movie, she decided as she washed off the week. Something that would take her mind off all her frustrations, something that would let her escape from her tiny apartment, her unexciting, stressful job, her much smaller world than she had once lived in. All she wanted to do was to escape from reality into her own little space and make the world go away.

She fixed her second drink after she called for the pizza. Now that dinner was taken care of, she could put her feet up and have her night. Tomorrow would come soon enough. She lay her head back on the couch and stared at the ceiling. Saturday was the powwow and she needed to make an appearance. Had to keep up the good relations when you worked with the Indians. Carlton should be the one to go, he was the executive director, but he had pressing family concerns demanding his attention. Diana snorted. In a pig's eye. He just hated the PR stuff and shoved it off on her every opportunity. And she didn't have much choice these days. No one really cared to hire her for anything financial when every financial record she worked on got audited, when there were Federal agents coming around. She had to work outside her field at what she could and in this case, she was Program Administrator for the Florida Native American Indian Society.

She closed her eyes. There was a party on Sunday and she needed to go. She had been isolating herself more and more, and friends were beginning to notice. She didn't know which was worse: the Feds coming around to have a friendly little chat or her friends coming around to check up on her. She wished they would all go away. Sometimes she wished *everything* would go away.

She sat with her head back, trying to clear her mind. She had never dreamed it would be so bad. Maybe she should have taken the offer to go into the witness protection program, get a new identity and just escape, start fresh. Why hadn't she? It wasn't like she had anything to hold on to in this life. Everything was gone.

There was a knock at the door and she got up, expecting pizza. Instead she opened the door to Jessie.

It is a sin, was her first thought, *that someone can change so little since I first laid eyes on her fifteen years ago.*

Jessie stood there, still long and lanky, again wearing blue jeans and white shirt with the sleeves rolled up. She was a little fuller in the face, had a few gray hairs, the same dark soulful eyes only now marked by character lines. The dark sunglasses were in her hands. Diana's mouth went dry.

And she has the same damn effect on me now as she did then!

"You're not delivering a pizza," Diana said when she could find her voice.

"No, I gave up that second job a long time ago." Jessie half turned to look over the apartment parking lot. "However, I do believe your dinner has just pulled in." She stepped back as the gangly kid threw open his car door, left the vehicle running and leaped up the steps two at a time to Diana's door.

"Thank you," he said breathlessly already turning and leaping down the stairs when she told him to keep the change.

"Well, come on in, don't just stand there," Diana said crossly as she took the pizza and set it on the table that separated the kitchen from the living room. "What are you doing here?" *Is Kentucky trying a new tactic sending you?* But she decided that was just her distrust and suspicious mind.

Jessie closed the door behind her as she glanced around the small apartment. "Oh, I'm traveling through. Thought I'd stop and look you up."

"Traveling through? Where're you heading?" Diana turned back to face Jessie, drinking in the sight of her. Her delight at seeing Jessie warred with her suspicion and resentment. The last time had been when Diana delivered her and Julie to the lawyer's office, and under normal conditions, that probably would have been the last of it. However, considering the role Jessie had played in her life, she hadn't been able to let her memory go. Thoughts of Jessie had preyed on her mind a lot in the past three years. Preyed: what an appropriate word.

Jessie stood just inside the door, not moving further into the living room. Diana knew she could see the entire apartment, small kitchen with an altar table separating it from the living room, the two small bedrooms at the far end, a doorway leading to the bathroom.

Quite a change, isn't it? Diana thought, but pride kept her from saying, *Not like the luxury of the cabin or hotel rooms we shared, is it?*

"Ocala," Jessie finally answered. She turned a questioning gaze back to Diana.

"Seems like you're close enough you could have made it. It's only a couple of hours further down the road." Diana moved over to her desk and started to search for her cigarettes. Months had passed since she'd had one, but she knew there was a pack in there somewhere. Ahhh, there they were.

"Am I stressing you?" Jessie asked as she eyed the cluttered roll-top desk, the bulletin board on the wall beside it. "I don't mean to."

"Of course not." Diana picked up the lighter and bent her head to light the cigarette and then tossed the lighter down. She turned back to Jessie, curious but not enough to ask, *Why the hell are you showing up now?*

"I promised Nicki if I got close to Tallahassee, I'd look you up," Jessie explained as if she had heard Diana's question.

Nice you promised Nicki. "Why?" In spite of trying to keep her voice neutral, the question came out sharp and demanding. *Why even bother after all this time?*

Jessie leaned back against the door. She looked a little surprised, but Diana could almost see her thinking that soon they'd be talking like they always had, like old times.

"Old times," Jessie said. She glanced around the apartment, taking in the two bedrooms. "You living alone now?" Diana gave her an appraising look. "I remember Nicki told me she thought you might be with someone but she wasn't sure."

"Kelly and I split up about eight months ago."

"I'm sorry."

"I'm not. I gave her a raw deal. She deserves better."

"Hmm." Jessie moved over to sit on the arm of the chair beside the door. "Where's Margaret?"

"In Europe."

Diana pulled the desk chair out with a jerk and sat down. "All right, Jessie. What do you want?"

Jessie pulled back, surprise on her face. "Just a conversation." She frowned, tilted her head as if in puzzlement, as if Diana had ripped up her script. The openness faded from her eyes and the guarded expression appeared as if it were finally dawning on her that perhaps Diana wasn't so happy to see her. This time Diana kept quiet and let Jessie fill the silence. "We haven't talked in a long time."

Diana still didn't say anything, didn't look away, but refused to speak.

"We used to have a lot to say to each other," Jessie said after several moments had passed.

"Did we? As I recall, we usually went right to bed," Diana said coldly.

"Not always," Jessie protested quietly. She waited a moment and then started again, this time on a different tact. "Nicki tell you she was pregnant?"

"No. The last thing I got from her was a Christmas card."

"Baby's due in early December."

Diana made no response.

"Did you know Julie and the clinic got some big award?"

"No."

Jessie sat there and searched Diana's face, frowning at Diana's coldness.

"Now that you have totally exhausted all conversation about people we mutually know, was there something else you wanted to say?"

Jessie looked down at the beige rug and then looked up. "I know I never called."

"I noticed."

"I probably should have," Jessie went on.

"So? You didn't." Diana ground out her cigarette. *I only saved your life. Not once. Twice. Can't imagine why you might call.* She ignored the thought buried even deeper. *Never mind that I loved you.*

"You know, we never got a chance to talk about everything that happened."

"I know." Diana pulled out another cigarette but only played with it. *Like, whose fault is that?* "I've been so busy for the past few years that I just couldn't find the time to fit such a minor conversation like that into my schedule."

Jessie drew back as if she had been slapped. "You know," she started again, still in a mild voice, "my therapist explained to me that sarcasm usually hides a hint of anger."

Diana thought about the statement for a minute. *A therapist. That's interesting.* She finally nodded. "Your therapist might be right. Of course, I didn't need to go to a therapist to figure that out. I simply pinned images up and used them for target practice." She turned to watch Jessie to see how she was responding.

Jessie paled and her nostrils flared as she took a deep breath. "You're angry with me," she said after a moment.

"Your hearing's improved."

"I was afraid to contact you because I didn't know how it would look, what it would cost me on the job. I was afraid it would cast doubts on my professional integrity." Jessie said it in an even tone, without looking up at Diana.

"And to think once I admired you for your openness." Diana shook her head as she ground out the newly lit cigarette. "That might be a true statement, Jessie. It's probably even part of the reason." She stiffly turned back to give Jessie a challenging look. "But I think it's more likely you didn't want to feel any gratitude toward the daughter of Czar Randalson for saving your life. Except for me, you'd be nothing but a name on the monument in the city park dedicated to those officers who died in the line of duty."

Jessie gave a sick little smile as she spread her hands, examined her fingers. "Something my sister reminds me of every year."

Glad somebody does. "She sends me a thank you note every year."

Jessie nodded. "On my birthday."

"I wondered if that was deliberate timing or just coincidence."

Jessie seemed to gather herself to start again. "I know I should have called."

"Why?"

"You saved my life."

"So? I'm sure anyone in my position, having the connections I did and knowing the danger you were in would have done the same thing."

Jessie looked up at her in shock, and Diana stared her down. They both knew there had been no one else who would have been able to do what Diana had done.

"I thought you did it because you loved me," Jessie said in an even quieter voice.

Diana fought down the rage she felt welling up. The past few years had taught her a good deal about not speaking when she was angry. "That's funny, at the time, I thought so too," she said finally, bitterly.

This time Jessie avoided looking at her. She shifted her weight in the chair, uncomfortable. "It's my fault. I should have reached out."

"That would have been nice."

"I was afraid to."

"I never took you for a coward."

Jessie flinched.

"I take that back," Diana went on abruptly, pouncing on Jessie's reaction. She knew she was getting ugly, knew it and couldn't stop herself. She clenched her hands to control her shaking. "You were a coward when you wouldn't look for Julie because she might reject you. You were a coward when you held on to her as an ideal instead of moving on and finding someone else. So why wouldn't you be a coward about calling me after everything I risked to save you?"

Jessie's head jerked up, her face went white and she jumped to her feet. She advanced a step toward Diana, her hands clenched into fists at her sides.

Probably, Diana thought distractedly, no one had ever called her a coward before. She herself didn't move. As angry as she was, she would have welcomed a physical struggle. But Jessie stopped after a step.

"Coming here was a mistake," Jessie said hoarsely through gritted teeth, her eyes narrowed.

"Well, it certainly falls under the category of too little, too late. So why don't you leave? You can tell Nicki you kept your promise and looked me up. And you can tell her what a mistake it was because I threw you out." She didn't even get up from the chair.

"Diana," Jessie started and her voice was shaking.

"What?!" Diana demanded curtly, feeling the cold anger shut down every other emotion.

This time Jessie heard the cold rage and stepped back. "I came to apologize, to say I'm sorry." She half raised her hand in appeal.

"Fine. If that's what you came here to say, you said it. Now leave."

"Diana, I don't want it to end like this."

"It already has. It ended years ago. So now you've said your piece. You've said you're sorry. Now leave, just leave." Diana stood so abruptly the chair fell over backward.

With a hurt and bewildered look, Jessie turned away. When she reached out for the door, she hesitated and started to turn back but stopped. She shook her head and went out the door, closing it softly behind her.

Diana went to the door as soon as it closed and locked it, latched it. She bowed her head against the door, listening, but only heard normal apartment-complex sounds. She heard, but didn't move to the window to see, a car door slam, the vehicle start and pull away. She could still see the surprise, the shock on Jessie's face, the hurt from Diana's attack.

Diana pushed away from the door, wiped the tears away, angry with herself for being ugly with Jessie, angry with Jessie for just dropping by like nothing had changed, that three years of silence hadn't happened, and just angry with the world. Suddenly the apartment was too small, too confining when she wanted...wanted what?

She went to the phone. "Hey," she managed to say in a civil tone when there was finally an answer. "I found some energy. You still up for that game? Fine, I'll meet you at the court." She glanced at her watch. "Twenty minutes? Okay."

A quick clothes change, stuff the pizza in the fridge, pull the racquetball bag out of the closet, and she was out the door. She had to remind herself to slow down. She had enough adrenaline to fly over to the park but a speeding ticket would not be good. She put Jessie out of her mind.

Brenda pulled in beside her before she even got out of the car. "Glad you changed your mind," the trim athletic woman greeted her. "Where'd you find the energy?" Then she stepped back when Diana slammed the Jeep door.

"Out of the past!" Diana snapped.

"Okay." Brenda retreated another step back from Diana. "I guess you're more than ready for a good game."

Good friends, Diana decided, are gold. She knew she was angry and shitty but she also knew Brenda wouldn't ask anything, at least not right away. Right now, she needed that, and she needed something to drain off all this angry energy without doing something foolish. Brenda was a good player, much better than Diana, except when Diana was pissed. Then her reaction time improved, her strength increased, as if every sense she had were determined to eradicate the ball from existence. On the floor, against the wall, in the air, Diana was determined. They were both winded in short order.

"The ball have a name tonight?" Brenda asked as she bent over, trying to catch her breath. Diana shook her head. "You know, if you could do this when you weren't pissed, you'd be a decent player."

Diana gave a short laugh and stretched up. She took a deep cleansing breath, released it. She felt better. "Sorry, Brenda. It's been a rough week."

"Uh-huh."

"Budget cuts," Diana offered in explanation. "Had to tell one of the interns the position's cut."

"Your position safe?"

"Yeah. It's funded by a grant. I'm good for a year. At least."

Brenda began to move around, indicating she was ready to start again. "So you're bushed at five o'clock and by seven you're ready to whip the world." Brenda cast a disbelieving eye, and Diana began to stretch.

"Yep."

"Order your pizza and movie?"

Diana bounced the ball and gave her friend a warning glance. "Just leave it right now, Brenda. Please."

Brenda gestured with the racquet. "Your serve, my dear."

Diana slowly began to lose her edge, her energy, and it showed in her play. She finally called it, signifying she'd had enough.

"Want to stop for a beer?" Brenda asked as they packed up. "Or are you really ready to go home and face those four walls?"

"You know I don't drink beer, Brenda."

Brenda shrugged and looked noncommittal. She still looked noncommittal when the waitress set the bottle and glass in front of her, the cola in front of Diana, and took their sandwich order.

"I don't understand human nature," Diana said slowly. "I've waited years for that woman to talk to me in some capacity. So when she drops in, I throw her out."

"Three years is a long time to wait," Brenda commented as she poured the beer. "And probably dropping in on you was not the wisest choice."

Diana gave a humorless sound. "When it comes to personal relationships, Jessie doesn't always make the wisest choices." She glanced up but Brenda merely looked at her with a bland expression on her broad face. "I know. I'm not the sharpest tack in the box either," Diana added, before Brenda might dryly point that out to her.

"We can always see more clearly into someone else's relationship."

Diana shook her head in disbelief. "I opened that door and saw her and the years just fell away. I literally couldn't speak. It was like the whole world disappeared, time didn't matter, nothing mattered except she was there." She was lost in the memory of Jessie standing there.

"She certainly has a pull on you." Brenda's tone was cautious.

Diana shook her head, coming back to the present. "Margaret used to say I lost all common sense when it came to Jessie." She glanced up to see Brenda bite her lip. "I suppose so." She sipped her drink. "The highlight of my life was seeing the surprise and pleasure on Jessie's face when I showed up in town."

"If she knocked on your door expecting that from you, she got a rude surprise. I don't think I've ever seen you so mad."

"And I had calmed down some by the time I got to the court." Diana shook her head. "I haven't been that mad since—" She stopped. Even as much as Brenda had gained her confidence, there were some things she couldn't say and *Since I wanted to break Waldo into tiny little pieces* was something she couldn't say. "Well, for a long, long time. I was so mad I was afraid to move, that I might shatter and explode or I don't know, something." She shivered at her remembered anger.

"Did she say why she came?" Diana shook her head. "Why she dropped in on you?"

Diana moved her drink at the approach of the waitress with their food. "She said she promised Nicki, that's her sister, if she ever got close to Tallahassee, she'd stop and look me up. That's all." She accepted the plate, took a deep breath, and waited until the waitress was gone. "You know what I think really pissed me off?"

"What's that?" Brenda began all the motions of modifying her sandwich, removing the pickle, adding ketchup, salt. "Want my tomato?" Diana shook her head.

"She said she was afraid to contact me in the years past because it might compromise her integrity with her co-workers." She looked to Brenda for confirmation, and Brenda didn't look up. "Is that strange or what?"

Brenda closed her sandwich. She didn't say anything, her expression carefully neutral.

"What?" Diana demanded. "You're in law enforcement, tell me: did I expect too much?"

Brenda avoided Diana's eye sas she spoke, which made Diana listen more carefully. "Every place is different. You have to work with those people. They have to back you up. Sometimes you get in places where you depend on them answering your call. You try hard not to give them any doubts." She looked up at Diana as if checking whether Diana understood what she was saying. "From everything you said, Czar was a powerful force. Anything related to him would have been—" She stopped suddenly. "Questionable," she finally finished.

Diana realized that Brenda had deliberately picked a more tactful word. She put her sandwich down. "Have I compromised you?" The thought had never occurred to her before.

Brenda shook her head. "No. You're not doing anything now. You've been under such a microscope that everyone knows you're clean. Oh, there's been some comments." She shook her head with an exasperated look. "Nothing substantive to speak of." She looked up to meet Diana's defensive gaze. "But you have to understand, at that time, with everything going on, it had to have been a different story."

Diana took a deep breath. She didn't like it. She wanted to defend herself that she had done everything she could to keep Jessie safe, but with the passage of time, she had gotten a different perspective. Years of time and dealing with prosecutors and lawyers and police. Oh, yes, she had a very different perspective. "All right," she said after a moment. "Maybe I expected too much. Maybe I did have the fantasy she'd love me enough to give up police work, but I knew it was a fantasy. I guess what pissed me off was that I never heard anything. I mean, once it came out I saved her butt, I figured I deserved at least a thank you. I didn't expect something so simple would compromise her integrity."

"I don't know," Brenda said. "I wasn't there."

Diana eyed Brenda as she ate her sandwich. There were times she could forget Brenda was in law enforcement. Short brown tightly curled hair, broad open face, soft-spoken, reasonable, pragmatic. Diana didn't know how she would have survived these past months without the friendship of this woman who exuded calmness, confidence and reason. Nothing seemed to excite her.

"So you think I was wrong," Diana said finally. That law enforcement had its own little code, its unspoken rules, should not have been any surprise. Maybe an oversight but no surprise.

"Depends on what you wanted. If you wanted to hurt her back." She raised an eyebrow as Diana's chin went up. "I repeat, if you were hurt and you wanted to hurt her back for the years of silence, you probably did a bang-up job. If you wanted to open a conversation, you probably blew it. I think a lot of it depends on what she wanted. If she was just looking up an old friend..." Brenda gave Diana a sudden look. "She knows you loved her, doesn't she?"

"Yeah, she finally got the picture. It was just late in the game. A lot of things started happening then and it got shoved to a back burner."

Brenda sat back, looked at Diana curiously. "She tell you she loved you?"

No, Diana admitted to herself. "At the cabin she said she missed me, was hurt I never came back, loved me but never understood me. But that was a reference to the past, not the present."

"Diana?"

"No," Diana finally answered. "She never said she loved me, never in the present tense." *And she never acted like it either. Friends with benefits*, Diana thought bitterly. *I'm a fool.* She took a deep breath. "So I've been carrying a torch all these years for someone who doesn't love me back? God, that makes me sound pitiful. Or stupid. Or both." Diana looked at the remainder of her sandwich. She wasn't going to be able to finish it. "Some fantasy person who looked like Jessie and didn't exist at all."

"I wouldn't say that she didn't exist," Brenda said slowly. "And it might well be she does have feelings for you, maybe just not what you wanted."

Diana buried her face in her hands. "God, I'm an idiot."

"No, not an idiot," Brenda assured her. "But maybe you've kept too much to yourself for your own good sometimes."

"I called her a coward." Through her spread fingers, she saw Brenda wince.

"Not exactly the thing to call someone in law enforcement, dear."

Diana didn't raise her head. "I didn't link it to anything about her job. I just said she was a coward when she didn't look up Julie, when she used her to avoid looking for a relationship. When she didn't call me."

"That might well have been true then, but it probably wasn't the thing to say."

Diana slowly raised her head. "I really blew it, didn't I?" She searched Brenda's face. "I've been doing the same thing I accused Jessie of, holding out for her the same way she held out for Julie."

"I don't think it's the same." Brenda took a long swallow of beer. "You had a few things going on that were obstacles."

"Like being tailed when you're trying to date?" Diana said with bitter amusement. At least she could laugh about it now, and it appeared that Brenda too could see the humor in it. Now.

Brenda did give a smile of remembering. "Well, there were difficulties, I'll admit. It wasn't easy but it wasn't impossible. You and I flirted with the idea of a relationship before we settled down to be friends. You and Kelly worked a bit more seriously at it. You never said a relationship was out of the question."

Diana ran her finger around the rim of her glass. "Should I have called her?"

Brenda shook her head. "Probably not. You still had a lot of legal issues. State of Kentucky still have charges against you?"

"Kentucky's a Commonwealth but no, all that just got settled. They were pissed at the Feds over the jurisdiction, and I was the bone between two dogs fighting over territory. I thought it'd never get wrapped up and they'd leave me hanging forever."

"It might well have been why she couldn't contact you—because of the investigations. Some jurisdictions are funny about that."

"So you are saying I blew it—I expected too much from her and then threw her out when she came to apologize?"

Brenda gave a sympathetic laugh. "I don't know, Diana. This is between you and Jessie. I just hate to see you hurt." She shook her head. "If you were hurt and wanted to lash out, then that's done. If she loves you, then maybe she'll figure out you wouldn't be so mad if there wasn't a lot of feeling there. Since you called her a coward, maybe she'll come back just to disprove it. If there was nothing there, then maybe she'll just pack up and be gone, figuring that, okay, she tried her bit and if that's your attitude, good riddance. I can't predict what someone I don't know is going to do. Hell, I can't predict what you're going to do, and I know you a good deal better."

"You're not alone in that department. *I* don't know what I'm going to do. All I know is I've got a splitting headache now and the past—" she paused to look at her watch, "the past four hours have been a nightmare."

"Thanks."

"Oh, you're wonderful, Brenda. What would I do without you, as a sounding board, as a friend, as someone I can count on?" She laughed even though it hurt her head. "You'll even tell me when I'm wrong. Now that's a friend. Let me tell you, I've had a lot of 'yes ma'am' people in my life."

Brenda finished her beer. "Well, now, friend, I'm going to tell you it's late. I've got a shift in the morning. You've got plans. It's time to go home and go to bed." She searched Diana's face. "Bad headache?" Diana nodded. "I'll follow you home, make sure you get there. You going to make it tomorrow?"

"Oh, yeah. Got to. People to see, things to do."

CHAPTER TWENTY-FIVE

"Oh, God," Diana muttered the next morning when she opened the apartment door to leave. "Florida sunshine." She squinted at the brightness then closed the door and went back to dig out her darker sunglasses. It wasn't like she had a hangover, she hadn't had that much to drink. It was just the combination of the anger, the crying, the lack of sleep. It was not going to be a good morning. She longed to hide in the computer room, darken the blinds, turn down the volume of the day and just hibernate. Not to be. Instead she had to go and make nice with all the organizations she worked with when she researched early Native Americans. So here she was, dressed in blue jeans, white shirt, leather vest and knee-high laced moccasins, going out to bright sunshine, and if experience proved accurate, listening to drums all day long.

"Oh, God," she repeated as she slipped on the darkest sunglasses possible. She glanced at her watch. "Maybe by three I can leave, come home, crash." She scanned the sky. Carolina blue, no clouds. The day was already turning warm. Great day for a powwow. *Ohhh, my head.*

The green-uniformed deputy sheriff stopped her from turning into the parking area filling the open field. Diana paused to look at the serious face behind mirrored sunglasses and the broad-brimmed hat. "Feeling better this morning?" Brenda asked.

"Pretty much, but the sun's too bright. Good turnout so far?"

Brenda looked out over the rapidly filling field, the traffic coming down the county road. "Hasn't stopped since nine this morning."

"Poor baby. You got your comfy shoes on?" She was always surprised how authoritative her friend looked when she was in uniform.

The signal came for another line to start for parking, and Brenda motioned for cars to continue. "See you later. Have a good day."

Diana parked the car and started across the field. She would put last night behind her, and she began to relax.

The feeling started about an hour later. She was at a booth looking at pottery when the hair stood up on the back of her neck. She rubbed her neck, not thinking about it and then it registered. She was being watched. She hadn't had such a feeling for a long time, and she couldn't imagine she had done anything recently for anyone to put a tail on her. Nothing was impossible, however. She moved along, skipping the jewelry, going over to watch the dancers' circle. While there were dancing demonstrations at posted times, any member could dance between times. The drummers were drumming and there were about four dancers demonstrating their skills, moving in the circle, and they had drawn a small crowd. Diana could watch the dancers and unobtrusively inspect the crowd.

When she got that restless feeling again, she scanned the crowd. She didn't get a clear glimpse except for the dark hair, but the movement was familiar enough for her to think she recognized it. *No, couldn't be. I'm seeing things.*

Just the same she moved back into the crowd, circled around and went down the row of demonstrations: cooking, weaving, drum-making, storytelling. She stopped and talked to people; after all, that was why she came. She got involved in conversation and was able to forget that specimen-in-a-tray feeling. However, when she moved, it came back. She glanced behind her and saw the individual moving through the crowd. She swore under her breath. *It just can't be.*

She turned abruptly and walked off by herself. Couldn't be Jessie. Had to be her imagination because of the previous night. After all, she didn't get a clear view, it was just a shoulder and someone walking away. There were lots of dark-haired women here. For Pete's sake, it was an Indian powwow. Tall, slender, graceful—the image tugged at her memory.

Stop it, she told herself. *First of all, it would be a hell of a coincidence if Jessie, just traveling through town, happened to attend the powwow. And why in your wildest dreams do you think Jessie would want to talk to you again after you threw her out last night? And what are you going to do if you do see her? Apologize? Cry? Insult her again? Get over it, Diana. That was just your imagination. Or wishful thinking.*

By the time Diana sat down with a plate of pulled pork and fries, she knew she had to clear her head. She ate mechanically, just because she had to do something with her hands. She had really screwed it up this time and now she was seeing Jessie in every jeans-clad woman out of the corner of her eye. That was not good. Hindsight was working overtime telling her how badly she bungled a situation she had been wanting for a long time. And the worst of it was she didn't have the faintest idea how to salvage it—if there was anything to be salvaged. Her headache was beginning again.

When the shadow fell across her corner of the table, she didn't even look up. The last thing she wanted to do was be friendly and pleasant to friends and co-workers. That was why she was sitting off in the corner all by herself, hopeful everyone would take the hint. Maybe if she ignored them long enough, they would go away. When the shadow didn't move and she finally did look up, there stood Jessie.

"We have to talk," Jessie said in greeting. She stood there, looking down at Diana, and she didn't look like she had a good night either. She looked reserved and closed off and hard to read—a cop.

Without a word, Diana indicated the chair across the table. She wasn't sure she could speak, her heart was pounding so. Well, this was what she wanted, another chance to talk to Jessie. Just to see her again, one more time.

"You had quite a head of steam last night," Jessie said as she pulled the chair out and sat down. She looked directly at Diana through narrowed eyes and for the first time, Diana could imagine the police uniform, a visible badge instead of the blue jeans, white shirt and jacket. It was a faintly disturbing thought. "Did you get it out of your system enough so we can have a decent conversation? Or are you going to get all ugly again?"

Diana's chin went up. She had sat across too many tables lately explaining things to people like Jessie. "I told you a long time ago. I don't like surprises. I don't do well." And all the time she was thinking *How the hell did you get here? What did you do? Tail me from my apartment? And why in hell do I have to explain anything to you?*

"It wasn't exactly the reception I was expecting when I dropped by to see an old friend," Jessie went on. "Seems to me you were pretty pissed and it didn't have a lot to do with being surprised."

"No, it had a whole lot more with not hearing from you for the past three years." *Three years of wondering what went wrong, if you even appreciated what I risked for you, if you even knew or cared what I did. If I even mattered. Wondering if it was all worth it.*

"Did you expect to?" There was an edge in Jessie's voice, a coldness Diana had never heard from her.

Yes, I expected. All of Brenda's questions from the night before came flooding back. *But that was my fantasy. Not you at all. I might as well admit that.* She caught hold of her temper. There was nothing to gain by getting angry. And she wanted to have a good last memory of Jessie, not an angry confrontational one.

"I thought it'd be nice," she forced herself to say in a mild tone. "But that was my expectation, had nothing to do with you." She paused. Apologies never came easy to her, especially apologies when she knew she was in the wrong. She did not like backing down, it went against every fiber in her. Even when there was nothing at risk. "I'm sorry I blew up last night. I was ugly and offensive. I apologize."

Jessie drummed her fingers on her arm. Her eyes narrowed even more as if she were weighing Diana's words. The minutes dragged on before she spoke and when she did, her voice was just as chilly as before. "You know I was quite tempted to go back to the motel, check out and drive on to Ocala. I really didn't expect to be thrown out when I stopped in to see you."

Diana said nothing. If Jessie didn't want to accept her apology, there was nothing she could do. Explanations had never been part of her repertoire. *Accept it,* she prayed. *Accept it, and say whatever you came here to say so I can go back to dismantling the fantasy of you and get my head back into reality. And let you go.*

Jessie waited a moment, still looking at Diana as if she wanted to dissect her. "You still never explain anything, do you?" she said finally.

Diana shook her head but she felt something within unbend. Jessie remembered that about her, acknowledged that much. Now she waited to see what Jessie might have to say.

"I must have spent over an hour on the phone with Nicki," Jessie went on when she finally realized Diana wasn't going to say anything. "She has the idea you wouldn't be so mad if there was nothing there. She's the one who convinced me we need to sit down and talk."

Diana felt like her heart turned over. Did that mean there was something there for Jessie too? She clamped down on grasping for straws. She had been down that road far too often. "And what do we need to talk about?" She tried to make her tone as neutral as she could.

Jessie said nothing but she lost the narrowed gaze, some of the chilly demeanor went away. For Diana, the police image went away and just Jessie sat across from her. She could see the changes, the physical changes the years had delivered. There were lines around Jessie's eyes, character lines from dealing with life. Her expression wasn't so open, there was a harder set to the jaw, lips compressed. The reality clashed with Diana's memory of a happy, eager-for-life Jessie, but she found the image just as endearing, just as enticing.

"We could talk about us. What happened. Where it went wrong."

"What's there to say?" Diana tried to just toss it off. She didn't want to give in to her hope that was part of her fantasy. "We started out as a one-night stand. You were hung up on a lost love, and I didn't want attachments. You wanted an itch scratched, and I wanted to touch someone."

Jessie drew back at Diana's bluntness. "I wouldn't put it that crassly." She looked positively offended.

"Why not?" Diana responded with a callousness she didn't totally feel. Their encounters might have started out purely physical, two horny dykes indulging an instant attraction but it had changed as those encounters continued. "Wasn't that the reality? You had a busy life and didn't have time for a relationship. Cops have a twenty-four-hour a day job. And you had a family to take care of besides. Julie was a handy excuse, lost love, guilt over abandoning her. Made you quite the romantic figure, the strong silent type with the faint whiff of a tragic past. I'm sure everyone viewed you with the idea of being the one who could redeem you. Made the itch easier to scratch, didn't it?"

Jessie leaned back in the chair. She looked at Diana with a slightly bewildered expression. "Is that how you saw it?" She frowned. "And you? You seem to have had my life figured out. What role did you see yourself in?"

Interesting that she doesn't disagree. "Mysterious stranger, mysterious background, probably money in the background, secretive. A lot of blanks for women to fill in any way they wanted to imagine. Here today, gone tomorrow." She gave a faint smile. "Undercover work, spies, anyone could fill in whatever turned them on."

"So what happened to change it?"

What indeed. How do you explain an attraction you don't even understand? Diana shrugged. She wasn't sure when it changed, only knew it had. Somewhere, sometime, she had crossed the line and she had begun to care about Jessie as a person. "I kept coming back."

"Why?"

Why indeed? Diana mused. Maybe because Jessie treated her like a person. Maybe because she didn't have a role to play, she could just be herself. "You touched me."

She looked away from Jessie, looked off in the distance. She could finally say it. Jessie touched her in ways she said she would never be touched. It had been an awakening, and it had thrilled her as much as it had frightened her. "I tried to tell you that night we had the fight about Julie. I wanted you so much it wasn't even reasonable any more. Even when I was away from you, I could feel you, like I was incomplete without you. I had to see you again. So I'd go back." She could remember how strong the urge was to return to Lexington, even when she suspected it might be dangerous, when she was setting up a pattern someone else could see. Now she understood what Margaret worried about, feared for all those times Diana had forbidden her to come along.

"Why didn't you tell me?"

Diana turned back to Jessie in annoyance. "Did you need it said, written to you in big bold black letters on the side of a building? Damn it, Jessie, why didn't you see it?" That was something that always bugged her, why hadn't Jessie realized Diana's feelings? Why did it have to be said?

Jessie looked down at her lap, uncomfortable. Evidently it had bothered her too. "In the beginning you said you wanted it in the here and now. You gave every indication that if I questioned anything, wanted to know more, you'd be gone in a heartbeat. You never shared details of your life, anything, what you did, where you came from. Nothing." She looked up at Diana, defensive, as if Diana was blaming her when she was only trying to follow the rules Diana had established. "Why should I have seen it? You never said anything to indicate conditions changed."

That was true enough. Diana couldn't deny it. She might have been compelled to return to Lexington again and again but every time, she had the impulse to flee. It wouldn't have taken much to have made her leave. But surely she had said something to tell Jessie how important she was. Even if she didn't, why else would she have returned to Lexington so often?

Jessie pressed on, leaning against the table. She must have sensed Diana's lack of defense or maybe she just thought it unfair Diana thought her so blind. "Even the night we had the fight over Julie. Do you remember what triggered it?"

Diana struggled to remember. She couldn't exactly remember what had been said except Jessie had erupted when Diana said she was still holding on to Julie.

Jessie continued when Diana didn't answer. "I asked if you were sorry about us always ending up in bed when you came to town, and you told me how wonderful you thought I was. And then I asked why we hadn't done something about it."

Diana slowly nodded. She had been so full of anticipation when she had come to town. She just knew this was the weekend that was going to change things. When Jessie had asked the question why, Diana had thought …oh, hell, after this many years, what did it matter what she had thought? "And I said you were still holding on to Julie. It was like turning a fire hose on a campfire. Not even the embers survived."

Jessie wouldn't look at Diana. Maybe she also thought it was an opportunity missed. "I wasn't exactly thinking of Julie at the time," she admitted. "In fact, I had been thinking about Julie less and less. I thought you were using her as an excuse, you didn't want me for anything more than just someone who would be there for you when you were in the area. Saved you from going out and having to find someone."

Diana looked at her in disbelief, her jaw slightly dropping before she realized it. She closed her mouth, but Jessie went on without seeming to notice.

"And then," Jessie plowed on, recounting the night according to her, "we tried going out to dinner. I tried to bring it up again and you still didn't say anything about how you felt. In fact, you brought up that other woman, the one you loved but who was already committed. Everything you said just reinforced the idea I was only there to be on the side, good enough to sleep with when you were in town but nothing more."

"Jessie," Diana protested, "that other woman was you!"

Jessie looked up at her and came back with "I know that now but I didn't realize it then. Everything you said just indicated to me why you wanted me on the side. I felt like I'd blown it, asked too many questions. It was going to be all over, and I'd just lost you completely. I wasn't even going to have you part time." She turned away as if she couldn't face Diana with this admission. "I wanted you so much, I was even willing to accept that."

Oh, my God, what an idiot I was.

"And then we went back to the hotel. Here I thought I was out the door and couldn't believe you still wanted me that night." Jessie shivered as she looked over the open field. "Nothing I've had since has ever matched that night. I felt for the first time, I really had you, you gave me everything you had. And everything I had feared about being a diversion for you, like I was just some toy for your amusement, got blown away. That night, I felt like you trusted me enough to show me all of you, that there was true openness between us. For the first time I felt I could lean on you, and you'd be there, you knew I'd be there for you. I felt like we were the only two people in the world and we mattered to each other." Jessie's words stopped, her expression changed, relaxed.

And the next morning…oh, God.

Abruptly Jessie turned back to Diana and she was brisk again. "And the next morning, you found my badge."

Diana closed her eyes, remembering her fight-or-flight response, her sudden unreasonable panic. She couldn't say anything. Even now, she could remember the shock. She forced herself to look at Jessie.

"I know now why you reacted the way you did," Jessie went on. She avoided looking at Diana. "But I didn't then. And you were—" she fumbled for the word "—strange for the rest of the weekend. I didn't know what was going on. Then you were gone. I had no way of contacting you, knowing what happened. I didn't know what scared you, and to be honest, your discovery of my being a cop wasn't exactly at the top of the list."

Really? Like what else could it be? Diana's curiosity got the best of her. "What did you think it was?"

Jessie gave a careless shrug. "Oh, I thought maybe you thought you were being unfaithful to that other woman. Maybe scared because we'd had such an intense night. Maybe you were afraid you went too far with me, exposed too much. Maybe because what I thought was trust, you saw as exposure." She looked away. "You were gone so long. I didn't think you were ever coming back."

Diana took in Jessie's explanations. Maybe there was a bit of truth in what Jessie had thought. That had been a fateful summer for Diana. She had been so far away, unable to reach Jessie, and she had learned how much she really wanted her, wanted a life with her. When Papa had said it was time to decide, she had pretty much made up her mind. All she had to do was to see if Jessie was willing. "And then Julie arrived back in town."

Jessie nodded. She picked up the napkin from the table and absently began to shred it. "I was shattered. Vulnerable. Maybe if she hadn't returned right then, I'd have done something different. But just the timing. I think I'm just a side dish, and then you." She stopped and shook her head, then went on. "You made me feel like there was an *us*, there was something real between us. And then immediately you don't want to talk about it, you don't explain and then you're gone. And then Julie's there, apologizing, saying she's still interested. I still feel like I abandoned her years ago. She's attentive, she's there, every day. I'd been using her as an excuse for so long, I felt like I was obligated."

Diana drew a deep breath. *If only I had said something. Margaret was right. Brenda even said it last night. I don't share enough.* "Timing." She looked at Jessie and now she could see vulnerability. For the first time she could see she had been part of the problem, it wasn't just Jessie. "I'm sorry," she said quietly.

Jessie gave a deep sigh. "By the time you did come back to town, I'd already given a commitment to Julie." She looked up at Diana and her eyes narrowed. "I was pissed too. You would waltz in and out of town whenever you pleased. No communication. Me never knowing where I stood. You just always had to be in charge. I wanted to show you I wasn't there just waiting for you." She looked back at the napkin and her voice dropped. "I didn't think you would just leave and not come back. So I decided I really wasn't important to you and Julie was a good choice for me."

"Ohhh, Jessie," Diana said with a moan. She buried her face in her hands at the thought of the lost opportunities, the mixed messages, the words that didn't get said. She looked up when Jessie sighed again.

Jessie straightened up, seemed to gather herself. She shook her head and looked down at her hands, evidently just realizing what she had been doing. She began to pick up the pieces of the napkin. "The story of my life," she commented. "Pieces and shreds. In college I couldn't keep Julie because of family obligations. I couldn't hold on to you because..." She stopped and looked up at Diana. "I don't even know why. Because I asked too many questions? Because I got tired of you making choices about my life? Because I didn't want to be taken for granted?"

"Maybe all that," Diana offered. "Maybe none of it." Her voice lacked conviction.

Jessie shrugged in dismissal. She wadded up the paper shreds like she was wadding up their past. "Doesn't matter anyway. It ended." She got to her feet and reached for Diana's discarded plate. "You done?" Diana nodded and Jessie took the plate. "I'm going to get something to drink. You need anything?"

Diana checked her cup and shook her head. Jessie took the plate and napkins to the trash barrel in the corner and then walked over to the counter. Diana turned to watch her go, watched her scan the crowd before she approached the counter. *So many missed opportunities,* she thought even as she drank in Jessie's form, watched her pull change out of her pocket. *Damn, she has turned into one handsome woman.*

She took a drink from her cup, reflecting on what Jessie had said. *All the stupid assumptions we made, my thinking she should know because I kept coming back. And I guess in a way she did because when I didn't come back, she assumed it was over. Stupid. Stupid. Stupid. Why didn't I say anything?*

"And you're still doing it," Jessie said as she sat back down across the table.

Diana blinked, Jessie's words merged with her thoughts as if she were a mind reader. "Doing what?"

"Making choices about my life." Jessie popped the can and poured it into the Styrofoam cup of ice. "Even when you're out of my life, you made an impact. You warn me about a bad sting, tell me not to go. I go and damn near get killed. Chalk one up for you. I get kidnapped and you coming running to my rescue. Chalk another one up for you." She took a drink, watching Diana over the rim of her cup, her expression less vulnerable now. She swirled the drink in the cup, mixing it with the ice. "I could not believe my eyes when you came bursting through that door. On the other hand." She gave a cynical look up at Diana. "Who else would show up?"

Diana considered Jessie's change of subject. Was she following the time and event sequence? *Or is safer talking about almost getting killed than being romantically rejected?* "Didn't look like anyone else was able to do anything."

Jessie tipped the cup, watched the dark liquid flow over the ice. "I saw you at the funeral," she said carefully without looking up at Diana. She lifted her cup for a long swallow. "The mysterious woman in black."

Diana stilled. That was how the papers had dubbed her at her father's funeral because they didn't know who she was. The funeral had been a crowded event, as many from law enforcement as family members. Diana had never before felt so on display, and it was then she realized just how alone she was and how much she missed Margaret. "Why were you there?"

"Identification," Jessie said simply. "Normally I wouldn't have been but there were individuals there who we were not previously aware of. I would be able to recognize some of them." She seemed to be making an effort to remain casual, as if she guessed talking about Czar's funeral might be touchy.

"Like me."

"Well, yes," Jessie admitted, "but you had such an escort we knew who you were. There were others we were interested in."

An understatement, Diana considered. There were people there to pay their respects, yes; and, it was an opportunity for potential leaders to size each other up as they jockeyed to fill the void. "Yes," Diana admitted. She made the effort to keep her tone neutral. "There were lots of people there. You must have run out of film," she added dryly.

"We don't use film anymore, Diana. But I get your point." Jessie took another drink. "The Feds kept you pretty well under wraps. You disappeared after that."

Safe houses. Interrogations. Frequent moves. Seeing no one. "Yes," she could say now. "Hurry up and wait. I was never sure if they thought I would skip or someone would kill me." *And in the end...*

"I couldn't find you."

"That was hardly my choice."

Jessie shrugged. "Wasn't mine." She met Diana's gaze. "Seems like I never knew where you were, Diana. I was always waiting, first on you, then on the system. Even when I knew you were down here, I had to wait until the Feds and Kentucky were through with you. And all the time you're sitting here, getting pissed as hell because I haven't talked to you." She took a piece of ice, chewed on it, watching Diana. "How do you like waiting?"

Diana frowned at the new edge in Jessie's voice, not exactly antagonistic but there was something there. "About as much as I like surprises."

Jessie nodded. "I figured as much. I never liked it either." She thoughtfully ran her finger around the rim of the cup. "You know, I used to keep a log on my calendar trying to figure out the best guess as to when you'd show up." She looked up at Diana expectantly.

"I didn't know."

Jessie nodded again. "No, I don't suppose it ever occurred to you. Or the fact that I took extra duty, extra shifts so I would have the time banked when you did show up so we could have some time together." She raised one eyebrow as she looked at Diana. "Never occurred to you, did it?" Diana shook her head. "Thought not. So why am I surprised that I rearrange my life to come see you and you throw me out?"

Rearrange her life?

"After all, you just pop up in the damnedest places, and I'm supposed to be just delighted to see you and just go along with it?"

Jessie lifted her hand, holding up one finger before Diana could say anything. "Don't get me wrong, that last time I was damned glad to see you even if I didn't have the foggiest idea what you were doing there. Somehow the 'how' and 'why' just wasn't germane." She dropped her hand. "And it all got explained. At least most of it. In due time."

Diana said nothing but she felt the warning bells go off.

"I suppose," Jessie went on casually, "I might as well ask questions about those missing parts now while we're talking. All the investigations are over, cases are closed. You should be able to tell me the things I want to know. I might never have another opportunity." She paused with a questioning look at Diana.

Still a cop, Diana thought with resentment. *Might have known.* "Go ahead. I can't promise you I'll answer but you can ask."

"Well, nothing ventured, nothing gained." Jessie moved around in the chair. "That little drug deal that went south: how did you manage that?" She gave Diana a more than inquisitive look. "I mean, I know what you told me at the cabin but there had to be more. All the hoopla with what's-his-name getting killed, and my surviving must have caused some commotion inside the Family."

Diana speculated as to whether she was being paranoid about Jessie's questions. One of her flights of fantasy during the years she had watched Jessie being a cop was just this: being taken in and Jessie being the one to interrogate her. So she wasn't taken in, but it still had the feeling of interrogation. The long table, the cop sitting across from her. This was where her dreams had led her.

"Perhaps Czar thought if daddy's little girl saved her ex-lover's life, he'd have another cop in his pocket?" Jessie suggested.

Diana felt her face flush with anger at the insult. She had to force herself into calmness. "Hardly," she replied in a frosty voice, not sure which she disliked more, Jessie thinking Diana would let herself be manipulated by Papa or that Diana would even consider the possibility Jessie might be for sale. "Papa didn't know anything about you. And he had old-fashioned ideas about women. They weren't supposed to be cops."

"No," Jessie agreed in an infuriatingly calm voice. "Women were supposed to stay in their place, and you and I both know what kind of places Czar Randalson had for them."

Diana set her jaw but said nothing. She should be accustomed by now to having her father used against her. She had finally gotten past arguing that his rules weren't her rules. She just hadn't expected it from Jessie. But then what should she expect? If she got defensive,

Jessie would just pounce on it like every other cop had. So she said nothing and wondered why Jessie was baiting her.

"Well, we'll set that to one side," Jessie said mildly after a long wait. "Czar had his cop anyway. Henderson going down must have cost him a pretty penny. Can't convince me that didn't cause a rumble in the backrooms." She eyed Diana in a speculative way.

I can't believe she's doing this. I can't believe we're having this conversation sitting here under a tent, out in the open. "I wouldn't even try to convince you," Diana said in controlled even tones. "It did cause quite a rumble."

"And I can't believe Czar Randalson just ate a few million because of..." She paused and cocked her head at Diana. "Why?"

Diana debated about answering. She hated that bland, noncommittal look on Jessie's face, hated more that Jessie thought she was part of that operation. She had struggled so long for a way to live with herself with Papa, and now to have Jessie, of all people, sit there and ask questions like Diana was part and parcel of it.

"He thought it was a double-cross," she said finally. "Only the thought of a bloodbath that would leave no one standing kept him from retaliating."

Jessie raised an eyebrow. "And where did he get that idea?"

"He put someone he thought he could trust in place to investigate, no holds barred, they could go anywhere, ask anything. Anything held back was just suspicious in itself." *That should be neutral enough to answer her and maybe satisfy her.*

Jessie leaned forward as if this was suddenly getting interesting. "And who, pray tell, did he trust that much? Czar Randalson trusted no one: that was how he survived so long. And it doesn't answer the question of how you managed to survive. How did you evade detection? What did you do? Bribe them? Or did you get away with it because you were daddy's little girl?" The last came out in a grating patronizing tone.

Diana leaped to her feet, choking back the *Sanctimonious bitch* comment she was ready to spit out. This cop was just like every other one she had dealt with: they all took her for some birdbrain piece of fluff who just had some influence because she was daddy's little girl. She could stand all the others thinking that; it kept them from digging too deeply. She couldn't stand Jessie thinking that of her.

"I didn't have to evade or bribe anyone," she said in acid tones. "He put me in charge."

"You!" Jessie came to her feet so suddenly she tipped the table.

Diana jumped backward, stumbling over the folding metal chair, catching her balance even as the chair collapsed and the table came back down on its four legs.

"My God, Diana, what did you do?!"

"Like I said," Diana spit back. "Convinced him a bloodbath would leave no one standing and he'd never recover."

Jessie came around the table after Diana. "Good God, woman. You could have been killed!"

Altogether a most likely possibility. Thought Margaret was going to kill me herself when she found out what I was doing. "I wasn't." Diana still stepped back from Jessie, who was reaching for her. "No one was. Not even you. Especially not you."

"Why?" Jessie grabbed Diana by the upper arms, shook her. "Why did you take the risk? What made you do that!?"

"Because I loved you!" Diana spit out. *Why else do you think I would do it?* "Because I didn't want to see you killed. Because it was your life that was in danger." She never meant for it to come out like this. What other reason would she have had and why couldn't Jessie see that? "Because I couldn't bear living in a world where you didn't exist anymore even if I couldn't have you."

Jessie let go of her so suddenly Diana almost fell, stumbling backward in an effort to regain her balance. She still would have fallen if she hadn't bumped into someone, someone who caught her by the waist and steadied her onto her feet.

"Ladies. Ladies, some decorum, please."

Diana turned with an apology even as she stepped back, and then she saw the green uniform. "Oh, shit," she muttered, even as she stepped back. *Someone called Security.*

Brenda eyed them both, her gaze sweeping, rather pointedly, at the overturned chair. "Are we having problems here?"

"No, Officer," Jessie answered immediately. "I can explain."

Brenda gave her a speculating look. "I'm sure you can." She turned back to Diana. "Problems, Diana?"

Diana shook her head, appalled someone had called Security. At least, she thought with some relief, it was Brenda instead of any of the other officers. "No, Brenda, we're fine. Just—just some discussion." She bent down and picked up her chair in an effort to hide her lack of composure. She set it up against the table and stood by Jessie.

"Discussion," Brenda repeated. The gaze she fastened on Diana was more than curious. Reluctantly she turned to Jessie. "And you might be?"

"This is my friend, Jessie," Diana supplied before Jessie could speak. The last thing she needed was Brenda to think there was an altercation. "You've heard me talk about her, Brenda." She felt rather than saw Jessie's glance at her use of Brenda's name.

"Yes, I believe so," Brenda answered in a noncommittal tone. "You have identification?" she asked politely of Jessie.

Jessie was already pulling out her identification and her badge. "Is there a problem?" she asked as she handed it over, looking directly at Brenda, at her name plate. "Officer Harless."

Brenda examined the identification, glancing at Jessie several times before she handed it back. "When you bought your drink," she explained, "the owner saw your gun. He thought Diana looked distressed, was concerned."

Both Diana and Jessie glanced at the drink counter where the owner was hovering, trying to see what was going on. Diana gave him a weak smile.

"And then when I was coming up, I could see what looked like an altercation." She looked from one to the other. "Can you explain?"

"It was just," Jessie fumbled for some words. "Some exciting news," she finally got out.

"I'm sure," Brenda said dryly. She rubbed the side of her nose. "Diana said you had dropped by. You were passing through?" Somehow it came out as much a suggestion as a question.

"This time," Jessie answered, glancing at Diana.

"Uh-huh." Brenda glanced at Diana then back to Jessie. "You mind if Diana and I have a few private words?"

"No, of course not," Jessie acquiesced.

Brenda moved a few steps away and Diana went with her. She certainly hadn't expected Jessie to react so explosively. Really bad timing since the guy had already seen her gun and was suspicious enough to ask for Security. Diana hadn't thought about the gun, but even if she had, she wouldn't have been concerned. Jessie was a cop.

"Are you okay?" Brenda questioned once they were a distance away.

Diana nodded; her head was still swimming with Jessie's baiting, her reaction. Her armor must be getting thin. Still, she didn't expect Jessie to react so strongly.

"When did she show up? Did you tell her you'd be out here?"

Diana shook her head. "No, never mentioned it. I don't know if it was just one of those things or what. I just felt her tailing me after I'd been here for a while, then she came over while I was eating and said we needed to talk."

"Well, proves one thing," Brenda commented with a glance to make sure of Jessie's location.

"What's that?"

"She's no coward." Diana gave a chuckle. "So how'd it go? And what's this exciting news if it's any of my business?"

Diana rubbed her face as she tried to put things together in a way she could answer Brenda. "It's surprising," she said slowly. "She—I don't know. She saw things differently than I did. I guess we both missed things."

Brenda hooked her thumbs over her belt, glanced around to check Jessie's position. "What made her grab you?"

Diana didn't know what to say, how to explain it. "She just wanted to know how some things happened, was surprised when I told her. She wasn't intending to do me any harm, Brenda."

"You're sure?"

Diana nodded. She gave a sigh of resignation. She might as well tell her. It wasn't like Brenda didn't know the background. "She wanted to know why I saved her butt and I told her it was because I loved her."

Brenda paused for a moment. "Oh, well," she said finally. "I can see why she might have been surprised. It's a standard reaction. Of course, everyone reacts to being told someone loves them by grabbing said person and shaking them." Diana gave her a get-off-my-case look. Then she looked away, unable to face Brenda again.

"Diana, look at me." Diana looked back into Brenda's concerned face. "Tell me, as your friend, are you okay with this? Is this something you want? You tossed her out last night."

Diana softened. It wasn't fair to drag Brenda into the middle and there were details she had never explained to Brenda. "I know, Brenda. I was really pissed. I didn't give her much of a chance." She sighed. "I really don't know where it's going from here; I don't know where it can go, but she did take the step to come see me. I owe her the courtesy of listening to her."

"Sounds like you did a fair job of declaring yourself as well."

"Past tense, Brenda. Past tense."

"Yeah," Brenda said dubiously. "You haven't stopped thinking with your head, have you?"

Diana shook her head. "I don't think so." She gave a soft laugh as she thought how her stomach turned over when she looked up and saw Jessie standing there. "Not yet, at least."

Brenda nodded. "Okay. I just wanted to check." She gave Diana a meaningful glance. "You call tonight if you need to, no matter what the time."

Diana gave her a smile. "Thanks. I don't think I'll need to but it's nice to know you're here."

They walked back to where Jessie stood waiting. Brenda gave Jessie a meaningful look and then Diana. "I understand you two have a lot to talk about, probably about things you'd rather others didn't overhear. You might want to pick a more private spot." She glanced around at the few people watching them. "Don't want to make the locals nervous." She touched the brim of her hat. "Good meeting you, Detective Galbreath. I imagine we'll be seeing each other again." Then she turned and walked over to the drink counter to reassure the owner Jessie was a safe person.

Jessie watched her go and then turned to Diana. "What did she mean by that?"

"Brenda's a good friend. If you're around me any length of time, you'll be running into her."

"How good a friend?"

Just the tone in her voice made Diana turn around to face her. She looked at Jessie curiously as Jessie watched Brenda move off through the gathering. "A good friend," she repeated.

Jessie turned back, cocked an eyebrow. "You have a magnet for women in law enforcement?"

Diana thought of Jessie, Brenda, Kelly, all of them in one branch or another of law enforcement. "Never thought of it, but I guess so." She took a look around and then back to Jessie. She was on pins and needles wondering what Jessie might be thinking. Her only reaction to Diana's words had been to let her go, and then Brenda was there. She waited but Jessie didn't speak.

"Well," Diana said finally as she picked up her leather shoulder bag. "I guess we're finished here." She looked at Jessie. "Unless there's something else you want to ask?"

"What do we do now?"

Diana considered carefully. This was the woman who said she'd never had a choice, Diana had made all the decisions. "I don't know. What do you want to do?"

Jessie moved closer to her, too close, Diana realized, but she didn't move. "I want to talk some more. Is that all right with you?"

Diana caught her breath. It wasn't over, not yet at least. Her heart began to pound more. "I believe so." She stepped back from Jessie so she could open her tote and search through it for her car keys. "Have a place in mind?"

Jessie suddenly looked more hopeful. "Maybe this needs to be a bit more private?"

Diana thoughtfully nodded. "Maybe so. You want dinner out on neutral ground or—"

"How about your place?" Jessie cut in. "Maybe dinner later?"

"Okay," Diana agreed. "I've got to stop at the organizer's tent before I leave. Shall I meet you at my apartment?"

CHAPTER TWENTY-SIX

Jessie got to the apartment first, parked the car in the shade. She opened the car door and just sat there a moment. Diana had said she loved her. She had risked a drug war to save Jessie without getting killed herself. That wasn't exactly new information, just more details. It was quite one thing for an unknown informant to tip her off, funnel information to her. Minor players on the fringes heard things all the time and passed them along. Even if Jessie had had the very vague suspicion it was Diana, she'd had no proof where the information was coming from. By the time Diana's identity was confirmed while they were at the cabin, there was so much else being revealed that Jessie never even considered the details of the drug bust. It was history.

It was quite another thing to realize Diana was at the heart of the organization. Jessie had seen some results of drug wars, and Diana had waded in and walked out. Jessie had a difficult time reconciling the woman who could manipulate those events with the woman who had been her Lexington lover. No wonder the Feds had kept her under wraps. Diana was not to be underestimated.

Jessie got out of the car. The afternoon heat was still too hot for her to sit there and wait. She needed to move around, stretch her legs as she considered these new revelations. She took the opportunity to see the neighborhood where Diana lived now, what it might mean.

The apartment complex was small, just a couple of buildings sitting between what she guessed from the sounds of traffic to be one of the main streets through town and one of the old residential neighborhoods. Nice enough, nothing fancy, very basic, low-key. Compared to what Jessie remembered of Diana's lifestyle, either she was pinched for money or trying to stay under the radar. Maybe a bit of both.

Diana had never really seemed to enjoy high living for all the expensive hotels she had been at when she and Jessie were starting out. Jessie had tried hard not to be impressed although she recognized they had been out of her league. She had been a little nervous when she had taken Diana out for dinner and it was, well, less than five stars. Diana had always seemed comfortable at the neighborhood diners and easy-on-the-pocket places Jessie had chosen when she came to town. As she said one time, she didn't come for the food; she came for the company.

Jessie walked around the apartment complex, down the shady street. Nice quiet area, enough economic mix, business and residential so Diana wasn't really isolated and still had some privacy. Old houses converted to lawyer and accountant offices. Jessie walked up the block and back, didn't want to miss Diana's arrival.

She went up the steps and sat on the railing outside Diana's door, contemplating. Diana had changed. Certainly she was not as carefree as she had been, less of a free spirit. More guarded. Suspicious. She had a barrier up if you even looked sideways at her. Jessie had definitely seen that after she brought the drink back, when she sat down and they talked about events after Diana had bailed out on Jessie.

Bailed out. That was how Jessie looked at it. Diana hadn't even stuck around long enough to challenge Julie. Jessie rested her head back against the corner post. Cut and run. Up until then, she had been possessive. Jessie gave a slow smile at the memories. Very possessive. Staked out a claim and exercised it every time she came back to town. It would have been nice if she had been forthcoming with information, but Jessie never pressed. After years of stalking women and going after them, someone coming after her, claiming her, was refreshing. Diana blithely assumed Jessie would be there for her. And she wasn't so dominant that she upset Jessie's butch mentality. Just, *I'm a catch, I'm special, I know it, and aren't you the special one I chose to come back and want to see, enjoy?* And Jessie really felt that way; she did feel special. Diana only had one question every time she came: are you available? It was Jessie who rearranged her schedule, her life, in order to be available.

Diana bestowed the favor of her presence, and Jessie basked in that favor.

If only. Jessie closed her eyes and soaked in the hot sun. If only they had talked more, shared more. Well, that was one mistake she was determined not to repeat.

But this was a different Diana, she realized. If Diana had been puzzling before, now she was an enigma. The years and events had changed her, made her harder, more cynical. But then, Jessie realized, couldn't she say the same about herself? If she had come seeking Diana looking for something she had lost in her past, Diana wasn't the answer. If she wanted to go back to that more lighthearted time and thought Diana would bring her back that joy, that idealism, that pleasure in life, she was making another mistake. So the question was, what did she want from the Diana who was in the here and now?

A vehicle pulled in and parked. Jessie didn't have to look to know it was Diana. She didn't get up to meet her, but sat there and watched as Diana got out of the Jeep, looked over the top and saw Jessie sitting there. Diana gave Jessie a slow smile and Jessie got a warm feeling through her that had nothing to do with the late afternoon sunlight.

She watched with appreciation as Diana crossed the parking lot. The old Diana would never have worn jeans, just wasn't her style, so Jessie had been surprised when she had finally found her in them at the powwow. She hadn't expected the moccasins, the leather vest, the white shirt, a costume much like her own. She had to admit Diana wore them well. She watched Diana come up the stairs. And the package was still definitely enticing.

"Been waiting long?" Diana asked as she hit the top step.

Jessie shook her head as she looked Diana up and down. "Years."

Jessie waited until Diana unlocked the door, stepped inside and turned around. "Coming in?"

Jessie stepped into an apartment cool and dim after the bright sunshine. She closed the door, flipped the lock. How many times had they done this? Diana unlocking the door, turning to invite her in. She could smell the same scent, Diana's signature perfume, the smell of her after the afternoon in the hot sun. Everything was different and nothing had changed.

"I'm curious," Diana remarked as she set her leather bag down on the desk. "How'd you know I'd be at the powwow?"

"You had a flyer on the refrigerator. It was worth a chance."

Diana turned around to face her, just stood there, and Jessie knew what she wanted, what she was going to do. She hadn't known until right then, until she saw Diana standing there. But now she knew.

She walked over to Diana, took her face in her hands, cupped her cheeks. "I want to thank you." She heard Diana's quick intake of breath, felt Diana's hands over hers, felt Diana's soft lips as she kissed her. "For my life." She kissed her again, a little longer as she felt Diana yield. "For all those years I've lived since." She wrapped her arms around Diana and Diana moved closer. Jessie closed her eyes, feeling Diana against her, knowing this was what she wanted.

"I'm not saying I don't want to talk. We didn't talk the last time and look where it got us. But I also want what we had." She stopped, feeling Diana's stillness. "And I want more." She rubbed her face in Diana's hair. "I have missed you so much."

"We're not the same, Jessie. I've changed, you've changed." Diana didn't move away in spite of her protest.

Jessie turned Diana's face up so she could see her expression. "Tell me you don't want me. Tell me you don't still have dreams of blue jeans and white shirts and sunglasses." She caressed Diana's face with her fingers, reveling in being able to touch her. She gave a slow smile at Diana's softening expression. "Tell me your heart didn't stop when you opened the door and I was standing there." She felt Diana slide her arms about her, press against her. "Throw me out again, tell me there's nothing between us and I won't bother you again."

Diana rubbed her face against Jessie's shoulder. "I can't."

Jessie buried her face in Diana's hair. Diana's two words untied the knot in her heart she hadn't even realized had been there.

"But I can't have you either." Diana stepped out of Jessie's arms and stepped away from her.

Jessie gasped, in surprise, in shock and she reached out to recapture Diana.

"Don't!" Diana said sharply and then her voice softened. "Please, Jessie. Don't make this harder on either one of us." She moved further out of reach. "You and I." She shook her head. "It isn't going to work. Too much has happened, too many complications. No matter how much either one of us wants it."

"It will work," Jessie cut in before Diana was too insistent. "We can make it work."

Diana shook her head. "We can't change who we are. There are too many complications."

"We can deal with them," Jessie protested. "We don't need to change who we are. There aren't so many complications. There's nothing here we can't deal with."

Diana still shook her head. "Margaret always said I lost all common sense where you were concerned. This time I'm going to hold fast."

"Diana," Jessie pleaded. "Don't. Please." She couldn't believe this. Just when she thought everything was finally coming together, Diana was ripping it apart. "Please, Diana. You made the choice before that there was nothing there for us. Look what happened."

"Yeah." Diana turned away, her back to Jessie. "I was in the right place at the right time to save your life."

"And I appreciate that." Jessie went and slid her arms around Diana. "And I'd like to tell you that every day." She was encouraged when Diana didn't break away, even leaned back against her. "You liked it before when I appreciated you, didn't you?" She felt Diana yielding to her but this time she was cautious.

"Um-humm." Diana gave a small sigh. "But I've changed, Jessie, in lots of ways. I don't want to be a rolling stone anymore. I've had my fill of one-night stands and empty rooms in my lifetime. I want to matter to someone."

"You matter to me." Jessie cautiously ran her hand up and down Diana's arm.

Diana went on like she hadn't even heard her. "I want someone to come home to at night, someone to curl up with. I want a home where there's love, not just a place to open my suitcase. I want someone there for me when I'm down, to share things with when I'm up. I want someone to miss me when I'm gone, to worry about me."

"I worry about you," Jessie coaxed. "Especially now when I know all these things about you." She nuzzled Diana's neck. "I've missed you."

Diana shook her head again. She unwrapped Jessie's arms and stepped away. "I thought—I thought I'd be over you, I could see you and there'd be nothing, and I could put you behind me. I'd be able to go on with my life, stop measuring everyone I met against you." She turned around to face Jessie.

"I want those same things you do, Diana."

Diana shook her head. "We're not the same people anymore, Jessie. I've got more baggage now." She took a deep breath, as if gathering her nerve. "For a long time, I've held on to the fantasy that you might be that someone, but..." She hesitated and then plowed on. "I need to give it up; it's not going to happen. I need to get on with my life."

"Why isn't it going to happen? We want the same things. We love each other. At least you said you loved me once. Are you saying you don't love me anymore? I know I love you."

Diana closed her eyes, as if to shut out the sight of Jessie. "Jessie," she began again. "It doesn't matter how much we love each other. It isn't going to work."

Jessie laid a hand on Diana's cheek to make her stop shaking her head. "Why can't we?"

Diana gave a bitter laugh. "You're a cop," she pointed out as if Jessie might have forgotten. "Times may have changed so the police might accept dykes in their ranks but not with a lover like me. I might not have a record, but I'm always going to be suspect. That's the biggest thing."

Jessie carefully wrapped both arms around Diana and held her. This was going to be a jolt for her, something Jessie hadn't been able to tell her before. "Well, you're right; that might be a problem. If I were still a cop. Or if I wanted a job in law enforcement again."

"If *what*?" Diana pulled back as if she hadn't heard Jessie correctly.

"I turned in my resignation. I'm taking leave time so I don't lose it. I'm on my way to Ocala for a job interview."

"You—you did what!" Diana pushed back to look into Jessie's face. "When? How? Why? But—why didn't you tell me?"

"I told you, we still needed to talk." Part of her was so amused and pleased she had been able to finally rattle Diana but at the same time, she knew this was going to open some serious discussion. When Diana pulled away yet again, Jessie released her. And then she waited.

"I don't believe it." Diana moved away from Jessie, moved around the living room, picked up her leather tote, put it down, picked it up again and looked at it like she didn't recognize it. She took it into the bedroom, stripped off her vest and came back out. She paused long enough to look at Jessie and start to say something. Then she abruptly turned to go into the kitchen. "Can I get you some iced tea?"

"Sounds good." Jessie recognized the impact the information had on Diana. She was going through all the normal everyday things in an effort to deal with it. Jessie had seen her do the same thing when Diana learned she was a cop. Ironic that learning Jessie wasn't a cop was just as big a shock to Diana as learning she was.

"And take a seat," Diana called from the kitchen over the rattle of glasses, the refrigerator door opening and shutting.

Jessie looked around and picked the loveseat, glancing at the coffee table covered with books, television schedules, the TV remote. She took off her jacket, folded it and laid it across the back of the loveseat. Then she removed her weapon and holster and laid them securely on the bookcase. She sat in the corner, wondering what Diana was going to say. At least, she consoled herself, Diana hadn't thrown her out.

Diana brought the two glasses of iced tea. "Just like that," she said abruptly as she handed Jessie the glass. "You get a wild hair and turn in your resignation and everything's gonna be okay?"

Jessie didn't answer right away, drank some of the iced tea. Diana took a seat on the loveseat but turned so she was facing Jessie.

Jessie carefully set the glass of tea down. Talking about this was going to be difficult for her but she needed to share this, and she had always been able to talk to Diana. "No, not 'just like that.' I had a lot of sleepless nights and gut-wrenching conversations. I even took a leave to decide just what I wanted to do and where my priorities were." She changed position on the couch so she could face Diana. "It wasn't just getting a wild hair and going off half-cocked. It took over a year to sort things out and really decide what I wanted to do and why." She paused, thinking what an understatement she was making. "It was a hard decision."

She waited, needing to hear what Diana had to say. Diana didn't say anything. Jessie waited for what seemed like forever before she couldn't stand the silence any longer. "So you see, we can have something together. We want the same things; we love each other. There aren't as many problems as you think."

"Did you do this because of me?" Diana sounded a little more sympathetic.

Jessie shook her head.

"Then why?" Diana frowned, leaned forward. "Law enforcement is in your blood."

Jessie hesitated. She'd had to tell lots of people she was leaving. "Why" was a constant question except from other cops. She had multiple answers. "A lot of reasons," she said slowly, not sure how she could explain it to Diana. She looked away and didn't meet Diana's gaze. Finally she shrugged. "Been shot, kidnapped, threatened with torture. Seemed to be pushing my luck. Time to get out."

Diana said nothing.

It was a simple, maybe superficial answer, Jessie realized. Part of her hoped Diana would accept it at face value. Another part of her wished she wouldn't. "Maybe I'm burnt out," Jessie continued slowly. "Maybe arguing with Julie all the time about police work took its toll. Maybe I don't feel the same about it. Maybe I'm just tired."

"A lot of maybes. Maybe none of them are the reason."

"I am tired," Jessie defended herself, looking back at Diana. "Cops get burnt out all the time."

Diana nodded. They did. They both knew that. Suddenly Diana reached out and took hold of Jessie's hand. She moved closer to Jessie, held Jessie's hand between her two warm hands. "What happened, Jessie? Tell me what really made you decide." She rubbed the back of

Jessie's hand to give reassurance, brought it up to her cheek. All the time, she watched Jessie's face.

Jessie's gaze finally slid away but she gave a lingering caress before she withdrew her hand. Diana still understood her, even after all these years, even on such a thing as this. "It seemed like nothing," she said finally. "There was a bank robbery. Four guys. Coordinated. They split up and hit two banks at the same time." She paused. "We tracked them down to one of the old warehouses out off Versailles Road. One took off and this rookie and I were chasing him. Anyway, he got away. So we were searching and I found him, called for backup." She stopped there.

"They didn't come," Diana supplied.

Jessie took a deep breath. "No, they came. There had been a smash-up, the first car got hit coming through an intersection—just a stupid, run-of-the-mill accident, so there was a delay, but there were others and we got the guy, got the money back. Got the conviction." She took a deep breath. "I just had a panic attack, just knew they weren't going to back me up, were going to leave me out there hanging at some point."

"Ahhhh." Diana understood. "Why would they do that?"

Jessie drank some tea. "The whole investigation of the kidnapping," Jessie said slowly. "Julie and I told everything—except the past relationship. That never came out." She gave a rueful laugh. "God knows, there were enough other things to keep the investigators busy." She sobered, glancing at Diana and then looking away. She didn't want to watch her expression. She didn't want her to think she was ashamed of their relationship but there were—how did she term it? Complications. "The investigators went over it and over it; they knew there was something. Yet everything was right there. You'd been in contact with the Feds, you didn't want to be party to a cop killing, you were keeping Julie safe because of her taking care of your father. If anything, they saw it as Julie being rescued and I just happened to be along. And we didn't dissuade them of the idea." She looked up at Diana. "That was the official story."

"And the unofficial?"

"Some collusion. For some unknown reason. I heard about everything, from you were deep undercover, hence the tip-offs in the past, to the idea that we had a torrid sexual free-for-all during the time at the cabin."

Diana had to chuckle. Sex had been about the last thing they had been thinking of while they waited for her papa's death.

"But no one really knew anything and business went on as usual. It was just...I guess...I'd hear all those stories. Okay, you always hear stories, no matter what you do; it gets blown out of proportion. Cops aren't any different about gossip than anyone else and lesbians on the force always have some story spinning around them. The change was in me. I had never doubted they would be there to back me up until that day. It was like something moved within me, some surety wasn't there anymore. And I didn't know how to get it back."

She looked up at Diana and she felt the loss all over again. Beliefs were the core of the work. You had to trust your team. Diana knew enough to know that, didn't she?

Jessie ran her hands through her hair. "Peterson retired, his heart was an issue. New partner. And then there was you."

"What about me?"

Jessie looked up at her, feeling the conflict all over again. "What was I supposed to do about you? I wanted you; I loved you for years. We had a relationship—all right, it was a haphazard one, but it was there. And all that time, I never picked up on anything. What kind of cop was I to miss all that?"

"There was nothing to pick up on, Jessie. I wasn't doing anything. I was going to school. I was running a legal business."

"You were doing favors for your father!"

"There was nothing illegal about sitting in and watching a trial, nothing illegal about examining books of a legitimate business." Diana kept her voice calm like she had gone over this a thousand times before. She probably had.

No, she supposed not, Jessie thought. Yet it still bothered her. Jessie pursed her lips, her eyes narrowed but she said nothing more.

"Jessie, I'm tainted, there's always going to be guilt by association. But I can't help the family I was born into any more than you can."

Jessie looked up at the ceiling, regaining some of her composure. "I couldn't stay in if I didn't trust the people I worked with," she said finally, turning back to Diana. "And I couldn't stay if I wanted to pursue anything with you. I didn't even know how you felt except at the cabin you said you loved me. I just knew I had to find out and I couldn't do it as a cop. So when Broadrick asked if I knew anyone who might be interested in a security position, I said I was." She turned back to Diana, defiant and vulnerable, braced to deal with anything Diana might possibly say.

Diana started to say something and stopped, her eyes clouded with pain. Belatedly, Jessie realized, as much as she hated the comparison, that Diana lost a family too, had to change a life. They were both dealing with loss. They had that in common.

"I know that was a hard decision for you," Diana said finally. "I'm sorry you got to that point." She leaned forward to lay her hand on Jessie's thigh. "Really, I am. I know what being a cop meant to you. And I know it wasn't easy to decide. But I'm glad you made the decision to get out rather than to stay in and be terribly unhappy."

Jessie looked away. She still didn't like reflecting on it, possibly second-guessing herself.

"So when is your interview?" Diana asked, effectively changing the subject.

Jessie breathed a sigh of relief, relief she wouldn't have to talk about it; relief Diana still understood her. "One o'clock Monday."

Diana drew back, taking her hand from Jessie. There were still issues to be considered. "Where at?"

"Serenity Farms. It's outside Ocala. It's a horse breeding and training operation." Jessie sat back. "Broadrick said it was a big operation, had some high-priced horses, both theirs and others there for training."

"So, you're finally going to do it," Diana said with a straight face. "Huh?"

"You're going to become the person I thought you were in the beginning." Diana gave a faint smile to assure Jessie she was teasing.

Jessie gave a small laugh as they both remembered Diana's misconception of Jessie working at one of the Lexington horse farms. "I guess so."

They sat still for a moment, saying nothing, lost in memories. The silence dragged on almost to the stage of discomfort when Jessie cleared her throat. "Are you going to stop being attracted to me now?"

Diana came back to the present with a jolt. "What?"

"Well, you admitted out at the powwow you're a magnet for women in law enforcement. If I'm not in law enforcement, do I still attract you?" The image of the green-clad deputy sheriff rose up in front of her and she had a sudden stab of jealousy. The realization came to her suddenly that she knew nothing about Diana's life here. The remark Jessie had made just to tease was more than a little bit true.

"Well, I was certainly attracted to you enough in the beginning and I didn't know you were a cop," Diana said with a laugh.

Jessie didn't look at her when she asked, "Would you have kept coming back if you had known?"

"Are you kidding?" Diana looked at her in amazement. "I would have run like a bunny who just sniffed a fox. You were the enemy, everything I'd been warned against." She reached out to take Jessie's hand. "Ignorance was bliss." She gave a slow smile. Bliss indeed. "By the time I did learn, I was so into you…" She trailed off. The things she had done didn't have to be said again.

"So didn't I deserve some sort of explanation?"

Jessie watched the debate in Diana's eyes and she drew back, protecting. She had crossed a lot of barriers to be able to get to this stage with Diana. She needed Diana to drop her barriers as well.

"Ignorance was safer," Diana said quietly. "And I was a coward."

Jessie waited. She had learned many new aspects of Diana but there was nothing to indicate any cowardice.

Diana drew a deep breath as if she had come to a decision. "Czar Randalson was a conniving, manipulating bastard," she began. "It didn't matter to him that I had a female lover. He probably knew about lots of them. Women were safer than men; women couldn't move ahead in the Family by marrying the boss's daughter. If he had known how much I cared for you, never mind you being a cop, you would have been someone to hold over my head. I spent a lifetime making sure there was nothing he could hold hostage to manipulate me. So I hid you for the same reasons he hid me, so the ones we really loved wouldn't be held over our heads."

Jessie recovered enough from her surprise to point out, "That didn't make you a coward. Prudent perhaps," she amended as she considered. She took hold of Diana's hand again. "So how were you a coward?"

"When Papa told me I had to make a choice and I went to see you, I was afraid. Turning Papa down had its risks. I knew a lot, stuff I didn't even realize the importance of until later. I still think he would have let me go, counted on loyalty to him not to say anything or maybe he just thought because I was a woman, I wouldn't be able to do anything. So I had that on one hand. And then on the other hand, assuming you were agreeable, there were two venues: either I could tell you about my family and you could reject me because of them, or I could not tell you and put you at risk." She paused, wondering if Jessie could even understand.

"And then Julie showed up."

Diana nodded.

Jessie rubbed Diana's hand, absently. "She didn't have quite the hold on me that you credit her. But I don't know, considering all you just said, you had many other choices."

Diana pulled her hand free and got to her feet. Talking about her father, those times past, made her edgy. "Well, it turned out well. I was in the right place at the right time to keep you alive. That wouldn't have happened if I'd never joined the Family."

Jessie turned around to watch Diana pace the living room. "But how did you do it? How can you call yourself a coward when you managed all that under your father's nose?"

Diana gave a mirthless laugh as she stopped in the middle of the living room, looked back at Jessie. The smug knowing look, the defiance, the uncertainty, all those emotions went across her face. "As they say, the apple doesn't fall far from the tree." Jessie frowned in puzzlement. "I did it right back; I manipulated him. If the ability to manipulate is genetic, I inherited it. I turned out to be definitely my father's daughter."

Jessie drew back and Diana's knowing smile challenged her.

"Can you deal with that, Jessie?" she asked in a quiet voice. "You had a terrible shock when you found out who my father was. You hated me because I might have contaminated you."

"I dealt with that," Jessie said quickly, too quickly.

"Well, it's easier to deal with when I'm saving your life. But I'm not saving your life now. In fact, just being with me might put you at risk." Jessie's head came up, the unspoken question. "Someone might decide I'm too big a risk running around loose and decide to silence me."

Jessie leaped to her feet, advancing on Diana as if she could hold off any danger. "No." She looked around the room, drew Diana away from the open window. "No," she repeated as she shook her head. "Not while I'm here." She drew Diana into her arms. She couldn't lose her after finally getting past all the obstacles.

Diana buried her face against Jessie's shoulder. She moved closer into Jessie's arms, slid her arms around her.

"So what do we do now?" Jessie murmured in her ear. She ran her fingers through Diana's still curly hair. "We seem to have the major issues out of the way."

"We could do what we always did," Diana said without opening her eyes.

"And that would be?"

Diana looked up at her. "We could go to bed."

CHAPTER TWENTY-SEVEN

Neither of them spoke as Diana took Jessie by the hand to lead her to the bedroom. Then Jessie stood at the foot of the bed while Diana turned down the coverlet and pulled back the sheets.

"How often have we done this?" Jessie asked when Diana returned to her, slid her arms around Jessie's waist, her hands lower to feel Jessie's ass, pull her tighter against her.

"Lots," Diana said with a sigh. "Not often enough."

"Do you know how often I looked for you?" Jessie took Diana's face in her hands, her fingers spread through Diana's hair. "You spoiled me; you were always popping up in unexpected places so I was always on the lookout."

"I thought maybe you'd stop wanting me." Diana unbuttoned Jessie's shirt, spread it open. This is real, she's really here; her, not some substitute, she told herself as she reached around to unfasten Jessie's plain cotton bra.

Jessie pushed back and the bra slid down her arms, exposing her breasts. "Are you serious?"

Diana nodded, her attention on Jessie's breasts, still slight but fuller than she remembered, the dark nipples. She stroked with fingertips and felt the old familiar response causing Jessie to catch her breath. Her own nipples tightened as Jessie gripped her shoulders.

"Do you remember that night in Lexington?" Jessie took a deep breath and began to unbutton Diana's shirt.

Diana gave a soft laugh, half at Jessie's remark and the rest in the sheer pleasure of Jessie's touch. "Which one? They were *all* in Lexington."

"When you tried to make me forget Julie?"

"Oh. That night." Diana closed her eyes and leaned into Jessie, their breasts touching, pressed into each other. "The dominatrix night."

They undressed each other with slow deliberateness, knowing each other and yet exploring the changes time had made.

"I don't know how many times after that, I'd do something inconsequential and it would trigger a memory. I'd shiver and remember what we did, just like you wanted me to. No one ever touched me like you did that night." Jessie buried her face in Diana's neck, a tongue stroked against the sensitive flesh. "I don't want to lose you again."

Diana felt the warmth begin to flood her, not the hot pounding excitement they used to have, a sexual demand that had to be met. She closed her eyes. This was a merging, a recovered part of her self that had been absent for so long. "I was so jealous. I wanted you to want me as much as I wanted you." She caught Jessie's hand, the long fingers, kissed her palm. She noticed the tan lines, the dark tan at the V of the neck, the forearms, the lighter tan over the shoulders, the legs, the whiteness of her breasts, her hips. She ran her hands over Jessie, all of her, stroking her arms, her shoulders, her back.

Jessie froze, closed her eyes, intent on Diana's touch. "Diana," she breathed. Then with great deliberateness, she pushed Diana back on the bed. "I did. I do."

Jessie pulled off one moccasin, then the other, pulled down Diana's jeans and threw them on the floor between the shirts. "I want to come home to you at night and wake up with you in the morning," she said as she rested her knee on the bed between Diana's legs. "I want to reach out and touch you." She ran her hands up the outside of Diana's legs and smiled when Diana shivered. "I don't want to wonder where you are and if you're all right, and I don't want to wonder about who you might be with." She threw her body over Diana, supported herself on one arm that she slid beneath Diana. Her tone darkened slightly as she gazed into Diana's face. "I don't want you imprinting yourself into someone else's memories." She settled herself against Diana, hip to hip, breast to breast. "Or turn into a vampire and take their life's blood."

Diana shivered at Jessie's possessiveness. "You seem to have remembered a lot about that night." She drew up her leg between Jessie's, rested against her. She ran her hands up Jessie's strong arms, marveling that Jessie really was here.

Jessie's dark eyes smoldered. "Everything." She ran her tongue over Diana's lips, teasing, tantalizing, her free hand caressing Diana's arm, shoulder, ribs, hip, touching as if claiming. "Tell me I was the only one you did that to," she demanded in a quiet, husky voice. "Tell me I was the only one who mattered that much." She withdrew, raised up so she could look down into Diana's face. She brushed her breasts against Diana's, smiled when Diana arched her back to maintain the touch. "Tell me."

Diana shook her head. "No one else ever came close." She pulled Jessie down to her, hungry for her now, needing her. Her hands went everywhere, exploring Jessie, and she felt Jessie's hands all over her as Jessie's mouth, tongue met hers. She relished the weight of Jessie against her, the nearness, the reality. She moved from Jessie's mouth to her neck, her shoulder and then pushed her back so she could move down to Jessie's breast.

Jessie stiffened at Diana's touch, her mouth enclosing the taut nipple. "Oh, God," she moaned. Diana pushed her and she fell back, her legs opening. Diana's hand slid over her hip, down and over her thigh, moving with terrible slowness. "Please," Jessie murmured as she raised her hand and found Diana's breast. The nipple stiffened against her palm and she pressed hard against the soft flesh. She felt the nipple sink into soft flesh and yet retain the firmness.

She felt Diana turn as her mouth moved downward, breast, ribs, across her stomach. Diana's breast escaped her and she explored instead Diana's ribs, hips, stomach. She gasped at Diana's touch, as she slid through the pubic hair and between the lips. She felt Diana shudder and touch her in response.

The first touch was enough to undo Diana, not with the raw sexuality of years past but with the comfort, the intimacy, the completeness she had missed for so long. Jessie opened, welcoming her like a long absent missed lover. She moaned with pleasure, the excitement coming now not because of the newness but of the return. She wrapped one arm about her hips, pulling her closer as she stroked. To love and to be loved. To touch and be touched. She felt the trembling, heard the moans. Moving a bit, adjusting positions, she could not deny herself, her lover anymore. Opening and being opened, she tasted, and then slid both arms around her and held her as she gave and felt tongue to clit. Pleasure washed over her in waves as she struggled not to lose herself in what her lover was doing to her but to match her. She felt a hand on her breast, a nipple pinched. She stiffened, trying not to close her legs as she felt the jolt and then release, relax, and breathe again.

The ceiling was apartment white, the light covered with a standard square frosted glass shade. The room was dim from the late afternoon sun on the other side of the apartment. There was the sound of a heavy breathing slowing down and then Diana moved, to reverse herself and lie beside Jessie.

"That was different," Diana commented lightly as she trailed her hand over Jessie's stretched out form.

Jessie turned toward her. "I couldn't decide," she said seriously.

"About what?"

"Which I wanted more. To love you or be loved by you." She caught Diana's hand, turned slightly on her side and pulled Diana to her. "I missed you. I didn't even know how much until now." She pulled Diana tight against her, slid her arm around to hold her there, slid one leg between Diana's.

"Hard decisions," Diana commented. She was content to be held as long as she could hold Jessie too. "Are you sure you made the right one?" Jessie drew back to look at her in surprise. "I mean," Diana said idly as she traced her finger over Jessie's shoulder. "We could do a replay, and see if it still works."

Jessie looked amused. In so many ways the years apart just disappeared. "Is this like testing the theories?"

"Well, yes," Diana admitted. "If you're interested."

Jessie moved to put Diana on her back. "I think I could be." She straddled Diana, low enough to pin her legs down. "But I have an issue with you first. And I need to say it now because if I don't, I'll stew about it and then we'll have a fight at some point in the future."

Diana frowned as Jessie caught her wrists and pinned her down. She felt the flash of anger in her belly, she narrowed her eyes. *Might have known it was just a ruse.* "What?" she demanded coldly. She looked up at Jessie and Jessie looked entirely too amused, as if she knew exactly what Diana was thinking. Then Jessie's expression softened and she bent down to kiss Diana, kissed her until Diana responded and kissed her back. "What issue?" Diana repeated in a calmer tone. *She did say in the future, so it can't be a deal breaker.*

Jessie looked down into Diana's face as she shook her head. "Still like to be in charge, don't you, Diana?"

Diana didn't move, forced herself to relax. *This is Jessie*, she reminded herself. "I guess so."

"I don't appreciate decisions being made for me," Jessie said quietly as she leaned over Diana. "Especially when they have a major impact on my life."

"I don't know what one you're referring to." *Or rather which one. God, there were so many I made. It wasn't like there was time for a consultation.*

"Any of them. But maybe especially when you came to Lexington and I told you about Julie. Why didn't you tell me about your 'opportunity'?"

Diana drew back into the bedding in surprise. Of all decisions, she wasn't expecting that one. "I told you," she protested. "Before, out there in the living room. You even said they were good reasons."

"No," Jessie corrected. "You told me why *you* decided. And I agreed they were good reasons for *you*. You. I want to know why you didn't tell *me*."

Diana frowned in puzzlement, so Jessie tried again.

"If you wanted to be with me, and I was that important to you, why didn't you ask me? Why couldn't you let me decide whether or not to take the risk?" She leaned over above Diana as Diana looked up defiantly. "I wasn't some naïve little civilian. I would have known what the risk was. I would have even been able to help."

Diana's defiance faltered, suddenly uncomfortable under Jessie's gaze. She could have, maybe she should have, but she hadn't.

"Why didn't you trust me enough to ask?"

"I was afraid," Diana admitted in a low voice, and to her chagrin, she felt tears form and threaten to spill out.

"Of me? Of what I might do?" Jessie released Diana and sat back. She stared down at Diana with a puzzled expression. "Come on, Diana. Tell me."

"I wasn't sure you'd want to have anything to do with me when you learned about my family." *Cops and robbers. Will the handsome sexy detective lower herself to deal with the product of a family such as mine?* "And then when you told me Julie was back and still interested, I didn't figure I had a chance. You loved her. She was beautiful; she was smart, a professional woman. And there had to be a big ego boost of having someone who wouldn't come through for you before now coming to you and saying she'd made a mistake." She turned back to Jessie. "What did I have for you?"

"Ohhh, Diana." Jessie got off Diana and stretched out beside her, took Diana in her arms. "If only you had told me." She bent down and kissed Diana, stroked her face in reassurance.

"What would you have done?"

Jessie thought about it. "I don't know." She gazed off past Diana to the plain apartment white wall. "Trying to reassess your life if you had made a different decision is always iffy," she said, delaying an answer. "There are so many twists and turns." She looked down at the woman in her arms. "I might have had to leave the force but then I wouldn't have gotten shot. I might have stayed in and then you wouldn't have been there to save me. I might have been frozen out because of you or just been a cop on the beat assigned to harmless duties which would have been just as bad." She brushed back Diana's hair. "That's not the point. You made a decision for me, about me. You didn't trust me."

Diana opened her mouth to protest and then said nothing. She couldn't argue. Whether it was her fear or her own insecurity, she hadn't trusted Jessie. "I'm sorry," she said finally. "I wanted to protect you and I wanted to protect myself. Maybe not in that order." Her eyes clouded. "I couldn't have stood then for you to look at me the way you looked at me at the cabin when you found out who Papa was."

"You did a good job handling it then."

Diana looked back. "Let's face it. I wasn't handing you my heart, I was handing you your life. And I'd had a few years to build up some armor, get tougher. I had more choices."

"And I came around," Jessie pointed out.

"Yes." Diana nodded and she looked up at Jessie. "I underestimated you." She shrugged. "Or overestimated myself."

"A failing of most individuals from criminal families."

Diana jerked and then caught the look of amusement in Jessie's eyes. "Sounds like a cop," Diana shot back, but this time she wasn't angry.

"Occupational hazard." Jessie brought up Diana's hand, kissed the palm, watching Diana with a speculative gaze. "Habits die hard."

"Probably on both sides," Diana warned.

Jessie nodded agreement. "But if we're in this together, we make decisions *together*." It was not a question. "We talk things over. We don't make assumptions."

Diana nodded carefully. "We can do that."

"We *will* do that."

Diana nodded in agreement. Jessie gave her a warning look.

"I suspect," Jessie said, carefully picking her words, "there will be things you won't want to share with me."

Diana felt herself withdraw in response. She could see it coming.

"I can accept that," Jessie went on to Diana's relief. "I'm afraid that's simply going to be the fact of our lives." She paused then went on. "Just don't lie to me. I can deal with anything, but not that."

Diana examined Jessie's troubled gaze. Such a simple statement. "As long as you can accept it when I tell you I *can't* tell you." Then she held her breath as Jessie considered.

Jessie finally nodded. "I guess I can deal with that. You've certainly demonstrated you would go above and beyond your safety to protect me."

Diana breathed a sigh of relief.

"It isn't going to be easy, is it?" Jessie asked softly.

"No. But after all we've been through, I think we can manage."

***

Hours later when they ran out of things to say, laying on the love-seat together, the remnants of the pizza from the night before on the coffee table along with the empty wine carafe and the two almost empty glasses, Jessie and Diana laid comfortably, more or less, in the crowded space.

"I'm sorry I called you a coward last night," Diana said slowly.

Jessie sighed. "You may have been right," she admitted reluctantly. "There were a good many times I would have rather faced a drugged-out perp with a gun than talk about my emotions. I didn't search out Julie when I could have. And I didn't look for another relationship. I thought anyone else would see me the same way Julie did, they would rank somewhere behind my family and then the job. I built walls for protection so I wouldn't get hurt again." She slid her arm around Diana more. "It didn't work."

"I'm sorry."

"Learning," Jessie said. "Can I ask?" and then she went on. "When I told you Julie came back, did you really think you had nothing to offer?"

Diana turned away and reached for her almost empty glass. "Like I said, what did I have for you?" She examined the few drops rather than look at Jessie. "Besides, you had held onto Julie for so long, I was afraid if we did get together, Julie would always be there in the background. Every time we had difficulties, you would wonder if you could have made it with her. I couldn't have stood that." She set the glass back on the table and looked at Jessie. "So I thought you needed that chance with Julie, even if it failed." *Even if I lost you.*

Jessie raised up to look at Diana. "Have you been talking to my therapist? She said the same thing. I needed to try and the relationship needed to fail in order for me to let it go completely."

"Were you able to?"

Jessie lay back down. "Pretty much. We were working at being friends, and then we got thrown together at the cabin."

"That should have either drawn you together more in mutual support or torn you apart." Diana had a sudden thought. "Did she blame you? I mean, if it weren't for her connection to you, she never would have been there."

Jessie reached over for the wineglass. "Sorta kinda, and then not really. It wasn't anything I did; but it was still because of me. She doesn't hold it against me, but we're not exactly bosom buddies anymore. She had a lot of aftereffects so when the opportunity came to staff the clinic in Cincinnati, she took it." She drank the last few drops and set the glass back down as the desk clock chimed midnight.

"This is nice," Jessie said slowly, without moving. "We've never been able to do this before."

"No. We were always too rushed. Things to do, places to go." Diana ran her fingers through Jessie's hair. "Speaking of," she said slowly. "I've got a party to go to tomorrow. Want to come along?"

"What kind of party?" Jessie still didn't move so Diana guessed she was either too comfortable to move or didn't dare because one of them would fall off the couch.

"Casual thing, backyard barbeque."

"Sounds fine. Who's going to be there?"

"Bunch of friends. General mix. Most of us go to basketball games during the winter, sorta get dispersed during the summer. I don't know who all are going to be there so I can't really tell you. You'll probably fit right in."

"They know about you?" Jessie asked casually. "Just so I don't put my foot in my mouth. You know, innocent questions come up, like how we met?"

Diana thought about it. "More or less. I assume anyone who knows me knows what's on the Internet, past history. It was a big deal when I first came to town and started meeting people. A few were paranoid when it became obvious I was being tailed all the time. Didn't want the guilt by association. Then it settled down. Occasionally when someone new enters the group it flairs up again. Sometimes I forget and tell stories and get halfway through before I realize I need to change details." She took a breath. "For the most part, I've tried not to hide anything. I lived a double life for a long time. When I came here, I told myself I wasn't going to do that anymore." She shrugged. "There's a big mixture in the group. Our only common thing is we're all dykes. There's a reporter who may or may not show up. There's a city cop." She frowned. "And Brenda works for the county sheriff's department."

Jessie made movements to get up and suddenly stopped. She looked down into Diana's face, her eyes narrowing. "Is this going to be a statement, you taking me to a party with all your friends?"

Diana hadn't considered it in that light but as she thought of her friends, her past, her present and now maybe her future. "Sorta kinda," she admitted. "Can you handle that?"

Jessie grinned, a pleased, knowing grin. "Oh, I think I can manage." She gave Diana a quick kiss. "And just what time might this shindig be?"

Diana had her own pleasant feeling. "Starts about eleven and will go most of the day. She staggers the crowd so not everyone comes at once."

Jessie stiffly got to her feet, stretching. She looked around and finally looked at her watch. "It's after midnight."

"I know. I like the nighttime hours, they're quiet."

"If that party starts at eleven, I need to get going back to the motel." She gave Diana a hand to pull her up to her feet.

Diana slid her arms around Jessie's waist, rested her head on Jessie's shoulder. "I don't want you to go. I don't want this feeling to end."

Jessie stroked Diana's hair. "I don't want to go either but are you sure?"

"I know I want to crawl into bed with you, curl up against you. I want to wake up with you in the morning." She sighed, a comfortable, contented sigh. "We could swing by the motel in the morning for different clothes." She pulled back from Jessie. "Unless, of course, you still have the habit of having a change in the car with you at all times."

Jessie laughed. "As a matter of fact…" They both laughed and then sobered. So many things had changed and yet nothing had.

Jessie looked into Diana's eyes, stroked her face. "Are you sure? If I go out and get my clothes, you're not going to change your mind and lock me out, are you?"

Diana shook her head. "No. I promise. I'll be standing at the door, waiting for you to come back."

And she was, greeting Jessie with a kiss. "I missed you," Diana murmured as she pulled her in the door and closed out the world.

Bella Books, Inc.

Women. Books. Even Better Together.

P.O. Box 10543
Tallahassee, FL 32302

Phone: 800-729-4992
www.bellabook.com